A Prisoner of Memory
A Novel by Maren Altman

First paperback edition August 2019

Book design by Maren Altman and Mehhma Malhi
Cover Illustration by Mehhma Malhi

ISBN 978-1-0870-4067-7

Refined by The Artful Editor
www.artfuleditor.com

Dedicated to Sarah

Prologue

I'm heaving and out of breath as I burst into his office, but I don't even stop to inhale before bursting out of myself.

"You knew! You could tell, and you never said anything! Anything! For months, hundreds of— Not even— Nothing! I was just a goddamn *specimen* for you to fucking psychoanalyze and watch self-destruct! *How...could...you?*"

He doesn't even look *at* me, he looks *through* me, beyond me. As I stand there, with the residual smoke of betrayal fumigating the space between us, he says nothing. He simply sits on a pedestal made of a PhD and inauthentic professionalism, not responding. I might as well be as inanimate as the parquet-framed photos scattered along his office walls. An overwhelming urge to rip these images off comes over me. I run behind his green leather armchair and slice at all of the little glass boxes like a rock climber with talons. If he won't look at me as an actual person, if not something more meaningful, then I will not act as such. Three, four, five, of these perfect little cells fall to the ground and do not shatter but still crack the air with the noise of glass hitting laminate. A wife and son gaze up at me from the posed Easter photograph that always used to catch my eye as I looked at the clock obsessively each time we met. Jarringly reentering reality, I turn back to make eye contact. Now, his eyes brim slightly with the gleam of tears, and he opens his mouth to speak but chokes on his breath, swallowing reflexively. His sadistic control has crumbled into animalistic surrender.

Without my permission, his display of grief catalyzes my own, and I cannot contain the silent streams of tears that race down my sunken cheeks. What feels like a lifetime's worth of experiences flashes between us as our gazes fuse in a momentary slice of immortality. I fracture even more, becoming torn, trapped, melted, consumed. All I am is a prisoner of memory, locked in the cell of my own mind.

Chapter 1

"Chocolate?"

No response.

He sighs. Sets the bowl back down on his red plastic side table. Adjusts the red glasses resting on the very tip of his ski-jump nose. Different red, though. Rustier than the cherry of the table. My eyes dart around the room, finally resting on a framed photograph of a couple and a child sitting in an Easter-egg patch.

"So, as you know—"

"Yeah, okay, I'll have a piece." He is more comforted than bothered by my blurting and quickly grabs the bowl to his right, holding it out to me.

"There's some white, some milk, some almond—"

"Any dark?"

"I'm afraid I've had all of those."

"Never mind, then." I sit back down. He places the chocolates back onto the table and sits once again in the green armchair. He chuckles.

"I guess we have that in common to begin with. Dark's always been my favorite, too."

"I mean, I don't mind the other kinds, but I'm vegan."

"Oh... Oh! How... Alright." He comes off strangely neurotic for a shrink. Typically in these situations, they project a kind of calm authority that may or may not be real, since they are supposed to be detached professionals and all, so I am slightly thrown off by such childlike meekness for a man who looks like he's nearing forty. Perhaps it is a facade designed to make me feel comfortable and overshare. I guess it isn't oversharing if it is your therapist, though.

"So, Valerie, how has adjusting been so far this first week at school? Everything going as expected for your freshman move in?"

A not-so-surprising first question. I bite my lip and shrug.

"If you mean feeling even more as if I'm just wasting time and waiting for something to end that never will, then, yeah, I guess so. Pretty much expected that."

"Met your roommate and all? Done the whole small-talk thing?"

"Yeah, a lot like what's going on here, honestly." I blink several times as I look down and cartwheel my long fake nails across the phone in my lap.

He chuckles, so softly it probably wouldn't be audible to anyone besides me. "I mean, we can't exactly start off a first session by probing into the brain's deeply embedded traumas."

Another shrug. I haven't had much of my usual energy to play the contrarian teen role any longer, so I won't. I slide farther down into the beige love seat, my torso shrinking and my attitude becoming even more foul.

"My roommate looks a little bit like Bette Midler. Bette Midler mixed with whoever played Lolita in the nineties version. That's the only impression I've really gotten so far."

He scribbles on his yellow notepad. "Do you like the film? *Lolita*, I mean?"

"Yeah. Yeah, I do. Have you seen it?"

"When it first came out, in fact. Always was a fan of Nabokov."

"I mean, *that* movie isn't really as much of a reflection of him or his story." I scoot up a little in my seat. The camel tweed brushes my denim grain up; friction warms my thighs. Looking up, our eyes meet for a split second too long before he responds.

"Very true. You're quite film literate for your age."

"I'm a film major."

"How fitting. I do remember hearing that now, yes. And apparently you're a really good one. So. I suppose we should get down to business."

I fucking hate that saying. Immediately, any openness from the moment we shared is turned off, obliterated. I'm reminded of where I am, why I'm here. Awake again.

He continues, "I understand you've had some difficulties with prior treatments and, as a result, you've come here."

It isn't as much difficulty with past treatments as much as little-to-no progress with past therapists, who were all female, but I nod along anyway.

"I'm also sure you're familiar with my success working with those affected similarly to you through talk therapy and, at times, medication."

My thoughts interrupt his voice and create a time chasm. That one word, *medication*, causes me to shudder, making me think of how such a simple term can hold so much change. Not even change. More like *forced mutation*. My mind resumes interpreting his spiel.

"Along with the support system of loved ones, of course. And I don't want this to be one-sided for you. I see it as more of a discussion between us. However, none of this will work without *effort* and *willingness* on your part. I know you want to get better, I'm sure of that, but I do need to know that you are going to commit to this process." His dark, round eyes bounce through those circular red frames and make it clear to me that I truly will need to play by the rules. No fucking around, no bullshitting. Actual cooperation this time. I nod in understanding of his implied proposition and then make eye contact in agreement. A contract is signed through our pupils, and at the moment, I really do intend to follow it.

I really do.

Chapter 2

I'm no stranger to insomnia. Her presence is familiar, expected, almost welcome. One of the characters who truly exist in my screenplay.

Tonight she isn't someone I try to wrestle or negotiate with. I surrender and let her win. Along with my restlessness, my roommate's sandpaper snoring coaxes me to leave my dorm room with even more encouragement than usual tonight. Just out of the four thin walls, I step into the fluorescent tunnel that is my dorm hallway. White light pierces my unadjusted pupils, and I squint, my senses startled. I consider returning to my room but am further motivated to stay up when I half-awakedly remember there are, sent from nonexistent God himself, peanut-butter-pretzel bites in our floor's communal kitchen. They're someone else's, but I doubt having just a few will bring about any suspicion of thievery. Seconds later, I am perched cross-legged on the laminate counter with a handful of square, thickly salted pretzel cubes in my left hand as I pop them into my mouth with my right. My obsessive-compulsive brain quickly approximates the nutrition as I become more conscious. About two hundred calories right there, probably about an equal number of milligrams of sodium. Fuck it, I'll have more and just won't eat breakfast in the morning.

"Ah, when someone buys those, it's the tits, man. Usually, there's just the normal pretzel-bite shit, but when they get peanut butter filled... *Ooh* yeah."

A short, stout figure hops onto the counter next to me. At first, I am unsure if they are male or female, but the nuanced curves of small breasts and protruding pouty, full lips are undeniable giveaways. Her bleached hair is buzzed especially tight and accentuates the *love me* tattoo on the upper right corner of her forehead, right on the hairline. In fact, she is covered in tiny tattoos—most appear to be stick 'n' pokes, probably done in high school with India ink in someone's basement on a Friday night.

I give a closemouthed smile. "Peanut butter is my crack." Another one shoots down the pie hole. She holds out a soft, round hand.

"Di."

"Valerie. Or Val. Whatever." We shake. She takes a few pretzels out of the bag resting in the space between us, and we share a silence filled with only the sound of obnoxious chewing of enriched wheat flour. It is devoid of the awkwardness or the typical forced dialogue found in most first encounters; there is a shared indifference and a relaxed camaraderie. It is powerful, it is quick, it is almost undetectable. A front-frame photograph of us could've made a great ad for some millennial roommate sitcom on ABC Family.

In between bites during this aphrodisiacal binge of stolen snacks, I gauge that Di is bipolar and recently attempted a second failed suicide. She doesn't flat-out mention this, but it's clear to a fellow psych ward regular. The fluorescent lights of this dorm remind us both of being committed, and we joke about the PTSD we'll experience during our stay here as a result.

She doesn't really have to mention much for me to understand her. It's all in between the cracks of her curse-filled language. Her family is also forcing her to go through the intensive mental-health counseling program at the Student Health Center. For her, it's mostly her mom, while for me, Dad is the only one in the picture for me, so it's the converse. And it seems that I'm a bit more sympathetic to parental guidance than she is. Or maybe it's just one of my good days where I do want to get better, where that part of me is winning out over the nihilistic devil digging into my bony shoulder.

"This is damn well the best situation I've been in so far, though," Di says. "So many fewer rules than when I was inpatient in Massachusetts, and a *hell* of a lot better than my lockdown shit in Vermont. I pretty much needed that, though. They had dank hot chocolate, I do admit." The bag, once completely full, is now completely empty as she grabs the final pretzel. I'm a little hurt.

"How long have you been in the therapy program here?" I ask, rimming my teeth for remnants. Di's comments imply she's been here for some time, which perplexes me since this is a first-year dorm. She scratches her temple, just adjacent to *love me*.

"Oh, it's my first year, too, but I came early for the summer session to fill in some credits I'm behind on from high school. So, almost three months? Not long enough to get *really* fuckin' tired of it or anything, but still long enough to feel like I should be somewhere further than I am."

"I feel that."

Though not relatively very long, three months seems eons longer than I'm willing to contemplate. Just a few days here, and I already feel like the Soviet army should be here to liberate me from the expectation of recovery—recovery in more contexts than I even want to consider.

Di yawns and slides off the counter. Her gray sweats and white tank top ruffle up as her short frame ribs against the sharp angle of linoleum. I find her confidence, even at this hour and in this situation, enigmatic.

"I'm out. Peace. See you around, Pretzels." My eyes follow her magnetically as she waddles back into the fluorescent abyss.

Chapter 3

Di and I were, I suppose, friends from that point forward. Now we spend a lot of time playing card games and shoplifting together. A strange pairing, I know, but I guess it's just as strange as we both are. We more so do things than discuss things. An action-oriented friendship. And she has taught me various skills. Like how to get around meds. Or, at least, how to convince myself I really shouldn't be taking them. If I don't convince myself now, I'm worried I won't have the awareness to stop later. I can't risk being numb to rationality.

I was first given meds after Really Bad, during my last year of high school, because it was clear something needed to change, and apparently that was my brain chemistry. Things got better, but mostly for everyone around me, not necessarily for me. It was like I was in a haze. From the outside, I seemed better because there was less of me—less of me to take up space and do anything at all, not just do anything problematic.

It feels better to have the company of what I know to be true, what I know to be real for me, than what works and what is real for anyone else. There is no chance of me returning to the lifeless underwater existence that comes from those little capsules.

The nurses at the Student Health Center really are sweet ladies. I'm sure they aren't aware of what they're really doing, suffocating our true souls for the sake of making themselves and the rest of mainstream society feel at ease. Knowing that others exist on a different plane is disconcerting to those insecure about their own intellectual abilities, which happens to be most people. So here we are, having to shove capsules down our throats to anesthetize any lingering individuality.

I'm not crazy. You're just quite ordinary.

"Make sure your mouth is really fuckin' dry before your med time," Di told me earlier that day. "Like, use a paper towel and shit to make it as parched as possible. Then keep the pill under your tongue while you drink the water from the Dixie Cup. There's no way around that shit, they *make* you drink from the fuckin' cup. Just don't get the pill wet—that's the key. And spit it out once you've left the clinic. Flush it, if you can. Sometimes you can see meds in the trash. And worst case, a one-off dose isn't going to do shit. I know you know that. It's just a pain in the ass that they think they're being nice or whatever, conveniently watching you take that first dose. And this is all just if meds really do fuck you up that horribly. Until you can talk to your shrink about some that do help. Like what I figured out finally now, with what works for me. But, for today, just tongue it and then run to the bathroom." Di raises her eyebrows.

I nod in understanding and brace myself to enter the medical area ahead. I'm nearly twenty. This sort of rebellion is pathetic and outdated given my age and my experience being on meds for nearly a year before breaking free, but it's necessary. After a sharp inhale, I proceed toward the metal doors and stand awkwardly in front of the frosted glass window. It slides open, and a woman with round spectacles blinks at me.

"Name, hon?"

"Uh, Valerie Updike." It feels like I am lying, like I'm sixteen again using a fake ID to try and trick a bouncer. She types something on a computer, leaves for a minute, and then returns with a small paper cup and a slightly larger Dixie Cup. It's startlingly chartreuse.

I take the cups from her hands and gaze at the little orange circle threatening me from the white paper sheltering it. The nurse stares at me, waiting to see me put the little orange circle into my mouth. Which I do. She then waits to see me drink from the goddamn Dixie Cup and swallow.

Which I don't.

My heart wrestles as my tongue pushes down that orange circle of death in a chokehold. I'm too scared to try and swallow the water circling in my mouth, so I offer a closemouthed smile to the nurse, turn around, and quickly leave. I've done it.

Or, at least I think I have, until I spit everything out in surprise when I lift my gaze to see Dr. Ellis directly in front of me and slam right into this torso. Immersed in his phone, we collide into one another as my mouthful of water explodes onto his perfectly tailored blue button-down. A damp, slightly orange tinge on his shirt now screams out at me. Fuck. Fuck. He's going to know; it's written all over my face. Dammit.

He blinks, mouth slightly open, then brushes down his shirt. My eyes dart to the little orange circle on the ground next to his foot.

"I'm so sorry, Valerie. I should've looked where I was going." He notices the stain is orange and ponders it in a seemingly scientific sense. "Fanta?"

A vacant two seconds of silence asphyxiate my heartbeat.

"Um, uh, just orange juice." What the hell am I saying?

"Ah. I see. Well, I do look forward to our next meeting in a few days. Take care." Dr. Ellis looks down at me from above the red glasses resting on the very tip of that sharp, almost too-chiseled nose.

"Uh… Oh! My bad, I'll—" I cut myself off and dart out of the way.

The minuscule tangerine circle grins eerily back at me as the sound of wooden-soled loafers echoes down the hall of the Student Health Center. I grind my boot heel directly into its face and, finally, force a swallow down my throat.

Chapter 4

Once again, I find myself eating alone in the middle of a crowded

restaurant. Though daunting to most, I am familiar enough with

this to feel at ease in the uncomfortable routine: the awkward

millisecond pause of the hostess after I say, "Table for one," the

pitying stares from the other guests, the vapid presence of silence.

I'm way uptown without the time to head back to my dorm and eat

there before my therapy session.

    At this restaurant, I don't get too much notice. Hole-in-the-

wall cafe with socialist propaganda covering the walls and mason-

jar drinking glasses posed next to hemp purses, so the crowd

doesn't really seem to give as much of a shit. Or at least they've

gotten fucking good at pretending behind their John Lennon

sunglasses. I slide into the shiny yellow booth and sink down like a

small child, placing my feet up on the other side. A red-haired

waitress glares at me. I comically grimace and shoot up in my seat.

I could never fully master badassery.

The same woman comes over and raises her eyebrows at me. "Know what you want?"

"Uh, I'll take a green tea for now. Still looking." She purses her lips and turns back around. I nearly choke as a figure sitting at the old diner-style bar to my right catches my eye. The red-and-black-checkered flannel, the silky black-brown hair. A flip-book of a thousand and one little hand-drawn images plays in my mind.

I can't, I can't, I won't let this happen again. I grasp the white laminate and wince. When I open my eyelids from their death grip, judgy waitress is standing right there again, staring through me hazily. My gaze jolts to the menu, and I order the first thing I see.

"Um…the portobello burger with…sweet potato fries, please." Dammit. I fucking hate mushrooms.

"What kind of bun?" She asks the question in a strangely accusatorial tone.

In return, I decide to be as difficult as possible. I'm also incredibly pissed about the mushroom thing but too cowardly to go back on it now.

"Do you have gluten-free bread?"

"Yeah, for two fifty extra."

"Okay."

Silence. She blinks. I look down and purse my lips tightly.

"So?"

"Okay, I'll have the gluten-free bread. And low on the salt." I speak with my hands and keep my gaze hidden. Flippantly, the waitress kidnaps the menu from my hands, and I slink back down into the overstuffed lemon cushion.

My eyes don't stray from the man at the bar. I can't help but stare; my mind will not escape memory's throws. I'm trapped.

It's the night of my senior prom, about a year and a half ago. We both sat on top of the chain-link fence outside the gym in ripped jeans and sriracha-stained tees, peering in at the drunken amoeba of teen hormones.

"I can't believe I'm outside a high school right now. *Your* high school, your high school *prom*; God, I need a fuckin' hobby," Vic said.

I giggled, warm and stoned, and he tousled my hair as I leaned against the bony crook of his shoulder.

In a rupturing instant, our shadows were backlit and my neck became warm from the beam of a headlight. I instinctively turned around. Thankfully, the lipstick-stained joint had slipped from my fingers into the sewer below, but the smell was still pungent.

A tall, muscular cop slowly approached us. In the midst of this, all my hazy mind could focus on was that he could use a good rhinoplasty.

"What do you think you're doin' out here at this hour all by yourself? I see you're not takin' part in the dance inside." There was a good twenty, thirty, feet between us. Maybe the cool spring wind was saving us from the culpability of the stench. Or he was congested.

I waited for Vic to respond, but he said nothing and stared. I jumped in.

"Yeah, not really our thing, Officer. Just watching." My voice ascended six octaves.

"*Our* thing? And who might be out here with you, young lady?" He relaxed slightly, settling into his right hip as his stance adjusted. His angular head cocked to the side, his mouth ajar disconcertingly.

"My boyfriend here. Sorry for— Oh, he must've left, I guess."

I snap out of it when a server drops off my portobello burger. I frown. Why didn't I take back my order? Redhead waitress is watching me from afar, and I fake contentment while struggling to bite around the impressively tall mass of mushroom.

Its sliminess makes it considerably hard for me to swallow. Not even distracting my taste buds with green tea helps. I wrestle with it, struggling from within. Outside, though, I inconspicuously blend in. Oh, I can pretend.

Chapter 5

The glass bowl today is filled with Skittles, and there is no offering held out to me upon entering the room. However, even before making eye contact with Dr. Ellis, I walk over to the candy directly next to him, submerge my hand in wrist deep, and writhe out a handful, picking out four orange pieces and dropping the rest back into the bowl. He says nothing, just watches me, and my heart rate spikes in residual paranoia. I'm not truly high anymore, but Di and I met up a few hours earlier to smoke and attempt to write convoluted literary masterpieces for the experimental writing class we'd both signed up for. Needless to say, we didn't really write anything coherent or remotely submittable and mostly ended up eating more pretzel bites. Whoever keeps buying and leaving them unhidden for our thievery is a godsend. However, regrettably, I'm still a little hungry. I decide I just won't have dinner tonight. So I grab the Skittles. Orange only, though.

"How is your afternoon going, Valerie?" He sniffs and blinks at me.

I shrug. "Lots of homework and studying, the usual. Nothing really new."

"Are you finding your medication and these sessions to be making things easier so far?"

I crush a Skittle in my back molars and nod. Easier since Really Bad happened last year, yes, I guess so. But perhaps not. Perhaps things gradually get worse as looking back in agony ignites more pain than the initial event itself. I dread the day when the train tracks of my mind can no longer support the thousand tons of memories claustrophobically crowded into each car.

We discuss my academic goals and what's going on in my personal life. I want to get my shit together so I can really make the films I want to. So I can stop feeling like such an imposter, a panicked psycho amid creative geniuses, and can feel centered enough for my creativity to come through. I somehow came to this school on a full ride because of this film I made last year, in high school, that compared adolescence to a butterfly's chrysalis to a rose budding. It was called *Bud*. I didn't expect it to get so much praise, but it did. I made it the beginning of my senior year, before Really Bad, when I was in love with Vic, and he was in love with me, and nothing felt heavy. Everything in me easily flowed into *Bud*.

Because when things are good, or even decent, creativity flows, and my art emerges, but when things aren't, and they usually aren't, I feel energetically constipated. Which makes me isolate myself more. Which makes me hear the clamoring of hatred in my own brain more and more, so loudly that it keeps me from realizing I can leave the cycle altogether. I have yet to figure out how to escape. But I find peace in my projects. I can create that safe reality for myself in a way that has never been created for me by those who were supposed to love me enough to do so. I tell Dr. Ellis that I want to tell myself the story that was never told to me.

His white plastic timer rings and shakes the red metal side table.

"I look forward to seeing you next week, Valerie."

My phone vibrates as I nod and rise to leave. It's a text from Di.

sitting outside at harrys if u want 2 join. pls do

I smile at Dr. Ellis, excited to go meet Di at our usual coffee shop near campus. They have the best cinnamon to mix into our black coffees, we've decided.

Within five minutes, my backpack is hanging on the metal chair next to Di, and I'm pulling a five out of my pocket. "Be right back," I quickly mutter.

"I already—" She motions to the second cup of coffee in front of her.

"Oh, thank—"

"—got you one."

I grin slyly, then we share a laugh. I was initially a little bitter that she chose to sit outside in this cool weather, but I often forget that my discomfort is typically not the result of others' malice. Unlike me, she is probably not perpetually cold.

"So? Still writing?" I motion to the tattered Five Star spiral notebook in front of her, which is covered in anime-style doodles that mark her territory.

"Ha, yeah, actually fucking getting somewhere now. Kind of, I think. Trying to explore some deep cosmic shit through limerick."

I sip my coffee quickly, trying to warm myself up. It is bitter and too hot for my tongue, but I long for heat. The corner of my eye catches a prepubescent boy in a yellow sweater, and I choke on my drink, almost spewing out the fiery liquid. My conscience is enveloped again, twisted in agony. I reenter the inescapable portal.

Broken bottles were arranged in a perfectly disheveled way around his body as if they were the corpses and he was their god. A pile of chartreuse vomit balanced on Greg's yellow shirt, blinding the innocent, faded Pokémon characters from seeing what was going on in front of their eyes. The whole scene was foreign to criticism, untouched by assumptive eyes, and I felt as if I were violating it by acknowledging its existence at all. Just weeks prior, that same body had been standing right there instead of lying, preparing to jump into the pool instead of lifelessly waiting to attract flies, surrounded by friends instead of remnants of poison once quarantined. That's what the past was now, quarantined within my memory, never integrable with the immortal scene just feet away. The floor-to-ceiling glass windows framed my vision in such a way where I felt like a museum spectator viewing art. His bruised head in the golden mean, surrounded by a vignette of shattered glass. The grim reaper's half-assed signature scribbled in the bottom right corner.

All because *she* did this. All because he had nothing else to look toward, nothing else to see as the end result besides booze and bile. He was only twelve. I think it was his first time drinking—no, I am sure of it. Until then, he was a partial witness to alcohol's noose, familiar with the "almosts" and "close ones" but never understanding its choke hold until the chosen one was to be him. And even then, it would have been too late for him to realize that. *She* killed him, she killed *Greg*—not directly, I admit, but in the overall scheme of things, she was the one who set off the convoluted Rube Goldberg machine to drop that very first ball in the hole.

"A Tragic Victim of Underage Alcohol Consumption." "Binge Drinking Claims Yet Another Minor." Bullshit, bullshit, bullshit. *A Mother Teaches a Son How to Drown Himself.* That is more like it. That is what truly happened, with her laughing as she denied her own inability to escape her personal sea of sorrow.

The boy turns back around after removing a laptop from the backpack hanging on his chair. He lounges in his seat, legs mindlessly splayed wide. Greg wouldn't have sat like that. Greg wouldn't be wearing a knitted Ralph Lauren sweater and neon wireless Beats. The boy is nothing like Greg, nothing at all, and yet my mind still sees him there, his face present and clearly animated. I cannot tell myself it isn't there, because it truly is.

Di doesn't notice my crisis as she scribbles over and over dozens of lines, drawing a huge X over the whole page.

"Absolute shit. I'm dropping this goddamn class. Like, right now." She twists awkwardly in the metal chair and reaches for her phone in her back pocket. Just like that, she gets out, she escapes, she eliminates. I'm still trapped. Greg smiles at me from afar.

Chapter 6

Di lays on my dorm bed, halfway between the fetal position and a perfect Savasana. She has been tripping on acid for most of today, and I'd begrudgingly agreed earlier to be her babysitter. However, within the last few hours, she's slowly begun to reenter reality. Her voice only barely still contains hallucinogen-induced wavering, the metallic edges of her typical speech patterns gradually returning.

"It's *embarrassing*, honestly. You think you're going to have this fuckin' dramatic exit, and then it's this uncomfortable *thing* that you don't know what to do with. Do you recycle it? Burn it? Do you frame it? Keep it as a memento of your unintentional survival? That's the part you don't think about! Sure, you're like, 'maybe this won't work,' but you're not like, 'what happens to the fuckin' note if I live?' and all." Di sits up and leans back on her palms, crossing her legs. I worked to steer our conversations away from anything too intense for fear of triggering a bad trip, but I trust that she is coherent enough now to discuss what she wants to.

Which happens to be the suicide attempt that kept her out of college for a year.

"Ten Hydros. Goddamn, I even threw that extra one in there after Reddit fuckin' *told* me nine was easily lethal. And I thought, *I'm a small person. Nine is probably more than enough.* Then I bought ten for good fuckin' measure, but *nooo*, I guess my liver was already used to being overworked and shit."

"Are you hungry yet?"

"Nope."

Patricia, my roommate, enters loudly, carrying reusable shopping bags filled with God knows what. Scratch that, they're probably filled with clothes made in sweatshops by the same children her sorority so proudly throws "fund-raising mixers" for. And I'm the insane one.

"I don't think I've talked to her since, like, before graduation. Maybe junior year, even." Patricia presses the phone into her shoulder as she throws the heavy bags onto her bed and continues talking to who I'm sure is her boyfriend. "Stop it! No! Don't remind me!"

"Want to get out of here?" I ask Di, who immediately nods and jumps off the mattress. We find ourselves sitting once again on the kitchen counter, and Di, as not-hungry as she just claimed, begins to inhale pretzel bites.

"Are you...better now, though? Feeling better, I mean? Mentally?" Her unchanged expression proves that she knows what I'm referring to.

"I have good days, and shit days, so sometimes I am, I guess. I think people feel like they need some huge joyful life or whatever to feel better, but I'm just glad for shit to be still sometimes." Salt and peanut butter ooze from the torn, chapped edges of her mouth in percussive chews.

"That's true. Like sometimes feeling neutral, or indifferent, seems like relief. You know?"

Chomp. "Why I loved being a file clerk. The monotony is totally numbing." Di hops down from the counter and sighs. "Alright, I think I'm out. Shit looks normal now, and I'm exhausted. See ya." Di takes a few steps, then waddles backward, grabs another large handful of pretzels, and skips off as her chewing noises reverberate against the fluorescent-lit walls. Still sitting on the counter, I roll up the near-empty bag of pretzels, which was completely unopened minutes ago, and reach to stuff it back into the cabinet when I hear shuffling near me.

"So *you're* the one eating my peanut-butter-pretzel bites." Melancholy dark eyes look down at me, confusedly coupled with a toothy smile, and I'm not sure whether to apologize or laugh it off. The limbo in my mind is obvious as I open my mouth, shut it, and end up staring down at my checkered pajama pants.

I finally begin to speak. "Um…sorry? Sorry." I nod, avoid all eye contact, and return to placing the bag back when this boy speaks again.

"I'll have some, if that's okay." Once again, I can't determine whether the statement is meant to be firm or ironic. The whole interaction reminds me painfully of middle school and feels far too juvenile for a college dorm.

"Oh, sorry. Here. Um, thank you, by the way? I won't be taking them anymore or anything. But, yeah, thanks," I muster up, half laughing, half serious, fully uncomfortable.

"It's alright. I don't really mind. Jett." He holds out a hand, and I put forward the plastic bag before realizing he meant to shake hands. We both laugh without releasing an ounce of the controlled tension isolated within each of us. Finally, I complete the handshake.

"Val. Or Valerie, whatever. So you…live here, too?"

"Yeah, kinda." He stands there leaning against the counter too elegantly for his Old Navy pajama pants.

"Um, I should, like, pay you for all your shit that I ate. Because Di and I totally had most of what you bought."

"No, no, don't worry. Really." He pushes back his messy dark hair, which is long enough to seem unkempt but conditioned well enough to make it clear that it's perfectly, intentionally disheveled. I look down at his shirt and laugh.

"Skid Row, huh?" I take a sip of the tea beside me before realizing I did not make any tea. It is stale and cold, and I end up spitting it out in the sink.

Jett looks down at his shirt and seems not to notice this. "Everyone is trying to bring back grunge, but I think hair metal is so much more worthwhile. You don't have to hide all the effort you're putting into how you look." He counts out the three remaining pretzel bites and nimbly eats them one after another.

"Yeah, those pants are hair metal at its finest."

"Even rock stars have to wear pajamas occasionally." Jett picks up the empty bag and throws it away as he leaves, then walks to the opposite end of the hall from my room.

I wipe off the leftover crumbs from the counter onto the ground and tie my hair up in a bun as I walk back to my room, praying that Patricia is gone or off the phone. When I enter, I see her sitting at her desk, holding her phone to her mouth. She's speaking really loudly.

"Premeds are just so competitive. *So* competitive, you have no idea, babe—"

"Oh, I bet—" Goddamn. He's on speaker. Patricia's already spoken with him on speaker several times in the past few days that we've lived together, and I am not interested in hearing more about her sorority sisters or the drama in her premed track. Patricia's unquestioning identification with everything I could never be stirs me every time I look at her. Patricia will never feel alien in herself like I do.

It seems that, even here, in the space that should offer me the most solace, I'm more irritated than ever. I can't escape the madness no matter how hard I try.

Out of habit, I think about going to get more food from the kitchen as an excuse to leave, but then I decide it's best not to reenter what I've just left behind. Jett, Skid Row, Old Navy. An inspirational mood board if there ever was one, I'd say.

Instead, I sit down at my desk and look into the dirty vanity mirror balanced upon my yet-to-be-read stack of Vonnegut novels in a way that perfectly matches the height of my face. My eyeliner has smudged from tears of laughter at Di's drug-induced commentary, and my liquid lipstick has split on the edges and completely given me butthole lips on the inside. I let my hair down and stare at the face I see in the mirror. I pretend I'm at a Skid Row concert myself in the eighties, hair messily strewn about and makeup cracking like old plaster. Maybe I'd be wearing a faux-leather jumpsuit, or some animal-print crop top. Chunky black platforms and silver jewelry to top it all off.

"Like, I would *kill* for that internship. How dare she!"

Chapter 7

I sit in Dr. Ellis's beige love seat perpendicular to the normal position today, leaning against one arm with my legs strewn over the other. I pick at my nails as he apologies for having to answer some emails before starting, though he has no need to, as I'm early.

"I really should have done this beforehand. My, how responsibilities creep up on us."

He is an unbelievably fast typer. If it weren't for the number of backspaces I see him making, I would assume he was writing a novel in each email reply. He then slams down the almost-vintage MacBook and picks up his yellow notepad. His small handwriting fits succinctly between the prison bars of red lines, never touching the boundaries. Dr. Ellis flips the page over and crosses his legs, placing the notepad on the slope of his knees so that I can no longer gaze at it. He looks up at me, writes something at the top, then smiles. It's a little phony. I swallow.

"How is the afternoon treating you today, Valerie?"

"Decently, I suppose. It isn't too cold, so that's a plus."

He scribbles something in his yellow notebook. What the hell could I have said worth writing down? Maybe my near-positive commentary was especially noteworthy.

"Any weekend plans?"

"Um, Di and I are going to a concert. This small band we both like. On Saturday. Nothing planned for tomorrow night, we'll probably just stay in and watch a movie or something."

To "watch a movie or something" is always adult-speak for getting high and pretty much doing nothing. It's a euphemism I learned to habitually swap in years ago. I know I can tell Dr. Ellis I smoke weed without him being shocked or feeling uncomfortable or whatever, but I also know that being aware of others' illegality, no matter how indifferent you are to it, makes you feel a little unsettlingly culpable. At least that's how I always felt with past boyfriends and shit. I'd personally rather not know, and maybe Dr. Ellis is different—I mean his job *is* to get to the bottom of other people's shit—but I truly attempt to uphold Jesus's Golden Rule at all times.

"What band?"

"Oh, you wouldn't have heard of them. It's, like, three total including the openers."

"Hmm. Rock?"

"Yeah, basically." I pause, running my fingers through my dry-shampoo-coated, root-touch-up-needed stringy tendrils. "Any weekend plans for yourself?"

His eyes perk up from his notebook at the question, and he leans back in his green chair slightly, hands gripping the arms.

"Tomorrow my wife is hosting her book-club meeting for most of the afternoon, so I'm trying to arrange something to avoid that...mess," he eloquently finishes.

"Not your thing?" I cock my head to the right and meet his eyes inquisitively.

Dr. Ellis chuckles. "No, critiquing half-read self-help manuals doesn't hold much appeal."

I guess Mrs. Ellis doesn't use the valuable resource of having a self-help machine as a husband to her advantage.

He sits up straighter and shakes his head enough to reveal hints of being flustered. "How have your mood swings been? Any luck in using the techniques we've discussed?"

"Definitely. I've felt more chill." *Chill* belongs nowhere near any reference to myself, but the further from the truth, the less it resembles a lie. Dr. Ellis half smiles and sniffles. Something is scribbled on the final line of the yellow page and is gently folded over; the following virgin page is then smoothed out with the back of his callused yet expensively moisturized hand.

Following the session, I find myself walking in zigzags through every street of the neighborhood. I woke up three pounds heavier today, so I will walk extra. It's how the Rules work. The Rules of how, when, and what I can do to my body. I didn't ask for them, but they're always there, scribbled in every hallway that connects the neurons in my brain. They came after Really Bad, when my mind got the extra energy it used to put toward falling in love with people who turned out not to be who I thought they were. It also seemed to get the extra energy I used to put into filmmaking. I blame medication for stealing that spark from me.

I listen to podcasts to pass the time, not really listening, just using them to drown out the ever-present white noise that would probably help solve things if I were to ever let myself listen.

As the season progresses, the sun sets much earlier, and had the darkness not already begun to claim its territory by five, I probably wouldn't have noticed the pale-blue lights surrounding the basement-level entryway. Through the bubbled glass windows, I see various beaded cushions strewn across a white daybed, illustrated on by the dim shadows of passersby. The floor is uneven wood coated with layers of grit and glitter, and a dull neon sign I can swear I've seen on Amazon flickers *Psychic Readings* in dark-purple cursive. The Rules never said all my walking had to be uninterrupted.

A bell rings and echoes gently as I struggle to turn and push the rickety doorknob. A middle-aged woman, petite and adorned in metal jewelry, walks out from around a corner and simply piercingly looks directly into each of my pupils, not one or the other, but back and forth between the two like a Ping-Pong match. Startlingly, she wears bright-blue circular lenses, cheap enough to reveal her naturally dark eyes.

"Um, I saw you offered readings."

"Fifty dollars for thirty minutes, plus however much longer I decide to go on for." She pats off crumbs from her ripped jeans and long gray top. "Tarot. Interested?"

I agree to a fifty-dollar tarot spread and follow her through a black velvet curtain down a narrow hallway, eventually sitting down across from her at what appears to be a breakfast table, judging by the coffee and sugar. I guess she works from home, or, more seemingly, lives at work. Without asking for my name or even introducing herself, the woman opens a deck of oversize golden cards and then holds them out to me, asking me to shuffle and then split the deck in half twice.

She begins to draw out the sequence, placing each card between us in a specific, intricate pattern. Some of the cards face me, some her, and some are placed on top of others perpendicularly. The process is overwhelming to me in its unfamiliarity, and yet I feel strangely calm. Probably the incense.

"So, I'm just going to ramble for now, and then we can chitchat after, so I don't get any bias while I'm going through the cards first off." She raises her eyebrows and huffs, picking up the card farthest to the right on my side. "You're coming from a place of absolute meaninglessness. Shallow relationships that don't really exist." She lets out a sharp laugh. "They aren't working. At *all*. And you're *beginning* to realize this but haven't really let yourself hear the truth. That's what I'm really getting from this right now, a lot of Pollyanna thinking. Listening to people who empower delusion over and over. Okay." She discusses the next few cards, which relate to my past, apparently. In one of the piles, a card labeled *The Hierophant* stands out to me in its perpendicular opposition to the rest of the stack.

As she speaks, I feel unable to breathe, like a weight is pressing down on my chest to keep me still. To keep me taking up as little space as possible. I'm becoming as small as I can to avoid getting struck by the daggers that it feels as if her words are turning into. Once she's done speaking, I try to disguise a gasp for air as a yawn. She looks at me to continue, and I nod.

"Something institutional isn't being recognized. I would suggest a marriage, but you seem... How old are you?"

"Nineteen."

"So *probably* not marriage?" I shake my head, biting my lip. "But maybe something of institutional value such as a degree

or label…that just is not being taken *seriously* or *acknowledged*…"
She emphasizes certain words very distinctly, as if I should underline them in a textbook for future reference. Her intense energy throttles my psyche, causing me to sweat underneath my countless layers of not-warm-enough-for-winter clothing.

The woman, through her doll-like contacts, goes on to describe my present situation of blockage and denial. She keeps accenting words like *fantasy* and *fear* with a widening of her fake-blue eyes and routinely comes back to *denial*. It is a confusing maze of ideas connected in a frame that fits well but is barely hanging together.

She pauses. "You're energetically sensitive. Be mindful of your presence around others and what *others* means to you." At this, my gaze darts down in slight discomfort. I'm not sure if *energetically sensitive* is psychic-speak for being psychotic or if she's implying some supernatural shit. I'm going to go with supernatural shit for now while I'm feeling relatively into it.

The next two cards are the Queen of Wands and the Queen of Swords, one after another reversed away from me. "So basically you see yourself as a go-getter, and everyone else pretty much sees you as aloof, maybe even a *bitch*!"

Her enthusiasm and confidence alarms me, and I jump in my seat.

"Which you aren't, and you don't have to care about, but it does show a sort of disconnect from how you see yourself and your outer image. Something to think about." We progress further, and she goes on some more about this *divide* or whatever until we reach the cards on my far left, which she explains refer to my future.

Her black-polished fingernails point to the illustrated image of a soldier on a battlefield holding a sword while surrounded by other swords and dead soldiers on a beach. It is an intensely troubling image to me despite its bright colors and serene background. The ironic juxtaposition reminds me of children's Christmas stories, lightly sprinkled with mentions of crucifixion and torture.

"You're going to have to think about what went wrong in past battles as you scrounge up some courage and move forward to the next ones. Reconsider your plans of action because they obviously aren't working." The last card is something-of-cups, which she explains is a positive outcome. I snort and don't hide my amusement at this, which she does not acknowledge or let interfere with her psychic magic mojo headspace.

The dark circular lenses look back up at me. "Basically, removing whatever block you're experiencing is going to take getting up off your ass and actually going for something tangible. Because you keep running into the same wall"—she knocks on the wooden table, then throws her hands up—"and you're starting to realize that finding a way *around* that wall is the only way out of this situation, whatever that may be. Being assertive is the key. This making sense?"

I bite my lip and nod. Her intensity is making it difficult to remain present. "Yes, I guess I am blocked. In what I thought was my craft, I guess, and I'm starting to realize I'm actually literal shit at filmmaking, whether it's me on my creative decline or something external to blame for fucking me up, and I'm not sure what to do now. At all. I have so much to say, so many ideas, but nothing translates into real art. My stories just seem so *fake*, so empty…" My use of *yes* makes me feel like I'm speaking a character's lines in a script. *Yes* is a scarily definite choice for my safe zone of ambiguous vocab. *Mm-hmm* or a simple grunt is usually my go-to, but *yes* holds much more gravitas than I'm comfortable carrying. It is assertive, that's what it is. Maybe I'm starting to live my happy-ending truth already, right here in this black wooden chair in this candlelit lair.

I pay her the fifty plus tip and walk back out into the sludgy alley. *Assert* myself. I can do that. I can beat the crosswalk before it counts down the seven seconds it has left despite being at the total other end of the block. Totally.

I can't, and I end up fucking up some cab's driving trajectory and almost being hit by a biker attempting to dodge the swerving vehicle. Maybe I already asserted myself with that *yes* as much as my confidence battery allows. Tomorrow. Tomorrow I will beat the crosswalk. For now, I will continue following the traffic signals and the Rules.

Chapter 8

The elevator rattles as it slams the underground floor. They really should fix that before it gives someone a heart attack or blows out my knees. I begrudgingly drag out my laundry, which spills over once I exit the elevator, a towel ending up trapped in the closing doors. It rips in half as the metal slams shut and rises. The leftover scrap apologetically drops at my feet.

"Shit."

I pick up the pink terry cloth from the ground next to my Batman slippers and sigh as I gaze at the rest of my dirty laundry. A shadow forms over the clothes, and I peer up. It's peanut-butter-pretzel-bite guy. Jett. His lips are moving, but I don't hear much. Humiliation and surprise distort my vision through an opaque veil, and I can't read his lips, either. Feeling powerless and turning red, I rip out my headphones and try to catch up to what he's been saying.

"—any help?"

I blink twice. "Oh. No, I'm alright. Thanks." I'm still hunched over in a squat, and my headphones are now tangled with the rest of the mess. Obviously, he's aware I could use some help, but he knows it would be more embarrassing for both of us if he acknowledged it. The opposite elevator shaft opens, and Jett enters, still looking at me and my disheveled mess.

"Cool slippers, by the way." The sound of the doors closing reverberates me to a shudder. At least I'm getting a thigh workout in this squat I'm somehow still maintaining, but my white robe is probably picking up dust mites that will just further irritate my shitty fucking sinuses. Goddamn. It's not even nine a.m. I could already use a fucking joint, or anything really, to distract me right now. If Di weren't the furthest possible thing from a morning person, I'd probably text and harass her right now, in this moment, on this basement linoleum floor surrounded by food-stained T-shirts and half of my favorite childhood washcloth.

We do end up smoking, later that afternoon, out of her dorm window. My mouth switches between chewing bites of a baked sweet potato and inhaling molasses-thick hits.

"I've never seen someone eat a potato like that. But it is efficient, I'll give you that."

"I already told you, it's a fucking *sweet* potato, Di. A Japanese one, that's why it's purple and white." Di grabs the foil-wrapped whole potato out of my hand and chomps down on the corner. Her small mouth leaves a perfect tooth-lined crescent. My mind races. Maybe that means I can take a few grams out of my weight calculation of exactly 225 and be able to use those leftover calories in my dinner later. Except I had an almond when Di offered me one earlier. So that probably evens it all out. Yes. The caloric density translates. Perfect. It's all in order.

"Damn. Good shit." She hands it back to me, and I nibble next to her bite to bring the potato's surface back to an even line. Di lingers in her savoring too much to pay any attention. She doesn't really ever comment on my rituals, just like I don't comment on the dozens of empty peanut butter jars in her trash that she lazily covers up with a blank piece of paper or two. Except her lack of commentary is due to ignorance, while mine is due to knowing it all too well to bear acknowledging her shit, too.

"The most embarrassing thing happened to me this morning when I was trying to do laundry. That guy I told you about who buys the pretzels? He saw my hand towel get caught in the elevator and rip, and all my laundry spill over the whole goddamn floor. And, *and*, I was in my fucking robe and slippers."

"The Batman ones?"

"Yes, the fucking Batman ones."

She coughs out a feeble laugh. "Jesus. I still need to meet this guy. Thank him and all, for aiding in my recent weight gain."

I snort. My heart races uncomfortably. Despite the inevitable feeling of panic and the alien out-of-body dissociation that weed always brings me, I smoke anyway, as a painful distraction. I can feel my nerves rejecting the incoming substance in each inhale. They don't seem to sink into softness like others' do. I experience the depth, the mellow, and the lowness it brings, but my veins begin pumping at hyperspeed to try and clear it out before I can settle. An airplane never able to find a cruising altitude between every layer of turbulence. I'm prevented from enjoying any relaxation as my body jolts me into an unwelcoming limbo between states.

Di's eyes are closed as her mouth barely opens to allow for a pristine exhale. I look down at the half-eaten sweet potato in my hand and rub my foot across it viciously, trying to coat the thing with as much filth and toe jam as I can. Guess I can't eat the rest now.

I wrap the loose foil over the now-dirty potato and stuff it into my backpack. At least this anxiety always prevents my appetite from being able to skyrocket as is expected.

Walking out into the hallway, my heart races erratically. It is a jagged musical score of staccato and crescendo that leaves a ringing in my ears and a clenching in my jaw. I lean against the wall near the large metal elevators and grind my stone teeth as my gelatinous brain melts into a thick, boiling vapor. The musical score of ringing elevator bells from floors above and below reverberates the vapor between the wooden sides of my skull until it cracks down the middle in a perfect dichotomy. The vapor dissipates. A melodramatic auto-lobotomy.

I sink to my knees. My memory jolts to experiences at high school parties where some well-meaning guy, two or so grades above me with awkward intentions, would tell me I was "just greening out" and to "try and take some deep breaths." The past embarrassment rises in me and brings about the neural muscle memory to attempt those breaths anyway. I end up getting very light-headed and make myself stand up to pace around, slamming the elevator button to my right. Perhaps a walk will calm my mind.

Outside, the cold, humid air causes my nose to run upon impact. My upper lip is quickly painted with makeup-erasing snot. I reach for a cigarette to distract myself but cannot light it in the whirling wind, so I throw it down, aborting it with a heel grind.

Greg stands across the street from me, staring at his toes-together, heels-apart feet, like he always does. My mind suddenly becomes much clearer as the chaos softens within me. I breathe in, breathe out, and close my eyes. The wind rips my eyelids back open and tornadoes my hair to cloud my vision, but Greg is still right there. I haven't seen Greg since before Really Bad, when I hadn't gotten on meds yet. Now, being in his presence here, something is activated in me again. The part of me that is creative, alive, and full of feeling has turned back on after long being subdued. Manic electricity races up my spine.

Greg's gaze lifts forward to meet mine as his posture remains hunched and timid. Without allowing my mind to grant permission, my hand raises itself and waves violently in hopes of catching his attention.

"Greg!" I croak from my dry throat. "Greg!"

I continue crying out across the street. The wind thrusts his shaggy brown hair across his scalp, but his expression remains stagnant and unwavering. I'm jumping up and down erratically, my heart rate mirroring my jittery motions, my voice trying to slip through my heavy breaths.

"Val? What the hell?" Di stands barefoot next to me, her hands on her hips. "Who are you yelling at?"

Di doesn't know, and Di won't believe me.

"Val, come back inside. You're too high. I've been watching you scream at an empty sidewalk from my window. I don't want the security guards inside to hear you and make you leave for being a crazy homeless person or some shit."

"I can't, there's someone—"

She grabs my arm, and I trip over my own feet without breaking my gaze. Greg's still standing there, a perfect porcelain statue, as Di drags me away.

Chapter 9

The night before Really Bad, Vic and I went to the movies for the premier of *Haunted Skullrider*. It ended up being a shit horror movie. I fell asleep.

"Val," he whispered, shaking me and laughing. "Val, wake up, come on." I slowly rose up from the old red velvet theater seat and stretched up my arms. We exited the building and made our way to his twenty-year-old Mercedes station wagon, his arm around my shoulder to shield me from the wind, and I nestled into his prominent shoulder as perfectly as a puzzle piece.

"Agh, sorry," Vic muttered as he dropped his keys and bent down to pick them up next to the driver's side wheel. I sniffled and waited for my door to unlock as he climbed in and reached over to let me in.

"Your nose is awfully pink." He gave a pitying purse of the lips and grabbed my hand. I could tell he was surprised by how cold it was, and he gripped it firmly as he turned the wheel to reverse with his left hand.

"Your nose is awfully small," I replied. He'd told me pretty early on in our relationship that someone had compared his face to Dwight Schrute—in particular, the small proportion of his nose to the rest of his face. He exhaled a soft, slightly insecure laugh and looked at me while slowing the car down to a stop. I could tell something serious was about to escape from his mouth, something whose weight would surpass its length. It would be exactly what I wanted to hear, what would save me, what would barely lift me from the flatline I was constantly at risk of fading into. My eyes granted Vic permission to speak, and he preemptively swallowed. With a honk from the car behind us, the moment broke. Our eyes immediately retreated and locked on to the road. It reminded me of getting my hopes up about my parents' empty promises as a child. I bitterly bit my lip. I was expecting to hear what would squeeze some serotonin out of these defective neural pathways. Could've been some dopamine in there as well, a pure delicacy.

As we drove up into my driveway, the disappointment buried me, and I couldn't bear to meet Vic's dark gaze.

"I'll text you tomorrow." God dammit. I guess I had been obvious enough to make him lock up, too, even if he hadn't been the same level of pissed off about our disintegrated moment. I slammed the car door and felt overwhelmingly guilty for causing him such discomfort. *Why do I always do this to people? Fuck. Fuck. Fuck. You piece of shit. That could've been salvaged. Vic would've told you he fucking loved you. Vic doesn't fucking love you now. He's rethinking the whole thing, thinking about how that honk was a goddamn sign that he shouldn't even be near you or interpret your codependency as "commitment." He's glad he didn't utter those words. He's thanking the impatient driver of that falling-apart PT Cruiser behind us for nearly hitting his bumper and completely obliterating that delusion he had. If you hadn't been so fucking awkward after, he definitely would have retrieved his courage and given it a second go. But you closed up, as always, and caused both of you to suffer. In a utilitarian sense, the whole equation would end up more positive than negative if you weren't there at all. It's that way with every single equation you're a variable in. Omission makes the most sense.*

As I entered my house, my dad was sitting at our kitchen table doing some work on his computer; he looked up and blinked. He didn't say anything. He was always fairly decent at reading me.

But he was also always too afraid to ask any further about my true mood. I could tell he always hoped my darkness was simply on the surface but knew deep down that it wasn't. Denial is a hard cycle to break once it starts because it roots itself at the base of the spine and coils around each vertebrate in knots of titanium.

Tomorrow will be different.

Tomorrow will be different.

Tomorrow will be different.

I kept telling myself that as I tried to fall asleep in my fluffy pink bed. I think it was a mantra I'd heard on *The Secret* documentary as an example of a positive affirmation that claimed to actually change your reality if you used it enough. I think the secret is really that you know how everything's going to end up. And for a good amount of people, it does end up fairly well, like they're sure it will, because so many people's dreams are based on what they see right there in front of them. They're caught up in their surroundings. When those appearances happen to not *actually* amuse you, there is no fucking secret because you understand the truth, you see the nuances in 20/20, and you're the only one wearing the 3D glasses out of the whole audience. Winston Smith in 1984. Joan of Arc. Jesus goddamn Christ.

I woke up sweaty under the same pink taffeta duvet despite the fan whirling all night. There wasn't the usual morning delirium that allowed for fleeting relief. There was just overwhelming recognition of my fail ure, of my fuckup, of my inability to be loved. Usually, I'd have woken up to a "good morning" text of some sort from Vic at this point because I fucking knew he had work in an hour and was already up because his boss was a hard-ass and he needed a promotion and he wouldn't be late even if his boss wasn't a hard-ass and he wasn't almost broke from spending all his money on his guitar because I knew him. I knew his OCD and his always-being-on-time despite also always-being-stoned. He was my always.

I knew I had to do it now or I wouldn't have the guts again. I was pretty sure most people did this kind of shit at night, or at least midday, when they'd had the chance to savor their final moments. The last meal on death row after getting approved by the current administration of severe mental illness.

It was a shame that the ten grand that went toward trying to make me happier with myself would also end up supplying me with a ticket out. I'd known that post-rhinoplasty Vicodin would come in handy sometime; I'd just assumed it would be for extra income.

So there I was, before ten on a Sunday morning, preparing my own release, holding the circular white pills in my hand while snot-crying naked on the bathroom floor. Little did Di know how much we did have in common.

Except I didn't actually have the guts to swallow when it came down to it. I looked at the little white circles like I expected my vision to suddenly vanish, tears dripping down onto my bare thighs. The beast rose and took hold of me, angry at me, angry at the world, angry at Vic, angry at the fact that I was angry all the fucking time.

"I just wanted an *I love you*," I mouthed to myself in the mirror. I leaned forward onto my palms and began punching the mirror and surrounding black tile with my frail hands until it began to look like what I imagined the core of my mind looked like. I was howling, chugging back mucus like I hadn't eaten in years—

which some may say I really hadn't, I suppose—and blood was spattering onto the off-white walls. I was Jackson Pollock in a passionately creative episode.

The door suddenly burst open even though I'd made sure it was locked before. It was my dad standing there, staring at me as if nothing was wrong. A beat boomed between us.

"*Ahhhhhhh!*" I punched the shiny black tile even harder, imagining it was his face. "*Do something for fucking once! I said fucking do something!*" His jaw dropped ever so slightly, and his eyes darted to the pills on the counter. He grabbed my thin biceps in each of his hands and dragged me into the hallway. Then he got two towels, wrapping me in one and wiping at my cuts with the other.

I don't remember anything after that until getting to the hospital and starting to talk with some doctor. I also recall suddenly regretting ever leaving that pink bed. I wanted to cry but was too tired.

"What prompted you to do this?" the calm female doctor later asked me as she sat down at my eye level in an attempt to seem more trustworthy.

"I fucked things up with my boyfriend." It seemed to be such a pathetic, meaningless statement in that moment, but it really was what had sent me over the deep end after piling it on top of all the other shit.

"Who is your boyfriend?"

"Vic Graham."

"Is there a number where we can reach him?"

I nodded but then realized I didn't have my phone on me and didn't know it by heart.

"He works at Revival Guitars, you can reach him there." Some part of me wanted to fight the system, but I was too tired, and at that point, I didn't even know what "the system" was.

The woman returned after a few minutes with a concerned look on her face. "No one at the store knows someone by that name. Are you sure he doesn't go by a different name or work somewhere else?"

Heat rose in my chest. "No, I'm sure. What time is it? He gets off at four."

Her sudden swallow shut me up in anticipation of whatever she had to say.

"Valerie, that's not the main reason I'm here. We're going to run some tests for some mental-health issues we suspect may be causing this."

"Wh-what kind of mental-health issues?"

A pause. "Possibly some schizotypal, or—"

"You think I have schizophrenia?"

"There is a range, it's not—"

I shut off at that point. I was diagnosed that day. And the meds did help for a little while, for the year I remained on them, but I no longer saw the truth. I knew that, and was okay with it for that time. I wasn't seeing in 20/20 anymore. I was watching the 3D movie in 2D with everyone else after having experienced the full version before. I wanted to go back to how I was, but I was too tired.

But Vic was the only thing that had ever made my life worth living. It doesn't matter whether my malfunctioning mind can take credit for him or if real biology can. Even my own self-created love left me, but better loved and lost than never loved at all. That's the saying, I think, though some might question the veracity of love in my case.

Then I moved here. I got a taste of the power of my untamed mind again. I felt the creativity and joy rising, little by little, waiting to become fully activated. And suddenly, I'm not too tired anymore.

Chapter 10

I give a closemouthed smile as I walk into Dr. Ellis's office. The walls are a newly painted bright white, and the furniture is slightly rearranged.

"You repainted," I say without thinking.

"All of our offices, yes. Not sure how I feel about it, though. It's a bit stark."

"I like it better than camel."

A laugh. "Yes, I would say the intensity of it is probably more suited to your liking."

"My liking? And what would that be?" I raise my eyebrows as he looks at his notepad with a chuckle.

"How was your weekend?"

I sigh and roll my eyes playfully at his disregard for my question.

"Di and I went to some museums because she had a project for a class, and I was pretty bored. I don't really like museums much, but one exhibit on zippers was cool, I guess."

"See anyone else besides Di?"

I begin to nod and impulsively decide to bring up Jett. "There's this guy who lives on my floor, I think, who I keep running into. It's pretty embarrassing, honestly." I recross my legs and shuffle farther back on the love seat.

"Tell me about him." The command feels forced, and a strange voice inside yells at me for mentioning Jett. I scratch my ear and look up at Dr. Ellis with my head slightly cocked to the right. After awkwardly explaining the peanut-butter-pretzel-bite situation and then eventually getting to the laundry incident, my voice tapers off with an insecure, "Yeah…" as I realize that Dr. Ellis isn't laughing or finding it as funny as I assumed he would. I tried. He takes a while to write in his notepad, then begins to speak as he keeps his gaze on his writing.

"Have these interactions caused an increase in anxiety for you at all?"

"Um, I guess in the moment, yeah, when I'm embarrassed and all. But I don't think I get too anxious about it otherwise. It's been nice, actually. Meeting new people, I mean." We go on to talk a little more about how my weekend went and what exhibits I saw. Our hour today is heavy with more meaninglessness than usual.

There is a numb sensation between us that disconcerts me here. We don't do any emotional mastery work like we began to do the last few times. Most of the session I'm just thinking about how I'd really like a sweet potato right about now.

On the way back to my dorm, I grab a few groceries, sweet potatoes included. Stepping out of my building elevator and into the hallway, I look down in extreme hunger at the inside of my bag and consider biting into one. I learned you could eat potatoes raw sometime recently and impulsively decide to nibble the end of one just to try it. I grab one with a thin, prominent tip and apprehensively graze off the smallest bite. Hearing footsteps, I look up and see Jett walking down the hall toward me.

"Are you eating a raw sweet potato?" Still with the small chunk in my mouth, I debate with myself for a few seconds, unsure whether to swallow it or spit it out or do anything at all. I go with swallow and decide not to try and act natural with him.

"Uh, yeah, it's safe and all. I was just trying the very end. It's not something I, like, actually do or anything."

He grabs the sweet potato out of my hand and hesitatingly takes a similarly puny bite out of the opposite end.

"What are—"

"Tastes kind of bland. I'll stick with cooked." He continues to the elevator, and I hear him click the button as I rush into the kitchen.

Forty minutes and exactly one hundred grams later, I am decently satisfied and text Di. We meet up in her dorm again, which smells like incense now. Her roommate, Anna, who is surprisingly decent, apologizes "since it might smell a little strong" upon my entrance but also asks that I "please not talk about it because my RA is a bitch and if she hears anything, it'll be my third citation and I don't want to get kicked out and all."

"No worries. Gotcha." She leaves quickly after I sit down on Di's bed so that she can "leave us to it." Her possibly Buddhist hanging chain of elephants and bells rattles on the door as she gently closes it.

"Damn, I expected you to wait for me to text you after what happened the other day. I guess you really are a grown woman, Val. I'm really proud of you."

"Oh, shut up."

"Just saying. You are a mature young woman." She pronounces *mature* "ma-too-er" and begins to smile, unable to take herself seriously.

"I'd ask if you have plans and shit for today, but I know you don't."

"Ohhh, she's *psychic* too!" Di is in an unusually energetic mood. Maybe she took an Adderall or something. I don't care enough to ask. "Yeah, no, I don't have anything planned. I was probably just going to finish my season of *UFO Investigations*."

"Want to go to Harry's?"

"After I finish this episode."

I sit on my phone as she slouches in an ergonomic desk chair in front of her sticker-covered MacBook. Twenty-one minutes later, she shuts it and stands. "Okay. Can you reach my umbrella?" She points to it high on Anna's shelf. "Anna borrowed it and just put it there." Understandable, as Di's side doesn't seem to have one free inch of space. I can barely reach it myself and realize how tall Anna must be.

"Does she model?" I ask curiously.

"Used to, then quit and is pretty against the whole industry now. She's super into, like, meditation and yoga, I think. We could've probably ended up being friends if we hadn't been matched as roommates and all."

"Understood."

Ten minutes later, our porcelain mugs clink onto the wooden table in between us as we sit down. Di tries to stabilize the table slightly when she realizes it's wobbly, quickly giving up. She slouches down with her legs splayed and wrists resting on her thighs.

"You think I should keep letting my hair grow out or re-shave it?" Her hair has lengthened considerably within the last few weeks, her waves and dark roots becoming more pronounced.

"Maybe let it grow out just to see. Are you going to redo your roots?"

"Yeah, I think I want to go blue, though. Like, ice blue."

"Mm. Should be cool."

"Okay." She pauses in thought. "I think I'll shave it tomorrow."

"Cool." I'm already a little hungry, which reminds me of seeing Jett earlier, and I retell the story to Di.

"This shit sounds like a fucking sitcom. Hopefully, I'm with you next time. Fucking hilarious."

"I told my therapist today about all the shit that's happened with him, and he was, like, stone cold. He didn't find it funny at all, it was so fucking awkward."

"Hmm. Probably just uptight."

"Yeah. Probably."

Chapter 11

"I mean, it's an ethically valid choice for me to keep avoiding my meds. The pills have a good chance of using lactose binders. Totally justified; I would expect no less." I'm on speaker with Di, pressing my phone against my shoulder with my ear so tightly it hurts the cartilage where it's pierced.

She huffs. "I'm convinced I'm completely fuckin' rewired. I think it's the yoga."

"Dude, you've done, like, one class."

"Three! I've done three. I got a class pack." I used to do some yoga. In the pre–Really Bad and pre–pre–Really Bad days. Back before there was even a buildup. Back when things were numb and I was even numb to the numbness. Patronizing Di does make part of me want to get back into practicing, though.

"Okay, I'm gonna go. I need to do my peer-editing shit before I get too tired."

"Responsible. I'm headed to see Sweets. Talk later." She hangs up. I get a nervous twinge whenever she brings up her drug dealer. I never really could master the art of casually buying an ounce of weed; it always seemed like a life-or-death game of roulette with no adrenaline reward upon surviving. Thankfully, I usually don't have to employ much manipulation to get Di to do the face-to-face part for me; she just asks for a little extra payment on my end.

As I bring the phone down from my ear, a text from my dad appears. He's telling me about the unexpectedly cold weather back where he is. I say *where he is* and not *home* because no place so unwelcoming can be considered home. He signs the text with a *love u* and an accidental click of the return key, which extends the message blankly an extra line. I sigh in amusement.

No matter how docile or loving, there is a rubber band of past history causing constant strain on our momentarily non-problematic relationship. Being connected to me has meant seeing me experience the death of a brother, a child that tried to be but never was his, and, with that, uncharted moral territory. He and my mother divorced shortly after I was born, for circumstances unknown to me, and the same happened with my mother and Greg's father a few years later. Denial of it all was always easier for my father, and due to this, I punished him, constantly and dismissively. An eloquent, advanced silent treatment executed by an overgrown child disguised as a gifted young woman. I don't think I've said anything more to him than *yes*, *no*, or *'kay* in years. It's like the memories form a straightjacket around me the second we share air.

Before I get the chance to respond, he asks when a good time would be for him to come visit. I bite my lip. It's not so much that I don't want him to visit; it's that I don't want the emotional proximity to everything I've tried so hard to run away from.

maybe thanksgiving or the week before, I type back quickly. I hope, in his impatience to see me, he chooses the week before so that I don't have to think about eating around him on Thanksgiving. Thankfully, he immediately confirms he can't wait to come up and would love to do the earlier dates.

I head over to Harry's with my computer to actually do my peer-editing shit. This kid in my creative writing class only puts out these anime-esque short stories that I swear are straight transcripts of *Naruto*. I find a table in the corner, sit on the side looking at the rest of the room so that my computer screen isn't facing everyone else, since that would make me too self-conscious to distractedly roam, and cough as I pull out my computer. I'm not wearing makeup, but I feel a little confident in my new dark-maroon corduroys. Comfort in wearing color one small step at a time.

I nearly choke as I notice Jett is sitting at the table closest to mine, still several feet away. I swear he wasn't there when I sat down. Maybe I just wasn't paying attention. He's reading what appears to be a biography about Skid Row. I try to read the title without getting noticed, but to no avail.

He begins speaking to me loudly without even looking up. "It's pretty boring. If you were wondering." My cheeks immediately flush in hopes that no one else hears. I quickly try and make myself calm down since I have no foundation on to hide my giveaway red cheeks.

"I'm editing a bullshit anime short story, so probably not as boring as that."

"I don't know if you can call a literary piece *anime*, technically. Maybe narrative manga?"

I smile. "Whatever it is, it's shitty and grammatically horrendous."

He gets up and moves over to sit in front of me. "What are you doing tonight?"

I hesitate and end up making the incredibly daring choice *not* to tell some lie I think he'd find impressive.

"Probably smoking with my best friend."

"Do you smoke a lot?"

"A fair bit. But I don't really inhale much, honestly. It can give me bad anxiety, and I prefer cigarettes."

"Yeah, I get panicky sometimes with that shit, too. I don't know, just doesn't sit with me as chill as it does with other people."

"Oh my God, exactly!" I say a little too enthusiastically. A twentysomething in a beanie and clunky wireless headphones on top glares over at me. "I mean, same with me. I just can't get super into it, but I pretend it's, like, worth spending money on just because I always have, I guess."

"Fuck that shit. Spend your money on, like, I don't know...more sweet potatoes or something." He sets the book down and leans back a little in his seat.

"What do you have there?" I ask curiously, nodding toward his mug. He laughs.

"I'm kind of embarrassed to say this, but a matcha latte with soy milk. I don't know, I just really like the way it tastes."

"And you're straight?" A few more people look over to me. I must be a lot louder than I think I am. And right here, right now, for once, I don't really care.

"Why do you assume I'm straight?"

"I don't, now that I know you order matcha lattes." He laughs as pushes his messy dark hair back. He's wearing a navy bomber over a white V-neck and light-wash jeans. I suddenly wish I'd smeared a little dark eyeliner on. Not to seem put together or anything—quite the opposite, like I'd had an eventful-enough night to wake up with perfectly disheveled day-after makeup that I never actually have because I don't really go out or, God forbid, forget to complete my skin-care routine before bed.

We make a little small talk about Skid Row until the conversation runs its course, and he slowly segues into leaving.

"I don't have an umbrella and don't want to get caught in the snow when it gets heavy," he explains, zipping up his bomber.

I think of offering him mine but decide against it. Probably overkill.

I return to my computer after saying bye and notice that the gray-haired man at the table in front of me is eyeing me curiously.

"Convincing monologue," he projects confidently toward me, nodding. I give a confused closemouthed smile and force a cough as I quickly gather my things. Time for me to leave, too, I guess. Still no peer editing done.

Chapter 12

Walking back from class late in the afternoon, I realize it is Greg's birthday. He would be sixteen today. His prepubescent image, forever carved into the cave wall of my skull, progresses into a taller, older figure with slightly darker hair but just as wiry of a body. He would be still wearing that goddamn yellow sweater, though higher up now on his torso, and I imagine him in black, fitted skate pants and matching sneakers. He wouldn't be blowing out any candles but instead digging into spaghetti. The kid always fucking loved spaghetti. He'd still love spaghetti at sixteen. He would continuously exist young at heart, only getting older physically. We'd be at Mandolino's, his favorite restaurant, now that I see the space more clearly. I'd lean across the table to hug him. It's something I never felt comfortable enough doing years ago, but now that we're both older, the juvenile awkwardness surely would've faded into mature comfort.

My way of creating the life I'd dreamed of, even if I was only successful at doing so for a few years, was with filmmaking. Enough to get me that scholarship and a bit of confidence in something. That something isn't there for me anymore, and I believe it to be stolen from me by doctors and pills and the medical system, but I always wondered what Greg's way of transmuting so much dreaming would be. We'd talk about how different things were going to be for each of us once we got to eighteen and were out of there. I got there and thought it would be smooth sailing. I saw that it isn't so simple. I wonder how he would've seen it, too.

I light a cigarette under the alcove of a vacant store space and wonder if Greg would've smoked cigarettes. I don't think so. I think the smell would've irritated his delicate senses. There was little boundary between him and the world; he was constantly being hammered by anything and everything around him. At our celebratory dinner, he'd be slurping down his noodles and his orange juice (he'd still order orange juice at dinner, I'm sure of that), and he would tell me I should stop smoking, actually. Yes, he'd suggest it in that way where you can tell the person cares about you enough to not try to make it sound any type of way but instead translates their feelings into language without an agenda. He'd hold eye contact with me until I gave him an adequate response of agreement. Then he'd blink with those long, straight eyelashes and sip on the straw of his orange juice. Suddenly, I feel a pang of guilt when I realize that I'm still imagining him at sixteen acting as the twelve-year-old who actually wants my approval. No, at sixteen, he probably wouldn't still be going to Mandolino's with me on every holiday, since it wasn't like we had some typical phony family gathering to go to. This birthday, he'd probably be smoking weed with a friend, just one friend, because I know him, and he wouldn't be one to have a big posse or anything. They'd be playing video games or doing some other dumb shit. They'd probably order in fucking Domino's and drink Diet Coke until their stomachs hurt. He'd hate me for being related to Mom at this point in his life, and my obligatory birthday text would be read but not responded to.

I throw down the cigarette and stub it out before continuing to walk back to my dorm. The dry skin on my knuckles roughs up against the grain of my coat as I slide my hands into the large pockets. I think someone gave me L'Occitane hand cream awhile back. I really should find that in whichever drawer I crammed it into.

It's five. That means an hour and a half until I'm allowed to start cooking dinner. Dinner won't even be ready for another hour after that because I have to measure and weigh out everything before cooking and wait until the oven is totally heated up before I can put anything in it. And then I'll eat later and won't be hungry before bed and might (but not actually) be less hungry in the morning.

Dr. Ellis has told me before that it seems like my diet is my form of exerting control because I feel out of control in other ways. Whatever. I'll stop this shit when I feel like it.

It's six thirty. I race into the kitchen. I go to pull out my scale and preheat the oven when I realize Jett is leaning against the counter, scrolling on his phone and eating peanut-butter-filled pretzels. The pang in my chest is so internal I'm sure he can't sense my molten anger reverberating.

"Oh, hey there," he muffles calmly. I smile forcefully and turn the dial to 400. Maybe if I take long enough to get everything out from the fridge and cut it, he'll be gone. Maybe I can weigh my vegetables and tofu without him noticing.

Five minutes of pretending to examine each and every floret of cauliflower later, he's still there. The fact that he's mindlessly eating absolute shit pisses me off even more, and I debate putting everything away and explaining, *Oh fuck, I have plans*, as I rush out to meet my mystery date. No, I bet I can eyeball this. I know how much sweet potato is about 150 calories, and I know how much tofu is around that, too. My mind itself is a fucking calculator.

I cut everything awkwardly as only the sound of my blade and Jett's chewing fills the five or so feet between us. After finishing, I step back and panic. This looks like way too much. I know if I plate all of this for myself, I won't be able to keep from eating it. Heat rises jarringly into my temples.

I bite my cheeks and impulsively half yell at him, "Do you want any of this? My stomach hurts, and I don't think I'll be able to have all of it." Jett looks at me in surprise, still chewing. His eyes shoot down to the baking pan in front of me.

"I mean, yeah, sure, thanks, I'll have whatever you don't, I guess... Are you sure, though?"

"Cramps," I say, raising my eyebrows. "I tend to lose my appetite." I don't expect him to get all embarrassed at me bringing up my period, which I haven't had since God knows when, but it should shut him up. Hyper-liberal white guys tend to avoid talking about women's topics unless they're damn sure it won't make them seem sexist. I often find avoidance is how they react to nearly anything controversial. Just as I expect, he doesn't say anything and nods as he puts away the aluminum bag of pretzels.

"Just leave out whatever, and I'll get it later. Thanks again."

"Yeah, no prob." I smile again, and Jett sways off. His strides are long and sturdy, full of gravitas.

I got into cooking out of necessity. Greg and I needed food, and I was around ten or eleven when our source for nourishment became increasingly undependable. My memory recalls lots of canned soups that I would bulk up with microwave-steamed vegetables found in the back of the freezer and minute rice with ketchup. When the processed food became too gross to bear any longer, I began to accumulate wrist burns from trying to make things in the oven. I think I made this awful meatloaf shit as my first successful oven recipe. Greg was in elementary school by then, around eight or nine, and would jump up and down in glee upon seeing me revel in the success of actually making something myself. We'd slather expired Heinz ketchup on the top of everything and gulp it down within minutes as we'd watch the six-thirty episode of *Wheel of Fortune*.

Now back in my dorm room, I jump up from my desk chair as the timer on my phone goes off. Time to take everything out of the oven. As I look down at the sheet of food, I bite my lip and cut every section in half. Half the tofu. Half the sweet potato. Half the cauliflower. Half the brussels sprouts.

Mixed together on my plate, I look at the scattered concoction for several seconds. Ten-year-old me wraps her arms around my waist and shakes me, yelling, screaming, "What are you doing?" I move everything into a little bowl so that it doesn't seem as small. She's still there, puny hands digging into my bony sides and pounding my vascular abdomen as she tries to get my attention. I look down, and she's still there. I writhe and try to wrestle her off, raking her head back.

I wish I could snap her neck.

Chapter 13

I've stupidly admitted to Dr. Ellis how I've been seeing Greg everywhere recently. He knows that when I say this, I don't mean thinking about him sometimes and imagining things. I mean really seeing.

"I'm surprised. You seemed to be on such an upward trajectory. Upping your dose may be called for, then," he declares definitively, followed by a cough. "You don't have to live like this. You know that." I clench my fists, digging stubby, damaged nails into my palms in hopes of painfully punishing myself. The bitten nubs barely touch my skin in the first place.

My mouth twists to the side, and my feet tap the love seat. He rearranges himself in his green chair.

"I'll put in a call for that. We'll see if that helps. I'm glad you mentioned the beginnings of this before...anything happened." So I under-exaggerated. But this strange, bursting force inside me needed to make itself known. I just wish it hadn't been to him, or anyone, anyone at all. I'm bigger, I'm better than this. I'm in power. Just a slipup.

Except I'm not. Except I'm a failing piece of shit with no self-control or self-awareness. A feral animal.

It would be easy not to take my meds once I got back to my dorm with them; it was putting on the facade during the visit that required skill and precision. And I knew this next particular visit they'd watch me extra carefully with the mention of reprised symptoms. Not that they could necessarily force pills down my throat once I left, but it was still nerve-wracking. Like I'd get in trouble and go to detention or something.

So that first Monday, upon my visit, I replayed in my head the relaxation techniques Dr. Ellis walked me through over and over again. Little did he know I'd basically be using his own psychology against him.

Tense the wrists, tense the forearms, tense the shoulders, release. Tense the toes, tense the calves, tense the thighs, tense the glutes, release. Fuck this shit, hearing his voice say *glutes* every time I go through this makes me get more anxious than I ever was beforehand.

I go up and smile. I say my name in a level tone to the short nurse, just as rehearsed, and the once even drumbeat in my chest begins to syncopate and become sporadic. I hand over my student ID and wait for her to finish pulling me up on the computer. I hope she can't tell I'm nervous about seeming like I haven't been taking my meds as she looks at me a second too long. Hopefully, it's my trying-to-look-slept-in makeup causing her to think about whether I actually went to bed in it or have early-onset Parkinson's.

"Thanks," I say, taking my ID back from her outstretched hand. I turn around and start heading out.

"Hon, you forgot your new refill!"

I go pick up the goddamn orange bottle and scurry away.

Once I'm back in my dorm, it's late enough in the day for me to be allowed in the kitchen. My food will take about an hour to cook. Yes. I'm perfectly allowed at this point.

Jett, in that same Skid Row shirt over some unfamiliar black jeans, is leaning against the counter and typing furiously on his phone.

"Oh, hey," he says happily, looking up. "I thought you might be coming in here soon. I'll pay you and all, but could you cook me something?" The tone of his voice is casual and direct, without the usual strain of having rehearsed the statement beforehand. "I'm really tired and don't feel like going anywhere." I let him take the comedic pause I know he's scheduled into the spiel. "If you don't, I may starve. I've only had a cinnamon-raisin bagel today."

I exhale and roll my eyes, acting as if I'm flirtatiously willing to agree to his request. Except inside I'm scrambling because now my next few days of what I'll eat are subject to change depending on how much of my shit he eats. Fuck.

An hour later, we're carrying our plates into my room at the end of the hall, each trying to manage holding both a plate and a mug as we open the door one after the other with a foot.

"Thanks, by the way. I think I forgot to say that earlier."

I shrug and clang the fork onto my teeth.

"So. I suppose I never asked you the usual bullshit. Major, place of origin, pronouns…" He cocks his head to the side a little. I cover my mouth and look down as I finish chewing. Not quite sure why I do that whenever I plan ahead to speak while food is in my mouth like others can't obviously tell I'm currently chewing. A surge of answers rise up to my mouth, a surge of so much I want to entertain him with, but the force of fear keeps it all down. Fear of saying something that will lead to bringing up Really Bad. Or Greg. Or Mom. Or Vic. I'm scared that if I say any of it out loud, it'll somehow be more real than if I keep it to myself. Though, the more I seem to ignore it, the more it blares in my head and plays in front of my eyes.

I swallow my bite and keep to the outskirts of my mind, where the trail to the core is least likely to be followed.

"I'm a film major right now, but I'm total shit at it, honestly. Like, I don't know how I got in, I've never really done anything outside of BS school projects on iMovie, and I don't care about it anymore. I mean, I do care about it when I care about it. But it feels empty. Maybe I'll switch to... I don't know." Saying that out loud makes me realize that I truly do want to change course, which feels heretical. I'm here on a fucking full ride. I was *that* girl who was going to create some beautifully witty documentary or surrealist film that would indisputably become a cult classic. My professors think that's who I am still. But now, it's beginning to really hit me that I never wanted to make great art, I wanted to experience great admiration, and I could only lie to myself in that way for so long.

"Aw, don't say that. You have to have *some* talent if you're here." He chews a carrot.

"No, like, really. There was some fuckup or misunderstanding of my mediocrity as genius, I think, or a fuckup of my application with someone else's. I should switch to something else, but…redefining yourself as something other than an 'art student' is kind of daunting. Especially when so many people associate that with you. I know that's really stupid, I know." Heat rises into my cheeks and cradles my dimples. I look across and slightly down at my red velvet sneakers that hang off the edge of my bed. Jett leans back in my wobbly desk chair.

"People associate that with you?" Jett asks, furrowing his brows.

"I won a film thing last year. It got me a lot of attention. Attention that helped me get in here."

"Like, a film festival award kind of thing?"

"Yeah. Something like that. It's whatever, I'm over it by now."

"Doesn't sound like *just whatever*. You sound talented. You *seem* talented, just by knowing you for this short time. You seem like someone who really could make some meaningful shit someday."

"Thanks. I hope so." I blush and look down at my remaining food, instantly estimating the caloric value left.

"Well, I'm a history major. I think I want to minor in French. But who knows." Another chomp of a roasted carrot. A damn perfectly roasted carrot, if I do say so myself.

"Do you know what you want to do with that degree? Just curious. I'm asking as a film major. No judgment."

"I want to run a company for historical reenactments."

I look up at him and blink. My mouth opens a little. I quickly shut it, worried that food is hanging out.

"Dude, I'm kidding."

"Oh my God, I really didn't know how to respond to that!"

We both laugh for a minute, and he sniffles. It's a delicate sniffle, not robust or snotty or gross.

"Yeah, no, I don't really know what I actually want to do in the end. Maybe teach, honestly. Anything but become a fucking museum docent or curator or some shit like that." Jett shakes his head as if to rid himself of even mentioning the topic.

"Any certain kind of history?"

"I like the Renaissance."

"I would *not* have taken you as a medieval guy!"

"Because I'm not. I said the Renaissance." Chomp. A potato this time. His mouth moves around in a circle as he raises and lowers his eyebrows assertively.

"Psh." I roll my eyes. "Alright. Where are you from, then, Renaissance guy?"

"Portland."

"Portland?"

"Portland."

He goes on to describe how non-Portlandia his life really is back in Oregon, how his parents don't really recycle, and how his mom has a Suburban with terrible gas mileage.

"Yeah, I got the hell out. It's a vortex."

I explained how that was exactly how I felt about my hometown, despite not being from somewhere as notoriously eccentric as Portland. He talks some about his typical American parents, his lack of siblings except for a distant older half-brother named Fred, and I probe him more than usual to delay and avert discussing my own family. Not because I mind or am in denial, but because I don't want him to think of me as bruised and delicate or see "mommy issues" written on my fucking forehead from this point forward. So I ask about his parents' occupations to a ridiculous extent, and his mind seems not to question the motives behind my curiosity. Without hesitation, he describes his mother's real estate job and his father's marketing director position for a supplement company.

"And you? Parents, any siblings, the gamut?"

"Um, yeah, the usual. Younger brother."

"That's it? Nothing special? I feel like you're someone to have grown up with, like, two moms or a stay-at-home dad or something unconventional like that."

I laugh.

"No, that's pretty much it."

Chapter 14

I remember waking up in the morning and heading downstairs before school. Twelve, braces, lower-belly pooch, mosquito bites, the whole shit storm. Six thirty or forty-five in the morning, pajama pants and a pilling school club T-shirt. Bare feet. It's one of the few memories that I can truly recall. Most of the first eighteen years of my life are a numb, dissociated blur of being drunkenly screamed at and hit. I suppose they're sealed off to protect me from them.

The wooden stairs beneath me felt starkly smooth. As I reached the second-to-last step, I jumped off over the final one out into the living area, just as I still do today on every second-to-last step. My toes curled under the very edge to allow for my push of just a few extra feet. It was early, but I still had the energy for that little soar.

I cannot specifically recall my thoughts. None of my thoughts from childhood seem to have made it through, just scenes and images and flashes of light. Or the absence of either when I wish they were there.

In all likelihood, I was probably trying to decide what to make myself for breakfast. The choice was typically cheap corner-store powdered donuts or strawberry Pop-Tarts. If both were either stale or gone, then maybe an oatmeal packet. I didn't touch those unless I had to or they were the dinosaur-egg kind.

However, as I turned the corner into the kitchen, I looked outside and saw my mother sprawled out on a lawn chair next to our poorly maintained pool. The green of the shattered bottles matched the algae. Both were proof of life past its right to exist.

I did not even care that her black minidress was hiked far above her hips or that her underwear was twisted grotesquely to the side. Overexposure to everything with her was nothing new for my tired young eyes. What was truly disturbing was not even her existence but rather her existence between states, not fully choosing either life or death but an uninhabitable place in between. At least in choosing death there would be a reality for which to draw upon, some peace in its definiteness. The surreal limbo of your unconscious mother surrounded by proof of her life last night and your own wish that it had been her death is not a stable place for the mind.

It was the first time I'd clearly heard the voice in my head hoping that there was no life left under that black polyester tube dress. Instead of wishing things would be different, I wanted things to be so real that the situation could advance no further. I was exhausted from the constant fear of her hurting me, whether physically or emotionally, and the only escape would be the death of one of us. If it weren't me, then at least it could be her.

Now, I recognize that same voice often, wishing that it were me now. Maybe that's why this memory replays for me, over and over again. Maybe it's the origin of the conscience within me that longs for the peace of withdrawal. Maybe it replays so I can understand her, that voice that's created the Rules and wants me to see Vic and Greg when I do. She's the devil restricting me from seeing clearly but also the angel fueling my creative fire, when she can. Which I'm not so sure she will do anymore.

As much as I wished my mother were dead, I knew she wasn't. Her chest, just barely, and far too peacefully, rose and then deflated like a tired party balloon. With my mind, I tried to be the piercing needle, but my aim wasn't strong enough to break through.

Like the poison circling through her veins that locked her away from reality, the poison of my mother's very being locked me out of my own body and propelled me into a bird's-eye view of the whole situation. I was in a helicopter, watching everything from high above and circling around to see the scene at every angle. My stomach lurched slightly as we dipped and dove. I was the pilot, the passenger, the cabin, the engine, the propeller. Everything but my twelve-year-old self standing in my kitchen looking out the floor-to-ceiling windows.

I wasn't the girl that looked in the pantry, pulled out the mostly eaten bag of powdered-sugar donuts, and mindlessly ate the rest. Sipping my glass of orange juice, it was empty in ten minutes and was left rimmed with sticky powdered-sugar residue.

I called my dad. "Dad, Mom doesn't feel well. Can you take me to school?"

Thirty minutes later, the Acura sedan pulled up on the curb by the front door. Door opened, backpack thrown to the other side, seat belt clicked. Except the person sitting in that sedan clicking that seat belt wasn't me. I was still in that helicopter with my sensitive stomach toppling everywhere high above the clouds.

Thoughts of what Greg would do never penetrated that helicopter, though I was aware of them circling around. The small part of me that wanted to address them convinced myself that with no one to wake him up for school, he'd sleep through the whole day or think it was Sunday.

I was not aloof or distant that day in school. I remember still answering questions, half-assing being a class clown, talking to friends. The helicopter was on autopilot with nothing in its way and nothing to make it stop until carpool, when the fire of trauma engulfed me from the inside out and trapped me to nearly burn to death inside the cabin.

My flesh raw and exposed and rotting away, I was faced with the open wounds gaping back at me as the flames slowly died down. My mother's Suburban approached. As the fire was extinguished, the true pain became evident, and the thick layers of pus pouring out of my skin snatched my focus away from my name being yelled out by the carpool monitor. Finally, my teacher came over and got me, scolding me for not getting up earlier.

"Come on, Valerie. You're holding up the rest of the cars in line."

As if in an automated trance, I followed the tall older woman to the tan SUV and climbed into the passenger seat. My mother's face was hidden beneath her usual mask of eleven-shades-too-dark Revlon ColorStay foundation and two thick halos of grainy black eyeshadow.

The second our eyes met, I entered my helicopter once again. My response to her "How was your day?" was a low-quality pirated recording. My mannerisms and breathing were performed by a stunt double. The actor didn't have asking her about that morning written down in the script.

Walking into my house and looking out where I had left my body that morning, I slowly reintegrated back into myself. The windows and pool were just like they had been when I left. Poorly kept but clean, orderly, unoccupied, and calm in my mind. Not a sight to see at all.

As I returned to my room, however, my wounds started to act up again and catch fire. The physical agony was not as intense as simply looking down and acknowledging that they were even there.

Instead of tending to them, however, I ignored them, and my body gradually became a mound of bleeding flesh turning into a shabby armor of scabs and dried blood. No clothing could entirely conceal the inhuman mess underneath, though, through layers and layers, I got pretty damn close.

Chapter 15

"Di, I'm not paying thirty dollars for that."

"Come on, it's not like you have class tomorrow morning."

Fuck. I knew keeping the fact that I didn't have class on Friday to myself would've come in handy.

"He's not even going to come on until, like, two a.m., the openers will be mediocre, I'll just be thinking about whether I should move my body or not the whole fucking time, and I *guarantee* I'll get pushed up against either a drunk perv or a coked-out bitch."

She sighs and sinks down in the wooden chair at Harry's. I sip my coffee and look to the side.

"Fine. I'll just go myself."

"Ask Anna if she'll go. She might be interested."

"Oh, fuck you."

I smile as I take another sip and internally punish myself for not ordering a matcha latte like I meant to. I figured if Jett always got them, I should probably try it myself. Actually, fuck that. I'm not wasting 150-plus calories on a drink. Good job, subconscious.

Each time I glance at Di, my eyes linger a split second longer than usual. Her buzz cut is reshaved really tight, and the black ink of her *love me* hairline tattoo is even more apparent now that the skin of her forehead is completely visible. I can tell she appreciates the attention of fellow coffee-shoppers trying to read it without getting caught.

"You know," Di begins as she wipes dried coffee stains from the corners of her mouth, "I think I'm going to become a female rapper."

I blink at her. "I'd ask if you were serious, but if you're mentioning it, I know you have to be."

"I just have a lot to say that I can't put into words."

"Rap is literally all words."

"Fuck you. I mean, like, speech words."

"So, conversation."

"Mmm. Yeah. It has to be...truly lyrical and shit. Real emotional."

I stifle a laugh, but she notices anyway.

"Oh, come on. I didn't make fun of you when you said you wanted to write a cookbook!"

"Di, I'm not making fun of you," I calmly state as I set my mug back down on the table. "Just how you're bringing this up and how you did it."

"Hmph. SoundCloud fame, here I come." She itches her scalp right above *love me*.

"Do you have a title for yourself yet? Or a name?"

"No, I wanted to bring this up so I could ask you for ideas and shit." She sits up a little bit higher in her slouched posture.

For the next few minutes, we half jokingly, half seriously think of possible rapper alter egos but never seem to settle on anything.

"It's fine. I have the rest of my career." Di raises her nose and pinky up as she sips her coffee.

"I should get going. I'm meeting Jett at four." Stating that out loud, even to Di, wavers my voice and causes a slight spike in the frequency. The fact that her eyebrows, and with it her tattoo, shoot up sharply doesn't help calm my nerves, either.

"Oh?"

I laugh, partially due to nerves and partially due to her expression.

"Yeah." I hike the long chain of my cross-body purse over my shoulder and push the chair in. The wind sharply hits me as I exit out the doors of Harry's and make the sharp right onto the sidewalk. Within ten minutes, I'm fighting with Jett about walking through my dorm room door first. He's trying to be all gentlemanly by opening it for me and letting me through first, and I'm trying to defy gender norms by refusing. A rude statement for the greater good.

"Come on. I'm already holding it open for you."

"Right, so you're closer to walking in anyway."

"Why wasn't your door locked in the first place?"

"I'm just irresponsible, I guess."

Jett rolls his eyes and slides into my room, and I follow close behind. He makes the daring choice to climb onto my bed, just right of my pillows, which were clearly my designated backdrop. I pretend not to notice or pay any mind. He pretends not to have consciously thought through the decision.

I untie my Vans and throw them into the closet across the room, either shoe falling on opposite sides of the nook. Jett laughs. I shrug.

"How was your *coffee date*?" His voice rolls out on an exhale and ends in a thud as he emphasizes *coffee date* sarcastically.

I angle my cross-legged body toward him a little more on the twin-size bed. "Fine, fine. Actually, pretty funny. Di told me she wants to pursue a female rap career." The moment I mention this, I feel a subtle thread of guilt pass through me. Not because I've said anything shitty behind Di's back or even implied something derogatory, but because I would always share these kinds of catch-up moments about others with Di herself. I feel like I'm betraying her, or at least transitioning into some new social realm for myself, by not discussing other people only with Di. The fellow scientist becomes the specimen herself.

He stops for a moment to take what I've said in, gazing up at the popcorn ceiling.

"Honestly, from how you've described her so far, Di is probably the only person I could hear that about and not be super surprised."

I shrug. He has a point.

"We couldn't come up with a name. But I'm sure she'll think of something out there."

There is a split second of awkwardness that Jett thankfully kicks away by bringing up some good documentary series he's watching online about the Vietnam War. I couldn't care less about the history behind it, but I feign some interest and try to engage in the discussion, nodding to points in his description that I recognize from high school history class. He asks if I want to watch some, and I oblige.

"Yeah, okay. Um, I'll get my computer." I pull my laptop off my desk and rip out the charging cord, then launch myself ever so slightly to make it onto my bed again. Jett laughs, and I am momentarily embarrassed before I realize that my small-person accommodations, compared to how tall he is, are probably really funny to him.

"You should get a step stool or something."

"I made it just fine."

"Yeah, but jumping to get on your bed every time must be a pain."

"It's a good quad workout."

I'm unable to follow much of the documentary's plotline. The parts I do pay attention to, I'm not quite sure what the terms even mean. I think I recognize *Agent Orange*. Not a definite, though.

Jett loosens his boots and pushes them off. As they hit the linoleum of my dorm room floor, they emit a shallow patter that harmonizes with my acute pulse. He yawns languidly and leans on his right forearm, angling toward me slightly. As he itches his scalp and shakes his long, dark hair out, the unpredictability of his motions impounds me with electricity. An inch more to the right, and he would probably touch my arm hairs, which would turn me into dust through a self-imposed lightning strike.

"I'm cold," I say.

My eyes meet his for a split second, then I look down at my hands. I can feel that his gaze remains locked on my maroon-covered eyelids.

"Um, do you want a jacket?" I keep my head a little down and stick my tongue out slightly as I concentrate on figuring out how to act natural.

"You're supposed to offer to let me get under your covers." His eyes dart to my unorganized, overflowing closet. "Do you really think I'm that skinny?"

"W-what?"

Jett launches himself off my bed and yanks out a cropped black bomber jacket, one that's already really fitted on me. He attempts to stuff his toned arms into the pinhole-thin straws. The jacket somehow goes on, sitting awkwardly at his elbows and making him look a little like a humiliated Chihuahua being forced to wear a fucking dog parka during winter. I burst out in laughter that rises deep within my navel and explodes out of my sore throat. I get red when I realize I haven't laughed like that in years.

Without being able to move his upper body, he walks over to my full-body mirror and looks at himself, then nods with an embarrassed smirk. The apples of his cheeks turn a pale pink, and his eyelashes point downward as he closes his eyes and giggles.

"Dear God, I guess I am that skinny." He attempts to shove the jacket back where he pulled it out from, and after a minute or so of painfully awkward maneuvering, I put him out of his misery.

"Just throw it on my shoes."

Now that his arms are exposed again, I notice just how intricate the tattoo designs are. Black and red dashes connect into complicated geometric forms and symmetric patterns. They look almost like cuts or lesions executed with the artistry of a painter. The translucence of his pale skin allows the ink to overlay directly above purple and blue veins in a rigid yet whimsical road map. As Jett lifts my white sheets and burrows beneath them, the quiet reverberations of deep laughter still present inside me all choke in tiny individual nooses. Just like I remember, it's me sitting up tall as Greg lies beside me falling asleep to a Disney movie at eight p.m. on a Friday. I clench my jaw to cut off the sequence of memory-coated dominoes from falling down. When I peer down at Jett's head again, he looks back up at me innocently, and I can't help but smile even with the chain of dominoes millimeters away from crashing. My jaw still cutting off my head from my heart, I climb underneath the covers as well, though not so close to Jett as to short-circuit my wiring.

For the remaining thirty minutes, I don't hear a word of the documentary. I'm too busy carefully keeping each domino upright and unwavering while also emitting my excess electric charge ever so slightly through all those open wounds I still carry on my body.

Chapter 16

I trot into Dr. Ellis's office with a steaming black coffee in one hand and my phone clenched in the other as I feverishly text Jett, my head pointed straight down. My mouth is in a half smile, and my mind is far away from being in the same room as Dr. Ellis.

"Someone seems to be having a good day."

My spine jolts in shock as I hear him speak. I shove my phone into my coat pocket and take a sip of my coffee. It burns my tongue, and I wince, then I look back up at Dr. Ellis and shrug.

"Eh, not terrible, I guess."

"How did your project go? The one you had to do on a location?"

My energy plummets with a slow sigh.

"Oh. It was pretty shit compared to everyone else's."

"I'm sorry to hear you say that. What did you end up doing it on?"

I sigh. "The fucking grocery store."

Dr. Ellis tries to stifle a laugh but fails and snorts. I wince.

"It was going to be cool, I thought, really… I was going to overlay some time-lapse shots and make some comparison about the kind of people that visit in the morning versus at night, or… Well, so, the manager thought since I kept coming back throughout the day that I must've been loitering or stealing or some shit, and…it didn't end up working out."

"Well, I'm quite sure it couldn't have been that bad. You're at one of the best schools for that, you must be quite adept."

"I'm not adept, though. Like, no, not at all, at least anymore."

He raises and lowers his eyebrows, obviously resigning from that fight.

"You and Di do anything fun recently?"

"She went to visit her parents this weekend. So I spent some of it with Jett."

His pen stops, and I can hear it pop out of the hole his firm grip has made in the yellow notepad. I tentatively decide to keep going.

"We watched some of this history documentary and hung out, so nothing too fun, I...I guess."

"Jett is the one who repeatedly causes you anxiety?"

I'm taken aback slightly by the question, which hits me more like a fierce statement. I scratch my leg to the loud rhythm of my heartbeat as I struggle to address the question.

"I wouldn't say he causes me any more anxiety at this point than anyone else does. Except maybe Di. Di doesn't really cause me any, really. I like Jett. Spending time with him makes me happy. It makes me feel kind of like myself again." My lips scrunch to the side as I swirl around a hot sip of coffee. *Happy. Like myself again.*

"Describe him to me." Dr. Ellis shuffles slightly to the side in his seat and leans against the green arms. His red eyeglasses fall to the very tip of his pointy nose, and his dark eyes forcefully demand an answer against his soft speech. I gaze up as I gather my thoughts.

"Tall, dark, handsome, and emo."

He laughs again and writes something down in his notebook.

"Anything memorable about his personality?"

"Yeah, yeah, sorry. He's really calm and...*fluid* about everything. Like, nothing could shake him."

"Sounds like someone you could count on."

I think for a minute.

"Yeah, I guess I could if I ever needed anything. He comes across as super reliable, definitely." I rim my finger around the lid of my coffee. "He's majoring in history," I blurt out to fill the silence.

Dr. Ellis shuffles again and rereads some of what he's written, then breaks his focus with a tight, closemouthed smile back up at me. We talk some about how taking my medication has affected me, and I assure him I'm "doing really, really okay." Nothing too memorable today.

"What about you?"

"What was that?"

"How are you doing?" I ask.

He sniffs and leans back in his chair in surprise but maintains eye contact with me. I sense an internal debate between telling me the socially acceptable *fine* he probably tells everyone else or matching me where I'm at and honestly laying it all out.

"A little tired, a little stressed, but I'm not complaining."

So. More to the safe end of the spectrum but not totally committed.

"Stressed, huh?"

"Old people problems."

"I wouldn't say you're *old*. How old are you, even? If you're allowed to tell me that?"

"I'm a little over twice your age."

"So, like, forty or so?"

"Around there." Dr. Ellis's gaze and, with it, his red glasses point downward. His smooth cheeks flush delicately.

"How's your wife's book club or whatever?" At that, he sighs and rubs his temples together. I guess my attempt at distraction was an epic failure.

"Among other things, not exactly the pinnacle of my existence, perhaps you could say." I drink some of my now-lukewarm coffee and wait for our session to turn back to its normal role play, but he doesn't probe me. Instead, Dr. Ellis gazes out the window at the tall buildings and the clouds that hang low today, just above our floor level. I take another sip.

"Um...I feel that. Yeah, I have some shit like that, too, I think." I shut up and join him in looking out the window. His phone buzzes, and he picks it up. I've never seen him get interrupted during a session.

"Oh dear God." He groans, leaning back in the green leather armchair. He exhales and rubs the bridge of his nose between his eyes vigorously. Seems like the guy could use some of his own relaxation techniques.

"You okay? Book club meeting? Don't have a place to hide out?"

He chuckles. "No, I wish. My babysitter, who my wife hasn't gotten around to firing quite yet, canceled on us last minute for tonight. June and I have an art opening for our dear friend that we can't miss... Dammit." It's the first time he's referred to his wife by name. June. I put my money on a blonde ectomorph, probably a Libra.

"I mean, I probably wouldn't offer unless it wasn't already five p.m., but if you need someone..." I raise my bent arms slightly to finish the rest of my statement. He furrows his brows and looks through me in contemplation.

121

"I can't imagine doing something more unprofessional, but this really is an emergency. We should be back by midnight. Is twenty an hour okay? It's double what we pay Azalea, the absolute…the sitter we have now." I laugh audibly at his frustration.

"Yeah, yeah, totally cool." He tells me how to get to his apartment and not much else. I debate between asking if I can bring sweet potatoes to cook there but then decide I'll do it anyway because it's not like I can go against the plan I already put into my calorie-counting app.

"I can't *believe* I'm having to do this and even *ask* this of you…"

"I won't tell your boss or…supervisor, or whatever. I won't say anything. Whoever they are. Not like I have some wild life where my Friday nights are always filled."

He blinks slowly at me and smiles faintly, then blinks forcefully and darts his vision down.

"No, of course not, don't worry. And we're over already. Same time work for you next week?"

Chapter 17

Dr. Ellis's son, Christopher, does not look much like him. Perhaps his dark-brown eyes are similarly round and his hair is just as full, but that could also be the equally-as-sharp haircut. It's quite impressive for a first grader. I didn't get the chance to see June before heading upstairs to Christopher's room as Dr. Ellis had suggested I do upon my arrival, but I was curious and hoped she would come in to say goodbye before leaving. Unfortunately, I heard the door slam and the living room TV turn off a few minutes later.

"I'm Val. I'm pretty chill with whatever, just don't burn the house down. I'm sure you know the drill. I'm just going to do some work on my computer....in the living room, I guess? Let me know if you need anything."

"Mmkay. I'm tired, I think I just wanna go to bed."

"Your dad said you already ate, right? So I don't need to make you anything?"

"Uh-huh. I had soup." I'm not typically a fan of kids, but this one is reassuringly calm. I'm pleasantly surprised. Or maybe it's because he's tired, like he said. Either way, I give Dr. Ellis some credit.

"Okay. Yell if you need anything, then. I'll check on you in a little."

"Mmkay."

I carry my bag over and sit at the sleek metal dining room table. My laptop makes a loud clang and screeches against the tabletop as I move it into place. Upon opening it, I see a few texts from Jett, and the energy current inside me surges a little faster.

Hey. Do you happen to be doing anything tonight?

Of course I'm kind of convolutedly possibly asked out by an actually decent male the one time I have plans on a Friday night. I groan and even exhale a little laugh as I ponder my luck.

babysitting 4 my therapist :/ at least the house smells like rosemary & the kid's quiet tho?

Instantly, I see the dots that mean he's typing. That's what I appreciate most about him on a shallow level, what seems like his no-bullshit approach to, well, most things. He doesn't fuck around and make me wait.

My roommates are driving me fucking crazy, any chance I can come over?

Two currents of opposing energy inside me begin to ignite as they cross. One of them wants so strongly for him to join me, and the other is firm in the responsibility I have to this commitment. I know I'm not some fifteen-year-old who wants to have her high school boyfriend over just to get to second base, but I still really don't want to fuck Dr. Ellis over at all. He's not on my Bad List of people who deserve no good whatsoever. Honestly, the only person who's ever lasted on my Bad List is my mother.

The energies keep warring inside me, sparks trickling out of my pores, until they finally both ignite and I text back.

only if u promise not 2 fuck anything up here & also bring me some spinach bc i brought stuff 2 cook w & totally forgot

Organic spinach?

lol i don't rly care. ill pay u back tho

Ok then I'm definitely getting whatever hydroponic shit you'll reimburse me for. See you in a little.

I send him the address and lean back in my chair. The energy oozes out of my scabs and surrounds me in a protective bubble that shields me from feeling anything but fear, excitement,

and shards of preemptive regret.

Chapter 18

Jett knocks on the metal dining room table with his bony knuckles. The languid sound reverberates as he gazes around at the living-dining area, which is equipped with a chef-level Viking stove and sleek white island seats that match the dining room chairs. I imagine June and her book club sitting where I am, drinking Pinot Grigio and arguing about how life-changing some Eckhart Tolle novel was for them.

"The kid?"

"Asleep."

"Oh, nice."

"I mean, I think. I can't really, um, you know, be sure, but…"

"If you're concerned for whatever reason, I can go check."

I roll my eyes and hit his shoulder playfully as I make my way to one of the white barstools and prop myself up with a little jump.

"Anything new with you?" I ask, speaking surprisingly calmly. He blinks as he continues to look around the space.

"I hope this spinach is fairly new," Jett says as he pulls the spinach out of a paper grocery bag and holds it out.

"Oh! Thanks, I almost forgot." I take the spinach and place it in the fridge by the rest of the things I brought.

"I also got you this. Don't worry, I remembered you're vegan and all." My heart races as I see him lift up a clear plastic box with a brownie inside, wrapped with a little red bow around it and a bright-yellow sticker labeled *VEGAN* on the side.

"Oh, I—I…" I sigh and look at him as sincerely as possible. "I'm not *really* a chocolate person. But I'll so take it back for Di, she'll love—"

"Ah, no biggie, it's chill. Two for me, then," Jett says without missing a beat, placing a second brownie next to the one he had bought for me. He folds up the paper bag and gives me a closemouthed smile. I return the gesture as a reflex.

"Thank you, though, really. Ice cream next time," I jokingly add. He nods.

"Got it. Not chocolate, though."

I exhale and nod sheepishly. If only I hadn't decided on a granola bar before I came, I could've had that goddamn brownie. I *knew* I should've saved some calories just in case. Now I've fucked it all up.

I get up and start prepping the rest of the food, putting cut sweet potatoes into the oven and wiping my hands on the dish towel next to the stove. However, upon seeing the olive oil on the counter in front of me, I quickly take out the pan of potatoes and drizzle a hefty amount over half. There. Now Jett has his and I have mine. I patter back to sit down on one of the island barstools.

"Are you still reading your biography about Skid Row?" I ask as I launch myself up, nervous energy powering my speech.

"No, finished it. Now I'm on to Pearl Jam." Jett scratches his right temple with his left hand and then tousles that messy, dark hair.

"A biography about them?"

"Eventually. Right now, I'm just listening to a lot of their music, watching a lot of their interviews. Firsthand stuff."

"Why?"

He cocks his head at me and pauses, looking down. "I think to understand history the best, you gotta look at whatever art was being made then. Art is just a response. If you can figure out what patterns the art is responding to, you can figure out how it was in that time period. Maybe. At least that's how I think about it." I swallow and let his words linger between us for a moment.

"What all have you found from studying... Hair metal and nineties rock, I guess?" I laugh a little, and he smiles.

"I think that whole period was when everyone who was too scared to talk back against the...*establishment*, I guess, began to find each other and gather together and all. Strength in numbers. Once there were groups, they could start homing in on what they stood against in the culture, and art was a means for them to articulate that. So, a lot of rejection of, like, baby boomer puritanical shit. I'm still figuring out the specifics of it all from where I see it. I like to think it all through myself before reading shit on it. Maybe my unbiased view is just about as important as any well-researched expert's."

"That's interesting. Yeah, I think there's something really fucking valuable about going into something empty-headed," I say as I walk over to my book bag on the dining room table and put on a little of my red-tinted ChapStick. Then I blot my lips together aggressively with my back turned to him in case it's too much. I'm just trying to add a pinch of flush without seeming like I'm trying to add just a pinch of flush.

"Empty-headed?" Jett smiles and swirls toward me on the white barstool. I feel my cheeks get a little red.

"Is that not a word?"

"Do you mean open-minded?"

I think on his question for a moment as I lean against the table, my palms cold against the shiny metal.

"No. I don't think I do. Because you could be open-minded but still have a bunch of other information piled up internally that keeps you from really internalizing anything…internally." Jett laughs at me. "Oh, you know what I mean. It's just…too cerebral for my art-student mind to articulate." I walk back over and sit next to him.

"Yeah, yeah. Totally. I'm so careful about what I consume these days with so much *bullshit* numbing everyone and turning everyone's mind into a fucking landfill. No one has any fucking idea what they're doing anymore."

"And you do?" I hike my left leg up onto the slippery seat and wrap my arms around it, hugging it to my chest. My excessively mascara-clumped eyelashes blink at him amusedly, and he flutters his lips, making a *vroom* sound.

"At least I admit I don't. I say stepping back is the only way to move forward."

After we talk more about actual serious generational shit, my timer goes off, and I go to plate our food. I fluff up the spinach in my bowl to hide the measly portion of brown rice (one-half cup exactly) and drizzle a little more olive oil over Jett's dish for good measure. Then I crack some pepper over mine and salt and pepper over his. Plenty of salt over his.

"You're actually a *really* fucking good chef. Like, this shit is impressive. I can cook simple shit pretty well, but damn, I need to hire you when I'm tired of sandwiches and pasta." Warmth rises inside me as Jett savors his meal, cutting the crispy, oily potatoes and stirring his cup-and-a-half serving of rice. The warm electricity inside me ascends with power, with conquest, with energy. I am powered by consciousness. Calories are my poison.

After we eat, we head to the gray tweed couch on the opposite side of the room to watch another history documentary on my computer. My laptop balances on a stack of books, which include *The Psychology of Sex* and *Art Deco's Rebels*. In trying to find a comfortable position, the lightning flowing through me gives me the go-ahead, and I lean against the side of the couch perpendicular to Jett, spreading my legs across his. Then, stretching down casually, I act as if I'm simply a touchy person and positioning myself like this is nothing personal. *You're chill. You do this with everyone,* I repeat back to myself, almost fooled into believing it. Jett's eyes open wide and look down at his lap, which has my jean-covered ankles resting upon it, then blink and meet mine. My pupils are wide enough to allow him access to my electricity inside, but his own internal currents cut through mine until all that is left are my scabbed wounds, spewing little sparks of fear.

Finally, he speaks. "That can't possibly be very comfortable."

I smile and pull my feet back into a cross-legged position, still facing him, then shrug. "It was, but whatever."

He sits up slightly, and I lean up onto my knees, the line of our gazes crossing in an X as each of us look at the other's lips. My hands reach his shoulders, and his grip meets my hips, my mind racing when I think about how bony they are and how he probably wishes there were more to hold on to. The currents of lightning inside me are strong enough to meet his and, with that, they break through the short-circuits of doubt that hide in the scabs. My wounds allow for quiet, for stillness, for simplicity to enter and combat the rope of fear coiling all the way from the base of my spine and to the top of my head. All that manages to still make noise is the rustle of my hair as Jett's fingers move through it and the echoes of his heart singing fearlessly over mine.

Chapter 19

"No, I didn't fuck him. He left after, like, an hour anyway. In case Christopher got up and all, which he did. So good thing he wasn't still there." I take a sip of my coffee and gaze around Harry's self-consciously.

"Damn. I really wanted a good story." I roll my eyes at Di as she picks up her fallen backpack from behind her chair. "Over the counter, in your therapist's bed... Man, the possibilities could've been *endless*." She's saying all this loudly over her shoulder while she's half bent over, and my cheeks flush with worry that people around can hear. Thankfully, everyone seems to have their headphones in, minding their own corporate-ass business.

"Yeah, next time," I joke, wondering if I'll ever see Dr. Ellis's place again. "I...I do really like him, though. Like, not in a *weird* way, just... I don't know." My cheeks flush as I quickly reach for my coffee again to occupy my attention.

"Oh God, you're getting all *sappy* and shit," Di obnoxiously announces. I giggle and twist in my seat, looking down at my tight black pants.

"This is why I need to third-wheel sometime. A guy you actually like? Life-changing." She pulls out a chocolate bar and begins to mindlessly eat it.

"I don't think that would work. You'd hate it. Third-wheeling is awful. Even with me and Jett, I'm sure it would be." I itch my arms and arrange myself to sit up tightly with my hands squished between my thighs.

"Ha, alright, then. Never mind." She holds the half-unwrapped chocolate bar in her mouth as she puts on her coat and lifts up her backpack. "*I* have a job interview in thirty."

"What the fuck?"

"Mm-hmm. Didn't wanna say anything in case I didn't get it, but I can't keep a secret for shit. Just a retail position down at Round Two, but still, it'd be cool. I'd probably be able to steal some thrifted shit."

"Better not let them on to that attitude."

"See ya!" She half yells, turning around to wave a couple feet from the door.

I gather up my things and head out a few minutes later, scurrying back to my dorm through the strong winds. I forgot my damn gloves, and my fingers are about to break off into gross, flaky icicles. As I get back and lie down on my bed, my stomach rumbles in pain, and I curl up into a fetal position on the right side of my body. The overwhelming emptiness embraces me lovingly, and I let the fogginess in my brain take over, bringing me as close to divinity as I'll ever get. I check my watch. Three twenty-one. Three hours and nine minutes until I can even think about eating something.

Except that's all the 5 percent of my brain that is still able to work fixates on; the bare survival mechanisms are all that's left operating in my broken, lobotomized shell. I open the heavy eyes that I previously slammed shut in agony and look at my desk chair. From where I'm sitting, it's sideways, and the whole world is turned onto its axis. There in that wooden chair is Greg, rocking back and forth on the wobbly legs not designed to rock at all.

"Val, come on. Val, please." His image flutters and pixelates as the current inside me ebbs and flows. I reach out to him, and he grabs the very tips of my fingers with his sweaty little palms. His grip tightens, and I feel him sucking every watt of energy out of my body. My wounds gape with electricity from deep, deep within, which repels the daylight surrounding me and cloaks me in a dark shield from everything illuminated. The electricity pulls me closer to Greg until I merge with him, unable to exist alone. I am a parasite feeding off his immortal youth.

"Val..." His voice echoes in reverberations that bounce between the walls of electricity that bind us together away from the world. My vision goes dark, and we're falling, falling, falling.

We're being wrenched down by the gravitational pull of fears lying within the magma core of my heart. I open an internal eye and realize that is where we're descending, through my heart space itself. Hitting the bottom means reaching myself.

The fear rooted at the base of my spine shakes and shudders. Each vertebrate it previously latched on to is now too fluid for the fear to hook. Inside me, it desperately searches for a groove to place its foot on to, for a handle to grip, but every attempt it has at remaining inside me falters. It is awakened from its sleeping state of autopilot. Now, I'm in control.

I wake up, hours later, to my phone vibrating. I look at the time. Five fifty. Forty minutes left. I can do this.

I see a text from Jett on the screen asking if I'm doing anything tonight. Me in this instant wants to say no and drown in my own darkness. Me, both inside and everywhere outside myself, knows to say yes. My severed, floating identity is torn even more, and I don't make a decision to follow either part of myself.

depends on how emo i'm feeling, I eventually type back. It's a shit reply that'll make him do all the fucking work in this conversation, but I'm not up for fifty-fifty right now.

I'll come over at 8 and bring a movie. I'd say a romcom but with you I think I know better.

anything but a historical reenactment, I reply instantly. A soft smile forms on my lips and creeps to the outside of my eyes. I throw my phone to the foot of my bed and sit up. Hopefully, my makeup really is perfectly disheveled now.

Chapter 20

"I brought you ice cream. It's plain fucking vanilla, so you have no fucking excuse not to like it. It's…it's a coconut milk one," he says, turning the pint toward him and reading the label. Thank fucking God I saved most of my calories for this dessert, knowing the possibility of something like this happening. I smile and cock my head, my hands on my hips, which are exposed above my low-rise jeans. Their familiar boniness comforts me. I'm proud of my planning, proud of how I've structured everything to go.

We sit cross-legged on my bunk with my computer out in front of us as Jett leans over and slides in the movie. My mind is too busy to ask what he's picked.

"I figured you were into horror. Maybe I'm wrong." His back covers the screen, so I place my hand on his shoulder to look above and see what's playing. My grip sharpens in a cadaveric spasm as the title flashes on the menu. *Haunted Skullrider.* Jett jumps up in pain.

"Jesus," he screeches. My heart falls to the pit of my stomach. I want to vomit it up.

"Shit, sorry. Hand cramp," I mutter, falling back onto my feet. He grabs his right shoulder where I pinched it and massages it a little. There's a tight wrinkle in the thin green shirt from my nails.

"Have you seen this one?"

"Nope, I haven't," I lie. "B-but I've heard it's pretty good." My heartbeat takes over my voice and wavers the tone.

"Where's your roommate?"

"Oh, Patricia's at her sister's wedding this week. Bridesmaiding," I answer.

Jett sits back and offers me a plastic spoon in both of his hands as if he's a ring bearer. I laugh and pick it up, then take a small spoonful of ice cream and grab it with my lips. The opening music sours the sweet, rich taste in my mouth into rancid bile. My stomach is overfilled with memories. I feel an increasing need to purge myself of potent toxicity.

Jett sniffles and jolts at the initial scare of the film, where a mutilated, decaying body suddenly emerges from a tranquil grave. I remember this part. I remember my head on Vic's shoulder and my heavy eyelids. I remember the motion of his jaw eating popcorn and rocking me to sleep and his shudders occasionally a2wakening me into a dreary haze. The velvet fabric of the seat still feels soft beneath me.

By the time I've come back to the film, it's already gotten to a part I haven't seen yet. I force myself to take another bite of the ice cream and curse myself for not being excited about these well-earned calories. I get a dull brain freeze and reenter the chains of the memory. The cold in my mouth becomes the cold wind hitting my inadequately dressed frame on that cool night. Vic's arm is around me again, protecting me, becoming me.

Jett stirs again, minutes later, when another half-dead zombie jumps out.

"Whoa, shit. Sorry. You're braver than me, I guess," he says, looking up at me and batting his dark eyelashes. I roll my eyes and lie down.

"I'm just too tired to show how scared I am, but trust me, I'm a total baby, too." He lowers himself to my level, exactly at my eyeline. I close my eyes and place my hands in a prayer shape underneath the right side of my face. I feel Jett's fingers push my fallen hairs behind my opposite ear. My tar-coated eyelashes flutter open just enough to see his red-and-black forearms and to lose myself in their labyrinth. I want to ask what his tattoos mean, if anything, but my mind cannot reach comprehension right now. I sigh deeply and feel Jett sit up. I hear a bite of ice cream, then the cardboard pint being placed onto my desk.

"I'm gonna go put this into the freezer," he says softly as he places a hand on my back. I nod, eyes still closed. The movie plays in the background, but the images of red-and-black twisted patterns occupy my mind. The wires inside me are pushing electricity through the maze, and I can't find my way out.

"You awake?" Jett asks as he climbs back onto my bed. I open my eyes and prop myself up on my forearm.

"Yeah, yeah. Just tired. Sorry, I always fucking fall asleep with movies. It's so bad," I croak, laughing at the end. Jett smiles.

"It's fine. It's kind of a shit horror movie anyway." He leans forward on top of me, meeting my lips again and combing back my hair with his hand. I touch his bony collarbone and sink into his stable frailty. My other hand creeps under his shirt, my fingernails scraping his ribs and feeling every small bump along his exposed muscles. He begins to do the same, and ripples of panic emerge deep from within. The fear inside me is still swimming around with no home, but it begins to latch on to the thought of my stomach after eating a few bites of ice cream. I *know* there is no difference from the sharpness I'd checked for before Jett came. But the fear finds a resting place in the cave of my stomach and causes my body to flinch once Jett's fingers glaze over the V of my lower abs. He retreats his offense and looks down at me, my shirt ridden up and half sideways.

"You okay?"

"Yeah. Just ticklish." The ominous depth of my voice says otherwise.

Memories replay of Vic being forceful. I'm not sure how to classify his transgressions—all I know is that sometimes they weren't what I wanted. I didn't always make that clear, but I think it was clear anyway, and now even eager muscles hold muscle memory of when they weren't. Nothing was ever major, and I was never hurt, so I don't hold ill-will toward him for anything specific.

Jett lowers back down and meets my mouth again, carefully not placing a hand on my midsection. I wrap my grip around the base of his skull and push myself over on top of him. My hair forms a tent between us. In it, my fear and my electricity are trapped.

Chapter 21

Dr. Ellis sniffles and pushes up the red eyeglasses that have fallen to the tip of his nose. His right leg crosses over his left and shakes a bit. He seems like the type to be over-caffeinated until ten p.m.

"So," he says with a perky gaze and a lifted chin. "How are we doing this afternoon?"

"Decent. Not bad. Maybe better."

"Anything new, or same old?"

I grip my knobby knees and lean forward a little, stretching out my lower back. "I guess I'm actually...seeing Jett, kind of. Nothing's *official*...or anything...but...yeah." I can't help but smile uncomfortably. My mind wants to be mature, and my words want to be honest, but the rumbling fear doesn't let either fully win out. However, Dr. Ellis's piercing gaze strikes right between my eyes and lifts my tucked chin. I feel my wounds becoming increasingly inflamed until I force myself to break away.

"Well, that's good to hear. I really hope this makes you happy," he says with precision. However, his arms are crossed and he's looking down at his yellow notepad without writing anything, his lips pursed to the side. His red glasses slip down and hit the brown carpet with a soft thud. I swallow.

"I—I haven't been having visions lately, either." Dammit. Impulsively lying makes me even more anxious.

"This is all very, very good news." Dr. Ellis's glasses slip again, but he catches them and hikes them up farther than usual. "Um, how have your classes been going? Any new projects?" Artificial interest swims in the sound waves.

"Fine, I guess. I'm just doing the bare minimum until I can transfer into something I like...if I can figure out what that is."

"Any possibilities?"

I shrug and exhale. "I mean, nothing I'm sure of. I wasn't able to take any classes outside of my required film shit this year, so it's not like I can say I really liked a different area or anything."

"Do you want to stay in art? Or are you looking into moving into something more academic?"

"Honestly, no idea." I look up and make eye contact. "I might just drop out. I don't know." He shuffles in his seat and recrosses his legs.

"I went through a similar dilemma my first year of college. What helped me was really asking myself what I liked as a child. Just simply what excited me. Then, it made it easier to pick what I wanted to study."

"Which was what?"

"Psychology. Initially, I was an architecture major."

"Hmm. Psychology. Yeah, I'd pick that over architecture."

He smiles lightly and flips a page in the yellow notebook.

"Well, then. So would I."

"Were you into psychology at all early on?" I ask.

He shakes his head. I swallow.

"I…I used to ask a lot of questions. But no, I didn't come out of the womb accusing anyone of having the Oedipus complex," Dr. Ellis explains. We laugh together, our smiles coordinating.

The rest of the session continues on, with no mention of Jett or Greg or anything daunting again. He discusses with me what my interests are in hopes of helping me navigate my educational troubles, but I'm still lost. All I seem to want is a river to carry me far beyond the barren desert I'm in.

"Oh," Dr. Ellis adds as I'm gathering up my things to leave, "thank you again for watching Christopher for us. We're still scrambling for a decent sitter in the meantime, but you really helped me out. *Us* out, June and I." He forces the door open widely, and I walk through.

"Yeah, no problem, anytime."

"Alright, then. Take care." I hear the familiar click of the metal knob as the door shuts, and I head down the elevator and out onto the street. It's warmed up significantly and is uncomfortably humid. I even washed my fucking hair today. My phone buzzes with a text.

ok so i fucked up, a text from Di reads. My breathing tenses. I see her typing once I open up my messages.

the concert is tonight, not tomorrow. im sorry im useless ok but can u still go

I sigh. I'd already planned out what I'd be eating tomorrow to work around the concert, but what I'd planned to have tonight isn't too different or problematic. I'm angry, but Di knows I'm not doing shit, so I don't really have a decent excuse.

ya ya no prob

I ruffle my hair back and grab the nape of my neck violently with sharp fake nails. It's too late to cancel my workout class tomorrow morning, which I scheduled early, thinking I wouldn't be extra hungry from moving around all night at a concert. *Breathe, Val. Breathe. You know you can work with anything.* Fuck it. *You can totally stay until around one, say you're annoyed at someone near you, and then tell Di if you don't leave you're going to have a panic attack or some shit. You're absolutely batshit, and Di knows that. She won't question you. Back by one thirty or two, you can sleep for five or so hours and feel decent when you have to get up at seven for the eight a.m. class. You might just be a little more tired than usual, but an extra cup of coffee in the afternoon will fix it.* Relief washes over me. Damn, I have it all figured out. Nothing can stop me. I work the system. I make the system. I *am* the system.

Chapter 22

Di leans against my bed while I delicately apply dark-purple liquid

lipstick around the corners of my mouth. Little violet streaks creep

into the creases, and I pout in disapproval. Eyes looking messed up

is hot; lips looking messed up is fucking gross.

Patricia's over at her desk, chewing gum and talking on the

phone loudly.

"I know, right? She shouldn't have gotten chapter

president. She doesn't give a *shit* about the chapter, she just wants

that internship. That's all I'm saying." I hear a deep thud. "Fuck!

No, yeah, I'm fine, I just hit my…my *elbow* on the corner of this

damn desk. I know, *right*? If I keep on talking about her, I'll

probably end up getting hit by a bus tonight."

Di glares at me through the small vanity mirror on my desk,

and I stifle a laugh.

"Hopefully," Di announces loudly, knowing full well that

Patricia couldn't have less room in her brain to process Di's

presence. I mouth, "Shut up," and get back to my makeup, pulling out my well-loved mascara tube for the final touch. Or, more specifically, the final ten layers of touch.

"*Oooh!* Okay, then. Go girl, you get him. Love you too! Mwah." Patricia's phone clangs as she sets it down on her wooden desk. In my peripheral vision, I see her turn sideways in her chair to face Di and me.

"Where are you guys going tonight?" Her gum clicks as an air bubble breaks. Di looks to me to answer, as if to say, *She's your fucking roommate.* In a millisecond, my eyes yell back to her, *Fuck you. But okay.*

"A concert," I reply flatly, fluffing up my hair. It needs another round of curling.

"Ooh, what band?"

I glance at Di. *Your turn.*

"Burned Edge. And Microdoser is the opener," Di answers with the coldness of knowing damn well that means fucking nothing to Patricia, and she enjoys every second of it.

"Oh. Cool." Patricia turns back to face her desk and scrolls through her phone. Di's gaze remains fixated on her, analyzing her caramel flat-ironed-to-shit hair and golden glitter phone case. I actually like the phone case. But I know Di would call it *millennial kitsch.*

Eventually, after I've re-curled my unruly mane and killed the ozone layer with gallons of hair spray, Di and I take a cab on over to the venue. Di's wearing a white crop top with a gray moon on each breast and loose camo cargo pants. Her feet are slipped into her usual black Keds, and a matching black bomber jacket slouches around her stout figure. A rare thin layer of eyeliner makes me take more interested in looking at her face than usual. Paired with my leather miniskirt, fishnets, and corset bodysuit, we're quite a scene to look at, but neither of us ever miss an opportunity to dress up.

I begin to feel a cold rush upon preparing to pull out my fake ID for the bouncer. I've had the same bullshit Maryland one since I was sixteen, the day after getting my braces off, and it's never failed me. Maybe it's karma's reward for never actually using it on alcohol and instead frequenting mature video-game shops in high school. I leap out of the cab and over a puddle onto the sidewalk right in front of the dark warehouse building. A fast-moving line has already formed, and Di and I shuffle to the end. I yank down my skirt.

"Birthday?" The bouncer asks Di in front of me as he looks over her ID, which is obviously shit. I'm pretty sure it's printed fucking crooked. But having a face tattoo does tend to make her invincible in these instances, and he lets her slide in as she unquestionably repeats her twenty-three-year-old birthday.

"Next," booms the large man. Without making eye contact, I shuffle up and hand him my card. He barely looks at it before handing it right back and moving on to the next person. The coldness escapes from inside me, and I excitedly skip to meet Di, who is waiting just inside, before remembering I can't take the chance of skipping in these damn platforms.

"*Excuse* me, thank you, yep, yep, thank you *so* much," Di confidently chimes as she cuts through the small crowd to the front. Somehow intimidating-looking people who act suspiciously nice have a free pass for shit like this. I hold her hand like a parasite hanging on to Moses as he parts the sea.

"Nice," I say to her as we grab on to the barricade. She turns around to look at the slowly growing crowd around us.

"Fuck, I need to pee. I should probably go now," she grumbles. "Be right back, don't fuckin' move." I make a clicking sound in agreement and turn back around to face the front.

"I *love* your outfit," says a woman to my right, about my same height with bleached hair and a red tube top. "Goth chic. Nailed it." I flush. *Goth chic.* I'll take it.

"Oh, thanks. You, too," I meekly reply, nodding to her top, then becoming beet red when I realize I've basically just stared at her boobs for an awkwardly long five seconds. She doesn't seem to notice or care.

"Cynthia," she says, holding her hand out. I shake it and respond with my own name. She leans over the bar in front of us, sticking her butt out a little as she places her weight on her forearms. "Here for Burned Edge or Micro?"

I half roll my eyes. "Neither, kind of. I mean, I've heard some of Burned Edge's songs, but I'm just here with my friend. She's peeing," I explain.

"Is this girl on E already?" I hear someone behind me whisper. I look around and don't see anyone entertainingly professing their love. Damn.

"Gotcha, gotcha," Cynthia replies. Her voice is gravelly and languid, and her small hooded eyes barely peek out from long, straight-across bangs.

Di returns. I look to introduce her to Cynthia, but she's gone. A small part of the current inside me slows. I would have liked to speak more with her.

"The bathroom's good for grungy mirror pics, I figured I'd let you know."

"I may just have to take an intermission to check it out, then." We stand around on our phones, re-scrolling down the same feed since there isn't any service and pretending to find it all fascinatingly interesting. Eventually, thirty minutes past the call time, Microdoser comes on and begins to play their distorted, hallucinogenic pop. Di groans the exaggerated words with the lead singer as I calculatedly try to move naturally with the beat. In the right corner of the stage, I see a figure peek out from the wings. My stomach lurches. He's here, with his silky hair barely touching the nape of his flannel. He's looking around the stage for something when he notices me and freezes. Our eyes, powered by all of the memories racing through our connected brains, a flip-book whirling like an accordion, trap us from the sounds and the lights and the people crowding the dark room. Suddenly, I'm right back at Really Bad, eighteen years old, wishing I'd done something different on that car ride, begging from a voice deep within for him to finish that sentence. He swallows. I lift my chin and bite my lip. The song suddenly ends in a loud guitar chord, and both of us turn in surprise. When I look back, Vic is gone.

After Microdoser has played their set, I wave down one of the roadie guys moving the set offstage. He suspiciously approaches me and leans over the edge of the raised platform.

"Yeah?" He's short, with fiery-red hair and a blue sweatshirt on.

"Is Vic your sound guy? Does he work here?" I screech. He flinches his face back in confusion.

"Sorry, I don't know who you're talking about." He flips his hood up and gets back to work, unplugging the guitars and moving the amps.

"Vic Graham?" I scream out to him. "Long black hair? I just saw…" The guy leaves the stage carrying a guitar.

"Who are you talking about?" Di asks, coming up beside me. I clench my jaw and don't meet her eyes.

"I...I saw a guy I know come out a little from the wings. He must be working as a sound guy here..." I shake my head and feel fear latching on to the broken shell of my head. It's much closer to my mind now, much less hidden and much more apparent. It's tangled between the mess of my consciousness. I see it clearly. I'm afraid to see Vic. But the other half of my mind yearns to.

"Oh. Weird." She hunches back over her phone, illuminating her small mouth and piglike noise. I sigh.

"Yeah." I know Vic is back there. I need to find him.

Chapter 23

"Di, I'm going to go find, uh, just that guy," I quickly say after Burning Edge has played their encore and the crowd has begun to recede. She nods.

"Yeah, okay. I'll wait here." I shuffle off to the right and try to catch the attention of one of the security guards.

"Hi, excuse me?" I whimper. One of them cocks up their head at me. "Um, I think my friend works here. I saw him onstage in between songs, and I was wondering if I could just say hi?"

"What's his name, sweetie?" the guard booms without an atom of warmth on his face. My throat closes up some.

"V-Vic, Vic Graham." He turns around and says something to the shorter guard next to him, then nods and turns back to me as the shorter guy walks away.

"He's checking for you." My heart jumps around and syncopates below my quick, shallow breathing. Part of me, upon seeing Vic, wanted to sprint through the crowd and out of the room at the speed of light. But more of me knows there is too much left to say to waste any more time. I lean on to my left hip and tap my right foot, the grooves of the platform sole sliding on the smooth concrete floor. After a few minutes of waiting, I walk past the oblivious remaining security guard who is on his phone and head backstage. I push back the black velvet curtain and enter the long, thin hallway with several doors on the right and steps to an onstage entrance on the left. Echoes of clanging metal and heavy weights being dropped reverberate between the thin walls. There is no visible end to the dark hall, a never-ending tunnel with Vic trapped somewhere within it. In the darkness, I see light reflecting off of silky black hair. I run toward it, not caring if I break a heel in the process, not caring if my shoes fly off and hit the sides of these thin plaster walls, not caring if I ever get out.

"Hey!" I hear a voice yell. "Do you have permission to be back here?" I turn around. Red-haired guy is peeking out of one of the doors behind me, blinking. I sigh and drop my head, try to start saying something, then give up and just walk out.

"Wait, what did you say your friend's name was?" My neck rips around instantly.

"Vic. Vic Graham, Vic." My heart leaps. I hear the guy ask something I can't entirely understand. There are some audible *no*'s and *dunno*'s I can make out, followed by redhead guy peeking out again. He shrugs and shakes his head.

"Think you have the wrong guy. There are a lot of people who work here, but I dunno anyone by the name of 'Vic.' Sorry." He slams the rickety door shut, and the silver knob locks loudly. I bite my lip, expecting a rush of tears I'll have to fight, but I am too empty to create anything. I feel a flake of my lipstick move on to my tongue. I spit it onto the ground and chisel the spot in the concrete with my foot, pivoting back around to face the end of the hallway. It calls for me and holds out the offering of security, of predictability. There, I can hide; there are no sudden Really Bads or hiccups in my control. There is simply fluidity where I can release everything and yet gain it all. Through the darkness, I gain Greg's peace and his immortality.

"Oh! Yeah, there she is. Thanks."

I flip around and see Di waving at me. "Shit, I was getting worried. Come on, I'm starving."

I stand for a second gazing beyond her, looking for the same solace I had felt turned the other way, but I'm met with a flat black velvet curtain.

"Sorry, yeah." I patter over to her, and we take a cab in silence back to our dorm.

Like old times, we're back and sitting in the kitchen. She's eating some potato chips, and I'm guzzling down water.

"You're pretty fucking quiet. You okay?" she blares between teeth crunches out of an oil-and-salt-rimmed mouth. Her short arm reaches deeper into the Lay's bag, which ruffles loudly. "Looks like someone fuckin' stepped on these chips. All fuckin' crumbs."

"Just tired. I'm gonna head out."

"No pretzel bites? I figured since you and Jett are tight and all, we'd get a free pass from now on." Her eyes light up. I can't help letting a little laugh escape from deep within my exhausted ribs. Opening the cabinet above my left shoulder, I find the peanut-butter-pretzel-bite bag in the corner and grab it by the teal clip sealing it.

"All yours. I'm out." She catches my underhand toss of the bag and gives me a salute. I'm carrying my black platforms as I do the achy post-heels waddle back into my room. Patricia is already asleep, so I take off my makeup and get undressed as quickly as possible. After washing my face and brushing my teeth, I hide under the covers and imagine myself fading into the dark hallway. I pretend the fluffy sheets are the black hole's embrace protecting me from everything. Most importantly, protecting me from myself.

Chapter 24

Last New Year's Eve, right before Really Bad happened during my senior year, Vic and I strolled beneath the blue Christmas lights counting down the hours until they'd be taken down. My small hand fit into his, and our feet navigated the broken cobblestones on our way to our friend's house. I knew most of the people who would be there, but I was still on edge, my anxiety heightened even more so from the weed and the cold weather. He turned to face me as we stopped to let cars go by.

"Come on, don't be scared. You know you'll have fun." He squeezed my right hand and swayed it back as he looked both ways and led me across the intersection. Once we got to the party, he went off to play pool with some of the other guys there, and I sat down in the corner of the messy garage on a ripped leather couch next to my kind-of-friend Melody. Each of us wasn't someone the other would hang out with by choice, but we were always available to ease social anxiety for one another at just the right times.

"Hey," she said perkily in her nasal tone of voice. "How are you doing?"

"I'm okay. Good."

"Yeah, same here. It's fucking freezing in here." I saw a rough Aztec-patterned blanket above her on a shelf and grabbed it, covering us both with it. She seemed drunk as she snuggled close to me. We sat in silence, looking out at the crowds of inebriated teenagers and college kids surrounding us. Protected by furniture made of skin, and warmth created by itchy threads, we became invisible and omniscient.

"Did you come here with anyone?" I asked curiously without thinking once we'd eavesdropped on incoherent phrases that jumped out at us for long enough.

"I *came* here with David, but there's no way in hell I'm leaving with him. I just wanted his Grey Goose, and I know he just wants to get laid, but he's harmless, so I'm just avoiding the asshole." Melody sighed and leaned back into the couch with her knees pulled into her chest. Her cheeks had the forced glow of alcohol consumption, and a wrench yanked deep within my stomach, yearning to strip out all the redness from her face to make her see the beauty it was covering up. My eyes pierced the flesh of her somewhat-chubby cheeks. I noticed the little texture on her smooth face, the smeared mascara at the corners of her brown eyes, and the sweat beads lining the muddy roots of her dyed strawberry-blonde hair. Melody was trying at all costs to return back to that little girl who probably truly had that strawberry-blonde hair and that glowing skin and that docile demeanor. She just didn't realize it. She was just trying to fill the silence that, if she let herself hear, would remind her of whatever fucked-up shit she was trying to run away from. My overthinking, marijuana-clouded brain spun in circles, trying to figure out why she chose alcohol as her noise. It created trails beyond her, weaving in and out through each person standing in that crowded garage, being pushed by everyone's internal concert they refused to ever let end.

"Fuck that," I finally responded. "Don't encourage shitty douches like that." I saw David just off to my left drinking a beer and patting another taller guy on the back. I yearned to make him truly accept the emptiness he refused to acknowledge so much so that he smothered it with the physical meaninglessness of insecure girls and cheap booze. I hoped Vic wasn't drinking. He often didn't with me; he knew it made me upset, and he didn't really do it much anyway, aside from the occasional whiskey.

Melody giggled and dropped her head onto my shoulder. I looked down at her scalp like a small alien and blinked. There was a little flake of what could've been dandruff or dust on a frizz of light hair sticking up, and I gently picked it out, flicking it off into the shelves behind us. Then I placed my head back on top of hers and peered out into the crowd, which was full of people too busy trying to forget themselves to remember me, though I wasn't sure if I was even visible or there to begin with.

I felt my hair being lightly pulled and shot up. Melody's head fell into the cushion, her mouth drooping open uncomfortably. I propped her up somewhat and patted her head for good measure.

"Hey. I'm not really feeling it here. Wanna head back to yours?" Vic asked me as he twirled a silky lock of my hair between his fingers. I'd been really into straightening it back then, until Really Bad when I gave up on most everything.

I nodded and grabbed his hand with a slight smile. On my way out, I told some random girl to check on Melody, and Vic and I ventured back down the row of houses illuminated by the moon and the blue lights.

"Your hair looks *awesome* right now," he said, peering down at the top of my head. "It's, like, reflecting the blue and shit." I looked up and placed my hands around his neck, leaning in for a kiss. Our tongues tangled into a knotted rose, a messy barter that we comfortably fell into.

Back in my room, our skin bare and reflecting the light of the moon that was coming in through the window I irresponsibly left open, the space between us closed until his silky black hair meshed into my equally forced-to-be silky black hair, and our bodies combined with that. Both of us melted into one another. I had never felt so whole or so giving, like I had both provided and gotten exactly what I needed for once. I wasn't overthinking or winding in roundabout circles within the cavern of my mind. I wasn't paralyzed by fear, which at that point was still hiding in my bones as my inconspicuous pilot. We guided and followed one another in circles until there were no more breaks to be smoothed together. Vic wasn't there for me or for him, and I wasn't there for him or for me, but we were there for and as the person we created together, a creature of the imaginary and the real becoming a demigod between worlds. Straddling the tightrope between morphing into a single being and forfeiting our identities completely, all of our energy used to heal one another eventually died out, and our eyes faded into the darkness of tomorrow.

Chapter 25

"Well, at least I have my computer on me," my dad says, patting his black mesh briefcase as we climb into the yellow cab, sans his luggage. It somehow ended up in Chicago and is supposed to be getting in later tonight. The driver slams the door after me and enters the driver's seat. Cigarettes, fried food, and weathered leather linger in the trapped air.

"Could you turn the heat up?" I yell against the plastic barrier. The bearded, chubby man does nothing, so I plop back, defeated.

"So? How has everything been since you moved in?" Despite having most of his belongings hundreds of miles away, my dad still smiles widely. He sits facing me, no seat belt, as I slump down with my hands stuffed in between my cold, tightly crossed legs.

I shrug and look down. "Okay. Nothing much."

"Feeling okay?"

"Yeah."

"You sure?" he asks.

I turn my head, making eye contact for a second as I nod, then move my vision out the window behind his head.

"Good, good. I'm glad to hear things have settled down for you." He readjusts to face the front and opens his briefcase, pulling out a manila envelope. He holds it out to me, and I look to him before reaching out to grab the tan paper. He nods, and I clamp the corner, then notice my name written in his messy childlike handwriting in the center. In his typical left-handed struggle, most of the ink is smeared in a fog across the rest of the word, *Valerie* wavering sideways as it stands firm on the paper.

Inside is an old photograph of me, at maybe two or three, standing on my father's seated lap, his hands on my tiny waist to lift me up. I'm holding a strawberry in one hand and reaching out to the camera with the other. His decades-younger face with just-turning-gray hair is cocked to the side in a huge grin. I'm in a pink gingham dress, and he's dressed in an outfit he still wears today, a baby-blue collared shirt and orange khaki shorts. In an outdated style, his feet are adorned with high white socks and clunky Nikes. My eyes study the scene through protective blinks. I want to apologize to that toddler; I want to warn that man; I want to rip the strawberry out of her hand and starve her to death before she gets the chance to slowly do it years later.

"Look how cute you were. And little. I wish you were still that size," my dad says gleefully with a joking lilt in his voice. He picks up the image out of my hands and purses his mouth as he looks at himself.

"Damn, I looked good then. I need to lose weight."

I chuckle lightly as he sets the photo back between us on the seat angled toward me. "It's for you. Keep it, I have a copy back home." I place the shiny, drugstore-developed paper in my black purse and lift the corners of my lips slightly as I look back at him.

"Thanks, it's nice."

"Uh-huh." He leans back proudly. I know inside he's patting himself on the back. It's the kind of thing he'd see as a little victory in his daily battles with me.

We pull up to his hotel to drop off his briefcase and check in. He had offered me a room for the few days he's visiting, but I felt bad making him waste extra money on me, so I refused despite his pestering. After my dad confuses the receptionist with winding jokes and failed attempts at complimenting her jewelry, we make our way to a restaurant my dad made reservations at, that he's promised is "the coolest thing in this area of town" and "a place you can take your friends to impress them." Both are unlikely statements, but his enthusiastic energy is a somewhat nice change.

"Look! They even have vegan cheese!" he excitedly yells out once we sit down and get menus, holding his up at me and pointing. I nod.

"Yeah." I sip my water and tap my foot. My eyes travel to the open kitchen and the line cooks flipping skillets over open flames. Illuminated by candles, couples and pairs of girls sit beneath that open view into the inner workings of the restaurant. My dad thinks I don't notice him staring at me, blinking as his face droops in seriousness. He sighs loudly.

"Was your flight here okay?" I finally say after we've exhausted using our menus as an excuse to not speak. He reaches for his illuminated phone. I blink.

"Yeah, yeah, sorry, I…" He breaks into laughter and types something, then scrolls and laughs more. He answers a call, complains about "this case being absurd," and returns to scrolling and exhaling occasionally in amusement at whatever email subscription he's reading this time. I remain looking straight at him, my eyes unwavering and my posture straight. My dad shakes his head amusedly and types more, not putting his phone down until our waiter returns.

"Interested in any starters?"

"No, I think we're ready to order," I quickly mention.

"But they have fried okra," my dad boasts loudly as if it's a genius statement bound to astound me. "Your *favorite*."

"I'm fine." He smiles at the waiter.

"Well, then, *I'll* have the fried okra to start, and we'll see how that goes." The man nods and we finish our orders, with me ordering some mushroom stir-fry. My dad returns his focus to his overly bright phone. I sip my obnoxiously refilled glass of alkaline water.

"You know you came here to see me—I think, at least," I finally declare, frustrated. My father's blue eyes dart up, little lines of text reflecting off of his shiny eyeballs. He sighs, sets his phone down, then smiles at me.

"Then, tell me about your whole new life here. You don't seem to have much to say."

"Sorry."

"Don't be sorry, I just… Okay. Tell me about your roommate, then."

"She looks like Bette Midler mixed with…yeah, she looks like Bette Midler to me."

"Interesting. She nice?"

I shrug. "We don't talk much. *She* talks too much for that."

"What?"

"She's, like, always on the phone, I don't know."

"Seems outgoing. Could be nice for you to be around." My eyes dart from the ground to meet his in defense. "You know what I mean."

"Okay." The waiter brings over the fried okra, plated with an oil drizzle and a pinch of cilantro. I take a sip of water.

"Mmm!" My dad's eyes light up, an immediate one-eighty. "Val, you *have* to try some." I know I won't get around this one, but a single bite won't change anything, especially if I factor that out from my meal. I take a nibble off the corner of a piece the farthest away from the oily crescent and fake enjoyment.

"Oh wow," he says, savoring the food. He continues to grab at the little brown-green chunks while I pretend that it's taking me five minutes to eat this whole sliver.

"Be right back," I eventually mutter as I place my napkin on the table and head to the bathroom. Locking the door behind me, I peer over the black porcelain sink and place my hands behind my neck. My lips tear a little as I yawn, so I pull out ChapStick from my purse and run into the photo of me as that little girl again. In my hand, that strawberry is perfectly bitten into with itty teeth marks. Looking closely, I had some red juice outlining my smiling mouth. I don't think I've smiled like that ever since. Who was taking that photo? I'm not even sure where it was taken; it looks like a park in the background, but I'm not certain. I pee and head back out.

"Who took that picture you gave me?" My voice is steady and direct. It shakes my dad enough to drop his phone two inches onto the tablecloth.

"W-what?"

"The photo of us you gave me. I…I was just wondering who took it and all." I'm a little quieter as I place my napkin back in my lap and straighten out my silverware. The plate of okra, I notice, is empty.

"Oh…well, it would've been…your mother, yes. She would've been the one to take this. We were in Arizona." He drinks his iced tea and blows his nose. My empty stomach is suddenly filled with the surge of memories that are always waiting for the floodgates to open.

He changes the subject, and I talk some about my classes and school. I don't mention my plans to change majors, not because I'm concerned he wouldn't approve, but because it pains me to see him excited about me. And I know he would find my confusion exciting in his optimistic, oblivious way.

A white bowl of mushrooms, broccolini, and brown rice plops down in front of me. I make a tiny indent in the rice where I'm allowed to eat to and scrape off some of the teriyaki sauce from the vegetables to move onto the off-limits section of my plate.

"I didn't know you liked mushrooms," my dad states, peering at my dish.

"Oh, I…well, taste buds change." I clear my throat. He looks up.

"That's right, every seven years. You're right." He nods and takes a loud, crunchy bite of a carrot in the pasta he ordered. I try to bite into a mushroom and gag. We sit in silence as we eat, him scarfing everything down as I pick out individual grains of rice and ribbons of green. I'm not even trying to keep myself from eating at this point; my appetite has been sated by that little girl eating a strawberry. I grab my napkin and wipe away the leftover juice.

Chapter 26

I groan as my phone vibrates and wakes me up. I went back to sleep after working out, using the time I'd usually take to get ready. It's Jett texting me, asking if I want to go to a cat cafe *because it seems like the kind of thing you'd be into*. I snort and explain how I have class in an hour.

Why does it matter if you don't care about film anymore

I flip over onto my back and blink at the ceiling. It's my film theory class. I hate my film theory class. But I'll still go to my film theory class. My phone buzzes again.

You're switching out anyway... I sit up and see Patricia curled up on her side, her eyes closed and her chest lightly rising and falling. I pick up my phone and avoid addressing the issue— that I have about thirty-five minutes to solve.

wheres the cat cafe

About a block away from Harry's. I'll buy you a coffee on the way.

Warmth inside me hides the cold, obligated drive to go to my pointless class. I'm convinced.

ya ok, meet u there then? n like 30?

Jett agrees. I roll out of my fluffy sheets and slip on jeans and a fuzzy gray sweater, then quickly smear some black liner and purple shadow around my green eyes. Pulling my coat on, I fluff up my messy hair and pop my hood.

Jett's already waiting inside Harry's once I get there. He's zooming into something on his phone before he sees me and his eyes shoot up. Behind him, on the island countertops facing the windows, are two drinks.

"A coffee with just cinnamon," he says, handing me the smaller cup to the right. I smile as my face flushes, and I take the cup, nodding my head in thanks.

"Matcha latte for you?" I point to the other cup behind him.

"You know me too well." Jett picks up his drink and knowingly waits for me to open the door for him.

"I'm so thankful chivalry isn't dead for a real gentleman like you," he sings in a high voice. I roll my eyes and hit him playfully.

"Just making up for the millions of women who've probably never held the door for someone else in their lives." The coffee burns my hand slightly through the cardboard sleeve, but it helps to warm me even more so. We walk stride in stride for a few minutes until we reach the cafe, sipping our drinks and aligning our steps. I walk to the wooden door under the pink cat sign and am greeted by a young Asian woman smiling at me.

"You have an appointment?" she asks in a thick accent.

"Oh no, we don't," I say, looking past a cracked pink curtain at guests playing with cats.

"Sorry, all booked." I blink back at her firm face, shake my head tightly, then look back at Jett. He thanks her, and we walk out.

"Well, shit," Jett says, shrugging. "Sorry. I thought you'd really like that. Oh well."

"We can just go back to my dorm, unless you have somewhere else you wanna go."

"I don't. Sounds good."

Another documentary. More making out. Less thinking about my playing hooky. Until he asks:

181

"Wish you'd gone to class now?" I roll my eyes and meet his lips again, his arms moving my body from above to underneath his in a quick motion. We both lift each other's shirts up in a tangle. Two soft drops sound one after the other as they hit the floor.

He reaches for my belt, and though I let him, I feel my electric guard going up. *He isn't Vic. You do want this. Wait. Do you?* The force within me manages to transform into words, and I break away before the plastic strap is pulled out of all the loops.

"I…I need to pee. Sorry." I jump up and grab my shirt, then head down the hall.

"Val? You okay?" I hear him yell out from the room before the door slams shut.

He's not Vic.

His hair is similarly dark.

And he towers over me about the same amount.

But he's not Vic.

And I shouldn't feel like he is.

But I do.

I pee a little even though I don't have to and lean over my knees, my face in my palms. Maybe he's like Vic was in the beginning. Maybe he's Vic before Vic became not-Vic, or maybe he's Vic before Vic *really* became Vic. Either way, I'm sweaty and thirsty. After drinking some tap water and splashing my face under the sink, I leave the bathroom without washing my hands. When I reenter my room, Jett's sitting up and pulling his shirt on.

"Sorry, sorry," I say, head down and cheeks flushed. He's also facing toward the ground as he pats his shirt smooth.

"It's fine. Just scares me when you freak out like that." Jett sighs, cocks his head to the side, and picks up his phone. "I'm gonna go get some work done." He looks up at me. "You sure you're alright?"

"Yeah, yeah." He gets up, and I open the door instinctively. "See ya." No, not worth playing hooky. Now I've fucked up the whole day. I deserve to get whatever shit comes my way.

Should've just gone to class.

Chapter 27

"I swear to God, Creed doesn't sound like Pearl Jam," I tell Jett.

"Play 'One Last Breath' and tell me Scott Stapp doesn't twist his voice to sound like Eddie Vedder. *Tell* me."

I laugh and set the phone down on my desk, putting it on speaker. I play the song on my computer and hear Jett singing along carelessly in the background. A puny smile forms on my lips.

"Okay, maybe," I admit loudly over the music. "I hear the resemblance. Somewhat."

"*Bullllllllshit*. But okay. We're getting there." I let his scratchy voice hang in the air a little. His light breathing provides steady background percussion to the staccato chords in my mind. "Val? You there?" A car horn plays through on his end.

"Yeah, yeah. Sorry. Was on my computer. I—" I suddenly stop as my phone vibrates with another incoming call. It's from a number I don't recognize. "Hold on a sec, I'm getting a random call."

"I gotta get to class soon anyway. Call me later?"

"Of course. Have a good time in historical reenactments."

"*Bye*, Val."

I laugh and answer the call with an ill-fitting glee in my voice. "*Hello?*"

"Valerie?" It's Dr. Ellis. The instruments inside me crash to a thud.

"Dr. Ellis? Um...."

"I'm sorry to reach you like this; I got your number from your medical profile... Anyway, we're in a pinch for this unexpected thing tonight with June's mother, and we, well..."

"Do you need a babysitter again?"

"Well, yes, and I was wondering if you happened to be free again."

"Yeah, I can do it. What time?"

"I'd need you here by about six, and we should be back by midnight again. I'll compensate you extra for the short notice; June was supposed to have another girl lined up by now, but... Right, six, if that works."

"Sure, yeah. Okay."

"Thank you so much, Valerie. See you then." I hear his phone click down, then I save the number as his contact accordingly. My mind runs quickly through food plans for the evening. Take-out salad. I can pick it up on the way. Double-checking the nutrition facts online, I cheer inside for already having a plan in place to work with after getting thrown a curveball. No nukes on my planet.

I get back to looking at required texts for an essay class, but after dozens of pages, I don't really read anything. My eyes scan the characters and phrases but don't fuse anything together as language. They're dead symbols to me, inactive, unbusy little bodies piled on shelves in morgues with no more life to thrive on within my mind. Thirty pages later, and I'm no more educated on the use of jump cuts in *Life Is Beautiful* than I was beforehand. I don't even have an iota of an idea of what *Life Is Beautiful* is about. I'm a great film major.

Hours of mindless eye-scanning later, I'm in a cab headed up to Dr. Ellis's shiny apartment, my salad, computer, and charcoal face mask in tow. It's about time for a pore clearing, and I'm not going to wait until after getting back to my place past midnight for that shit. The doorman acknowledges me with a nod, and I take the elevator to the sixth floor. Dr. Ellis already has the door cracked, and I gingerly step in.

"Hi there," he greets me. I notice a bottle of wine and two glasses sitting on the island countertop, one half empty. Christopher is at the dining room table playing on an iPad.

"Hey," I say, and Christopher looks up and waves at me accordingly. "Hi, Christopher. How are you?"

"I'm okay. Dad, may I have some juice?" He speaks with the same poignant, mercurial tone as Dr. Ellis.

"Steven, remember, we stopped giving him sugar at night so he could fall asleep." A slim, frantic woman with shoulder-length dark-blonde hair steps around the corner as she adjusts one of the many bracelets on her wrist. Guess I got the blonde part right, but I'm still unsure if she's a Libra. She curls the shorter pieces framing her face around her ears, and her dark eyes under blunt, rounded bangs notice me.

She blinks a few times before speaking. "I'm June. Valerie, right?"

I swallow and nod.

"Uh-huh, yeah, yes, that's me." My eyes seem to be unable to meet hers as she forcefully gives me a once-over. Suddenly, I feel naked in my loose ripped jeans.

"Well, thanks for stepping in again. Hopefully, this won't happen once more." She turns to put away some dishes. The porcelain clangs loudly, and I furrow my brows. In my peripheral vision, Dr. Ellis is staring at me, but I decide not to embarrass him by acknowledging it. June suddenly drops a bowl, and the broken pieces fly across the smooth black floor.

"God *dammit*." She bends down in her black kitten heels and sighs as she picks up the large pieces. I run over to help but end up standing there, uncertain about what to do.

"Um…do you have a dustpan?" I finally say in a wavering voice.

"I'll get it, don't worry," Dr. Ellis declares as he steps in front of me and pulls out a broom with pan attached from the pantry. I walk back by Christopher, who is totally immersed in his game, and peer at the couple uncomfortably. June whispers something I can't make out while they're both hunched behind the island counter, but when Dr. Ellis eventually rises up, he's shaking his head at her. He pops down again for a moment and is looking at me as he stands up again, brushing imaginary dust off of his khaki pants. He smooths out his baby-blue button-down and pushes up his glasses. June puts away the wine and grabs her purse from next to Christopher. June and I make a millisecond of eye contact, which is quickly decided by both of us not to be worth committing to.

"Bye, Christopher, have a good night," Dr. Ellis says as he opens the door for June and she walks through.

"Bye, Dad, love you!" Christopher's head remains down.

"Love you, too." Door click. Lock. Suddenly, seconds later, it bursts open again. Dr. Ellis runs into his bedroom.

"Cuff links," he explains as he returns and exits for a second time.

"It's my *mother*, Steven," I hear June mutter outside.

"June, we have almost an hour…" Dr. Ellis's voice trails off as the elevator rings in arrival and then shuts loudly. I sit down across from Christopher, and he suddenly looks up at me.

"Could *you* get me some juice? I swear I'll fall asleep. Mom just thinks they stop me when they don't really."

I laugh and make my way into the kitchen, opening the fridge. "Yeah, okay. What kind?"

"Apple, please." I hand him the pouch and sit back down, pulling out my computer. He excitedly takes a sip and thanks me.

"No problem." My stomach rumbles as my mind overpowers it with memories of Greg sipping Hi-C juice as we played Scrabble on my bedroom floor. I almost ask Christopher if he has any board games he wants to play, but I stop myself. I can't let my mind go here. Too risky. I call Jett to distract myself, but he doesn't answer. I pick at my ripped jeans and focus on the tiny frays, once connected, once whole.

Chapter 28

My fingers tap the dining room table anxiously. It's midnight, I'm beginning to get hungry again, and Dr. Ellis and June aren't back yet. I lay my head on the slick surface and push the chair back as I lean forward. Suddenly, the table reverberates with the sound of someone's voice. It's a young boy's voice, just starting to crack, and it tears me away from focusing on my aching stomach. Greg's sitting across from me.

"Val, Val, Val," he repeats until I raise my head and sit up. His hair is matted, like he's just gotten out of bed. My lips part, but no sound escapes.

"Val. Why are you doing this to yourself?" Greg's voice cracks on *yourself.*

I inhale sharply. "W-what do you mean?"

"You know what I mean, Val. Why?"

"I need to."

"You need to?"

"I... It's just something I like to do. It's not like it's doing much, it's just...something to think about."

"It's all you think about."

I swallow without meaning to.

"Val, you need help."

"I am getting help. I'm seeing Dr. Ellis, and I'm on meds—
"

"You're not on your meds—"

"How… You… Yes, I am." I stand up to push the chair in, and it squeaks against the floor. "I'm living my life. I'm on my own. I'm fucking *doing* it. You have no goddamn idea what the…the real world is like." His big brown eyes blink up at me.

"I don't think you're really living your life."

"The hell would you know?"

"Come on. Have a banana or something. I don't think they'd mind." I look over at the fruit bowl.

"They're fucking green, Greg."

"Val, you look like a little kid."

"*You're* the little kid."

"I'm not kidding! You… Please, Val. Please do something." I run over to the fruit bin, grab the banana, struggle to rip the hard, unripe skin open, and mash it on the table right in front of Greg. I grind my wrist into the metal. Yellow goo spills out all around my hand as I pierce Greg's pupils with my own.

"Is this enough? Am I *doing* something now!"

"Valerie." A heavy voice booms from behind me. When I blink, Greg is gone.

Slowly, painfully, I turn around to see Dr. Ellis and June standing inside their entryway. June has her arms crossed, and Dr. Ellis is in front of her. I look back at the mess on the table, all in front of a perfectly pushed-in chair. The heat inside me rips open my scabbed wounds and surrounds me in flames, engulfing me as I fall to ashes. Dr. Ellis and June simply watch and stare at the spectacle. Boiling tears well in my eyes but turn to steam before they can pour out; my neck tenses in a choke hold of my own doing.

"Valerie," Dr. Ellis says, "could I speak with you outside for a moment?" My eyes lock on to his. I don't breathe. He opens the door, and my body follows without question out into the hallway. June scurries to the kitchen, and as Dr. Ellis closes the door behind me, I hear a paper towel rip. I wince at the sound.

"I'm so, I'm—" The words begin to pour out of me like stewing magma.

"Don't—"

"I didn't mean to, he was—"

"Valerie—"

"I can't—" He grabs my shoulders and looks down at me over his red glasses, which are nearly falling off the tip of his nose. In his grip, I inhale as if he's stabbing me in the core.

"Get home. Rest. I'd like to see you before Friday. Are you free Monday at our usual time?" Without thinking, I nod. I don't know if I'm free. I hope I'm not so I can get out of class.

"My things… I'll…" I point back into his apartment as he drops his hands. Dr. Ellis turns bright red and shakes his head quickly, then pushes his glasses up.

"I'll get them. Are they on the table?"

"Yeah, they are." He rushes inside and reappears seconds later, gingerly holding my black book bag. The huge red pentacle on the side is an ironic contrast against his perfectly tailored, pressed khaki pants.

"Thank you. I'll—I…" He hits the elevator button for me, and I look down at my shoes.

"I'll see you Monday, Valerie. Please get back safely." I keep my eyes down as the elevator doors close, but right before they shut, I look up for a split second and meet eyes with Dr. Ellis again, who hasn't stopped staring at me since handing me my bag. I purse my lips and furrow my brow. Then, the metal doors clang loudly, and I'm short-circuiting from within again. In a rumbled daze, I make it back to my dorm.

Chapter 29

Jett's head leans forward as he sips the smoothie he's brought. Behind him, the snow swirls and falls like drunk confetti. The sound of the strong winds echoes under Alice in Chains coming from my computer. My eyes flutter open each time the whirling gets really loud. Jett pauses the music and begins searching for a video to watch.

"You're really tired awfully early," he says, pushing my ratty hair back. I haven't washed it in a few days.

"It's been a tiring few days."

"You've only, like, babysat and gotten a massage."

I blink a few times at him. I've gone on two runs each day. "I guess I needed the rest." I sit up and pull my hair up into a ponytail, which I immediately regret upon remembering I look like a Founding Father like this. Before I get the chance to undo it, Jett grabs the end and twirls it. His eyes are fixed on the YouTube video he put on of World War II submarines.

"Jesus Christ," he mutters as the narrator with an Australian accent spews out some meaningless specs about whatever the hell this submarine is apparently capable of. I lean against his shoulder and close my eyes as he takes another slurp from the purple cup in his hand.

"What's Di up to?" he asks as an ad comes on. I shrug against his body.

"Dunno. Maybe recording some rap for her SoundCloud."

"She ever decide on a name?"

I laugh.

"Yeah. Miss Carbon, or something. I think."

"Miss Carbon?"

"Di... Diamond... Carbon... I think because diamonds are made out of carbon. At least that's what she said."

"Yeah, yeah, they are... Funny."

I snuggle more into the crook of his arm and try to keep focused on my computer, but my heartbeat slows and my mind traps itself into sleep.

Hidden in the cavern of my broken skull, I sit in a room across the table from a hooded figure. The table is ornate and wooden, and the figure's face is shadowed so that I cannot see them. I'm seated in a red velvet chair, frozen still, eyes fixated on the person in front of me. There is a shiny metal goblet sitting directly in the center of the black wooden surface. The figure takes a sip, and I see some dark-red wine swish up the side of the goblet as they set it back down. When they begin to speak, their voice is androgynous and unfamiliar.

"You must be scared," they declare. The sentence echoes within the creaky wooden dome.

"I'm too tired to be scared."

"Too tired or too used to it to realize?"

I breathe deeply and continue to look at the formless black shadow under the curve of a thick hood. "Where am I?"

"You know where you are." The ceiling is cracked, with the faint glow of neurons firing. It looks like a futuristic cave drawing etched onto the cosmos.

"Who are you?"

"I am not anyone." I lean forward on my knees and peer as persistently as I can at them. My eyes burn with focus, but I can't make anything out, and I eventually lean back in defeat.

"You pretend I don't exist. Now you see me for what I am."

"Which is what?" I ask.

"What is."

I shake my head in confusion. I know I'm dreaming, and I try to force myself to wake up, but I continue to be seated on red velvet no matter how much my brain yells at my muscles to move.

"You don't understand the nature of what I truly am. I am no one, but you think I am someone else. You think I am one to engage directly, to think of you at all costs."

"Are you...?" The words taste slimy as I force them out, too bitter at the thought of something higher to complete the phrase. I swallow to rid myself of the pathetic voice I let myself use.

"I suppose, if that makes it easier for you to understand."

I laugh. I need to get more sleep.

"I'm sitting across from…who knows what, who I can't even see the face of, who's drinking wine from an…an antique fucking goblet, all in the broken wooden cave that is my skull. Alright."

"I'm not here for you, but I am here." As they reach again for the cup and take a sip, the wine pours down from their mouth, flooding the whole room instantaneously with dark, thick waves. I take a deep breath as my head goes under, and when I open my eyes, I'm blinking sharply at YouTube on my computer. Jett is laughing lightly at some joke about Lincoln. I cough.

"Oh, hey. You're awake." I sit up, my ponytail lopsided and asymmetrical. I yank it and pull out a significant amount of hair along with the band.

"What time is it?" I ask. Jett looks at the watch on his left arm.

"Almost five."

"I'm getting dinner with Di tonight, if that's still on. I should probably start getting ready."

"Okay, I'll head out, then." He sits up and stretches his arms over his head.

"No, I mean, you don't have to. I just…"

"I need to work on some shit anyway. Medieval astronomy shit."

"Riveting."

He kisses my forehead and hops down from my bed. The sound of the door shutting behind him lingers in the wooden space of my head for a little while before letting up and allowing me to leave freely. Looking in the mirror, I see through my green irises to my dark pupils, and in that tiny tunnel, I see the reflection of a dark, faceless hooded figure drinking wine staring back at me.

Chapter 30

"Slowest goddamn elevator I've ever been in," my dad mutters as we finally reach our floor and get out. The air is sharp with chlorine. A museum docent stares me down, partially like he has to, partially like he's judging the shit out of me. Out of everyone at this exhibit, he probably is right in suspecting that I'm the most likely to fuck something up.

"Sorry," I say as I accidentally step on the back of a woman's shoe while death-staring back at the docent. My dad whips around to see what commotion I'm causing, and I pull my phone out quickly to distract myself.

"You don't like the art?" he asks, seeing my head bent over the screen.

"Oh, sorry, no, I do. Just a text. Sorry." What is Jett doing tonight? I wish I had a text from him.

I follow my father around the large room like a small child unsure how to walk. My eyes glaze over the postmodern-kitsch sculptures and paintings. There is a crowd gathered around an iron bathtub bathed entirely in reflective gold paint with *NO*

SALVATION graffitied on the inside in hot-pink sponge strokes. Photography is allowed, so I'm not enticed to take a picture. In fact, my mind writhes as I watch families happily photograph the art around me, smiling and pointing at their favorite pieces. I stand in the center of the room and cannot imagine the riveting pull of amusement, the intoxication of interest. My dad is holding his phone horizontal with both hands to try and photograph a red painting in front of him. He turns back to look for me, makes eye contact, then waves me over. I walk up to his side. He motions for me to move in front of the art.

"What?"

"Come on, I want a picture of you." His right hand still holds the phone perfectly stiff and sideways as if in a cadaveric spasm.

"Dad—"

"I want a picture of you to remember the trip by, Valerie." I do not have the energy to argue. I move adjacent to the rectangular canvas, the metal chains on my pants clanging as I press my ankles together and force a closemouthed smile. As soon as my dad looks at the photo on his phone, he bursts out laughing.

"You gotta come see this." I slump over and wince when I notice my eyes, terrified and uncomfortable, juxtaposed against my mouth in a pinched smile. It isn't funny to me at all.

"Alright, alright," he says, giving up, and I back away to the opposite end of the room. Eventually, we make it through the rest of the museum, with him focused on the art and me focused on pretending to be focused on it, then head to our dinner reservation at his favorite restaurant here. It's a little Chinese place with less than ten tables and an annoying bell that clangs every time someone walks in or out so that the single host/waiter/chef/whoever the hell he is knows to come out. As I struggle to pull open the metal door, my dad grabs it behind me and holds up two fingers to the host, who is already in the dining area setting down silverware. He motions us to a corner table, which is shaky and unstable and covered with a red paper tablecloth.

"Water," I quickly mutter when the waiter returns. "Oh, and the veggie delight, with brown rice and the sauce on the side."

"Not the General Tso's tofu?" my father asks, flabbergasted. I keep my head down toward the menu and shrug.

"And *I'll* get a Diet Coke and the orange stir-fry with the vegetarian duck, please," he says confidently. At this, I do look up at him in surprise. He always gets the normal duck.

"I thought I'd join you for a change," he mentions after the waiter leaves. I smile, and my face flushes with embarrassment. He nods and drinks his Diet Coke proudly.

"Thanks," I blurt out.

"What are you up to tomorrow after I leave?"

"I have class in the afternoon, then just seeing my therapist. Not sure about plans afterward."

"You like him?" I almost spit out my sour lemon water.

"W-what?"

"Your therapist guy. I mean, is he easy to talk to, you get along and all?"

"Yeah, yeah. He's cool." I don't want to bring Jett up to my dad. He'll pretend not to see him as another Vic, as another internal weapon of my own doing.

"Good to hear. You busy this week?"

"No, not particularly. I…I think I'm going to be changing majors." My dad's blue eyes nearly spring out of his long face before he yanks them back with a firm blink.

"Changing majors? What to?"

"Maybe…maybe psychology. I'm not certain yet. The required classes for it next semester would all be eight a.m.'s, which would suck—"

"I mean, if that's what you really want, then great. And you've never been much of a late sleeper anyway." I begin to play devil's advocate, then bite my tongue.

"I'm just not entirely sure yet. Just letting you know. Because I don't know how my scholarship for film would carry over…or if, you know, it can… I'm just, like, updating you." My dad has always made it work, but I don't know if that would be possible without my scholarship. It's not something I've wanted to consider, because I can't honestly imagine not being able to do what I feel like in this kind of a situation. I *will* study what I want, and it *will* be financially okay. I look back up at him as a big swallow enlarges his Adam's apple.

"I appreciate it. Just surprised you're switching from film. It was always your passion."

I raise and lower my eyebrows while holding eye contact. "Not so sure anymore."

"Well, you'd always make those movies with your friends when you were little. I watched them on that big desktop we used to have, you remember? Playing dress up with my things, and I'd have to clean *all* of that up the next day... You were very considerate."

I laugh and nod, remembering what I'd forgotten. The waiter brings out our food, made as quickly as ever in this seemingly always empty joint. The porcelain plate clangs down in front of me, vegetables slathered with thick teriyaki sauce.

"I—I... Never mind." The waiter looks to me, then leaves as my dad finally says thank you.

"Is something wrong?" he then asks, turning to me.

"I asked for the sauce on the side because it's always super salty, but it's fine."

"Well, here. I'll send it back." He begins to raise his hand.

"No, no! Please. It's cool." The waiter sees us causing a commotion, but I wave him away and smile. One-third less of the plate can be eaten, then, if my mental math at guesstimating the nutritional profile of this amount of sauce (one-fourth cup, maybe?) is decently accurate. Then half of the little mound of rice. Yes. Perfect. I smile and cheers my dad's dark drink with my lemon water.

"You know," he starts, swallowing, "I'm really proud of you, Valerie. You've come a long way, and you're doing really well for yourself. And you look stronger than ever; you look good." Another slurp of fake duck.

"Thanks, yeah, I really am. Stronger than ever."

Chapter 31

Di clicks the space bar on her computer and looks at me eagerly.

"It's cool, Di. Poetic, like you said. Where'd you get your beats from?"

"Dunno. Some guy who was selling them for five dollars a track on Instagram so he could pay his rent. Looked into it, and they were pretty fuckin' legit, so I bought a few."

"Oh. Cool."

"So, you think it's good?"

"Yeah, it really is. I'm impressed." It's okay. It isn't bad, I guess. I couldn't really pay attention for the whole three minutes, though, so I'm more ignorant than I am dishonest.

"Really?"

"Goddamn, Di, yes, I mean it." We both laugh and lean farther into the green sheets of her bed, each of us on opposite ends. Her room smells faintly of weed as I turn my head to face her cabinet.

"Wait, don't you have a two thirty today?" Di asks.

I flip my face back toward her. Di leans up on her forearms, her loose black T-shirt falling off one shoulder. I shrug and roll my eyes.

"I'm transferring out of this damn major, I don't give a shit!" I yell as I hug a pillow to my face.

"You could still probably use the credits as, like, electives or some shit."

"*O*-kay."

"Do you know what you want to switch to? Wait, let me guess. Gender studies. Maybe fuckin'…Ancient Greek. Theoretical genocide."

"What the hell?"

"Gender studies? I'm right?"

"No, Di." I fall back and put my hands on my stomach. With a sigh, I state, "Psych. Maybe."

"*You're* wanting to major in psych?"

"I mean, who better to understand and apply it than a crazy person?" We pause for a moment as the statement lingers between us.

"Yeah. Guess so." Her breath is soft and wispy, and I can hear small hairs in her nostrils wavering when I pay attention really closely. The electricity within me is shut off, flipped onto that *O* symbol on its plug. My wounds are still gaping, inflamed, infected, and oozing green pus, but so are hers, and we lay together in a mess of our own doing, of our own lack of doing. Little streams of secretion turn into puddles, which fuse with hers into a filthy mess of sickness, surrounding us like castle walls. I wonder if we'd still be here, lying down together, if they were to be torn down.

"You wanna do something tonight?" Di asks, lightly cracking the glass silence.

"Can't. Therapy, then I made plans—"

"*Jett*, I know. Alright. We should make plans for something this week, though."

"Okay."

"Okay?" I suggest we see a movie Thursday. She says there are no good movies out. I ask about dinner. She agrees. I leave. Her breath keeps whistling through wispy nose hairs until I shut the door completely behind me.

Back in my dorm, I put on some music and try to focus on writing this bullshit film analysis essay. My arguments are plagiarized, and my analysis is only vaguely relevant, but it's weight toward the required three thousand words. I look at my paper and realize I've been typing the song lyrics as I've heard them.

And either way you turn

I'll be there

Open up your skull

I'll be there

Climbing up the walls

I almost hit delete when I decide to keep them there and do some bullshit citation integration claiming they're relevant to my film. *Addiction increases exponentially at the rate at which the user takes drugs.* Boom. *Fear and Loathing in Las Vegas* pseudo-psychoanalyzed and half related to distorted Radiohead lyrics. An hour later, I've hit my completed my word requirement and sit back, scrolling up and down the pages to make sure there aren't any red squiggles to indicate I should actually reread what I've written. Revision is second-guessing. I believe in gut instinct. It's the mind reconsidering itself that fucks everything up.

A notification pings up in the corner of my screen. Jett.

Sorry, I'm not really feeling well. Rain check?

I click away the banner and tense my eyes, then decide not to put off responding.

Ya no prob. hope u feel better

He replies with a heart, and I go to text Di about hanging out tonight but then decide against it. I don't want to. I'll probably be too exhausted from therapy anyway.

I get a text from my dad: *Just landed. Love you.* I click it away and don't respond. He may think he loves me, but it isn't true. He loves feeling like he's doing something right, belonging to the communal agreement that family must be loved. Family is arbitrary. I have no goddamn family. My family lives within me, in my head, of my own doing. I am the ultimate artist; I depend on nothing and no one for my materials. I need no canvas. My own existence is my goddamn canvas. Every bloody, oozing droplet morphs and grows into an extension of myself, a separate entity entirely up to me to create. Of its own agency but willingly within my own rules. Responsible for itself but responsible in answering

to me. It's those who betray me who I take issue with.

I reread my essay. It's incoherent and jumbled, but so much

so that it may just pass for genius. Electrical charges from my

brain form ties between words and phrases that loop and

convalesce into roller coasters of language. It isn't up to me to

decide for anyone else to get on board. I create my own world,

without impeding anyone else's, without destruction, without

harm.

Chapter 32

"Hello, Valerie." Dr. Ellis opens his office door wide. I slide my phone into my back pocket as I stand up from the waiting room chair, then quickly pull it out as I prepare to sit down again on his office love seat. My heart pumps fast. I can feel myself crumbling within, finishing up the destruction that wasn't finished the last time we'd seen each other.

Sitting down in his green armchair, Dr. Ellis sighs and crosses his legs, then reaches behind him onto his desk and pulls back the yellow notepad and trademark black Mont Blanc pen. He flips a page over and scribbles in the corner. Sniffles. His eyeglasses fall, then get pushed up.

"How has your day been today?" His voice is calm and edgeless.

"Kind of busy. I hung out with Di, then wrote a paper."

"What paper?"

"This film analysis thing. I bullshitted it, but…yeah, it's on *Fear and Loathing in Las Vegas.*"

"I saw that when it came out. A while ago, now that I think about it."

I press my lips together and don't respond. Not bringing up what happened is making me lurch over the line on the track, causing me to make a false start and screw up the race every time Dr. Ellis speaks. He hasn't blown the whistle yet, and I'm worried I'll lose the sprint when he does, but I'd rather lose than wait here dying of stale electric shock.

"I… I'd like to know what happened on Friday, Valerie. I'm not upset at all, believe me. Apparently, I had the impression that you were…you were at a much different place in your journey. I just want to better understand what went on. What's *going* on."

I swallow as his deep-brown eyes look over his red glasses and meet my pupils.

"I'm sorry."

"Look, you don't need to apologize. In fact, *don't* apologize. Just walk me through what happened."

The buildup inside me stirs; it burns my organs, it melts my brain, but it steams open my throat. "I saw Greg. He was there, at your table, yelling at me."

"About what?"

"I think asking me to eat, it's kind of a blur."

"Asking you to *eat*?"

"Yeah."

"So Greg was seated at the table, with you across from him, and you two were arguing about you eating or not."

"Yeah."

"Then what happened?" I notice the notepad about to slip off of his knee, and I point to it as he catches it just as it falls. "Valerie?"

I shake my head quickly. "Then I was telling him he was, like, a little kid, and to shut up or whatever, and he was telling me to eat one of your…one of your bananas."

"So *then* you brought it to the table." Dr. Ellis cocks his head to the side and furrows his brows. I feel nauseated as his pity permeates through the open cracks in my scabs and floats in the puddles of my wounds.

"I was really, really angry and just wanted to fuck with him."

"Have you been taking your medication, Valerie?" The question follows my comment so quickly that I feel as if it's been waiting on the tip of his tongue for longer than the duration of the conversation. My chest feels like a wire hanger, inverting and then snapping. However, the constraint suddenly allows me to feel controlled, connected, and I raise my chin slowly.

"Yes. I have."

"Maybe we'll switch you out, then. I'll write in for a different kind."

"Did I build up a tolerance or something?"

"Maybe, maybe just…just chance. We don't have a perfect system to work out these things definitively." Dr. Ellis scratches his head and sighs. His hair has grown slightly longer and messier. A tendril of brown gray hangs down on his moisturized, barely wrinkled forehead. Instinctually, I find myself wanting to push it back, to bring him once again to his pristine image of shined glasses and pressed khakis.

"Yeah, I get it." I squirm a little in the crevice of the beige love seat. Thunder booms in the distance.

"Do you know why Greg was telling you to eat?"

"He was telling me I looked like a little kid. Telling me I needed to put on weight, basically. Pissed me off at the time."

"Was he mocking you, making fun of you?"

"Not really. He was, like, *concerned*, which was the worst part."

"Concerned that you aren't eating enough?"

"I guess so. Came out of basically nowhere, it was weird. Just threw me off, which is why I was angry, I think." He scribbles in the notepad and inhales to say something, then pauses. Another inhale.

"Have you gotten other comments about your weight? From anyone else?"

"No, which is why it was so, so weird coming from him. Like, it wasn't something I'd expect him to say." Rain begins to hit the windows to my right.

"Expect him to have said, you mean."

"Yeah, yeah." Speaking of Greg in the past tense doesn't put me any more in the present.

"I'd like you to see a dietician, Valerie. Just, you know, as a precaution."

"What?"

"Well, if food-related anxieties are coming up through these hallucinations—"

"I really only had this one. It's not like it's a big *thing*, or whatever."

"Valerie, I just want to make sure nothing is wrong on that end. So that we can rule that out as an issue impacting your mental health as well, vitamin wise, and in general." I swallow and suddenly regret wearing tight clothing. I adjust myself, trying to push my thighs down to appear larger.

"Okay, sure." He jumps up, types something on his computer, then writes down a name and number on a Post-it.

"Here." He walks to me and hands over the note. My eyes dart up to meet his as he towers over me, and my half-remaining fake nails graze his hand as I take the paper.

"She probably won't answer this evening, but you should try tomorrow morning. Okay?"

"Yeah, I'll call her then." *Maya Kensington, RD* reads the yellow Post-it Note in wavy cursive. The writing is more feminine than I'd expect from him. Delicate, like a computer font I'd pick for a Jane Austen presentation or a PowerPoint on the history of Aphrodite.

"W-was June upset? I was just…I was worried I really upset her."

Dr. Ellis's eyes widen and bloom. "Don't worry, please. Just a paper towel or two. June…she isn't a part of this. This isn't about her."

"Okay."

"So, everything going well with you and Jett?" I pull back a little at the way Jett's name sounds in Dr. Ellis's voice. It's ill-fitting, like a wiry child wearing his grandfather's letterman. It feels a bit like retaliation for me bringing up June. I'm not sure why it feels combative to speak about either of our relationships, but I have the sensation of being punched in the gut nonetheless. Once I get past the divisive weirdness, though, I find myself grinning a little at the mention of Jett.

"Yeah, yeah. Really well. I was supposed to see him after this, but…"

"But what?"

"He wasn't feeling well. I might ask if he wants me to bring him soup or something. He didn't say what kind of sick he was, though."

"He lives in your dorm?"

"Right down the hall, I… Yeah. We always meet in my room, but he comes from that way, so…" I shrug. Dr. Ellis blinks sharply, then scribbles and seems to either underline or scratch through something heavily. The Mont Blanc grinding through the notepad bothers my eardrums.

We speak more about Jett and me, mostly on what we'd done and talked about the past week, and then we speak about Di and her rapping. I make sure to draw that out, because Dr. Ellis finds it amusing, and his smile is reassuring to see. He looks like Christopher, with straight, square teeth and a sliver of his gums showing ever so slightly when his grin gets roaringly stretched. As his timer goes off, I feel myself sinking deeper into the crevice of the cushion instead of picking up my things to go. Dr. Ellis doesn't stand up either until I look to him in confusion. He quickly uncrosses his legs to rise.

"Friday, as usual?" I nod and turn around to grab my bag.

"Okay, then. Take care of yourself, Valerie."

"You, too." I smile a little, and his eyes reflect unfamiliar warmth.

Chapter 33

I stop and lean over my knees at the crosswalk, breathing heavily.
The cold wind laces up my ribs in a tight corset and prevents me
from fully inhaling, and my vision is slightly out of focus. My skin
is tight, unable to produce sweat due to the force of the air, and my
hair is blown back in a frizzy ponytail. Twenty seconds later, I
make the final run into my dorm and exhale in the warmth of the
building, immediately turning to trudge up the five flights of stairs.
My right ankle creaks each time it hits the ground, piercing pain
running up my leg as it struggles to balance on the final uneven
step. I let the heavy door slam behind me. The shower is cold, as
usual. I'm cold, as usual.

The full bottle of pills on my desk stares at me as I enter,
my spine shaking while I try not to chatter my teeth too loudly as
Patricia sleeps. I accidentally hit my shin on an open drawer and
yelp in pain. She stirs a little, then sighs, and her chest returns to its
labored, steady rise and fall. Gingerly, I get dressed, firmly
cupping the zipper on my baggy black pants to trap in the sound.

I sense the little orange pills in the little orange bottle rumbling, bubbling, crying out as if to ask for freedom. My heartstrings are pulled in hopes of evoking pity, but I hold firm, raising my chin triumphantly and grabbing the plastic tube viciously. If I take them, I'll lose the only real company I have.

The shaken contents clang, and Patricia's eyes flicker open. My heart skips in a panic as her hazy eyes lock on to me. I swallow, set down the bottle, and reach farther along the shelf as if to look for something in the mostly empty section of my desk. Thankfully, there is a small tester vial of perfume nearby that has rolled out of my fragrance bin, and I spritz some across my neck. I see Patricia turn back over and throw her covers over her messy brown hair. Letting my held breath go, I pick up the pills, grab my backpack, and head out into the hallway. On the way to the elevator, I drop the pills into the trash. I peer over. The orange tube face-plants right in the center of someone's munchies from last night, what looks like a creamy rice dish and mashed potatoes. The bottle is slowly devoured by the mess and sinks into a pile of decomposition.

Walking to Harry's, I pass by a restaurant bordered by green ivy and baby-blue shutters. I don't read the sign, but I stop and stare at the customers visible through the painfully clear glass: families seated around bowls of artisanal bread and meager servings of pancakes. My eyes pick out a couple on the far left end of the windows, directly next to the glass, sharing a pitcher of mimosa between two champagne flutes. The identical levels of orange liquid in their glasses make it seem as if they've recently sat down, and the woman's perky, energetic posture confirms this. She leans forward on her forearms, cocks her head of short, curly black hair, and reaches for her mimosa. As her full crimson lips meet the pristine glass, my mind retreats back into itself, and I escape from the doorstep of the restaurant as I'm pulled within myself. I regress.

My mother swished her tall, thin flute as she swallowed. My tiny hands picked at stubby nails, as stubby as they are now. My hair was dyed a brassy blonde, which I thought looked natural, and I told all my middle-school friends "that it was just the sun." She went back in for another sip, finishing all of the liquid, and got back up for more. From the corner of my eye, I saw her reaching up to the liquor cabinet and drawing down a tall white bottle to add to the orange juice and champagne.

"So, do you have any plans for the summer yet? Camp?" asked the man whose name I had already forgotten. He blinked at me and chewed his tenderloin in unappealing circles. My jaw clenched, but I pried it open to speak. Nothing got the chance to come out, though.

"She's doin' a movie camp up in North Carolina, only the most intelligent students qualify," my mother said. She sat back down. Glass clanged and reverberated. I nodded to the man without looking at him, then dipped my finger into my wineglass filled with water and swirled the rim in an attempt to play a tone. I was initially excited to hear my mother speaking about me so positively, since she never said anything like that directly to me, but deep down, I knew that the statements weren't meant to reflect on me as much as they were meant to reflect on her.

"God, stop that."

I drew my hand back and wiped it on my towel. It hadn't made any sound. I felt my mother's sharp gaze as I kept my head down and my hands hidden.

"You going to eat anything?" she asked. My hands, without thinking, reached for the fork, pierced an overly seasoned breakfast potato, and stuffed it into my uncooperative mouth.

"And you? I see you stirring around your plate."

Greg quickly scooped up some eggs and also kept his eyes down.

"I make all this goddamn food for it to just be *played* with. Wish there was some goddamn *thankfulness* in this house." Another long swig. I gingerly raised my gaze and watched how her throat rippled as the poison descended lower and lower.

"Well, movie camp. That's awfully cool. Are you an actress?" Male Guest adjusted himself as I took a second too long to respond, in case she was about to interrupt me again. Finally, I rose my chest to inhale and speak.

"No, I make films."

"At thirteen? Well, shit, you're ahead of me." He looked to my mother, and they both burst out laughing. Their smiles were parasites living off of stealing the little bits of life within Greg and me, sucking all of our light out until we sat there like starving animals, withering away with the food.

"Wonder where she gets her creativity," my mother said flippantly. Smiling wryly at Male Guest, she lifted the flute again and tilted it back. Just the month before, Greg's dad, Carl, had been in that seat. Neither of us blamed him for running for good this time; it was long overdue, twelve years overdue, and if we could, we would, too. My dad left her before I'd even turned one, as opposed to Carl divorcing her when Greg was twelve, so Greg did have a more difficult transition. I enjoyed Carl. He was serious and hardworking, often spending full days and nights at the office, which was probably why he lasted for over a decade on and off with the woman.

I cursed fate for piling us all together in this endless inferno. Greg and I both looked forward to the days we got to spend in our respective households with our own fathers, away from her, but being away meant constantly worrying about coming back. It was easier to adjust to living in the flames than prepare to be burned at the stake.

"That's it," she boomed, standing up and leaning over to grab Greg's plate from the table.

"I wasn't—"

"Just leave. Brats aren't welcome."

I rubbed my temples. There was no room to be confused; the reasons behind her behavior were her own boredom and sadness. Greg could've eaten his whole plate and gotten sent away for taking too much from everyone else.

"Well, *I* sure appreciate this tenderloin. Wow," Male Guest boomed. I stared at my own plate, the meat untouched but mashed and severed so as to seem so.

"Why, thank you, Evan. Made it 'cause I knew you were a tenderloin man." Evan, or whatever his name was, hit her shoulder playfully, and my jaw shut so tightly I was surprised my skull didn't break down the middle like the *Titanic* being cracked by hitting an iceberg in an unforgiving sea.

"May I be excused?" I asked, as calmly as possible. My mother looked at my plate, sighed loudly, and met my pupils with hers.

"I guess so."

Quickly, I wiped off my plate, dropped it into the sink, and took a final drink of my water before placing the glass there as well. The last thing I saw before walking back upstairs was her finishing the rest of her drink as Male Guest (or maybe Evan?) grabbed her thigh.

I blink back to reality. The curly-haired woman sets the mimosa back down, and an old waiter approaches the couple. The wind encourages me to keep walking, so I follow its whistle, continuing down the street to finish my homeworrk at Harry's.

Chapter 34

My shirt smells a little strange. I must've spilled vinegar on it.
Walking back from the kitchen to my room to get deodorant, I see
Jett coming out of the elevator.

"Oh, hey there. Feeling better?" I ask. Jett's eyes are
slightly dark and appear sunken in.

"Maybe a little. I'm gonna go lie down."

"Well, let me know if you want or need anything... A
Benjamin Franklin impersonator..."

"I'm leaving now," Jett says with a slight giggle. I continue
on toward the end of the hall and turn my doorknob, forcing the
uneven door open. Patricia is sitting at her desk with her phone on
speaker. Her eyes dart toward me as I enter, but she doesn't bother
to move or turn down the volume.

"I don't know what to tell you," says a deep male voice on
the other side. "It's not like I didn't...like I didn't give you the
benefit of the doubt."

"I just… You can't expect me to be—" her voice cracks. I suddenly remember that I came for deodorant and try to quietly move toward that drawer in my desk.

"Look, I've said everything I can. I have to go."

"Have to—have to go?" There is a piercing silence. Patricia inhales sharply through congested nostrils. "Have fun fucking your pregnant cunt of a wife, asshole." Her arms jolt to hang up, but she misses initially and hits a number on the keypad. "Shit! *God!*" She slams back into her rocking desk chair.

"Is everything okay?" I regret my question even before it's released from my lips. Patricia's swollen eyes send a somber glare down to my feet.

"No. No, everything is not fucking okay." She blinks, then turns back to face her desk and sighs. I set back down the deodorant I'm still holding and scurry out, making sure the door doesn't slam. Shit. My computer and books are still in my bag, on my desk. When I reenter to grab my things, Patricia has her head on her forearms, and she's sniffling over her desk. Trying to keep the door open while leaning over to reach my bag, I slip and hit the ground. Patricia launches up and peers down at me from across the room. Like a guilty dog, I gaze up at her with wide, forgiving eyes. Her mouth emits an uncomfortably loud burst of laughter, and I push myself to smile, uncomfortably squeezing into a dress that's far too tight to fit properly, then decide I'd just rather be comfortable in my smelly shirt. I rise up, gingerly examine my impacted and soon-to-be-bruised knee, and pick up my bag.

"Um, if you want anything, just...call me?" A lock of wavy hair drops in front of my right eye. I try to blow it away but am unsuccessful. Patricia emits a giggle from her blotchy red face, then nods. I turn away. Patricia snorts back tears.

"I just can't believe someone I trusted so much would be so dishonest," she whispers. I'm surprised and shoot back around to face her.

"I've been lied to, too. In shit like this," I say without thinking it over first.

"Shit like this?"

"Love shit. With someone older. That turns out to be fake."

"Oh. I guess you do get it, then."

"More than you'd know. Sometimes you just have to let the memory exist in your mind, back when it was real, and not hold on," I tell her firmly. We hold eye contact for a second longer than usual before tears start running down Patricia's face again. I maneuver quietly out of the room and into the hallway. Immediately, I pull out my phone to text Di.

hey r u home

yeah

can i come over to do some work. patricia is having a meltdown i cant be n here

um well i was recording some tracks but yeah ok

i mean if ur n the middle of something then i dont have to

it's fine

I don't know whether to trust what Di's saying or trust what I'm feeling, but I go with her texts because I do need a place to work, even if Di rapping in the corner becomes my background music. I wind around a corner of the hallway to the other side of our floor and knock on her door, realizing it's already cracked open. Some soft acoustic beats are playing.

"Well, that's a surprising sound to hear you playing." Di doesn't move at all from her bed, remaining splayed on her stomach with her laptop out in front of her. Her head bobs up and down to the beat, then eventually turns toward me as the song fades out.

"Sorry. Just...shopping around. Dunno how I feel about that one."

"Someone's high." I examine the pink-tinted whites of her eyes and heavily lowered lids. She shrugs.

"Creative flow, man." I notice, once again, an acrid smell coming from my shirt.

"Can I borrow a shirt or some shit? Mine smells like moldy ass; I can't get it to go away."

"Sure," she languidly sings. "First drawer on the left." I pick up an oversize black shirt lying on top, then notice it has crusty blotches on it.

"Di, do you do laundry?" Silence.

"I mean, the very bottom of the drawer is shit I never wear."

"Does that mean it's clean?"

"Most likely." Chuckling, I throw the black top back down and dig out a distressed yellow tee from the corner, soft with wear yet compacted as if it's never been unfolded. As I bring it to my nose, it releases hints of chamomile fabric softener. I slide off my current white long-sleeved top and throw it onto Di's bed. It surprises her as it hits her feet, and her eyes dart back in confusion. When her focus hits my body, she sits up.

"Jesus Christ."

"What?"

"There's almost none of you fucking left, Val."

"What are you talking about?" My goose-bump-covered elbows curl in to hide by my chest.

"Val, look at your fucking self. Look."

I walk in front of the full-length mirror on Anna's side of the room and drop my arms beside my hips confidently. "I mean, my boobs have definitely shrunk lately. Kind of disappointing."

"Val! I'm not kidding here. I...I have some spaghetti left in the fridge. Have it."

My body turns to face her without my mind approving. My voice also ignores asking for permission. "You think eating some fucking spaghetti is going to do shit?" I'm more on edge than usual after that scene with Patricia.

"I'm just trying to help you! You're… You can't do this to yourself." Di's stocky chest rises and falls sharply. "You need help."

"I-I'm trying to gain weight. I really am, it's just hard for me."

"With black coffee and sweet potatoes?" Without looking her in the eyes, I grab my shirt from off her feet and slide it back on as quickly as possible.

"You're going to fucking die!" Her shaky voice shocks my veins like an overcharged defibrillator.

I gingerly smile and swallow, then walk out the door without shutting it, my bag launched over my shoulder like I'm a hitchhiker carrying a bindle with no plans of ever turning back.

Chapter 35

Dr. Ellis's bowl is filled with a different color of chocolates today. Tiny little squares covered in gold wrappers, reflecting the cloudy daylight coming in.

"Dark chocolate. No milk. I checked. Even *organic*, if that means anything to you." He blushes a little and itches his freshly trimmed hairline. I stifle a yawn and grab one from the coffee table between us. I feel cool air on my ribs and suddenly shoot up when I realize the neckline of my red V-neck has bellowed down to my knees. The chocolate mushes softly in my warm, clenched hand. Dr. Ellis clears his throat.

"Thanks," I blurt. I look at the uneven, melted square and unwrap it. I'll take out some of the rice from my dinner, I guess. My anxiety makes me nauseous, but I force the chocolate down my throat and smile at him. Another cold chill hits my chest, and I peer down, noticing that my shirt has fallen to one side and exposed my black bra. Readjusting myself, I sit on the shirt's back edge to keep it pulled up.

"Well, then, how have you been this past week? I know you mentioned some important papers."

"Yeah. Thankfully they're turned in now."

"Much left for the rest of the semester?"

"A few final projects. I don't know what I'll do yet."

"I'm sure you'll figure out something creative." I squirm a little, not sure if I will.

"How is June's book club going?"

Dr. Ellis is loosening the wrists of his button-down and rolling the sleeves up to his elbows as he sniffles reactively to my question.

"It's a bit hot in here," he mentions. "Anyway," he continues, raising his voice, "it seems they've...*disbanded*."

"Disbanded, have they? What a shame."

"Or at least June is no longer a part of the group."

"Too much commitment for her busy schedule?" A knife pierces my sternum as I realize what I've said. However, Dr. Ellis laughs, and my bones gently repair.

"I was hoping keeping her mind busy again would encourage her to get back into practicing law, but it seems a group of unemployed wives tends to…tends to perpetuate each other's, well, they keep busy talking about each other."

"She practiced law?" The taste of chocolate rides up in my throat, and I stifle a small burp.

"Believe it or not, she worked for a maritime law firm. I still don't fully understand how she *got* that job, at the time, at least, but…here we are." He smiles lightly at me and smooths out his notepad.

"What do you mean? How she got that job?"

"I… She was a…a *friend* of the owner of the firm, is how I've come to understand it… But…"

"Oh, I'm—I'm… My bad. Sorry." My clumpy eyelashes brush the hollows of my eyes as I blink downward in discomfort. Dr. Ellis rolls the sleeves on his shirt up one more time and fans himself with the yellow notepad.

"Are you warm? I'm awfully warm."

"I'm okay. But I'm always cold, so you're probably feeling it right." He stands up and adjusts the thermostat next to the door. As he returns, I notice how tightly and perfectly tailored his pants are. It's as if they're custom-made just for him, the pleats and inseam and everything perfectly proportioned.

"Sorry about that." Dr. Ellis checks his watch, then smiles up at me again. His face is slightly rosy with heat, almost reminding me of Vic's after he had something to drink.

"Valerie, any changes in your relationships? Any new ones?"

"Jett's been feeling like shit, so I haven't really seen him much. He said he was better this morning, though, so I'll probably text him after this. Maybe."

"What kinds of things is your relationship based around? Is it…a, well, serious matter or more…more fleeting, would you say?"

"I mean…it's nothing super serious right now, but it's not like we're just friends with benefits or any shit like that. So no, it's not *fleeting*, I guess." I hope it's not fleeting, or at least, I hope Jett hopes it's not fleeting. I get uncomfortable and automatically slide my shoes off and cross my legs on the love seat to distract myself. "Can I do this?"

"Sure, go ahead." He stares at my white socks for a second, then returns to scribbling roughly on the notepad on his lap. "So it isn't formed on a solely physical premise, I take it?"

"A *physical premise*?" I cock my head and can't stop my mouth from sliding to the left in a twisted smile. We both release shallow laughter. I look down at my thighs and blush.

"If you're asking if I'm just fucking him, no, it's not like that. We watch a lot of historical documentaries. I'm becoming a much, *much* smarter person."

"That's certainly good to hear." Dr. Ellis reaches behind him on his desk for a tissue and blows his nose politely, then drops it into the black trash can behind his chair and pushes up his glasses. "I just...wouldn't want you engaging in anything unsafe."

"Yeah, no, we're...we're cool."

"Di. What about her?" His eyes laser-beam to mine. "Her rap, and all?" I snort after he says *rap*.

"Oh...well, I mean, she's fine, I guess. We aren't really talking, though." He leans back in his chair in surprise.

"What happened between the two of you?"

"It was stupid. She was freaking out about, well, just about me, and I'm just not dealing with that."

"Freaking out about you? How so?"

"I was changing in front of her, and she started basically saying I looked like I was going to…to *die*. I mean, she's gained weight, so she probably is just not used to seeing someone who looks like me, I don't really know. Or care."

"She said exactly that you looked like you were going to die?"

"Well, she actually literally said I was going to die. Which is, like, fucking obviously." Dr. Ellis exhales a long and lengthy stream of air out of his ever-so-slightly parted lips as his eyes don't budge from his lap.

"Did you call that dietician I referred you to, Valerie?"

"Oh no. Shit, I meant to. I will today."

"Please call her. Because your weight *is* somewhat concerning to me, Valerie, and I would like you to speak to a licensed professional in case there really is a serious issue there."

My jaw locks, and my mind has to pry it open with huge titanium pliers in order for my voice to blast through. "Fine, okay.

I think this is all kind of unnecessary, but I'll *do* it, or whatever. If it makes you feel better."

"Yes, it would make me feel better. Has Jett commented at all on your appearance?"

I pause, staring out the window at clouds stabbed right through the center by the tall skyscrapers surrounding us. I imagine the feeling of opening and closing around such huge figures, having your formless ethereal body accept such chaotic and complex penetration.

"Valerie?"

"Sorry, sorry. I don't really think so. Like, if he has, it wasn't anything particularly serious. I can't remember anything specific."

"Does he comment on your appearance at all?"

"What do you mean?"

"Like, compliments, or suggestions, or just statements?"

I bite the corner of my lip. "Now that I'm really thinking about it…he doesn't really acknowledge my body at all, I guess. Like, it's there, he…*touches* it, I guess, but it's not necessarily something he's focused on? I don't know. He's different from past boyfriends with that." The sun is just beginning to set, and the daggered clouds absorb pink and yellow light. The rays reflect off Dr. Ellis's glasses.

"So he's an actual boyfriend?"

My heart rate speeds up, and I stop breathing to keep it down, but I end up inhaling sharply and loudly in a panic, making both of us jump.

"I—I guess so. Yes. I think so. It's something I should probably bring up with him at this point."

"Well, it's good to hear that he doesn't cause you any unnecessary worries about your body. An attitude of neutrality is sometimes the best help."

"Neutrality about your body from someone you're dating?"

He furrows his brows and blinks. "Perhaps I phrased that poorly. I would say his focus on other things about you besides just your physical appearance is probably a positive thing." My stomach begins to twist, getting wrung out by clenching electric fists inside my abdomen.

"Yeah, okay."

For the rest of the session, Dr. Ellis avoids Jett at all costs as we further discuss my body image, or what I decide to mention about it. My loud stomach rumbling bends the energy between us with its naive yells and makes us unable to directly communicate. I begin to speak in shrugs and itches on my crossed legs. The chocolate in front of me grabs the sound waves emitting from within me and ties them up, physically attracting me without question. My arm is strewn out like a puppet, and I grab one of the magnetic little squares. As I place it into my open mouth, Dr. Ellis's eyelids flicker obnoxiously. My writhing stomach screams back at my fuzzy, disoriented mind. After chewing and breaking eye contact with Dr. Ellis, my brain comes back online and flashes red lights to signal a misfire.

I'll just have half my serving of rice tonight. It's whatever.

Chapter 36

At this point, I haven't spoken to Di in over a week. Neither of us is going to be the first to try and reconcile. Including myself. Especially me.

"You're going to have to talk to her eventually. She's your best fucking friend, for God's sake," Jett says quietly, crouched over his computer at our corner table in the library. He leans back after I don't look up from my own laptop and keep on furiously typing.

"Val," he says. I slowly raise my line of vision.

"Yeah, I know. Whatever."

"Come on. You can't 'whatever' this."

"Jett, I'll take care of it."

"It just seemed like you wanted my advice."

I hunch over even more and curl further over my keyboard. "Jesus, I'll take care of it."

A student library monitor raises an eyebrow at me from the information desk in the middle of the room. I give a small smile back to signal I'll shut the hell up.

Resuming my attempt at brainstorming my next film project, my fingers are supercharged with the combative electricity between us, and I find my fingers booming down with all of gravity's might. They hit each key with the precise drama of a piano player at the climactic height of a concerto. In front of me are two thousand people at the edges of their seats waiting for my wrists to drop and for my fingers to land perfectly on the huge ending chord sequence, expecting my elbows to ascend and then plummet in release. As I slam the enter key in a declaration of finality, I receive a standing ovation, and I rise. Careful to mind my long red satin train, I bow and receive an equally-as-regal flood of whistles and hoots, respectful because of the elite mouths they're pouring out from. Exiting the stage, the light in the wings illuminates my surroundings: the third floor of the library.

"Can I use you for my film project?" My change of tone shakes Jett, his eyelashes fluttering in an attempt to dust off the burst I've sent his way.

"Uh, yeah, I guess so. Sure." He picks up his orange water bottle and takes a drink, then looks back up at me. "I guess I should ask what it's going to be about?"

I think of how to word my idea. "I... I'm thinking of it as a goodbye to film. My last project ever."

"And how the hell am I involved in this?"

"You don't have to be on camera; I haven't necessarily figured that part out. I want to get a few people to write a letter to their childhood selves, not as, like, a corny...a fucking looking-back-advice shit thing. More like...more like a spoken ego death, kind of."

"I'm somewhat...fucking confused." Our mouths spread wide to teeth-dominated smiles in unison. "A letter to childhood me... Ego death? What?"

"All the shit you thought you were as a kid. Write a eulogy to it." I lean back and curl my legs up in the sturdy gray block seat. Jett just keeps his eyes focused on mine, blinking, breathing, reading.

"Not gonna lie, I'm still a little confused. But I take it creative license comes with some interpretive leeway."

My eyes focus on the black swirls riding up his neck, like plumes of smoke floating up from his heart.

"Just try it. I don't know who else I'm going to ask, but I'll figure it out, I guess." The performance high has worn down, the euphoric imprint of applause on my brain returning back to a stable equilibrium. Jett inhales, begins to speak, then catches himself before making a sound and returns to the interior of his mind, reconsulting with the writer of his screenplay.

"You can ask Di, if you make up with her and all. You know you're going to run into her, I don't know, getting food in the kitchen or something. It's stupid to freak out about her commenting on what you look like, anyway."

"I have absolutely no incentive to try to do shit. She can approach me." My arms automatically cross in front of my white hoodie.

"She might really enjoy doing this for you, though. I mean, I don't know her, obviously, but who knows. She could be the kind of person who'd really be down for this." Jett peers down and smooths out his jeans. I furrow my brows jarringly.

"And you're not?"

"What? No, no…Val, I'm not… I'm just saying, she could enjoy being a part of your project. That's all."

"If you don't want to do this, you can tell me."

"Where the hell are you hearing me say I don't want to do this? I'll be a part of your damn childhood ego-death letter movie or whatever, Val."

"Never fucking mind," I mutter as smoky heat vibrates within the rickety wooden boards of my ribs, shooting up to reverberate at the speed of light within the cracked cavern of my head. I stuff my computer and books back into my bag and lift my hood to shield my face, insulating the electric shocks within me even more until my skin bursts into blue flames. The fires grow and rise as the flames are fueled by the propane pus never ceasing to ooze out of my infected wounds. I walk out of the room, losing myself to ashes, leaving a trail of bodily ruins in the middle of the silent third-floor study area.

Chapter 37

As I approach my dorm room, loud unknown voices echo out into the hallway.

"It tastes kind of like dentist toothpaste."

"Well, I like it."

"I mean, it's not like I'm drinking it for the taste necessarily."

"Oh, hey there." Patricia turns from her desk to face me as I enter in a coat covered in melted snow and my hair windblown back. "This is Rita."

"Hey. I'm Val." I wave slightly, and Patricia's friend smiles hazily. They're on either side of a large pink liquor bottle with some of our little kitchen glasses in their hands.

"Oh, do you want any?" Rita's voice is warm and hearty.

I shake my head. "I'm good. Thanks."

"Sorry, I should've warned you," apologizes Patricia as she props herself up to sit on the edge of her desk. "Some of our guy friends should be here soon. I didn't expect us to all be here, but…"

"It's…it's cool, it's fine." She's right, she should've warned me so I could've prepared for this ordeal instead of hoping to rip my coat off and fall into bed.

"I like your hair," Rita muses. Her big blue eyes, lined with dark-brown liquid liner and not-quite-blended concealer, give me a jazzy look-down. She is poisoned to the point of losing all animosity; she is inhuman. I swallow and begin to unzip the front of my coat.

"T-thanks. Yours, too." Her hair is brassy, bleached, and in need of a root touch-up. It's slightly teased at the top, bringing more attention to her natural brown hue.

"*You* should come out with us. You look great. You're so hot." Rita looks to Patricia, who shrugs and looks to me. My eyes quickly dart down to my ripped jeans and old Vans in a panic.

"I…I'm kind of tired. I don't think so."

"Oh shit, they can't find our room," Patricia mutters, typing on her phone. She walks over to open the door and peers out.

"Oh, hey! Guys!" Her voice rings out from the hallway. Deep male voices approach until three tall young men around my age stomp in, eyeing the room like it's a rare museum exhibit until they land on me.

"I'm Val, Patricia's roommate. Hey."

They wave, and one in a navy V-neck and dark-wash jeans holds out a hand to me.

"Peter. Nice to meet you." My eyes don't budge from the floor, but I accept his hand. Sitting down in my chair as they gather around the pink bottle, I look in my mirror and see that my face is in surprisingly good shape after walking through the torrential snowstorm and my hair, successfully protected from getting soaked at the end curled pieces. After making sure the group isn't looking, I pout and make faces to myself. Fury looks good on me. The electricity within me, catalyzed by stewing anger, brings an ethereal glow to my cheeks. All of a sudden, my mouth is open.

"On second thought, I'll take you up on that. When are you leaving?" Everyone turns around, and my face blushes in regret. *Shit. Never mind.*

"Um, maybe, like, an hour?" Patricia suggests. That gives me time to eat beforehand. Inside, I scream at the part of me excited to hear that. The real me wishes we were leaving right now so I had no choice but to skip dinner. The real me wants to waste tonight's black-bean chili and rice I'd perfectly prepped and weighed out for every day of the upcoming week.

"Okay. Cool."

"What's your name again?" asks one of the guys, in a black T-shirt and black pants. His hand is tangled with Rita's.

"Val. Valerie. Val."

"Oh, that's my mom's name."

"Really?"

"Dude, it's so not," says Peter. The third boy laughs and sips straight from the pink bottle.

"The fuck would you know?" Black T-Shirt defensively declares. The group laughs and resumes drinking.

I'd need to change before leaving, though I could probably wear this outfit without anyone caring since I was already going to be the odd one out. From the right side of my closet gleams a black satin slip I bought years ago, wishing I was thin enough to look like a beautifully adorned coat hanger. My arm holds out the edge of the dress, and I imagine how I'd look now in it, without the chest being stretched out by a bulky bra or the stomach poking out with pubescent bloating. Before I can think twice, I pull it off the hanger with a swift drop of the wrist. The slick fabric feels like woven gold in my cold palms.

As I turn around to grab some tights from my dresser, I notice that Peter himself isn't holding a cup or taking swigs from the bottle being passed around. My eyes linger on him, then return to searching for my ratty black fishnets in an overflowing drawer of underwear and socks. I shoot up with the clothes and my phone, then shuffle into the kitchen to eat before changing and becoming my true self.

A shiny fork mushes into the black beans and quinoa apologetically. My stomach groans, and the portion-perfect Tupperware is empty within five minutes. Another groan. I'm just dehydrated.

Crammed into a bathroom stall, I rake on the fishnets, which should've been thrown out after their last wear but are somehow still able to encase my frail stilt-like legs. I shudder as the cool black satin that ripples and flows up my thighs, hips, and stomach. Cold feet regretfully step on grimy bathroom tile, jeans and hoodie stuffed into the crook of my arm. Standing on my tippy-toes, I fluff up my hair in the mirror, still barely able to see my eyes in the overly elevated rectangle. Platforms would go well with this, but I don't want to overwhelm these pathetic look-alikes. Booties. I don't give enough of a shit to massacre my heels tonight. Okay, then. It's almost nine thirty. I can be back by midnight and get eight hours of sleep and go on a run early enough to not fuck up tomorrow's schedule. Saturday will go exactly as planned, exactly as it must be performed.

I force my dorm room door open and throw my dirty clothes into the hamper to my left.

"Jesus, girl!" Rita points to my dress and nods. My cheeks curl in a tight grin, my mouth slammed shut. Everyone else turns to face me, and heat rises to my cheeks.

"Come on, it's just *me*." The words glide out of my chapped lips, and the group laughs softly. One point for Valerie. I reapply some eyeliner and smear on ChapStick as they keep drinking and talking. Eventually, Patricia comes out from the corner of the room where I can't see her.

"Hey. Are you ready?"

I nod and stuff a few necessities in my purse, then grab my coat. Walking out, my eyes catch a glimpse of my body in surprise within the frame of our full-length mirror. The slip dress hangs perfectly on me, not a hint of a protruding, vile extra pound for the innocent threads to snag on. My long black coat opens widely to expose my chiseled collarbones while protecting the backs of my Sharpie-line calves. The last one out, I struggle to shut the uneven door, but I eventually do, locking it shut with a quick turn of my silver key.

Chapter 38

My legs sprawl over Patricia's and Rita's as I contort myself into the back of the cab, ending up wedged in the corner against the window and black-shirt guy. He smells of fruity alcohol and reaches into his pocket to pull out a flask, holding it out to Peter on his right.

"Man, you know I can't." Black Shirt shrugs and takes a swig himself, then slides the gold flask back into his oversize pocket.

"You don't drink?" I ask Peter, leaning forward to see him.

"Not tonight," he says with a sigh. His skin is tanned, and his light-brown hair is perfectly parted and smoothed. "I'm taking something I can't really drink with." My brows furrow in curiosity as his hands reach into his shined leather loafers and pull out a tiny plastic bag. Inside are three small capsules filled with white powder. The cab seems to stop moving as my eyes focus in, mesmerized.

"E?" I ask quietly, still gazing at his tanned hands.

"Actually, Molly, to be specific. Tested and everything. I don't fuck with fake shit." I look back up at his face, which is angled toward the bag in his left hand. Peter's lips are full and pink, and his eyes are wide set and dark. He definitely comes from money: the hair, the clothes, the ability to not only buy designer drugs but *test* them to make sure they're of quality. He suddenly darts his eyes to mine without moving his head, and I look away, embarrassed.

"Do you want one?" My neck whips back around in surprise.

"What?"

"Molly. *MDMA*. Basically E, like you said, just…just the high-quality shit." The capsules bounce as we hit a speed bump. My eyes blink but remain fixated, and my throat swallows repetitively. After a period of silence filled by only the cab driver's road rage muted behind a plastic screen, Peter shrugs and takes out one of the pills, then stuffs the baggie back into his shoe. I turn to gaze out the window to my left and pretend not to give it any mind, but I am filled with regret. I should've taken the goddamn pill when I had the chance. *Fucking child.*

I'm silent for the rest of the cab ride, assuming we're headed to a club, hoping we're going anywhere far away and driving fast enough to unravel my mind from my body and spin it into millimeter-thin strings, and strew them all over Earth, far away from each other. Eventually, the cab comes to a stop, Peter overpays the fare and makes sure to tell the driver to "keep it, don't worry," and we gather in front of a large purple awning.

There is a line of girls huddling together, dressed for the mideighties when it's fifty degrees lower, and the occasional male hiking his sport coat over the shoulders of a girl-of-choice nearby. It's comical: they hunch over and tuck their backs under in discomfort with a neon veil of desperation covering it all. My own knees begin to shake as a gust of wind strikes hard, but I don't close my coat because that would cover up everything I'm proud of. I'm the same as them, a pretty little suffering shell, addicted to the Nietzschean creator's pleasure of molding oneself into a sickly distorted ideal. Suddenly, Rita grabs my hand and we follow Peter to the front of the line. The barricade is pulled aside, and he pats the bouncer on the back, who nods. Damn. I was looking forward to the panic-then-relief adrenaline rush of whipping out my fake ID.

Purple lights spiral around in helices and matrices on the concrete floor. Shiny black booths border the sides, with shiny people packed into them like bales of hay and shiny glasses in their hands adorned by shiny fingernails. Rita stumbles into my shoulder, and I trip over my ankle boots. Right where they'd previously been stabbed, another dagger of regret hits me for not wearing heels. I've fucked up a possibly exciting night. *You don't ever get exciting nights. You are an ungrateful, unperceptive, undeserving imbecile.*

After regaining my balance, I gaze around me in all three-hundred-and-sixty degrees. It's a fun house of clowns and freaks and animals magically intertwining, unaware of the spectacle they are until they tire. A bartender shoves a tray of Jell-O shots into a lingerie-clad waitress's dark arms. A girl hikes her pastel-pink skintight dress up and bends over, grinding into a man twice her height with a watch the size of my head on his right wrist. I remain still as my mind swirls, but instead of spiraling out into equilibrium, it begins to implode, disintegrating itself through its own doing and tangling into an unfixable necklace chain that'll just be thrown into the trash as a cursed waste of money.

Peter checks his watch and looks around, irritated. The rest of the group is intoxicatedly holding hands and yelling about what shots to get.

"I want *Fireball!*" Rita whines, sounding like a nasally dolphin.

"We're getting Goose," Black Shirt declares. "I'm paying, I decide."

"Gentlemanly, Adam," Patricia snaps. He rolls his eyes, and I look back to Peter, tapping his foot and cartwheeling his fingertips along his thigh.

"You okay?" I question in a panic. I don't really give a shit if he's okay, I just don't want to focus on my own mental demolishment.

"I just want this goddamn Molly to kick in already. It's usually, like, happening by now." He doesn't make eye contact with me and instead keeps focused straight ahead, into the alien mess ahead of us. I sigh at his Grecian-like features, chiseled marble, and his marble pedestal, completely aware of it.

"Still have the rest?" My chin tilts downward, my dark eyes ascending to meet his in a penetrating demand. He blinks and exhales, pulling the bag out and waving it in front of his eyes before handing one tiny pill over. I smile without breaking contact and dry swallow the capsule. The screaming inside me is too occupied to also break out in a nervous rage about what I've just done—too occupied by the rabid external to contemplate the internal whirlpooling.

"Give it about an hour. If you decide to drink, know I told you not to—"

"Oh, I don't—"

"See you on the other side, then." Peter raises and lowers his eyebrows as his full lips twist to one side. He turns and walks away, a sculpture of stone turning to life.

Chapter 39

I lean against the wall as Patricia and Rita dance to a remix of a song I remember cursing as *basic* in high school. My butt hurts as it crams against the white brick. I'm still cold amid all of the warmth around me. Goose bumps prick up higher as everyone else breaks into a sweat.

"Do you *feel* it yet?" Rita screams out at me. I laugh weakly and shake my head.

"I'm starting to think that this shit is, like, cut or something." I'm getting restless and feeling robbed. Peter and the rest of the guys are nearby, leaning against the booth to our left. I walk up to Peter and tap him on the shoulder. When he turns around, I see that his pupils are big and dilated, like black-hole saucers spinning on a record player. It takes me a second to stop staring and remember what I wanted to ask.

"Hey. Can I have the last one? I'm not feeling anything, and it's been, like, an hour."

"You sure?" His voice has a Technicolor viscosity that my eardrums ride effortlessly, like playing Rainbow Road in *Mario*

Kart. I nod. After digging into his shoe with difficulty, the last tiny oval rests firmly in my palm, and I drop it into my mouth, then grab the drink out of black shirt guy's hand to wash it down. It tastes like watered-down cheap vodka, and I wince a little at the fact that I've let poison infiltrate my iron castle, but I quickly shake it off in hopes of melting into the mindless energy of everyone else around me. Peter's body moves slowly throughout all of this, languidly, sliding from hip to hip with his eyes closed.

"Can I have my drink back?" Peter asks.

I break character and drop my jaw in surprise, then smile and hand back the tiny glass. Suddenly, Peter grabs my hand and pulls me to the rhythm of this stupid, basic song. I calculatedly step and twist like I think most people do, my dress fluttering out at the edges. Patricia and Rita join us, and Rita grabs both me and Patricia by the hand. They dance together like amoebas joining and separating on each beat, and I haphazardly pretend to do the same while not getting stepped on by their pointy heels. I suddenly appreciate not having worn any myself, as I probably would've had even more trouble pretending to have fun. We continue on in an ever-morphing circle.

About twenty minutes later, as I've begun to tire of calculating every formless motion of my hips and feet, my body shivers as if gallons of ice have been dropped on me. Every tendon in my body tenses, every muscle freezes, and my eyes begin to narrow in with a heavy vignette around the edges. I try to catch my breath, my chest slammed shut like it's waterlogged, and I feel a heavy grasp on my shoulders. Through my tunnel vision, I can see Patricia holding me tightly and staring directly into my eyes.

"Hey. Hey. Stay with me," she repeats a few times. My heart spins out of control, triple, quadruple, quintuple, anything possible from cardio exercise. Her mouth moves like a tortoise in slow motion. Her words enter through my ears into the cavern of my mind but are immediately sped up into high-pitched white noise, further fueling the increasing pedaling of my heart.

"I…" My breath falls ten thousand feet. Forming a sentence is a struggle with all my focus on the patterning in my chest.

"I have to go," I force out. I don't know what my voice sounds like.

"You think you're going to get out of this crowd easily?" Black Shirt whirs. His tone further stabs my chest, the blood spewing a million times more forcefully than usual due to my heart rate. I can feel myself melting into a flattened crepe of dried blood right here on this club floor. All of the energy in the world is being powered into hammering me into a millimeter-thick slab on the concrete. I'm breathing so quickly that the little space I can still see into becomes increasingly fuzzy. The cold continues to fall like acid rain bullets directly into my pores. All I can think of is somehow getting out and crawling into my bed. This was a mistake. I need to go home and sleep this off.

My heavy, almost-flattened feet stagger once. Suddenly, my head rams into a chest, but I'm too focused to care. They'll move. My knees buckle. The body I'm digging into presses me up and holds me with a firm grip.

"Breathe. You're just coming up." It's Peter, singing in an eloquently inebriated melody. "Inhale with me. Come on. Inhale." With all of the power in my breaking bones, I raise and lower my chest with his. My body seems to realign, standing up straighter, intertwining each ligament back together from the splatter on the dusty ground. My heart continues to sprint at the speed of light, but after a few seconds of breathing, my mind has caught up. The cold shivers down my spine one fierce last time before a deluge of hot water encompasses all of me. The next time I look up at Peter, I realize the comforting shower is raining down on both of us, just us, and I smile with all the energy and electricity of my being pressed into a single spreading of my lips. All of my gaping wounds are sealed shut and glossed over with expensive creams; all of my scabs have healed to reveal baby-soft virgin skin, and my body holds all the wisdom necessary to make exactly the right movement at exactly the right time. His palms move down my arms to grab my hands. I grasp the tips of his fingers as I laugh electrifyingly fast.

"Told you." Peter's head cocks to one side. We look at each other like best friends from a past life, like twin flames joining together into a burst of blue fire. My mind, enjoying this new speed of consciousness, not only hears the music but understands it on a spiritual level. Each note strikes a different point on my body, as precise as acupuncture and as deep as a massage. We move more together, even more so than Patricia and Rita, as we speed above the sound of the music and ascend above the crowd to a halo outside of everyone and everything. I'm not overthinking; my mind has found its cruising altitude to avoid all unbelonging turbulence.

Peter's hands make a ring around my waist. We're both submerged in the overflowing hot spring of crystal-clear water around us that shields us from the chaos. Viewing it all through the waterfall, everyone suddenly makes sense as being exactly as they are supposed to be. Patricia's and Rita's clumsy motions are perfectly choreographed for their beautiful bodies. The two guys farther away gleam in poised confidence, drinking absolute poison that is entirely what they need at this moment. They're complete, whole, perfect, integrated. Nothing is how it shouldn't be. Peter's grip is warm on my stomach through the cold, slick fabric of my black dress. I turn around and wrap my arms back around his neck, wedging myself into him like a polymer puzzle piece. My legs, frail and withering away, feel as if they are strong and agile underneath a gleamingly vibrant body. I turn my porcelain facade back to face him. He smiles down, and I break into euphoric laughter rooted all throughout the electric field inside me. The fear lying dormant in my spine is not activated but rather totally and utterly demolished. The water has drowned it. We swim in a pool of ecstatic laughter as we realize the perfect placement of everything around us. I realize how *full* I feel, how I haven't considered food at all for the better part of the last hour as I've been swaying against Peter. This new level of existence doesn't require any material sustenance, just appreciation and acceptance. I connect to each and every club-goer around me who is taking shots, grinding, screaming, waving their arms to the rap song blaring outside of this liquid shell. I am them, I see through them, and I wish to reach out and physically show them, but I more so want to remain entirely immersed in this cradled bliss with Peter. As our cartoonish eyes meet, a thousand words are said to greet each other after being disconnected for a thousand lifetimes. I see myself in the shiny exterior of his eyeballs, and at first I am slightly put off by my own miniature reflection, but I welcome the fright; it is in its proper place of belonging in my life.

"Hey, we should get some water. Okay?" Peter's grip loosens as he leans down to speak to me. I nod, taking his hand and following him to the bar where he grabs one of the little plastic water cups. I copy him, quickly gulping down two cupfuls. His elegant lips glitter as a little droplet of water displays all the color of every strobe light in its little oval. I embrace him in appreciation, and we return to the rest of the group, moving together once again to the music as they watch.

"Val, you look like you're having fun," Patricia hums into my ear while I'm pressed up against Peter again. Through pursed lips, I smile with all my might, turning my head to the right. "We might head out in a little. You should come with," she says. I nod.

My gaze strips straight through her blue irises, smeared with makeup, and cuts right to the circling light inside her. She is full of so much more than I let myself believe, more than her Valley Girl voice, more than her annoying sorority shit, more than her weird older-guy relationships. She is divine, reflecting back to me something within, which I don't see. I then let that vision escape me, and I turn around to face Peter, who rests his chin on my head and embraces me. I lift my head up and, without having to run it by my calculated set of rules first, I let my lips meet his. It isn't romantic, necessarily, but an essential motion. We continue to blend our own light together. It shoots out through the waterfall over us. I don't know how much time has passed, and I don't care. I am outside of time itself.

His motions stop, and he sighs out loudly. Peter pushes his hair back and looks at me starkly. I get the feeling he's exited the flood and left me alone, but I understand and embrace it, continuing to move on my own.

"Val, we're leaving now. Come with us." Patricia motions for me. Rita is holding her hand and blinking at me. I can't imagine leaving right now. I must appreciate the warm shower coming down on me, allowing me to rise up as myself in all my own love for everything.

"I… I'm going to stay." The high pitch of my own voice scares me a little, but I love the way it rests at the top of my throat like helium. Patricia starts to say something but stops as Peter's hand weighs on my shoulder and he begins to speak.

"I think she wants to stay with me a little longer. We'll head back soon, though."

I smile and nod.

Chapter 40

The tips of my fingers glide against Peter's arm as we watch the rest of the group leave and return to dancing. I have been smiling for so long that it feels strange to reposition my mouth back into neutral. His forearm exudes fiery heat up into my hands until I reach the stark cold of his watch, causing me to shiver. I love it, though. An eye inside me has been spread wide open to see all there is to be seen. I place my hands on my hips and stretch my shoulders back grandly to open up my chest. Suddenly, a feeling of lack permeates me, and I feel out of place in my body. Looking down, my bony legs overwhelm me. The size of my ankles disturbs me. It's as if I'm looking at me as someone else. I have no idea who this girl is. However, my worry is euphoric, exactly what I need, and I accept it willingly. I love my achingly bare frame. I embrace the creaky machinery I inhabit, with its dormant reproductive system, its broken extremities, and its saddened gaze. It's mine, and I cannot imagine anything but pure appreciation for all it entails. Peter's large hand reaches to grasp my waist. I snap back around to look at him with a smile.

"You should probably pee." Peter's voice doesn't have the ribbony weightlessness it once did.

"Ha, what? Why would I—"

"You can't really trust your senses when you're rolling. Trust me, you should go to the bathroom. And drink some more water, you're probably dehydrated. Here, I'll go with you." I grab his hand as he leads me through the crowd and into a back hallway. We approach a line of girls, but his hand pulls me farther along the hallway.

"Um, the line's—"

"Don't worry, just come with me."

I keep pattering on while grasping his warm fingers. I didn't want to stand there without being able to move, anyway. Peter knocks on a door at the very end to the left. There isn't a response. With a shove, he opens the door and pulls me in, then slams it behind him. In front of me is a shabby wooden desk with a few papers. There are a mop and a Swiffer leaning against the white brick wall to my right. I reach out and drag my fingers along the waxy finish; it is a luxuriously alien sensation. Fluorescent lights flicker overhead and catch my attention without letting it go

until Peter grabs my shoulder. I remember that we came here to find a bathroom, and a wave of distant confusion lingers in my mind until I feel my hips being rammed into the wooden desk. The fluorescent lights gently steal my focus until my heartbeat increases at the sensation of cold air against my thighs. I begin to dart around before large hands remove any agency I still possess. I'm trapped in a euphoric daze within myself as my body yells out, barely a flicker on my radar of attention. My dress then tickles my prominent backbone. I shiver. Deep within, I am screaming, but the sound is trapped within a thick layer of molasses that won't allow my mind to hear it. I'm traversing far above the crowds in a headspace I cannot dare leave.

Pressure between my legs leads to a sharp pain as the internal cries within begin to increase and increase. They just barely reach my mouth.

"P-Peter, I want—"

"Shh, shh." Fear rises within me, slamming to break the glass of composure and get me to run free.

"I don't—"

"For God's sake—"

"Agh!" I ram my elbow into his ribs, euphoria numbing me

from feeling the sharp jab myself. His hands instantaneously

release their death grip on my waist as he leans into his right side.

Hesitating for a second, I throw up my leg to hit his crotch and

uncoordinatedly miss but end up pegging his thigh. An empty

breath escapes from his statuesque lips, which are ever so slightly

parted, and I lurch for the door. It doesn't open. I'm yanking on it

as hard as I can, my tights still pulled down to my knees and my

dress wrinkled to the side. Screaming out in frustration, the door

finally releases, clanging as it hits the back wall. I fall forward but

catch myself, thankful to be in comfortable shoes, and lift up my

fishnets as I hobble as quickly as possible out into the hallway. My

legs start running, my knees scraping against each other, but the

lights and the sounds and the people revive my barren mind with

the warm waterfall of sensation. I stop for a moment as I'm

prodding my way through the crowd and look back on the scene

before closing my eyes and thanking it. Everything is just what I

needed, everything is in its perfect place for me at this moment. A

hand inside me waves goodbye like a small child to her parents

after getting dropped off at school. My eyes burst open when I

remember having to call my dad to drop me off at school when my mom was too drunk or too unconscious to even consider doing so. Jaw clenches. Hands grip. *It's not your fault. Don't resist. Don't. Resist.*

Walking out of the club, the memories pour over me like a glaze of lacquer, viscous and opaque. They are all I can see, but I am protected and covered. The hot deluge has warmed me but has moved on, moved through and past me.

There are already cabs lined up, and I slide into one. The driver stares an extra second too long into my eyes, but I allow him to, unashamed of myself. I am wholly broken and accepting of my ungratefulness. My head leans out the open window to my right. I prop my arm up on the edge once we reach a red light, and when we start moving again, the wind makes my eyes water. Instead of blinking them away, though, I allow them to fall. The little marbles cascade into my mascara and leave faded dribbles down my cheeks like squid ink.

Chapter 41

It's almost nine in the morning, and I haven't shut my eyes more than to blink. I would be worried about waking Patricia up with my unstoppable stirring in bed, but I know she'll be more deeply asleep than usual after last night. Her eyeliner is smeared across her eyelids, and there are also little lines on her light-blue pillowcase. I made a point to still run through my whole skin-care routine at half past three in the morning, not failing to wash, tone, and moisturize. I even considered doing a charcoal mask but didn't want to walk back through the hallway a second time. Even hard synthetic drugs have preferable consequences to alcohol.

A rhythm still beats through the tips of my toes, urging them to dance along to the sounds in my mind. Nearby sirens prompt me to leap out of bed. I do not feel underslept at all; in fact, I feel as if I have risen from years of hibernation. My usually aching feet hit the ground with a spring in each step. I tie my hair up in a rubber band and head out to the kitchen to get a drink of water, remembering to do so even though I'm not thirsty, because Peter reminded me to hydrate repeatedly last night.

Peter. Last night. I won't allow myself to relive such a confusing, out-of-place event. I am not even sure if anything actually took place or if my broken machine of a brain misfired, misinterpreted everything, and then misremembered it all. Trying to recall it at all is like attempting to watch a blurry pirated recording of an old, already-fuzzy home movie. It just doesn't make sense to try and pay attention in the first place. I don't know if I was acting stupid, like how I freaked out when Jett touched me, too, or if I really was harmed. I don't know if I can even blame trauma on Vic when I can't explain how all that took place. I can't decide whether I should be upset or not, which makes me upset at myself. My mind races as if it's been caffeinated a thousand times over.

In the kitchen, I prop myself up on the counter and tap my legs against the wooden cabinets. They're slightly loose and creak. I sway from side to side to the music I'm making as I sip my glass of water. The cold tickles my lips. Audible steps make me jump in surprise.

"You look awfully energetic." It's Jett, his hair strewn about from just getting out of bed. He's in long gray plaid pajama pants and red socks with no shirt on. I smile and bat my stubby eyelashes like I still have a full face of makeup on.

"I had an energetic night that's turned into an energetic morning."

He furrows his brows in confusion.

"You went *out*? Did you...?"

"I didn't *drink*, no, if that's what you're asking." He doesn't know the full story, just that I don't. He probably assumes it's some attempt by me to be holier than thou.

"Well, then, tell me about your adventure." Jett shakes the electric kettle on the counter and pours the leftover water into a cup, stirring in some instant coffee mix from the cabinet above him. My legs are restless, so I jump down and push myself in and out against the counter.

"Jesus, did you have, like, a gallon of coffee?" His raspy voice cracks on *coffee*.

"No. I took *Molly*."

"The drug?" It comes out much flatter than a question. It doesn't rise up at the end; it's reminiscent of a disappointed parent trying to force a confession from their guilty child.

"Yeah." I nod eagerly. "I'm still kind of, like, feeling it. Not too much in my head, though. I can't stop fucking moving." My sway in and out from the counter has slowed slightly. His eyes scan me up and down a few times.

"Well, I'm glad you had…or are having a good time, I guess."

"Thanks, thanks. Yeah."

He sips his coffee. "Hopefully, you don't have a Suicide Tuesday or anything."

I jerk back and stop moving. "What?"

"Some people have a really bad hangover from that shit a few days after. As the term implies." The possible underhanded punch doesn't quite strike through the thin veil of warmth still hugging me.

"Well, I hope so, too. I think the last time I tried to commit suicide it was on Saturday."

His dark eyes expand as if they're being pulled apart by eye clamps. "The last time you tried to commit suicide?" Again, his question lacks the momentum to lift the end in typical interrogative fashion.

"Come on. *Yeah*, I tried to take a bunch of pills, but my dad found me, naked and bloody from punching my mirror, and crying and—"

"Jesus, Val."

"I mean, we all have our shit—"

"*Our shit?* I-it's not even ten in the morning—"

"I've been up all night, actually."

"Who gave you this shit?"

I blink a few times. "Patricia's friend."

He turns the coffee mug on the table and watches it, not looking at me when he does decide to speak. "So you went out with Patricia's friends? Didn't know sorority girls were your thing."

"They're not. I was trying to be *fun*." I step to reach my glass on the counter and gulp down water to release some of the remaining energy needing to run out from within. Jett sighs, his bare chest expanding to highlight his ribs even more. The muscles rippling on his sides give the appearance of fish gills, and if I focus hard enough, I can even imagine little silver sparkles reflecting off of him.

"Were they on Molly, too?"

"No. Not Patricia and her best friend. This other...this other friend of hers was, so I got it from them, but everyone else was just drinking." Though I'm not nervous, I avoid mentioning Peter. Jett's brows furrow even more. My throat clenches, like I remember my dad's doing whenever he would ask about my mom. It has my best interest in mind, trying to protect me from myself.

"Them?"

"Yeah, just one of her friends."

He moves to the fridge, pulls out two pieces of toast, and drops them into the toaster next to me without asking me to move.

"Are you, like, mad at me for this?"

He steps back after pulling down the toaster handle and meets my eyes. His dark irises are more firm than usual, balancing out my porousness.

"I'm not mad, Val. I'm just worried."

"You shouldn't be worried about me. Like, I haven't felt this great in forever."

"Well, obviously. You're still rolling."

I flinch back in disagreement. "I'm not still rolling. Sure, I may be, like, happy still and all, but I'm not fucking seeing your aura." My ponytail begins to fall down as my hand motions speed up with conviction.

"You've been restless and moving since I walked in. I'm really not mad, Val. This is just out of character for you, and I'm concerned for fucking obvious reasons." We both stand there looking at the ground. My hips continue to move from side to side before I process what he's said and force them to stop.

"Be happy for me! I had an absolutely great night, for the most part, I mean…I don't know why you're acting all weird." My lips take another drink of water, my head cocking back as I don't dare break eye contact.

"Because I walk in here first thing, still half fucking asleep on a Saturday morning, and the first thing I see is my girlfriend rolling from the night before?" Jett doesn't breathe; his gills are stagnant and tense. Finally, he inhales and exhales firmly. My hips beg to keep moving, but I hold them in place with all my might. "Even your pupils are still dilated," he says.

"I'm your girlfriend?"

The toast pops up. He removes it, dropping the pieces onto a place and shaking out his burned hand afterward.

"Look, I'm sorry, I'm not dealing with you like this." Jett runs his hands under cool water and then pats them dry with a rag to his left and leaves, carrying the toast, a jar of peanut butter, and a banana back to his room. I stand there, confused and still shaking slightly, then head back to my room with my glass of water.

Chapter 42

Around two p.m., after knocking out most of my schoolwork at Harry's fueled by a lingering afterglow and excess caffeine, a rush of fear comes over me. It's not sudden. I've felt it coming on for a few hours now. The wooden table in front of me looks as unwelcoming as my childhood home, and I cannot stand to sit at it any longer. Pushing it away, it screeches across the concrete floor and irritates my sore eardrums. I stuff my computer into my bag and don't both throwing away the coffee cup.

As soon as I exit the door, wind whirls up into my nose and gives my brain instantaneous frostbite. My mind slowly freezes to death as my body struggles to hang on to consciousness, pushing through the memorized directions back to my dorm. My ID isn't buzzing me in at the front entrance. I slam it against the sensor. Nothing. I'm hitting the white plastic square with the little keycard like I'm trying to karate chop a block of wood, but nothing is moving except blood to my inflamed hand. A security guard opens the door and stares at me for a moment before breaking the silence.

"Sorry about that. Should be working now." He closes the door behind him. I gape and try, gently and softly, to place my ID on the sensor one last time. The door clicks open, and I run in, turning the corner to the elevator as fast as my withering legs can take me. My dorm feels alien and unwelcoming despite feeling like Venus emerging from her shell hours earlier. Patricia is gone, her bed neatly made. I jump into my own. The leap takes all of my own strength, as well as that of the generations before me, pushing me to barely hide under my dirty sheets, which are in desperate need of cleaning. I curl into the fetal position, fighting to warm up my mind from its hypothermia, but feel as if my own psyche is out of reach. I don't understand where I am or why; I cannot figure out what it truly is I am searching for, and all I want is to get it all to suddenly work out instead of work against me. For the world to become as linear as I am, to make as much fucking sense as I do. I'm not pretending. I don't bullshit. I don't evade. Everything around me is based upon a phony understanding of life right now as the end all be all. I see more; I want more; I am more. The cold inside me shoots up, and I am an icicle, here to pierce all that is without being able to survive.

My mind, slowly thawing out and calming down, jumps to

Jett. I think of texting him before remembering he hates me now.

I'm probably on his Bad List. I feel confused about Peter. My

feelings shut off.

At least I'm back to being the only one trapping and

violating me. I am the powerful agency at hand. I'm reminded of

why I make myself a prisoner instead of letting someone else fill

that role. If I don't, someone else will, and this way, I won't have

to experience the Stockholm syndrome attachment to my creator's

pleasure.

Beneath the covers, my breath humidifies all the

surrounding air. Cold sweat begins to form around my hairline. I

wipe it away with a wrinkled sheet. It eventually becomes

unbearable; I throw the covers away and sit up to breathe some

fresh air. Sitting across from me, perfectly comfortable on

Patricia's bed, is Greg. His prepubescent little-boy legs rock back

and forth below the elevated wooden frame. His yellow sweater

hangs slightly off-center, like he's just slid it on over his white

undershirt. His khaki shorts, which are a size too big so he can still wear them once he grows into them, droop down slightly with the curve of his knees against the mattress. I can't help but smile.

"Hey," I mutter. His lips lift up in reciprocation.

"Hi, Val. I miss you."

My heart palpitates, and I want to reach out, but I still don't feel close enough with him to do shit like that yet. One day.

"I miss you, too, Greg. I miss you, too."

"Val, I don't think you're helping yourself."

"Helping myself? I don't really, like, need *help*, Greg." I sit up a little more as my breathing increases.

"I think…I think you should talk with Di. Just talk with her more." His young brown eyes run deep with the heartfelt profundity of a sage.

"Di doesn't understand my shit."

"Maybe that's a good thing."

"You don't understand my shit, either. Neither does Jett."

"Val, *you* don't even understand your shit." The curse word sounds out of place in his delicate voice, and my muscles tense as the dissonance permeates the air. My chest cramps, not allowing me to breathe and exhale the statement. *You don't even understand your shit.* Maybe not, but I understand how it makes me feel. I'm wrapped up in a coil of misunderstanding, none of it of my own doing.

"I wish someone was there for me. I don't have anyone anymore." His legs click the wood of the bed frame in a steady beat.

"You have me. And Jett. And Di."

I thin out my lips and sigh. He's right. I don't need anyone besides me, and he does show up when necessary.

"I don't need Jett. I don't need Di. I don't even *have* them. I never did, I..." When I look up to finish the statement, Greg's gone, and I don't get to say it. Just like Vic didn't get to say it to me because of that goddamn PT Cruiser the night before Really Bad. Just like how Jett will never, ever say it because I won't ever let him.

I fall back on the mattress. It hurts my spine. I can't just lie here; I did that all night. I need to exercise. As I'm pulling on leggings and a tank top, Patricia walks in with a to-go box that smells of sesame. She takes a bite of pad Thai as she kicks the door closed behind her.

"You okay?" Her voice is muffled as she chews rice noodles. Through my eyes, I shoot bullets, not to kill but just to release the chamber, directly at her, and she looks away in embarrassment as some noodles fall from her mouth back into the paper container.

"Yeah?" I ask, confused but not wanting to hear any answers. Patricia shakes her head and sets her food down on her desk.

"You just look a little freaked out or something, sorry," she adds quickly with a lighthearted laugh. *Fucking phony. I look like shit, okay, alright. I've been up all night on fucking ecstasy, Patricia. Fuck you.*

I don't respond to her statement and instead put my hair up quickly into a ponytail, grab my headphones, and begin running down the stairs. I'm out of breath after the first flight but never received instructions on how to stop, so I accelerate, bursting out the door and forward into the street without checking in with my now-thawed-out mind. It's goopy, like frozen fruit that's been warmed up to room temperature.

Each step sends cracks of electricity up through the balls of my feet and out the top of my head, frying the warm gel inside my skull and whirling it around, paining the sides of my wooden chasm. Minute by minute, the cracks increase. Greg's voice screams from within. I hear it over the cars honking, the people talking, the dogs barking, the music in my headphones. He isn't saying anything I can make out, just *screaming*, and not like he used to before jumping in our dirty algae-filled pool for a cannonball. He's screaming like he's being stabbed, like his little heart is giving out, like he's realizing what fate would really hand him. My knees rise higher and my calves pound the ground at an increasing pace to silence his cries. I can't care. To do so would be to surrender myself to everything that would kill me.

Chest pounding and arms flailing, I have no idea how long it's been, but I know it hasn't been nearly long enough. According to my watch, I haven't beaten yesterday's calories at this time yet; I cannot allow my mind to consider slowing down, either. However, my brain is still a useless, electrified mess of polymer and goo, and it cannot reach my physical nerves even partially. My body continues to pedal on the sidewalk as if it's a bike riding off into the forest. I dodge people without registering their expressions toward me, because to do so would also mean to leave this safety bubble of motion. My knees shake with each stride. I wonder each time if it will be my last.

My watch vibrates because I've finally beaten yesterday. I fucking did it. I bend over my knees, then punish myself by jumping up and jogging harder on my way back. My ID buzzes me into the dorms, rewarding me for my efforts. As I labor up the stairs and my breathing slows, euphoria returns. Two, three, four, flights of not feeling the stairs underneath me, just warm clouds supporting me up and away. As I finally spot the sign for the ninth floor, I stop for a moment to prepare for the relief of showering and finishing this karmic necessity. Except, as I reach my leg up for those final few steps, they don't make it. I try to jump over the second-to-last step but fail. My arm flails, and my cheek slams against the floor like a rubber band, and everything goes black. Greg's screams are the last thing I hear.

Chapter 43

My eyes open to a vibration on the stairs. It's a familiar vibration. My ears are used to its resonance. Coming into focus, my eyes register Jett leaning over me.

"Oh my God, Val. Val, can you hear me?" He slides his arms underneath my ribs and scoops me up firmly. I furrow my brows and blink quickly at him.

"Yeah, yeah." I shake my head and look down. The right leg of my pants has ridden up to show a developing green bruise on my shin. "How... What are you doing on the stairs?"

"I was heading to visit my friend a floor down. What are *you* doing on the stairs passed fucking out?"

"I'm fine, don't worry. Probably just part of the comedown, I feel okay now."

"Let me get you some juice; I have some orange—"

"No, no! I... Thank you, I'll get it. You go ahead, don't worry." I smile unconvincingly. His chest rises and falls a few times as my mouth lowers into a frown, my eyes still squinting with artificial amusement. His clenched jaw proves he doesn't buy it.

"Jett, please. It's some weird exhaustion thing, I bet. I'll sleep it off."

"Why weren't you earlier, though? What—" He stops himself, sorting through his thoughts. "Come on, I'll help you get up." I grasp Jett's hand, and he lifts me to standing and opens the hallway door for me. This time, I don't refuse going first.

My groggy mind finds it difficult to balance my body, so I lean against the wall as I turn to walk back to my room.

"Hey, hey." Jett grasps me underneath my armpit and halts my movement. "Come on. Get something to eat or drink, at least."

"I can't imagine eating right now," I mutter. "I should just sleep. I'm nauseous."

"Let me bring you something for when you are hungry. Come on, I know Veg-House is your favorite." Without having the energy to stop it, I release an exhale, powered by stewing anger and frustration, from within my brittle bones. My head falls back, my eyes close, and I lean back against the wall.

"Jett, please just leave me alone. I'm sorry."

"Val! I'm not leaving you fucking alone like this! If you won't let *me* stay with you, go to the goddamn hospital, get Di to take you or something."

"Please fucking leave me alone." I would've made it worthy of an exclamation point if I possessed any electricity left in my body. All that remains are short-circuited static flares.

Hot tears suddenly emerge from my tired eyes. Their unexpected presence shocks me into detached numbness. I stop the domino chain from continuing on and refuse to let the hot stream fall. My head tilts back to contain the already present tears. Jett's sad gaze lands on me, but I cannot bear for him to see me like this, and I turn around, aching back to my dorm. Jett doesn't follow.

Patricia isn't there. I fall to my knees and let the pent-up tears rain down slowly and silently as I rest my head on my desk chair. The scratchy brown fabric begins to dampen and squish under my nose, which is painfully wedged into a stitched indentation in the cushion. My body feels so light here bent in half that I think about it snapping like a popsicle stick. I want it to break in half. I sit on the floor and curl my knees into my chest, lurching my shoulders into a painful hunch. My face digs farther into the chair, and I can smell the stale perfume I've sprayed over months and months right here.

I uncurl and lift my head to look at my watch: 6:01. I have twenty-nine minutes before I can eat, even though I still don't feel the need to. But I've done a lot today. I beat yesterday's calorie goal. I better take this opportunity to celebrate. I haven't eaten at all, so I could technically eat a day's worth of food, but I don't want to take the chance of going *over* today's allowed food by underestimating. I get a little more rice in my dinner and a little more peanut butter in my dessert. Shit. *You can't think that far ahead.* That's in three hours. Just more rice for now. Perfect.

Having stopped crying, I sit up on my heels, and within seconds, I feel a gush of air on the bare sliver of my lower back.

"I brought you some orange juice." Jett's voice invites me to turn around. He sets down a tall plastic cup on the corner of my messy desk, atop the change-of-major forms that I haven't begun filling out yet but that are already crumpled at the edges. I didn't eat at all today, so I can have half the juice. I *deserve* half the juice. I can *enjoy* half the juice.

I pull myself up into the seat and take a sip. It's overly sweet, definitely unnatural and processed like he wouldn't know any better to avoid buying. It trickles down my throat, ad a sour aftertaste remains. *Fucking enjoy it. FUCKING ENJOY THIS SIP OF HALF THE FUCKING ORANGE JUICE!*

Jett crouches down next to me. In his squat, he is nearly as tall as my seated height.

"I guess Suicide Tuesday came a little early?" I don't laugh. He has no fucking idea. I know this isn't even about the fucking Molly or a fucking comedown; it's about everything spiraling out of my control and whirling me around in the process. "Sorry, sorry. Uncool. Um, h-have more juice," he says. I take another sip and force it down my clenched throat. I can't enjoy this.

"Jett, I'm sorry. Please, go ahead and see your friend, I'm just...I'm just being dramatic." I manage to let out a laugh that I find highly convincing. One point for me today.

He grabs a chunk of his hair, then slams his hands to his side. "You *passed out* in the stairway. You're not being dramatic. You're probably really fucking worn out from...from, I don't know, whatever you were doing while high out of your mind last night."

Here goes fighting against divulging anything further.

"I really wasn't high out of my mind. I was just dancing and shit. Probably just haven't slept well and shouldn't have run—
"

"You *ran* today?"

I shake my head in confusion. "Yeah?"

His shock surprises me enough to make me feel a little more alive.

"Jesus. Okay. You need to chill with the exercise," he says.

I roll my eyes. "I go on light jogs occasionally. There's nothing to really, like, *chill* with." My mouth meets the blue plastic cup to further prove that I'm an easygoing, balanced person.

He lets me set the juice back down before asking more questions.

"Why were you crying just now?"

Heat rushes over me. Not like the warm, comforting shower I took previously but a burning rash I itch to rid myself of.

"Suicide Tuesday, or whatever, like you said. Should just sleep it off. I'll feel better tomorrow." He puts his hands on my knees and tilts toward me.

"I don't think you'd be bawling just from a Molly comedown."

"I wasn't bawling."

"You look like you were."

"I know, I look like shit without concealer." His grip tightens on my knees, not painfully, but firmly, and I jump a little. Somehow the broken fuses inside me ignite with power they cannot logically possess. "I'm sorry, I know I'm a mess; there's no good reason, I'm just fucked, Jett. Nothing to *save*, no mystery to solve or any of that shit. Just mentally fucked."

"Don't say that."

"What? It's an objective statement. I am literally ill. I'm fucked."

"Why? Because a list of arbitrary criteria designates you as being fucked?" Jett's chest inches closer until it's almost leaning on my thighs. If he decides to put his weight on me, I'm worried I'll break.

"Yes, the DSM had basically told me that."

"Fuck that! *Fuck* that, Val—fuck any of that shit that's making you feel like absolute crap. Like you obviously are feeling now. Because something isn't...isn't working here." His passion scares me, and his sudden stroking of my leg tells me he knows that he's scaring me. Tears send signals of their impending arrival, but I hold them in. *Abort. Not here.*

"You don't know anything, Jett. I'm sorry. Because you have no idea, and it's...all really damn complicated."

"Tell me, then. I care." My eyes start to roll, but I clamp them shut and only allow them to open when I know I have control of my reflexes.

"I can't just suddenly pour out all my shit, you know." It sounds more aggressive than I've rehearsed. Point taken away.

"We've been seeing each other for months, Val. I know, like, your favorite food and movie and what kinds of things you like to do on the goddamn weekend, but I know nothing about *you*. I've told you my shit, even though it's not that shitty, and I know that you can't just have had the fucking white-picket-fence and two-point-five-children household. You didn't just come here like everyone else looking to party and get laid, you didn't... I don't...

All I do know, though, is that you're keeping a lot of shit to

yourself when talking about it could probably be of help to you." I

think of the man in Harry's from a few weeks ago. "Convincing

monologue," he said. I yearn to bluntly declare that, right here, and

fuck up this beautiful moment with all my might like I'm designed

to. Instead, I let him be and sit in silence. I think about grabbing

the orange juice but can't make a decision and continue to blink at

the ground. Jett leans up and hugs me, wrapping his warm body

around mine and clenching me tightly. I tense up to avoid the tears

just millimeters away from release, but he turns my head to meet

his, and as his lips meet mine, I cannot multitask. The tears fall

sharply. Everything I had left is lost; I am a shell of a person not

even able to make out well. I pull back in embarrassment, then

stand up and lean over my bed with my back to Jett.

"Jett, I really do just need to be alone right now. I'll talk to

you, I will. You don't deserve to be treated like this."

"Like what, Val?" I don't answer him and instead place my

head onto my forearms and look at the white sheets as they turn

black with my shadow. After a few seconds, Jett sighs, and I hear

him pick up the mostly full cup of juice and shut the door behind

him.

Chapter 44

Dr. Ellis shuffles into the waiting room from a different end of the hallway than usual, tucking his crisp cream shirt into pressed navy pants. His belt is one latch too loose.

"Sorry, sorry. Come in, please." I follow him into his office and plop down on the very middle of the love seat. There's a new, small coffee stain on the right cushion. I scratch it with my broken pointer fingernail.

"My apologies for being late. There was a line to the bathroom, but never mind that. How has this past week been for you, Valerie?"

I sigh and look at the empty bowl between us on the coffee table.

"Kind of rough, I'd say."

His face sinks. "What makes you say that?"

"Di hates me, Jett hates me, I feel like shit, I don't know. Just to name a few."

"Why do you believe Jett hates you?" I blink at the black carpet, which is perfectly decorated with fresh vacuum zigzags. The warmth of Dr. Ellis's dark eyes burns me.

"I mean, he should. I can't ever manage to treat him well. No matter what I do, I always fuck it up somehow. Like, he really tries to help me, and I just... I don't what to do with that." Dr. Ellis readjusts in his seat and pushes up his red glasses.

"Let's start from the beginning. What happened most recently with him?" He flips a page over loudly in the crisp yellow notebook. I prepare to feel a rush of panic after saying what I'm going to say.

"He found me passed out in the stairwell, tried to help me, and I freaked. I don't know why, I just really couldn't let him help me at all."

"You passed out, as in fainted?" His voice is heavy with concern but filtered through professional distance.

"Yeah, coming back from running up the stairs. It was probably a combination of things. I'm fine now." His eyes look over the red rims down toward me, skeptical but tired, and

eventually return to locking on to the lined yellow pages. His pen scrapes the pad loudly.

"Okay. Rewind for me. To the beginning of this fainting, this whole scene. Take me through it." Dr. Ellis sits back in his seat and nods, giving me permission to speak with his full attention. I furrow my brows and scratch my hairline.

"Well…Friday night, Patricia…my roommate, she's my roommate."

"Yes, I remember."

"Okay, well…I went out with her and her friends unexpectedly. To some club. I don't even know the name or really where it was."

I go through the rest of the story, leaving out parts my mind doesn't yet want to consider are even parts, and he blinks neutrally, though I know he must feel *something* nonobjective. A few pages of the notepad get flipped as I speak. I wonder how much information worth noting is really packed into my scattered, jumping retelling.

"So, yeah. It just kind of ended with me not…doing…anything. And he hasn't texted me or anything since.

He's probably waiting for me to apologize." I slide my hands in between my tightly pressed thighs, and my shoulders rise up as I inhale. His pen loudly scribbles for a while after I've resigned my mic.

"And…this was your first experience with MDMA?" He turns back a few pages, rereading, then smooths out the fresh page he's just revealed.

"Yeah."

"Are you sure that what you took was actually MDMA?" His question swarms among the dust particles highlighted by the sharp sunlight. He should probably close the curtains.

"I guess not totally, no. But I'm here and alive, so, I guess whatever it was didn't kill me." He gives an exhale filled half with laughter and half with discomfort.

"And you…*hadn't* met this Peter person before?"

My jaw clenches and my voice rises an octave without meaning to. "No, no, I hadn't. I hadn't met any of Patricia's friends before that night."

He asks more about the physical symptoms, wanting me to describe the sensations running through me, and I find myself

reliving the warmth and Technicolor embrace that are no longer a part of my reality. It's strange, retelling my aphrodisiacal euphoria to Dr. Ellis, but there is no one I feel I could tell it to besides him. With Jett, I already fucked that over. With Di, I already fucked that over, too, and I would feel weird mentioning such an emotional experience to her anyway.

"And were you just dancing with the group during this time? With everyone?" The pen taps the notepad. His chest rises and falls. Mine stays tightly constrained as if being clenched by two iron hands of God. I nod and shrug.

"Yeah." As his eyes return back to looking down, the grip releases, and I inhale.

"So then you all headed back to your dorm afterward?"

"No, I didn't go with everyone. I stayed...er...yeah, with Peter just a little longer, then I went back." My eyes stay pinned down. I didn't lie, but adrenaline still rushes down over me like I'm worried I'll get found out. Dr. Ellis's gaze feels sharp through my thin sweater, like he's waiting for me to respond and push him away. I don't. I let it invade my heart and burst it into two halves still somehow beating but now ripped in two like my skull.

"I don't think doing this again would be a very good idea based on where you're at, Valerie. I think keeping as much equilibrium as possible would be of help to you. Did you call the dietician to make an appointment yet?" No words come out of my mouth, which is moving in slow motion to try and form a response but can't. "Why don't you do that now? I have her number if you need it again." I sigh, typing what he's reading out into my phone and begrudgingly pressing it to my ear. It's as if I'm an unwilling but resigned child with little motivation to rebel.

"Um, yeah, Tuesday at eleven works for me. Thanks. Okay." I hang up, and Dr. Ellis is blinking at me proudly. I'm not sure if that's as a result of me following his instructions or, as he sees it, doing something for my own good.

"I just have to fill out a food log and come in next Tuesday. I forgot the address, but I'll look it up." He laughs a little and nods.

"Good, good. So, back to this last weekend. Did anything out of the ordinary happen once you got back?" He brushes that one piece of fallen hair in front of his cowlick back and continues to blink more quickly than usual. My foot, which doesn't quite reach the ground, begins to tap the love seat.

"Um, I couldn't really sleep at all. I ended up just kind of lying in bed until the next day, when I didn't really do much except…except *run*, and then…"

"Then you fainted?" I nod, then go on to explain how I felt pretty much entirely normal until suddenly reaching the top of the stairs, and then how I woke up to Jett helping me. "Well, thank God he was there, Valerie. Your habits are beginning to concern me. I don't think you need to be running in your current state." My chin falls in, and I wiggle my neck as the words try to invade me. I do not let them permeate my skin like I did previously with his eyes.

"I know I'm, like, not the fittest, but I really don't do that much exercise. I hadn't run for a few days before that."

"Had you exercised at all for those few days?"

"Yeah, I did some classes…but, like, not *cardio* cardio. Really nothing hard." Shoulders back, chest forward, utmost confidence. I am the epitome of balance and self-care.

"Valerie, your…your appearance *is* concerning to me." Dr. Ellis's eyes wander to my visible ankles peeking out between my

jeans and my Vans. As I glare at him fiercely, he quickly moves his gaze back to his notepad.

"I would really like you to abstain from anything rigorous for now, at least until speaking with your dietician. Can you do that for me?" My head nods like a timed metronome to the tune of his professional pleadings.

"Totally, yeah, I'll do that."

Chapter 45

It's been a week since I went out. Patricia's desk is scattered with makeup brushes and uncapped lip glosses. I wonder if she's at Rita's dorm. I wonder if she's taking shots with Black Shirt and the rest of them. I wonder if Peter is standing there to the side with pills, wearing his polished leather shoes and eyeing the group as they start to get loose while he stands firm. I wish I'd gotten his phone number. I was stupid for freaking out on him. I'm ungrateful. *Jesus Christ.* Even I could somehow ruin what could've been the greatest night of my life. If I had just let go and had fun... If I hadn't let past memories convince me that something different was going on in front of me, in reality... But, somehow, I managed to freak out. Somehow.

Jett. He called me his girlfriend, but I don't know if that was just a move to make me feel guilty at the time or if he really meant it. If he *did* really mean it, I'm pretty damn sure the title no longer applies. My mind wanders, picturing me running into him in the kitchen, and I consider never eating there again. I could probably fit a mini-fridge in here by my shoes, stock it with juices,

and live better off than I would if I constantly had to worry about seeing him. Or Di. Both of them are on my Bad List now, permanently engraved alongside those who have done me wrong by no direct fault of their own but who make me feel shitty just thinking about them.

I text Patricia to see what she's doing. We went out once, so I have grounds to ask again. It's not like I'm just her annoying roommate trying to tag along. Am I her annoying roommate trying to tag along? *Fuck. Fuck. Shit.* It's already gone through. *No. You're fine.* She's probably drunk. She'll probably respond, intoxicated, in a few minutes with a welcoming invitation full of misspellings and some tacky emojis.

A few minutes go by, and I am still sitting at my desk wasting time on my computer while still also wasting time on my phone. I reopen the text and notice it didn't even deliver. Her phone must be dead. I throw the phone onto my bed and fall back into my not-meant-to-be-a-rocking-chair rocking chair. The uneven legs screech against the floor as an acute pain shoots up my spine upon impact.

It's snowing out. The final glimpses of daylight make each and every snowflake transparent and hauntingly golden as they descend. The chair beneath me suddenly feels like a vortex of quicksand, with all the dried tears within the cushion drowning me slowly. As the sand around me begins to pull me in a fierce undertow, I reach my arms up and hurl myself over the edge and out of my dorm room.

I'm in sweatpants and a thin hoodie, no coat, and wearing my Batman slippers with no socks. Through the windows, I see that the sun has almost set, its pink light barely escaping through a gloomily cloudy sky, but the moon has already become visible. It's glowing strikingly silver in contrast to the warm sun hues fading away. As I open the front doors to my dorm building and exit, my eyes are fixated on the prominent ball of beaming gray. It's chilly, but the wind isn't strong enough to make it unbearable, and I'm able to stay fairly comfortable with my hood up and my hands tucked away. I walk down to the edge of my block where there is an old church with a small park in front. Only one of the several benches is occupied, so I sit on the opposite side of the park, facing away from the old man on the other bench and his small dog. My gaze is still drawn toward the moon. It is bright enough to keep me fixated but soft enough not to hurt my eyes. In front of me is a black metal fence bordering the park and the building. The windows of the church are dark and wavy. As I stare deeply into one on the far left, I can make out a face. I recognize the face, the messy boyish hair, and the uneven yellow sweater. Screaming in my mind starts as the face's mouth opens and its teeth are exposed. I curl over, hands over my ears, and tap my feet against the dead grass as my elbows grind into my thighs. The screams are louder than the voice in my head encouraging me to calm down. It's Dr. Ellis's voice, reassuring and grounded, telling me to take a deep breath on the count of four and hold it for five and then exhale it for six and then do it over and over and over and over. I ignore it. I stand and look right into the window at Greg screaming. Slowly, a figure approaches behind Greg and places a hand on his shoulder. They stand, glaring straight into my eyes, with a single wooden windowpane dividing the space between them and me, framing them like a modern, misappropriated *American Gothic.*

Vic is silent and stoic while Greg's face flails. The wounds inside me are reignited like never before. There is no longer skin to burn to ashes but instead pure bone, and my own cremation begins at the sore balls of my feet. My body disintegrates slowly. I need to see Vic and Greg before the flames reach my skull and it's over, once and for all.

Balancing on the knobs of my knees, walking like a pirate with a wooden leg, I make my way to the large wooden door of the church. It's locked. I shake it, hoping for the metal to suddenly break, my almost nonexistent knees now being devoured by fire. One of the glass panes of the door is cracked and broken, so I slide my wrist into it and lean over to grab the knob from the inside. The sharp edges scrape my wrists and forearms as I struggle to reach far enough in until, finally, with little red trickles dropping onto the caramel-colored wood, the door bursts in. By now, only my upper body remains, floating upon the circulating ashes eerily supporting a body once existing, once surviving. Vic and Greg stand there, staring. Greg's screams have been replaced by the sound of my own blood dripping onto the smooth mahogany floor.

"Just leave, Val. You don't need us." Vic's voice charges me like never before; I feel as if all that is left of me is that electric current running inside of me and nothing else. I am only a chest and shoulders now, with a phantom body in place of a physical one.

"I tried to help you, Val. There's nothing more I can do. You weren't there for me, and now I can't be there for you," Greg says. I think back to all the times I hid instead of comforting Greg when Mom was yelling at him, hitting him, ignoring him. I think back to all the times when I called my dad to pick me up and left Greg there with her, not because I didn't care about him but because my mind was so focused on myself. I'm still so fucking focused on myself.

"Greg, I'm sorry! I'm sorry!" I choke on tears I didn't know could arise from a body made of just a skull and electrified dust.

"You're just like Mom. You remind me of her. You feel so bad for yourself when all you do is hurt people." The delicate pitch of his voice is at direct odds with the nuclear level of his statement. Now, there is nothing left of me but my skull, which is already broken in half and barely functional, taking longer to wither than my other bones because of its density. Vic starts to laugh. No, not laugh—he's wailing uncontrollably from the pit of his stomach

319

like I've only seen him do once before when we pulled a stupid prank on my neighbor.

"The fact that"—Vic erupts in laughter again, doubling over—"that you're actually *surprised*"—his convulsions take over even his breathing, and Vic has to calm himself down before speaking again—"*surprised* that this is happening to you! You're fucking evil, and you don't even see it!" There is no longer any protection for my brain. No intact skull there to cover it and keep it safe. I am at the mercy of the elements with no control over myself. The fire begins permeating the outer membrane of my brain. My thoughts are increasingly difficult to form; they no longer take sentence form but rather come in convulsions of panic and betrayal. When I look up, Vic and Greg themselves are immersed in the flames. The wooden floors and walls do not ignite but simply begin to turn to ash just as I have. Vic continues laughing, and Greg continues gazing at me like a wounded dog at his abusive owner. With nothing left of me but an electric current powered by overwhelming guilt, I watch as they disintegrate, fall to the ground as dust, and remove all life from the space.

I look down and blink. My arm is bleeding, not too heavily, but enough that it's beginning to go slightly numb. Taking over without thinking, the body that no longer exists in the world of my mind runs out of the church, leaving the door open. The old man on the bench's dog barks at me as I move past.

In the darkness, I slam my ID where I hope the sensor is at my dorm's entrance. Click. The security guard stares at my arm. My feet run toward the elevator, and my eyes check my watch as I wait. Six twenty-seven. Perfect. I can begin cooking and weighing and doing everything necessary according to the Rules.

My feet carry me through the hallway and into the kitchen. The light is already on, and I see feet peeking out from the counter. Small white Keds. I know those small white Keds, but my feet move faster than my mind can catch up to. Small chomping sounds emerge as I continue on and get ready to open the cabinet and get out a cutting board, but once I enter the kitchen, everything halts. It's Di, leaning against the counter, eating peanut-butter-pretzel bites. Her chewing stops upon meeting my eyes.

Chapter 46

Di cocks her head seriously, inhales, and opens her mouth to say something, but she halts when she notices my arm. It has mostly stopped bleeding by now, and the blood has dried and left scarlet trails of crust.

"Oh my! Jesus, here!" She dampens a paper towel and jumps over to me, lightly scrubbing away the blood flakes. "The *hell* happened to you?" I just keep looking at my freshly cleaned arm and its thin but deep scrapes along the sides. "Val, come on, talk to me. You look like you've seen a fucking ghost or something." I make eye contact with her accidentally, not realizing how painful it would be. I don't understand how simply focusing on her two small gray-blue eyes and the dark pupils encased within can cause me to writhe inside my own skin like a snake trying to shed.

"Just cut it accidentally. It's nothing. Thanks for helping and all." She keeps looking at me, as if she's expecting more, then turns around and tosses the bloody paper towel into the trash. She misses and has to go pick it up.

"Look, I'm really fucking worried about you, Val. Maybe you should start, like, *taking* your meds and shit. I probably shouldn't have told you how I tongue mine. I wasn't my place to, like, do that at all—"

"Di, this really has nothing to do with you, with any of that. I've just been a mess lately because of shit with Jett and…and *you* and shit."

"All I said was that you need to gain weight. That's literally all I fucking said." Her voice is calm and direct like she's thought it over a million times and doesn't have any energy left to deliberate.

"I'm sorry." My stomach rumbles on cue. We both sit in this fiercely ironic discomfort for much too long.

"Were you coming in here to, like, get something?"

"Yeah, yeah." I walk over to a cabinet. "Just to make some food." I don't have the energy to fucking weigh anything at this point. I can eyeball it, it's fine.

My revelation shocks me, and I immediately punish myself for considering such recklessness. But Di is here, so I don't really have a choice. I lay out the vegetables on the cutting board before Di rushes over and stops me.

"Hey, hey. Let me do that. I don't want you hurting yourself even more." I'm confused. I thought she was upset at me, but I move out of the way anyway. She cuts everything quickly and a little larger than I usually would, but I smile at her when she's done because if I had any energy left to have emotional responses, I'd probably smile in a situation like this.

"Um, you don't have to talk about this if you don't want to, but what all happened with you and, uh, Jett?" Di picks up the bag of pretzel bites behind her and continues eating them, offering me a couple. Whatever. I can have them. I know I used less than a full cup of cauliflower for lunch, so two peanut-butter-pretzel bites would probably be okay. A voice inside me, now my very own, begins to scream, but I take the two little bread pillows out of her hand and chew them before the yelling voice can talk me out of it.

"It's fine," I say, looking down at my feet as I finish chewing.

"Do you want more?" Di asks. "Sorry." She's about to clip the bag back, and I shake my head, unbothered and also uninterested.

"You're fine. I just fucked it up, got all awkward, and basically shut down when he tried to help me. It's my fault; I don't think I want to do anything about it, though."

"What?" She half laughs, jumping up onto the counter. "Your, like, boyfriend and you have some fight or whatever, and you don't want to do anything about it?" The same yelling voice inside me, not yet loud enough to scare me, begins to instruct me to get defensive, but I am too tired to obey and continue looking at my Vans as if they are an optical illusion I'm trying hard to figure out. The kitchen begins to warm with the aromatic smell of spiced roasted vegetables.

"I just know I can't possibly do anything about it, so there's no fucking point. Like, I'm fucking evil, I fucking do this every fucking—"

"You're not fucking evil, Val. What the hell? Where is this coming from?"

I look back up at her without any life in my eyes. "What do you mean, 'what the hell'? Like, this is fucking obvious to anyone. I screw every single thing up. I'm evil, whether you realize it or not."

She's shaking her little round head, her faded-blue grown-out hairs barely grazing *love me* to obscure the very top of the tattoo. "Are you talking about this with your therapist?"

"Yes, kind of. It's fine, okay?"

"Val, you need to, like, *tell* him this shit. You're scaring me."

"It's not like he straight-up asks if I consider myself evil or not."

"It doesn't sound like you're telling him totally what's going on with you, whatever the *hell* that is, because *I* have no fucking idea at this point." Eyes glued to my Vans, my hands dig into the countertop. My arm stings a little as flexed veins stretch my raw skin.

"I'm sorry."

"I just want you to be okay, Val! When you don't talk to me for weeks and I run into you looking like hell, I'm going to get fucking worried."

"It's not like you tried to reach out to me at all." I'm not complaining, just stating facts.

"We both fucked up," she says with a sigh. I bend over to check the oven, even though I know there's still at least fifteen minutes left until everything is done. I stand back up and shrug.

"I hope you solve this shit with Jett. I really do. If I see him, or if I think I see him, since I haven't really met him..."

"Di, don't worry. When I'm ready, I'll bake him some shit as an apology or whatever."

"Bake some for yourself, too." This time, I get angry immediately. The force behind my gaze makes her blink.

"Sorry, sorry. That was inconsiderate of me."

"It's fine," I mumble. I walk over to get myself a glass from the cabinet next to Di's head. The last time I saw her, she'd just re-dyed her roots, and being up close to them now, I can see how much they've grown out.

"Promise me you'll really talk to your therapist about all your shit that's making you act like this. You should ask for help."

"I know." I fill the glass with cold water, then take a sip and continue to look straight down, waiting for the floor tiles to somehow move as a result of my focus. Di opens the cabinet back up, grabs the bag of pretzel bites, and leaves.

Chapter 47

The chairs in the dietician's waiting room are comfier than the ones in Dr. Ellis's. I do not let them fool me, though. I feel like a small child in a pediatrician's office or a dog at the vet; I don't care if it's for my own good, it's fucking scary, and I don't want to be here. I should get up, leave, and fucking tell Dr. Ellis that I went and that I'll eat more now along with some more convincing word vomit.

"Valerie Updike?" The nurse, young and pregnant, stands across the room from me and stares out in anticipation.

Sighing, I grab my bag and head toward her, keeping my head down.

"Hi there," she says with a smile wider than my mouth could probably ever physically stretch, and I follow her down the narrow fluorescent-lit hallway. She closes the door behind me in a small, cramped room with a paper-lined bed and a scale at its foot. *Fuck.* I meant to guzzle water before this. *Dammit.*

"So, there's a dress in the cabinet up here," she says, pointing up above her head until I nod. "And there's a bathroom just across the hall. We'll need a urine sample from you. It's just a formality. There are instructions on how to do that in there. Maya will be with you in a few minutes." Another huge smile, so big her eyes squint shut. I stare at her protruding belly and swollen breasts. I hope I never fuck up so badly I end up looking like *that*. Fat, waiting to have my life, not to mention my body, permanently ruined by a parasitic infestation of my own doing. A sour cocktail of fear and judgment remains until I go to pee in the fucking plastic cup, label it, and place it on the white rack they have across from the toilet. There are almost a dozen little yellow containers standing there like soldiers in an army ready for battle. Different heights, different tones, but all one family of misfits.

I've returned from peeing and have been waiting for a while. With my back cold and exposed in the billowing hospital gown, I hear a dull knock on the laminate door. Before I even get the chance to respond, a different woman's face peers between the wall and the cracked door before her gaze lands on me. She's tall and smiling so wide I am concerned her face may rip. Her teeth appear especially white in contrast to her dark skin, and her long, braided hair is tied up in a hot-pink ribbon.

"Hi there, Valerie. I'm Maya Kensington. Steven Ellis referred you to me?"

"Yeah, yeah, he did." She sits down across from me in a black desk chair and begins typing on an outdated computer, her back facing me. Little braids sway back and forth with the motion of her fingers on the tall black keys.

"Okay, we're just going to run through some *general information*, get your weight and some other things, and then chat a little. Sound good?" Another smile. I nod. She instructs me to make my way over to the scale, and my heart begins to beat so fast I'm worried I'm going to faint right in the middle of this poor excuse of a room. Stepping onto the black pedestal feels like balancing on the edge of the plank on a pirate ship. The crashing waves around me are going to lead to me falling into a vast, unwelcoming ocean whether I feel prepared or not.

After Maya is done balancing the scale, the number looks back at me menacingly. It's a pound heavier than I was this morning. Writhing inside are two delicate forces, one slightly betrayed and one slightly relieved. Did I really gain a pound? Or is my scale at home wrong? I did eat. Damn. Except this is convenient; I may be up a whole BMI percentage with that pound. Maya sighs and tells me I can get off now. She types the number into the computer and pulls up a list of questions that are too far from me to make out clearly. Whipping around her ponytail, she smiles and prepares to speak again.

"So, Valerie, what was the date of your last menstrual period?" Her long lashes blink at me brightly.

"Um, about…about sometime during summer."

"Do you know what month?"

"J-July, I think." I haven't gotten a period in almost two years. She asks me more questions, including if I've lost weight, to which I admit, and then she asks how much I think I've lost and why.

"Around ten pounds. I've just been struggling with mental-health issues that have really messed with my appetite. I've been trying to eat as much as I can recently, but it's been really difficult." Even I don't smell a whiff of any bullshit in my earnest voice.

"So, I saw you uploaded a food log like I requested. And you're vegan, I see?" I nod. She doesn't give me any trouble, surprisingly, and some relief washes over me when I realize it's a bullet I won't have to dodge. She gives a few recommendations on what to include in my diet and strongly encourages an increase in my calories, so I agree to eat more than I hypothetically did on this nonexistent day.

"Yeah, I definitely know I need to. I'm working up to it."

"*Otherwise*, Valerie…your weight, especially for your height, is dangerous. I'm going to get some tests done to see if there are any issues we need to be aware of as a result. Okay?"

"Uh, yeah."

"Alright, then. The nurse will be back in to see you shortly. It was great to meet you. See you soon." We shake hands, and Maya leaves, her ponytail swinging wildly as she closes the door behind her. The nurse comes back in seconds later to take my blood pressure and perform an EKG. Her hands are warm as they stick little circles all over my body that feel like suction cups. I've been abducted by extraterrestrial aliens who are performing bodily experiments on my vulnerable frame.

A few minutes later, after she's watched a computer that apparently is showing my heartbeat or some shit, I sit up and notice a rubber strap strangling my arm as if to prepare for a heroin injection. Or so I wish. Three little vials of blood are filled within seconds, and I tell myself I don't feel light-headed, even though I'm pretty certain I'm about to pass out.

"We should get back to you with the test results in a few days. Until then, just follow Maya's advice, whatever that may have been for you. Okay?" She gives me another million-dollar smile that's worthless in my book. Must be part of the employee training for everyone here. "You can just leave the gown on the bed and check out with the front desk. Okay?"

I nod, and Smiley Pregnant Nurse leaves, not making sure the door doesn't slam like Maya did. I rip off the gown but stop to look at myself in the full-length mirror against the tan door. With my feet together, the space between my thighs is more than a gap. It's like I don't even have thighs to have a gap between, just a void that my legs barely exist within. Turning to the side, there is little shape to my body, once somewhat adorned with muscular definition in my backside and down my legs. I remember having a slight bulge in my calves, seeing my quads tense when I lifted my leg up for a step, and even having baby biceps beneath a thin layer of feminine fat. There are times when I look in the mirror and see a ripped bodybuilder, in pristine aesthetic condition with nothing more to improve upon. Then, there are times like this, when I am not on top of the world, and I see a shell with little more than an inescapable lower belly pooch. If I am at the point where I am now, not quite on death's doorstep but definitely familiarizing myself with the neighborhood, and still not able to get rid of that shit, there's literally no way out. All this shit is a fucking scam; I'll still always wish for a longer torso, for smaller arms, for wider hips. Visible rib bones adorn my chest like lights on a Christmas tree. Except the season is long fucking over, and I still have poor little twinkling gold bulbs up months after the holidays have ended. I can't decide whether the voice in my head is praising my body or yelling at it, and if that can or will ever change. I pull on my jeans and hoodie and shuffle out quickly without truly listening to what that voice has to say. I ignore it, and it remains, quickly chirping in the back of my superglued-together wooden skull like forgotten, broken furniture stuffed in the back of an attic.

Chapter 48

For what I think is the first time, I'm at Dr. Ellis's office without makeup. It's not necessarily something I've cared about, but I'm typically coming from somewhere, made up for some other part of my day. I didn't go to my one class this morning, though, so I had no reason to go through the whole masking routine, and I don't give much of a shit anyway anymore. I'm curious as to what Dr. Ellis's reaction will be, or if he'll just hide his surprise. Without concealer, the gauntness of my face truly shows, and I enjoy the stares I get out in public. I'm just not sure if I'll appreciate the same spectacle from Dr. Ellis.

"H-hello, Valerie." Dr. Ellis's eyes seem restrained, as if they are attempting to gloss over. I follow him out of the waiting room and into his sun-filled office, plopping down into my usual mid-love-seat position. He blinks at me a few times while I'm adjusting myself.

"Hi there." I sniff back my runny nose.

"How was your class this morning?"

"Didn't go," I say flatly with a shrug. Dr. Ellis's brows furrow in concern.

"Are you feeling okay?"

"Yeah, I just really didn't feel like going. No point, anyway, since I'm not, like, staying in film anymore."

"But won't it still count toward your GPA?" He turns in his chair to face me directly. I shrug again, and my big gray sweater falls off my left shoulder, exposing my collarbones. Dr. Ellis's eyes follow my top as it drops, then his gaze breaks to the side and darts around the room as if he's looking for something. He shrugs as well, smooths out his yellow notepad, and adjusts his glasses.

"Are those shoes new?" I ask, noticing polished black loafers I've never seen before.

"Oh. No, they aren't. June has a thing for not liking black shoes, so I tend not to wear them."

"Even when you're at work without June?"

He laughs and scratches his temple. "I guess just a habit of mine."

"Well, *I* like them. You should wear them anyway." Dr. Ellis's face brightens but also reddens. "Really," I go on, feeling like there's nothing left to lose in this already imperfect situation. "You have good taste, don't second-guess it." He smiles and nods once, pushes up his already-high glasses, and smooths the already-smooth notepad. I slump back into the cushions.

"You met with Maya, the dietician?" My relaxed muscles tense up slightly at his words.

"Uh-huh. A couple days ago."

"And how did that go?"

"Um...I mean, it just kind of...went? Like, she weighed me, did some tests, and did some other general stuff. Nothing much happened during the appointment itself."

"And the tests? Do you know how they came back?" My breathing somehow refuses to continue without my manual probing. My mind pulls each little rib out and then inflates my tired lungs, releasing them slowly so they don't pop and crash as ribs concave back in.

"Um, she, or, the nurse lady, called me this morning." He blinks, waiting for me to continue. I'm too focused on continuously breathing to multitask.

"What did she say, Valerie?"

"Low *lymphocyte* count, asking me to come in again, I don't really know. I'll listen again to the voice mail after this." I see his slightly tanned hands firmly grab the sides of the paper so that the stack puffs out around his grip.

"I… Th-that sounds like something you really should do. Listen to that voice mail, I mean."

A thin smile forms on my face as he shuffles in the green armchair. "Are you okay?" I ask.

His large, dark eyes widen like he's a deer caught in headlights, debating whether to succumb to conversational annihilation or make a run for it. He settles on the former.

"Most likely just over-caffeinated. I'm glad to hear you went to your appointment and are making steps toward improving your health, though. Very glad to hear that." I don't return his misplaced punctuation of a nodding smile. Dr. Ellis halts the gesture and looks down at his sparse notes. In fact, I don't think he's written anything besides the date since I walked in.

"What kind of coffee do you get?" I don't feel like talking about myself. I don't want to give Di's advice the opportunity to manifest again through his guidance.

"Dark roast with a splash of milk and two Equals."

My mouth twists to pout on one side as my head cocks to the opposite side.

"Try it with coconut milk next time. Trust me."

"I like almond. I did get an oat-milk latte once as well, but I prefer normal coffee."

"Me, too. But I like mine black. Try it with the coconut milk next time, though, really."

Dr. Ellis gives a closemouthed smile, which I, this time, reciprocate. "I will do that. Thank you for the recommendation."

"Of course."

"Any changes with Jett or Di?" Again, my chest requires extra help to rise and fall as my body's resources are mostly allocated to my screaming mind.

"I ran into Di in the kitchen the other day. It was just weird. Like, she wasn't...wasn't mad at me, I guess. It was awkward and all, but she wasn't screaming or fighting with me. She was just kind of sad and rigid."

"Why did you assume she would be screaming at you? Weren't you the one who was offended?" My mind pauses a moment from its endless commotion to consider the statement.

Why wouldn't she be screaming at me if she were upset?

"I mean...I just kind of thought that's what she...would...do? I don't know, it's just what I imagined her response to seeing me after our whole shit storm would be." Dr. Ellis moves his pen up to his mouth and taps it against the corner of his lips a few times. I blink in curiosity at the thought visibly forming, anxiously waiting for it to emerge through words.

"You mentioned your mother often screamed at you often when you were younger, didn't you?" Again, my chest calls 911, and I have to be the first responder struggling to keep my heart beating.

"Yeah, yeah. I did."

"Perhaps you're assuming Di would have such an extreme or violent reaction because of what you became used to growing up, with such a tumultuous mother."

"That makes sense."

He continues to ask me about my assumptions for different types of behavior, tying it back to what I experienced for years, when I was always prepared for Mom's breakdowns, the drunken or, even more painfully but not as frightening, sober ones. It's much more difficult to relive the real past than the imagined present that stems from it. Maybe the Greg and mother I'm seeing are, in my mind's roundabout, convoluted way, trying to get me to do just that. Dr. Ellis eventually senses the darkness rising in my eyes to eventually cloud all of my senses, and he decides to end the session a little early. Three minutes early, according to the ticking generic black Office Depot clock above the door to the left. He never ends early; in fact, he usually goes slightly over, which is surprising since I know I'm his last client before the weekend.

"See you next week," I mutter as I get up, my voice audibly higher than I intended it to be.

"I will update you on the coconut milk in my coffee." As he opens the door for me, I feel Dr. Ellis's watch snag a few strands of my tousled hair as I exit swiftly.

Chapter 49

Di and I swiftly walk the several blocks to our favorite Thai place. I agreed to go mostly because she *had* asked me a full day in advance, so I had the chance to really prepare, and she provided no indications of patronizing me anymore. Her pace is slower than mine, with shorter strides, which makes me feel a bit antsy to move quicker. I wish I could run right now. Di's hair is now just long enough to style, so she's poufed it up a little with a deep side part to really expose her *love me* tattoo. Somehow I both envy and appreciate her ability to always steal the attention, without wanting to emulate it myself whatsoever.

I yank open the heavy glass door and pass it to Di, who struggles just as much.

"Jesus," she mutters as it slams in the metal frame behind her. Warm orange and red light illuminates the tan hostess podium.

"Two?" the hostess asks as she scurries over from across the dining floor. I nod, and she seats us near the window on the far end. As soon as she returns with water, I drink half of it, anxious to calm my stormy stomach and keep it from taunting my shaky mind.

"Well, you're thirsty," Di remarks. I nod enthusiastically. I find overdoing shit often removes suspicion. Unless you overdo overdoing it, in which case you end up suicidal and hospitalized. But I wouldn't know about that myself.

"I sweat a lot today, had a good workout." My mouth clenches in regret after proudly announcing what I thought to be a perfect fit for the conversation she initiated. "I mean, like, at the gym and all."

"Don't tell me you fucking ran again."

"No, God no." Calm now. Sometimes underdoing it also removes suspicion. Rarely does accuracy work, because we're all faking everything all the time so no one has any goddamn idea what a real reaction is.

"I was doing some *weight lifting*, believe it or not." I smile, and Di laughs. Phew.

"With what, a one-ounce dumbbell in each hand?" I roll my eyes at her in a grandiose swirl. Neither of us touch our menus; we know our orders already, and when a waitress comes up to take our drink orders, Di continues on with her meal request as well.

"*So*, I'll have a lemonade, the peanut spring rolls, and green curry, please. With tofu. And extra potatoes." Di yawns and hands over the laminated red-bordered menu without looking up at her.

"Oh, and I'm good with, uh, water. Just the ginger lover with brown rice, please." I slide the menu, the plastic cover ripped down the middle, toward the waitress, and she takes it and walks away, writing on her little notepad as she heads back into the kitchen. The restaurant is fairly crowded, it is a Saturday evening after all, and I'm thankful we're already seated as several groups have come in right after us.

"So. Any updates with Jett?" Di asks.

"I don't think there *will* be any more updates with Jett."

"You don't miss him?"

"Of course, I miss him. Just not as much as I don't want to deal with making up." The waitress brings Di's tall glass of lemonade with a small pink paper umbrella in the straw, and Di yanks it straight out of her hands like a child hypnotically reaching for candy. Without thanking the waitress, Di takes a long sip and exhales. I tighten my fists as I imagine the amount of sugar there must be in that.

"Okay, whatever. Once you have something to eat, maybe you'll lighten up and call him or something."

"Di, I don't want to call him during our dinner or anything."

"I formally give you permission."

"If I want to, I'll talk to him, like, later tonight or tomorrow maybe, even. *If* I want to." I lift the wet, uncomfortably dripping-with-condensation glass of water and take a sip as Di does the same with her lemonade. "Do you know if you got that job from a while ago? I meant to ask, sorry—"

She shakes her head and lets out a shallow laugh. "No, no, they told me they wanted someone with retail experience. Like, how is someone supposed to get a job when every entry-level position requires two years working somewhere else? It's a sign I should focus on my music." She leans back in the wicker chair, so much so that the scarlet cushion beneath her requires readjusting so as to not fall on the floor.

"Maybe. I say go for it."

"I thought you were skeptical of my creative abilities."

"Di, I fully support your SoundCloud escapades." She eyes me like she's not quite sure what to make of what I've just said. "I'm serious! Totally down to be front row at all your concerts. Here, at least. I'm not going to be a groupie." She pouts and makes a heart with her two hands, placing it in front of her chest in the center of the baby-blue tank top she has on. We go on to discuss some class projects we're working on and my lack of energy remaining for film projects. Di tells me to "screw film" because "art programs are fucking cults." I nod and drink the last of my water. The waitress comes to refill both of our glasses, even though Di hasn't taken a sip of her water, and then returns with our food. Di's curry sizzles, and metallic oil bubbles smile creepily on the top edge of the coconut milk. I look away, frightened by each bubble's Cheshire cat expression directed at me. Within seconds, Di's already taken a large bite of a spring roll, then she scoops up almost all of the peanut sauce with the remaining half. I cut up my ginger broccoli into small pieces, sectioning them out across the empty corner of my plate, then pierce one and pick up a perfectly crinkle-cut carrot with it. The vegetables taste strong and overly

347

salted, but I am almost confident that I've had enough water today to eat slightly more sodium than usual. Not confident enough, though. I hastily wipe off excess sauce from every vegetable before consuming it.

"You want the last one?" Di asks me, her voice muffled with food, as she points her fork toward a spring roll. I shake my head, actually considering it, since raw vegetables and a sliver of tofu wouldn't change my intake much today. I can't go forward with a sudden change in plans, though.

"Thanks, but you can have it." As soon as the last word leaves my lips, Di takes the spring roll, dips it into the peanut sauce, and dunks it into her creamy green curry as well.

"Next fucking level." I laugh wearily as she continues to dip the remaining portion into her curry and then wipes her hands thoroughly, moving on to her entrée. "You really should have some of this. Coconut milk's great for putting on weight."

"I'm fine," I spit back, then take a deep breath in and out. "I'm seeing a dietician," I decide to divulge. "You can calm down." The vulnerability is curated, but it feels surprisingly relieving to tell her. Di smiles and nods at me meaningfully.

As I continue to take small bites of each individual portion of food, I notice someone sitting down behind Di's head, someone I recognize. He doesn't notice me, or if he does, he decides not to react at all.

He's with a girl, red-haired and dark-eyed, and he's wearing the red flannel I remember all too well. The girl's long red nails slide down the menu as she opens it gently, the exact same one with a giant chasm down the laminated center that I just held. I drop my fork and stare at her, hoping the same rip happens right down her middle and through the rest of her body.

"You going to have any of your rice?" Di's voice shocks me, and I jump a little.

"Oh, um…let me just take a little, I guess. You can have the rest." Di thinks I don't like rice because I've told her that several times as a scapegoat tactic. She takes the little bowl after I get a spoonful and dunks it into her large bowl of curry, stirring it up forcefully with the white rice she already got with her order. She's just ruined the separate perfectness of each portion of food. Except her meal was already tainted in the first place, her curry

being too complicated and mixed together to offer any of the satisfaction from eating each separate part.

My eyes move to right above Di's slightly hunched-over form and watch Vic as he reads his menu while pushing back his long black hair and tapping his feet. He'll either order pad Thai or pad see ew because he loves noodles. Kind of like Greg, except Greg doesn't like spicy food, so I never did take him to Asian places. Vic's current resting face molds into a smile as he begins to speak with the red-haired girl, and I replay him bursting out in hysteria at my suffering as more and more of his teeth emerge in conversation. My eyes slam shut as if to save me from fully dying of pain.

"You...okay?" Di asks, blinking at me. A little piece of bamboo shoot is right below her lip.

"I...I know that guy. Behind you, near the front." She turns around, and I look down in worry that he or someone else will see, but he remains focused on the girl in front of him. The girl leans on her forearms toward him as her long curls fall onto the white tablecloth.

"Uh...which one?"

"The one with the ginger girl, near the door on the left."

My eyes fix firmly on Vic like a jet locked in on a bomb target.

"There's another girl sitting across from that ginger."

"No, like, the black-haired guy. Red flannel, right there."

She turns back to watch as I nod toward Vic.

"Um…yeah, Val, there's another girl across from the one I'm looking at. Asian, with the bleached hair."

"The long-haired redhead?"

"Yeah, yeah, whatever." She shakes her head, misunderstanding and obviously looking at a different table. I give up and also become too on edge to keep much of an appetite, so I set down my fork and also put my napkin on the table as I get up.

"I'll be right back," I mutter to Di, then head toward the bathroom on the opposite side of the restaurant. Past Vic.

Striding past him, I expect his eyes to at least flutter nervously as I walk by his chair, or maybe the pull will be so strong, he'll turn to look at me completely. Maybe he'll feel so compelled by my presence that he'll even say hi, out of not knowing what else to say, and then introduce this mystery redhead with long hair and long nails and a camo coat.

He doesn't. Not even when I walk back to my seat extra slow and extra loudly, unzipping and buttoning my jacket right by his ear, and not even when I cough directly next to his chair. Sitting down, I watch both of them order with the same waitress we had, reading his lips as they say, "Thank you," in his typical one-word enunciation of the phrase. I wonder if he says *love you* the same way. I wonder if that night he will say *love you* like that or really draw it out, *I...love...you,* pausing nervously between each word as if balancing on uneven footing. In my mind, I reach out and grab his neck, pierce it with my stubby nails, and write out *love you* across his forehead in blood, then wipe the excess on his hair to hold it back so that the phrase is clearly visible. Di's forehead tattoo would serve as a reference to make sure I spelled everything correctly.

The clang of Di's lemonade glass onto the table shakes me into remembering I have food in front of me. I spent all day dreaming about this moment just to have it ruined beyond comprehension, pummeled and obliterated by the atomic bomb of an enemy's presence.

After our entrees are taken away, we agree to get sticky rice and mango, since I'd planned on factoring it into my daily calories and didn't have my afternoon snack as a result. Thankfully, Di doesn't remember that I've said I don't like rice. It's brought out, and I take a small bite of the creamy coconut-milk-saturated rice; it feels like a human carcass in my mouth as I watch Vic eat his noodles. From this distance, I take a guess that he's eating pad Thai.

The fatty, refined bite of food in my mouth morphs into Vic's corpse, specifically his brain, that I'm swallowing after stabbing and strangling him dead. Each grain of rice is really a string of cranial muscle. Each small piece of mango is a cluster of his neurons and memories, and I'm devouring them all, wishing I could do the same to some of my own. I'm destroying him from the core out, like he did to me, that one night last year, by deciding not to say the three words that my life depended on.

Chapter 50

Three years ago. My mother's head leaned back against the black leather seat, her chin tilted up. Her veiny hands grabbed the wheel just enough for it to remain steady. We were going well over the speed limit, all the way in the left-hand lane, with everything around us seemingly traveling backward in fear, going far, far, away.

I cracked the window to give me some relief from the overwhelming smell of alcohol and cigarettes, but her head jolted toward me as I reached for the button. My hand automatically darted back in between my thighs. Thighs bigger than I have now. Thighs I still promise myself I will never see again.

Somehow, she still possessed enough control to slow down as we exited the freeway. My heart did not slow, however, remaining on edge in anticipation of having to position myself auspiciously in the likelihood that we would get in a wreck. If it was on my side, I'd bend down and shield my face. If it was on hers, I'd quickly shove her toward the impact then shoot against my passenger door as tightly as possible.

"You really are lucky I decided to take you out here," she slurred.

"Mm-hmm," I muttered, hoping it was enough to please her ego but not too much to make her keep going.

"Hopefully you *pass* and all. That wouldn't be nice if you failed, making me drive the hour for all of no reason, now would it?"

"No, no." My hands were pressed so tightly together that I'm worried one of them will break in half from the pressure. My eyes and jaw were locked in their respective safes, with no known code to remove them, just attempts at mindless shaking and toying with the lockbox itself like my mother's voice was doing.

The SUV halted to a stop, parking diagonally in a straight parking spot. The front wheels sat unapologetically over the yellow line, and many other cars were piling into the lot. Probably on lunch break. I wished I'd stayed in school that day instead of getting permission to leave. I should've waited until Dad was back in town. Except Dad would've been working during the day. And Mom doesn't have an excuse not to take me to do my driver's test

because she doesn't really do shit. Then again, she doesn't really give a shit about not doing shit, either.

"Alrighty," she announced loudly. "Let's get this crap over with." Inside the unwelcoming, moldy DMV building, I pulled a ticket number and picked a seat in the waiting room. Part of me didn't want my mother anywhere near me. Part of me wanted her next to me so no one would think anything of us. She placed her dark-pink faux-leather purse on the plastic seat to my left and got up, walking around the crowded area and eyeing everything as if the room were an empty art exhibit. Her lavender off-the-shoulder dress that looked like she'd outgrown it in high school, which was probably when she'd gotten it, making her a point of even more scrutiny. Large fake breasts almost overflowed from the elastic top band, her gold chain necklace squished in between. I felt like that necklace. It was smothered in silicon while I was smothered in equally ill-fitting parenting. Finally, Mom came to sit down next to me. My jaw clenched even tighter to prevent myself from sneezing at the overwhelming scent of Jennifer Lopez perfume and lingering Corona.

After nearly thirty minutes of playing on my phone, my ticket number, 337, was finally called, and I got up to fill out my paperwork before my actual driver's test. The woman who greeted me was large and much shorter than me, with bright-blue eyeshadow. I leaned down significantly to shake her soft hands.

"Raquel," she said in a slight Spanish accent. "Valerie?" She pronounced my name carefully, as if sounding it out: *Va-ler-ie?*

"Yeah, yeah," I said, nodding perkily, relieved to have left my mother's life-sucking side. We walked outside to the row of cars used for the tests. Typically, it's standard to use your own vehicle, but given the size of my mother's car and the implied understanding that she would never let me touch the wheel of that Suburban (that her unemployed self paid off with "child support" meant for yours truly), we had to drive an hour out here to a location where they provided sedans. Raquel stopped at a small red Corolla and slid into the passenger seat. I gingerly stepped inside the driver's side, struggling to adjust the seat to my height, and eventually clicked in my seat belt with a sigh. Raquel continued to

fill out some paperwork as I sat there, and I began to sweat and tap my hands on the strangely oily gearshift.

"Okay, so, we, uh, we're gonna do the parallel parking first. So reverse the vehicle and park it between the two cones on the other side of the lot."

She handed me the keys, and I successfully reversed and approached the orange traffic cones labeling where to parallel park. I knew if I didn't pass this portion of the test, I wouldn't be able to get my license at all, since so many points were allocated to this section. And failing would mean upsetting my mom. Which I knew; I'd practiced this maneuver countless times in my dad's car, with him helping me pull in between parked cars on his street.

"Okay, good job. Now, exit the parking lot and turn right onto the expressway," Raquel stated flatly after I'd finished parallel parking. Despite her monotonous tone, my heart soared, and I felt weightless. Mom wasn't going to yell at me because I was going to *finish* this.

Following Raquel's instructions, I turned when she told me to several times, and we ended up in a dilapidated residential neighborhood with plywood houses and overgrown yards. The area

358

scared me some, but I was sure anyone living here was used to student drivers passing by. As she wasn't telling me to turn, I kept going until seeing a car to my right approaching a stop sign. I didn't have a stop sign on my side, but the driver eyed me nervously, an older man in a hood and a jacked-up purple truck. I quickly slowed and motioned for him to go in front of me.

"Why did you do that?" Raquel immediately stammered, annoyed. "You have right of way. He had a stop sign."

"I—I—I know, I'm sorry, I just thought I'd let him go—" I stopped as I saw her deduct points.

"Go, go, you're holding up traffic!" A car honked behind us as she waved her hands at me to keep going, writing more on the subtraction side of her sheet. The rest of the drive, I attempted to be especially precise, but there were still a few times when she remarked on what I was doing, saying I was turning on my blinker too early or not slowing down enough before turns.

"You got...let's see...thirty-six. You had to get"—my heart plummeted—"thirty-five to pass. So you did it." She quickly added her signature to the form and took the keys. "Take this form to the office on the side, and they'll finish everything." I didn't even get the chance to thank her before I saw Raquel and her blue eyeshadow walking back into the DMV. I squealed and danced my feet on the thin mat of the Corolla. In a jump, I picked up the form and ran to the line of students holding the same paper waiting to get their provisional licenses.

I signed the paper eagerly once it was handed to me, not even taking a moment to curse the braces that seemed to fill up the entire photo. My signature stood as proudly as I did, unabashedly traversing the line given for it to rest on. I then stuffed the paper into my back pocket and went inside to look for my mother.

She was just outside the door smoking a cigarette and talking to a man who looked like he'd be asking me for pennies on the street. Upon seeing me, she quickly stubbed out the American Spirit and blinked at me, pretending I hadn't seen. Often, I was convinced she didn't even pretend. She fully believed in whatever worked most effectively in the story engineered by her poisoned mind.

My mother continued to blink at me as if waiting for me to initiate the conversation. My pride began to wither, and I almost forgot what had just happened.

"Oh," I said, pulling out the paper license from my jeans. "I… Yeah." She blinked at me a few times, then gathered her purse from off the ground and coughed.

"Well, that's good, at least. Nice to meetcha." The man beside her nodded and breathed out a plume of gray smoke. I followed her back into the Suburban, hit with even more of the scent of death and degradation. Hopefully, she wasn't still drunk. How ironic it would be if I could've saved my life by driving us now. I could legally, but really, I couldn't, as to even suggest doing so would offend my mother deeply. Probably to the point of rage. Throughout the drive home, I gripped the door handle, uncertain of her state. Uncertain if I was hopeful for getting a safe ride back or if some part of me truly hoped this would be our last drive, my last breath, and I would never get my own first drive.

Chapter 51

Ever since passing out in the stairwell, I've been eating a little more, so I don't get all freaked out about my heart anymore. I watched some recovery video where the girl explained how not all calories go toward gaining weight, some just go toward repairing organs and shit, so I figured if I upped mine a little, they could go toward helping my heart settle the fuck down. Maybe. Except after a week, I've gone up two pounds, I can feel myself absolutely ballooning today, and I want to rip all my insides out and pummel them on the sidewalk. Three months ago, at my lowest weight, I remember waking up and feeling so lightweight, so ethereal, that I believed I could float away every morning as soon as my feet touched the ground. Now, looking in the mirror and turning to the side, I look like I'm five months pregnant. My stomach is already rumbling, like it was before going to bed last night, but I grit my teeth and pull out my workout clothes. Obviously, by the way I look, my heart is long repaired, and now I'm just a gross fucking failure.

I go to pee. When I come back, I silently pull out the scale from under my bed, as I do every morning. Patricia's never woken up from it, since she's a heavy, late sleeper, but I start each day in a state of panic as I eye her nervously before turning around to step onto the scale. I get on and off quickly, watching the weight calibrate high above what I truly am, then drop back to zero and invite me to step on once again. Maybe one day, the number won't change at all when I step on.

The number goes up two pounds from the two I've already gained. I keep stepping back onto the smooth metal, waiting for it to correct itself. It doesn't. In fact, it goes up one-fourth of a pound as I continue to stand on it. Without caring if I wake Patricia, I loudly stuff the scale back under my bed. I put leggings, a top, socks, and shoes on my pudgy body quickly without a thought, like it's second nature. Grabbing a thick running jacket, I sprint out the door, down the stairs, and out into the street without even stopping to put in headphones. As my pace quickens, I set my watch to track my calories and begin to escape out of my body. It will keep going even if I'm not there; it will stay steady even if my mind wanders; my legs will tread evenly even if my heart goes out. The cold wind strikes my rib cage, which is broken and jagged, and my untreated burn wounds, which are scarred and decomposing. They're hidden from sight by my clothes, this thick navy jacket nearly shielding me from even appearing as a person, but I feel them all too clearly. No matter how excruciating the pain is, my legs will still go on. My legs are immortal, rusting at the ankles and knees, but immortal. My heart will cease to exist. My mind will deteriorate. But I will always return to the paces and strides as I traverse the world.

I make it to the park at the far end of the city where I usually turn around, but I know, with my weight gain, my body can handle much more now. Maybe this is a good thing. Maybe I'm stronger than ever.

The road veers to the right, turning into a more industrial area with smoke plumes rising out of factories I didn't know existed in the city. Getting closer, I avoid running too close to the groups of homeless people huddled together. Like snakes at my feet, I dodge their legs and their trash. My legs know exactly how to maneuver and how to remain untouched.

I finally run so far east that I reach as far as I can go. My hands grip the chain-link fence overlooking polluted water as my chest rises and falls furiously. It's upset at my legs, but my legs know better, and my legs know my chest can handle more than it thinks it can. The water crashes against concrete beneath me. I can feel a sharp vibration with each wave. I begin to turn around but stop when I see someone in front of me. My mind stops, my heart stops, my chest stops, and even my legs stop. They are not quite strong enough to move my large body from staring right into the eyes of evil incarnate herself.

My mother stands directly in front of me, her hands on her hips, which are covered by a tight black mini-dress I recognize all too well. On her arm is a pink faux-leather purse. On her feet are clear plastic heels, yellowing with wear, banded around the ankle with a silver ribbon. Her face is the same as I last remember it three years ago when I left and never looked back: overly tanned foundation sinking into deep, clogged pores and cheap black eyeshadow rimming dark eyes. Her bangs are grown out and parted in the middle to reveal an only slightly wrinkled forehead, a misleading facade for the havoc within her. The smell of her rancid

perfume fills my nostrils as I begin to effortlessly leave my body. I'm the only human ever able to fly.

However, when she begins to speak, I find my legs pulling me down and forcing me to remain present with her. My thin ankles and knobby knees are adequate anchors to stabilize my half-functioning brain.

"You wouldn't be goin' through all this *bullshit* if you hadn't left me," she snarls. "You are too messed up on your own to know any better than to screw your whole damn life up. I'm the only reason you got through your childhood. The way you are now? *Not* how I raised you. Look at you! Look at you!" Her breasts bounce up and down grotesquely. I squint my eyes, hoping to see her go away, hoping for silence. All I ever want is silence.

"I'm sorry," I squeeze out from tense vocal cords.

"Oh, you're not *sorry*. Why don't you *love* me, Valerie?" When my mother says my name, the electricity inside me combusts and catalyzes my inevitable death. "I love you. My daughter, my *baby*... All I did for you? Raised you, fed you, cared for you? And you cut me out of your life for *years*?" The pain in my chest from the explosion inside is too much for me to bear.

Suddenly, I'm seven again, asking to be excused from the dinner table. Except I've gained weight, so I'm not eating today at all. I'm not even sitting down at the goddamn table.

My ankles overpower my terrified mind and soar me away from the fence, out of the smoky airspace of gray factory buildings, and back onto familiar sidewalk concrete on the way back to my dorm.

"Don't you dare leave me again! *I am your mother!*" Mom's voice booms in the chill air like dust rippling after a meteor crash. Her words echo endlessly in my mind, scarring the sides of my wooden skull with deep crevices of profanity. I am a school desk vandalized by reckless students.

Snot drips from my numb nose and seeps into my mouth, mixing with tears emerging from my wind-pierced eyes. I am not crying, I cannot imagine responding to such an unworthy person in such an intimate way, but my eyes burn at the speed of the wind hitting my face. The sensation of salt on my taste buds panics me as I think of gaining water weight from sodium, which stops me in my tracks on the sidewalk. It's just snot and tears. Without even considering it, my body shuts down as I contemplate how much

I'm bloating. I feel lost as I uncontrollably begin to spit out all the saliva in my mouth, possibly saturated with salt, poisonous salt, which I doubt is actually there, but I must ensure it isn't anyway. As I stand there, my chest huffing violently and my body shocked by the sudden stop, my eyes suddenly do begin to well with actual tears. My legs are no longer quite powerful enough to sustain running, so I walk the rest of the way back. I find it hard to balance firmly on even ground. I find it easy to choke on tears when my throat is already almost entirely closed up, parasitically absorbed by its creator.

The security guard stares at my swollen, puffy face as I saunter inside and make my way to the elevator. When I get back to my room, I don't even shower. I climb into bed and hope that I burned enough calories.

Chapter 52

"You sure you don't want any?" Di asks, holding out the end of her blue marbled pipe to me. She coughs a little on lingering smoke and blows away the tiny clouds hovering around her face.

"No, thanks. I think it makes me too panicky and shit." I fall back against the wall and scoot lower on her bed. The green sheets have a new dark stain that I point at with curiosity.

"Fucking ramen broth. Anna scared the shit out of me last night when I was trying to eat and edit some tracks." She lights up the bowl and exhales, sending a thick plume straight up like a dolphin spewing water out of a blowhole.

"Eh, it's not that bad. So, you said you *met someone?*" I pout playfully. She chokes on her breath again, loudly this time, and the shrieking sound hits the walls with the force of a baseball pitcher.

"Goddamn," Di says, reaching for her water bottle. "Yes, I met someone. Her name is Iris. She's pretty cool."

"Where'd you meet this Iris?" She rolls her eyes at my overly enthusiastic inquiry.

"She applied for the job at Round Two, too, and didn't get it, too. She got my number then but just recently texted me."

"Is her hair purple?"

"What?"

"Like her name. Iris means *purple*. I figured maybe her hair was purple." Di looks at me like I've said the most profoundly incorrect statement ever, and I burst out laughing. "Okay, alright, she doesn't have purple fucking hair." The smell of weed arrives in another wave as she lights the last of her mostly burned bowl.

"Her hair's brown. Just brown. Like poop."

"I guess I need to meet this Iris."

"As soon as I get to meet Jett." Her jaw goes limp as she acknowledges her unintentional stab. "Sorry, sorry. Didn't mean to bring him up."

"I know, I know. It's fine."

"Want a hit to make you feel better?" Against the better judgment of my pained gut, I accept the meagerly filled pipe and light the remaining little green fragments, sifting around the charred pieces that cover most of the bowl with the tip of the lighter. The smoke writhes around my throat like an octopus being eaten alive. Finally, the smoke surrenders to the acids of my stomach and lies dead within my abdomen. I exhale its indigestible remains.

Quickly, my heartbeat begins its rapid ascent to try and run away from the unfamiliar substance. My mind is too preoccupied by the discomfort in my chest to have time to fixate on seeing my mother like it has been nonstop for the past few days. It relishes in the present anxiety as if it were a knife blade striking across my arm, as if I were brave enough to totally escape the chasms of my thoughts by doing such a thing. Except my cowardice proves I deserve to wallow in the labyrinth of my own doing.

"Yeah, okay, maybe you shouldn't smoke," Di remarks as she notices my feet tapping against the bed frame. I nod and swallow, focusing on striking each heel against the metal with equal strength at the exact same pace.

"You only took, like, one hit, though. Just breathe," Di instructs. I nod vigorously.

"It's fine, I'm fine. Tell me more about Iris."

Di rambles about Iris's interest in film noir and Alfred Hitchcock, and I'm immediately slightly angered by this Iris, who I haven't even met yet, because she is probably more informed about film and cultured than I am. The burning inside me flares up increasingly with the extra gasoline of frustration.

"Have you, like, gone out on a date yet or anything?"

"I'm getting there, I'm getting there. Trying not to come on too strong. I might suggest coffee sometime soon, if it feels right."

"You can't suggest Harry's. Harry's is *our* place." Di looks at me curiously, then swallows and itches her forehead tattoo.

"Yeah, yeah, okay. I'll suggest, like, the Red Onion or something. So we can eat there, too."

"Fucking gross."

"Entitled vegan."

I throw the pillow I'm leaning on at her, and she lets it hit her slouched face without wincing. Di leans back and begins to laugh. I begin to feel disconnected, knowing she's descended out of my level of consciousness and will continue to get lower and lower. Di always gets so fucking tired when she smokes weed. She already has her eyes closed.

"I guess I'll head out, then, if you're just going to fall asleep on me," I joke, my voice still shaking from the unwelcome

alien substance. She lets out a grunt but doesn't move at all, so I slide off her bed slowly and make my way out of her dorm room quietly. I'm in old checkered sweatpants that belonged to Vic but that I kept anyway. And my Batman slippers. Even though I'm only going down the hall to my own room, I pop on the hood of my black hoodie to hide from anyone happening to pass me. I wonder if the people who don't know me on my floor are scared of me. I hope they are.

I get closer to the other end of the floor where my room is without passing anyone until familiar Vans appear several dozen feet ahead of me. My eyes blink slowly in frustration. It really can't be. I don't have time for this shit. I don't have the energy for this shit. It's all being spent on killing the poisonous smoke still running rampant inside my veins.

"Val." Jett's voice is firm, not loud. Just firm enough to reach me from across the hall. The red exit sign above him flickers. I feel like I'm in an old horror film, with his face illuminated in red with everything else oversaturated in fluorescent light. "Val, can we talk at least?"

I sigh, walk up to my door, and open it, allowing him to enter before me. Thankfully, Patricia isn't there. He pulls out my desk chair and slides onto it, leaving me alone to hop up on my bed.

"Look, it isn't you...*doing* anything, or anything like that," I say. "I'm just really, like, down right now. I'm sorry." Just like I did on Di's bed, I tap my feet against the bed frame as I lean back against the wall. I remember again that I've just smoked, and suddenly my mind punishes me for not panicking this whole time. I just want a fucking break.

"You're not making any fucking sense. I have no idea what's really going on with you. You're being so vague. I don't know what's happening that's making it so difficult for you." His dark eyes don't waver as they stare me down, though I cannot seem to pull mine away from the tips of my slippers.

"I don't think you...*really* give a shit," I say. "Like, you *think* you do, you really do think so, but there's no way you could care about me."

"Val—"

"And I don't say that for sympathy or to make you feel bad, I really don't. Like, at all." Now I do look him in the eyes, entirely serious and devoid of emotion. He itches his bare shoulder where his thin military green shirt has fallen, over a large mandala tattoo I seem not to have paid much attention to before.

"I *do* give a shit. If I didn't, why would I keep trying to get through to you?"

"Sex, probably. I don't know." Jett cocks his head in annoyance.

"Don't say that."

"Sorry. I told you I was fucked."

"You aren't fucked."

"Jett, I'm fucking evil."

"Are you trying to make some kind of a joke here?"

"What?" I grimace and lean back. He throws his hands up in an effort to calm me down, but I'm far too riled up already.

"You think this whole thing is a joke?" I spew the words from my mouth carelessly.

"No, Val. I didn't say that."

"Well, I think you meant it."

"Jesus…" Jett closes his eyes and rubs his temples. "Okay, you obviously don't want any help with…*whatever*," he says, waving his hands like he's talking about something make-believe, "*whatever's* going on."

"I can't believe you don't think that I am *actually* going through shit."

"It's not that I don't believe you, Val, it's that I can't fucking help you if you keep everything from me and then get offended at everything I do to try and get you to open up!" I keep my head down and fail to continue breathing. I just keep tapping my feet through the silence, waiting for him to get up and leave so I can curl up and pretend he doesn't exist. Pretend I don't exist.

"When you want help, I'll be here. But I won't while you're being really weird and acting like this."

"I do want help, though!" My oxygen-deprived chest lurches forward, and now I'm sitting on the edge of my bed with my forearms resting on my knees. "I just don't really know how to explain what's going on because you'll think I'm crazy."

"I already think you're crazy, Val." His voice is still tense and wounded, but we both laugh a little. Jett reaches his hands out to grab mine.

I sigh. "I told you...I told you my brother died, right?"

His dark eyes blink in affirmation. Heat within me stirs as I think of Greg, and it explodes when I begin to talk about him. I hope I can get everything out before grief burns me alive once again, my body already dust turned to ashes.

"I...I see him sometimes," I continue, my voice unintentionally getting louder and breaking at the end as I'm forced to swallow without meaning to. My breathing speeds up, and all of a sudden, I'm just trying to catch my breath and stay alive. Jett comes over and hugs me. I bury my head in his green shirt until I really am about to suffocate and then come up for a huge breath of air as if I'm a deep-sea diver. He grabs my hands again and looks at them, then looks back up at me. I see myself, tired and disheveled, in his eyes and have to look away. As soon as I gaze down, though, his lips softly meet mine unexpectedly and confuse me even more, and I have to focus on my breath once again.

Chapter 53

The door shutting after Jett leaves shakes the walls of my dorm

room. I curl under my bedsheets, too wrapped up in my confusion

to feel anything. I'm just trying to follow my thoughts, follow

them until I understand *some* part of myself. I hear Patricia's voice

echoing down the hall and panic, reaching my toes out long to grab

my underwear from the end of my bed without luck. I lean up from

underneath the covers onto all fours in search of the blue lace

thong and pull it up my legs as I hear the door open and close.

Patricia keeps talking, and I can just barely make out her shadow

through my covers. I pop my head up and see her staring at me,

confused, and then grab something out of her desk and walk out

again. I jump out of bed and get dressed before she can reenter.

I might've felt glamorous if I'd had my makeup done

beforehand, smeared, and accompanied by that post-sex glow

that's always in the movies, even though it's not like I really

experienced anything like that. At least, not *yet.* It was only my

first real time, I guess, apart from Vic, which I don't really know

whether to count or not. But even none of that was particularly glowing. Alright, it's not going to happen. Even with the most skillful, thoughtful partner, my thoughts would somehow get in the way and fuck it up. I'd fuck up the fucking. *Fuck.*

My flushed face looks back at me from the mirror artificially, like an exhausted old man appearing alert due to caffeine. The euphoric bliss begins to melt away, partially due to Patricia-induced panic, and partially due to my mind coming back online. Nothing had really been solved, per se. Jett was confused by my confusing explanation—an intentionally confusing one, so that he'd get painfully lost and accept defeat. Instead, he didn't, and he just kept trying to make a clear path through the litter-crowded streets of my words, and I ended up the lost one. I had become too engrossed in trying to make him confused to remain coherent myself, which ended in him comforting me, which ended up with him in my bed, which ended up with a condom wrapper balancing on my overflowing trash, which ended up with me confused, tired, and now hyper. I sniff back my suddenly runny nose and watch one snot tear drip onto my upper lip. I wipe it away with the sleeve of my long-sleeved shirt and push my hair back behind my ears, asking myself what I need to get done now. I reach for my phone and notice a text from Di from more than an hour ago. It's a photo, and I quickly open it.

I blink a few times to make sure I'm seeing it correctly. She's on the street holding a few hundred dollar bills fanned open in her pudgy little grip. She didn't send any text to go with it, so I quickly call her out of both concern and curiosity.

"Hey," she answers.

"Di. What the hell?"

"What?" She laughs, and I can tell from the surrounding noise she's walking.

"Your picture! All that money?"

"Oh yeah! I have a *jo-ob*!"

"Really?" I lean back against my desk, the edge painfully hitting my back through my gray sweatpants.

"Yeah. Iris hooked me up. I clean trumpets."

"What? Iris? You clean *trumpets*?" I look out of the window in front of me at the almost-set sun penetrating the room with its golden rays. Di's breath on the other end remains steady and unamused by what is probably a misunderstanding on my end.

"Yeah. Iris's dad owns an instrument shop. I said I was, like, a rapper and all—"

"Oh my God—"

"Oh, come on. I said I was, like, in the industry, even if it's not exactly what I think he assumed, and he said he needed someone to polish the instruments in his store. The last person, like, died or something. I don't know. Anyway, I scrubbed trumpets for *hours* today. He paid me triple because it was, like, triple overtime or something."

"Jesus. Wow, Di. I'm…happy for you? Sorry, I'm just shocked." I laugh, and she coughs a little. It's a heavy cough. She's definitely smoking.

"Yeah, no, you're good." She exhales loudly. "I'm gonna go, okay? See you, like tomorrow. Or whenever."

"Yeah, tomorrow's cool. Okay." I hang up first and drop my phone back onto my desk, pushing against the edge with my hands and dropping my head.

I still feel pangs of humiliation every time I visualize Patricia's confused face looking at me popping out from my covers in a panic. I don't know what she saw or what she thought she saw, and that uncertainty makes me embarrassed. And sleeping with Jett after all the shit I've done to him: *What the fuck have I just done?* I still feel residual guilt about ignoring Jett, and now I feel filthy over what I've just let happen. Not because of some premarital religious shit, but because I feel like maybe I took advantage of him. He shouldn't still care about me.

I'm nauseous on air and hungry but nonresponsive to food. My mind is electrified, running at too high of a speed for words to latch on to. I sit down and place my head in my hands. My crotch feels sore, so I try to squish my thighs together, but there is barely anything there to touch. I curl into a ball and try to breathe, feeling lonely, guilty, and cold. I'm shaking, chewing on my own tongue, imagining what my mother would say to me right now if she knew what was going on. Where would she be in this room? She'd probably lean against Patricia's bed and ruffle the sheets mindlessly. Maybe this time in low-rise light-wash jeans and that Harley-Davidson crop top she always said fit just like it did in high school. No. *No!* I slam my eyes shut in an attempt to do the same with my mind. *If you think of her, she'll come here. If you give your mind any slack, it'll take the whole goddamn rope and run.*

It'll run solar systems away while you're choking to death on the end of the fucking leash.

I've just called Di, so I can't really turn to her right now. I just fucked Jett, I'm mad at myself about fucking Jett, and I'm honestly a little mad at Jett for fucking me right now, so I don't want to talk to him. I do want to talk, though, to emit these noxious fumes inside, which I cannot make sense of. I don't really know if this is my official first time or if that even matters, but I guess it is, in reality, and it's a pretty shitty one to look back on when you think about how you lost your v-card. Not that I had higher expectations at this point in my life. In this denouement.

Scrolling through my phone, I open my contacts to see hundreds of names, meaningless names, I-Wonder-Where-They-Are-Nows and They-Knew-Me-Before-Really-Bads. I reach *Z*, which doesn't list any names, and race back up to the top in frustration. However, as the list zips back up, a name catches my eye. He's professionally liable to care. He's *medically* forced to answer my call. I click on the name, Steven Ellis, without giving myself time to feel self-conscious. The boiling stew about to pour out of my mouth is blocking any neuronic pathways of cautiousness.

The phone rings three times, and I pull it away from my ear, deciding to forfeit and hang up before a voice-mail message indicates my defeat. Suddenly, I hear coughing erupt.

"H-hello?" His voice is rough sounding once he recovers from his attack. "Hello?"

"Uh, D-Dr. Ellis?" My breathing is sharp. It interferes with my speech.

"Valerie?" I hear shuffling.

"Yeah, it's me, I'm sorry, I don't know if I can do this, b-but I'm not doing well, and I'm confused, and—"

"Calm down, calm down," he says softly. "Breathe. Now, what's happening?"

I sniff and swallow. I clear my throat.

"I'm scared, I just saw Jett, and—"

"Are you okay? Are you hurt?"

"No, no! I'm just scared, I keep thinking of my mom, and I keep…I keep thinking that I'm going to make her come here, and I'll see her, and—"

"Where are you right now, Valerie?"

"I'm at my dorm."

"Can you make it to my office?"

"Yeah, yeah, I—I can walk over—"

"I'm heading over from my apartment right now. You'll probably get there before me… Just wait in the lobby. I'll have to let you up, since it's a Sunday. Okay? Valerie, are you with me?" I nod to myself and grip the phone fiercely with my right hand.

"Yeah, yeah. Okay."

"See you then, okay?"

"Okay."

"Alright. Take care." He hangs up, and I step onto aching bones to pull on my shoes and coat.

Chapter 54

I wait on the black worn-leather couch in Dr. Ellis's office building
lobby, looking out the floor-to-ceiling glass windows and wishing I
hadn't called him. I should've just made myself cry or something. I
didn't even bring my afternoon granola bar snack with me.
Dammit.

The large open space, filled with outdated eighties
furniture, is empty except for myself and the security guard sitting
behind a desk who keeps eyeing me suspiciously. I do look like a
wreck, tapping my foot against the sofa frame with my hair matted.

"I-I'm waiting for someone who works here," I declare
across the space once my annoyance requires release. I see his tired
eyelids blink dismissively.

The revolving doors behind me whoosh open. Turning
around, I see Dr. Ellis, in Lululemon sweatpants and a short-
sleeved T-shirt, rushing in like it's an emergency room. I simply
stare as he eyes me closely and strides toward the black couch.

"Valerie. Are you alright? Come on, let's go upstairs." He
hits the elevator button, and it immediately opens. Inching forward

on my tiptoes, I pass his arm, which is keeping the doors from shutting. He continuously gives me a once-over, taking an inventory as if I'm a forensic case study.

"I'm…better. I should've waited a little while, then I probably wouldn't have needed to call." He's silent for a moment as the elevator comes to a stop, and then, as always, the doors wait a good ten seconds before opening.

"No," he says as we exit. "No, I'm very glad you called. Don't ever hesitate."

"But it's a fucking Sunday, I really shouldn't've."

"Don't apologize. This is what I'm here for." He unlocks his office door and flips on the lights. The beige love seat looks as if it's been freshly vacuumed. I feel too dirty to take a seat, but I do anyway and gently smooth out my loose gray jeans.

"Now. What's happening?" The heaviness in his voice demands I truthfully come forward with everything writhing inside me and vomit out all the parasites gripping on to my deflated veins. However, those same parasites hold me all together, wrapping me up like a poorly assembled Christmas present that no one really wants to open. In the seconds following his question, both his voice and the parasite battle it out viciously, and both end up intertwining into a suffocated monster and evaporating into thin air.

"I think I was just having a panic attack."

"About what?"

"It-it's been a really weird fucking day. I saw Jett, and…"

"And what?" I notice no notepad on his lap. He could probably get it if he wanted. Maybe he can't risk staining the Lululemon sweats with a slip of the pen. I shake my head and try to replay his question in my head as if it were complicated.

"We talked, and he really tried to, like, ask me what was going on, and I couldn't…I, like, couldn't *tell* him. My mouth wouldn't let me. He was really trying to help…" Dr. Ellis just stares at me, blinking, until I finish. "He was really trying to help me feel better, and I wasn't saying much besides the fact that Greg, like, *died* and all, and that I've seen him in the past…"

He crosses his legs the other way and puts his elbow on the arm of his green armchair. His red glasses have fallen to where he'd usually then push them back up, but he lets them sit below his line of vision and gazes at me over the rims.

"Breathe, Valerie. Take a minute. Don't rush." I close my eyes and inhale and exhale slowly a few times. I probably look so goddamn stupid. I start to fight a smile, an eerie reflex that seems to come out of nowhere in less than ideal moments. Dr. Ellis clears his throat, and I flutter my eyelids open to continue.

"Then he…" I look at the carpet, which is striped with vacuum streaks. "Then he kissed me, and we, like, hooked up, but then he left, and now I feel so bad and so...*gross*, and I'm really, really confused, and Di is, like, high and probably doesn't give a shit, but I—" I choke on my saliva and reflexively gulp.

"Breathe. Just breathe."

My feet sway. I don't want to breathe. I hold my breath. Heat rises to my face until I break and gulp in a huge gust of air-freshener-scented oxygen.

"I'm sorry. I just got freaked out b-because I started thinking about my *mom*, and I was so scared I was going to see her, I was so scared—"

"Have you seen your mother, Valerie?"

"Like, how?"

"In hallucinations, visualizations." His response is flat as if it's prepared.

I look at him sharply but cannot hold the eye contact for long before returning my gaze to the vacuum lines, following them from the love seat to his armchair and back.

"Have you? When?" he asks after I give a slight nod. Breathing begins to overtake me, sucking in my stomach as my throat lurches up to grasp at more air.

"I—I was running the other day and saw her, and she—she was yelling at me, and I don't want that to happen anymore." My shoulders are curled in, my head down, and I am surprised when I feel large hands on my hunched frame. They are the same hands that gripped me when I smashed a banana on his dining room table and he told me to get home safely. I look up and see Dr. Ellis's dark-brown eyes closer than ever before. There are little copper flecks around the center and a thin yellow-gold rim around the outside. They are an entire microcosm of warmth, not just brown, not just one color.

"Valerie. Are you taking your medication? I know it's not ideal, I *know* we often don't want to change who we are, but you don't need to live like this."

"I do, though! Greg, and Vic, and my mom, they need to tell me these things, I deserve to be told these things!"

"You do *not* deserve anything like this. You do not *need* to be going through life like this. You have to take your medication, Valerie." Dr. Ellis's voice softens around the edges. "Please. It is painful to see you like this." He returns to his seat gently.

"It's painful for *you*?" The smile comes back to my lips, displaying itself without any permission whatsoever. My eyes are cold, not allowing any tears, which I wish would come to prevent my mouth from spewing any more stupid words.

"Yes. It is painful for me, Valerie. Nowhere near as painful as I know it is for you, but it is. Do you have any medication on hand back at your dorm?" I shake my head meekly at him, embarrassed by my weak show of defiance. "I'm going to write in for another prescription that should go through tomorrow. Please go by then, okay?"

"Okay."

"Right now, it's imperative you stay on your medication. I don't want something to happen that requires hospitalization."

"I will, I will." I nod, truly committed in the moment but instinctively knowing my true nature. A nature that refuses to have its rug pulled out from under it, even if that rug is suffocating it to death.

"Now, did...did Jett hurt you at all? Did anything happen?"

"No! No, not at all."

"It doesn't seem like you feel comfortable about the fact that you were with him, though."

I clench my jaw tightly and continue staring downward.

"I'm not now, but then... I don't know, I don't... I'm just confused, and at the time, maybe I was okay with it, but now I'm, like..." I look down at my feet.

"What makes you not okay with it?"

"The fact that I'm, like, sleeping with him while we both hate each other, I guess."

"You hate Jett?"

"I...I don't know, I'm just pissed at him for sleeping with me, and I'm pissed at myself for sleeping with him..."

Dr. Ellis sighs as my voice trails off, and I look up to see his solemn eyes looking over red rims at my face.

"I *know* he must hate me, though."

"I don't think he would be as concerned about you if he truly did."

"He probably knows his concern makes me feel like shit."

"Why does it make you feel like that?"

"Jesus Christ! I don't know!"

Now I really wish tears would come, to shut me up, to paralyze my cruel mind so it can't reveal itself through words and scissor absolutely everything in my path to pieces until there is nothing left for it to do but come back and also shear itself, shear me, away. I inhale and exhale to calm myself, then continue speaking.

"If I knew, I wouldn't be freaking out, calling you after having a fight and then fucking my fucking boyfriend; if I knew, I wouldn't be a psycho *bitch* seeing my goddamn dead brother everywhere; if I knew, I wouldn't be talking to *you*." Dr. Ellis's chest rises and falls rhythmically. "*Do something...!*" I yell pathetically, trailing off at the end when I realize there isn't an attack to combat like I'd prepared for. The offense to defend myself is coming from my own mind.

As I follow the vacuum trails over and over, pretending to be fascinated by them seconds after bursting out in juvenile anger, I can feel Dr. Ellis calmly gazing at me. The silence makes me increasingly anxious, and I feign discomfort, moving around in my seat, my little home here right in the crevice of the cushions on this goddamn beige love seat.

"I'm glad you got that out," he finally says after my mind has trailed off so far in trying to occupy itself that it has almost forgotten what it's distracting itself from.

"I'm sorry," I mutter after further silence. Now Dr. Ellis hates me. There's no point in trying to make anything work anymore. "I should...I should, like, go eat something." I notice the clock approaching six. I hope I'm back in my kitchen by six thirty. Otherwise, I might be too hungry once I get there and might start having Jett's peanut-butter-pretzel bites. That would really piss him off, too. Shit. No. *No. You'll be back to the kitchen soon.*

"Please do, Valerie. Thank you for calling me." He holds the door open for me and I leave, entering the hallway and the elevator on my own, the tears I'd hoped would come earlier finally send warm flames up in preparation for their arrival. I can't cry now, though, when I'm about to walk back to my dorm. Just like I couldn't cry at home because Mom would yell at me. Just like I couldn't ever cry in front of Dad because that would show how bad things were with Mom. Just like I couldn't cry after Greg died because that would mean crying in front of Mom.

I swallow and prepare to enter my little mental helicopter. I'll watch out for my scrawny body down there walking back to my dorm, but I won't be in it; I'll just make sure from afar I'm not jaywalking too dangerously or going the wrong way. I open the cockpit door, slide in, and prepare to soar far above my boiling eyes.

Chapter 55

I start packing up right as the clock hits 12:15. My professor always goes a few minutes over, and I don't care to appease him today. Before this, I hadn't showed up in weeks, anyway. As I'm trying to slide out without a sound, my knee hits the metal leg of my desk with a thud, and the class turns around to see me leaving while the film noir lecture still continues on. Before my professor can notice me, though, I rush out and vow to never show up again.

I open my phone and see a recent text from Jett.

Hey. Are you free this afternoon? We should probably talk.

ya. im walking back now what about 2?

Two should be good. Two means enough time for me to eat but probably not enough time for me to get hungry again.

Okay sure. I'll be at your room then.

I slide in my earbuds and turn up my music as loud as possible, then I flip my hood up and cover the face I spent an hour painting this morning, blending dark purple vigorously into my deep-set creases. It's still cold out, but not freezing, and my nose immediately runs. I avoid eye contact with anyone on the street as the snot unavoidably reappears no matter how many times my hands wipe it, along with my foundation, away.

Oven preheats to 400. Premeasured vegetables reheated. Twenty minutes later, vegetables come out. One handful of spinach in the bowl. Premeasured beans on one side. Vegetables, once they've cooled enough, on the other. Premeasured sliced avocado in the middle. Drowned in spices, then eaten over a forty-five minute period as I watch YouTube videos on eating-disorder stories. Lots of sad music and slideshows of childhood photos. Girl is scarred by being called "thunder thighs" in elementary school and embarks on a sad journey of starving herself, ending up weighing seventy-five pounds at sixteen. She's hospitalized. Now she's fat and happy. Eating disorders just didn't work for them. They weren't in control enough to not have *too* much of an eating disorder. Not that I have a real eating disorder or anything. Fat or hospitalized. I'm powerful enough to avoid both and stay perfectly centered. They just didn't get it. They weren't using their tools correctly, and they got hurt. You can't use a chain saw unless you understand how to use it.

I hear two little knocks on my door and look over to see Jett's sharp face peeking in. I pull out my headphones and can't help but smile ever so slightly. He looks like he's just rolled out of bed, his hair tousled and sweatpants on. Skid Row shirt. I haven't seen that one in a while.

"Hey there." The words roll out of his raspy throat slowly.

"Hey. You look like you just woke up."

"I didn't, but my class was canceled today, so I didn't have an excuse to get out of my pajamas."

"Understandable." I stand up and jump onto my bed, Jett following me.

"I swear, I'm going to get you a step stool. It's fucking painful to see you have to do that every time."

"I mean, I'd only be using it for a few more months."

"But I'm pretty sure you'd benefit from carrying it around." I roll my eyes at him, an easy thing for them to do. Meeting his is not.

"So, I..." he starts. "I just wanted to, like, be clear? I really like you, Valerie. I know we've pretty much agreed that we're dating, and...and I *hope* that's what you want, to be really dating and all—" He cuts himself off as if he expects me to. I look to the side. "Um," he starts back up again, "I just wanted to say that I *do* really give a shit about you? I'm not using you, I'm not… I'm not fucking around. I…I care about you a lot, Val."

I clench my toes and hope he doesn't see my Vans bending, then cough to clear my throat. "I… I'm sorry I said I thought you didn't give a shit. I know you do."

"It's okay. I know you're going through a lot of shit."

"It's…it's really *not*, like, okay, though. I…I do really like you, too, Jett. I'm just scared I'm going to hurt you." Flex, point, flex, point.

"What? Don't worry about me. I'm more worried about you. I want to help you, Val; I'm here for you." Jett turns to face me directly, pulling his left leg up and resting it on my white sheets.

"I'm sorry, I know. I'm just scared for you." I'm scared in general, and I'm not really sure it's for him, or for me, or for both of us. Jett shakes his head, confused.

"Stop, don't think about me. I want to know that you…that you want this like I do." My breathing becomes shallow, and my throat swallows continuously, making it difficult to find words. The lack of oxygen slows my thoughts, and I struggle to make it seem like I'm listening to anything he's saying. Finally, through all the chaos, some speech drips out.

"I do. I'm sorry, I'm shit at expressing my feelings and all."

"I know, I know. I am, too."

"I really appreciate everything you've done. Even if it doesn't seem like it. I'm sorry."

"Thanks." We sit still. He's angled toward me, blinking at my white covers, as I continue to fidget in my black Vans.

"Um, anything…new with you?" I ask.

"Uh, I wanted to talk about the other day, too," Jett quickly adds. My breathing decides to hide once again.

"I…" He stops and itches his leg. "I'm not just having sex with you, like, meaninglessly or whatever."

"Yeah."

"Like, please know that. I mean it. It's meaningful to me."

"It's meaningful to me, too," I say, finally making eye contact. We pause for a minute, locking pupils.

"Okay, good." He sighs, relieved, while I begin to tense and roll my ankles as well.

"I'm sorry—"

"Please stop saying you're sorry—"

"If, like, I'm hard to get to," I say, not pausing for his interruption, "know that I've just had fucked up past shit. My last…my last serious boyfriend was kind of, like, forceful. Nothing major, like, I wasn't, you know, *raped*, but I didn't always want to do the things I let myself get into with him, I guess. But I know you're not him. I *know* that." As my throat opens up and my breathing flows ever so slightly more consistently, I worry that my brain is going to turn inside out and flurry up into more words, overflowing and drowning us in this cramped dorm room. My windows don't open all the way. We'd surely die within a few minutes.

"I know. That's why I'm not at all upset with you. I've had shit, too, so I get it."

"Thanks."

"Yeah." He extends his leg long, turning to face the same way as I am instead of sitting perpendicular to me. I feel more comfortable and let my feet and ankles relax now.

"So, I guess I'll go, like, get dressed and all," Jett says on a sigh as he slides off my bed. "I'm starving, if you want to go get food."

"I need to work at Harry's," I blurt out.

"Yeah, okay. I might meet you, if you're still there."

"Okay, yeah."

"Bye, Val." He softly shuts the door. I fall to my right side and curl up, wishing I could say more, wishing I knew *how* to say more without exploding. It's as if the faucet of my mouth can only drip or flood entirely, with no middle setting. It's defective. I need a replacement.

Chapter 56

hey r we still on for dinner?

Di hasn't texted me all day, and I'm fucking worried because I don't have backup plans for what to eat if she falls through. The message is delivered, like my last few, and I wonder if she's moping and heartbroken over some shit with Iris.

did u & iris have a fight or something i can pick it up & bring it to u if ur sad n all

Finally, three little dots form as she begins to type.

I'm flying home tonight. Emergency. Sorry

is everything ok?????

No it's not ok

???

My dad had a heart attack.

Her dad's either dead or going to die. I'm sure of it. An intuitive pang in my chest tells me without needing her to, maybe without her knowing it herself. I just stare at the screen and wait for the message to vanish, for it to combust with too much information all crammed into one micro-conversation.

oh my god. im so fucking sorry, it sounds fake but i really

am Di…call me if u need anything, i havent been there before but

ive been kind of there, u know. take a few days off from ppl if u

need. i love u. pls take care & take care of urself too

She sends a heart and says she has to head to the airport

soon. I've seen picture of Di's family; her dad does look like he

could have heart problems. Karma immediately sends me a pang in

the stomach for judging him as overweight and therefore deserving

of reaping the health problems. I'm fucking heartless. *Di's dad is*

probably going to die, and here you are casting judgment on him.

Except, isn't it his fault? Isn't all of our shit our own fault? I'm

allowed to feel bad for Di. I do feel bad for Di. But not for him.

It's a never-ending paradox; we cause pain that other people don't

deserve, which then causes them to hurt others who don't deserve

it.

Di may love her dad, but his own suffering is going to

break Di. She may come back "stronger at the broken places" (à la

required-reading Hemingway), but she may not, and the root of it

all may just be some bullshit Di's dad never worked through

because he didn't know how to. If I'm compassionate toward him,

I'm loving a sinner. If I'm judgmental toward him, I'm hating an overgrown child in pain. I guess I just won't feel anything. I'll hide in the dry, flaking-away wooden skull of mine that is so barren it could catch fire any minute from the flickering electricity currents darting up my spine. One of these days, it will, and I won't just burn to the ground in the presence of the characters in my head. One day, all the pus secreting from my never-healing wounds will ferment into alcohol and ooze into my brain, flooding it from the outside in. I can feel it approaching just like I can feel Di's dad's heart giving out. Just like I can feel Greg near me, always. It's all mine, even if it's not there. I am there.

I need to figure out what to do for dinner. I should start eating in about an hour and a half. There's stuff here, frozen vegetables and some prepped shit for tomorrow that I can pull together. My foot taps as I calculate the calories for what I can have. I'm pissed off because I limited everything earlier thinking I was eating out with Di. I guess now I should be happy that I can add more. But I'm not. Because I feel cheated and robbed. Alright, I'll have extra quinoa, extra beans, extra sauce. But not too much extra because then I might go overboard. Then I'll lose control.

Then everything I've worked so hard for, the only thing I've ever done for myself, the only thing I've ever been recognized for, will be ripped away. Maybe no extra beans. Or sauce. Just in case.

If Di's dad just hadn't been overweight, everything would be according to plan right now. I wouldn't be scrambling to weigh out a fucking sweet potato before someone else walks into the kitchen. I wouldn't be fiddling with numbers that never seem to satisfy me. *Fuck Di's dad.* I can't even recall his goddamn face as I throw the blame out, hoping it'll hit him. Hoping it'll make him feel all the collateral damage that he's caused. Even if it's just a pitiful consequence of unintentional micro-decisions.

My fork stabs two black beans. They curl into one another as if they're spooning on a bed. With my teeth, I snag them off into my mouth, feeling the duo obliterated to saliva and mush in every chew. I go for another few beans, but this time, they spew everywhere with the strong force of my grip. Some quinoa flies up and nestles into my hair. I blow it out. It lands on my computer keyboard, right in the center of a little fingerprint on the *J* key. It's an oily little fingerprint. I should probably cut down on my fats.

Fuck. I'm not eating slowly enough. It's 7:45 now, and almost all of my bowl is gone. I have another fifteen or so minutes before I'm supposed to be done. Because if I'm done earlier, that means I'll get hungry earlier, and that can't happen. Except, I guess it can, because it always does, and I always power through. What can't I power through? When *has* anything actually stopped me?

Eight oh five. Bowl in dishwasher. I did it. I waited it out. I got back on track. I'm back on track. People like Di and Di's dad are not on track. They are too caught up in their pain, too focused on just numbing it out rather than pushing through and embodying that pain. I *am* pain. I accept it, which allows me to work with it, which allows me to *do* instead of *settle*. It doesn't matter if I'm withering down to nothing, a gracefully minimalistic existence, because that's my own fucking creation. I'm the agent of my own doing, not the pain I am pretending isn't there, not insecurity I don't want to acknowledge. Everything I am is because I want it to be so. No meds will mold me. No person will take away everything individual that I am.

Eight forty-five. I'm allowed my dessert, a peanut-butter cookie I baked, and some tea afterward. After getting everything ready, it should be 8:50 before I take a bite. 8:49:55. Five. Four. Three. Two. One. *Perfect.*

Chapter 57

There's a small tear in the beige love seat. It's on the far right, flailing out to me as I walk in and sit again in the center. As my weight falls on the cushion, a little piece of cotton springs out from the cut. I point to it curiously.

"Another patient's jeans got stuck somehow. Happened yesterday."

"Oh." I look at it more, like it's a car accident I can't turn away from. Finally, Dr. Ellis clears his throat, and I jolt up.

"Sorry," he adds, coughing. "I'm not feeling too well. How have you been since the last time we spoke?"

I shrug. "The same, maybe a little calmer. Maybe my meds will start kicking in soon."

"Yes, they sometimes take a while to adjust. You have so much going for you, Valerie; I'm really glad to hear that you've…really committed to this journey now."

"Yes, me, too." I haven't even gone to pick up these new meds yet. I have a few days before they'll call. I don't have plans tomorrow afternoon. Guess I'll go then.

"How have your eating concerns been going recently? I know that's not something we've touched on for a little while."

"Um, Di's dad died." Di texted me last night saying she'd be staying home for a week or two, maybe longer, while everything gets sorted out. I said I understood. Because I do understand the cold shell forming, built by shock and disbelief, that will crack eventually. Hopefully, for her, it's not cracked by reappearances of the dead and the dead-to-me.

Dr. Ellis blinks rapidly in surprise, then brushes back his just-graying brown hair.

"I'm incredibly sorry to hear that. Do you know the cause?"

"Heart attack. He didn't live long after."

"It's so very difficult to lose a parent so young, even in college. I hope she reaches out for whatever support she may need."

"Yeah. Me, too."

"How has this affected you? How does it make you feel?" I'm taken aback a little by his question.

"I mean, it's not really my...tragedy, or whatever."

"Not directly, but since it is happening to your closest friend, it must shake you up somewhat."

"I mean, I guess I've faced my share of death. I'm more annoyed than anything that Di has to go through this. Kind of just mildly pissed at the world, maybe." I sway my legs back and forth against the love seat. Then again, I've really only faced one death. Maybe two, if you include me leaving my mom's house once I turned eighteen and never looking back. I cut her out completely right then. I don't have any idea what she's doing now. So maybe I haven't had my fair share.

"That's understandable. Do you know how Di is handling this?"

"She seems to be trying to pull the whole *strong* card, taking some 'time for herself' and saying she'll 'be back' and all. I want to tell her to just fucking grieve and get it all out before it creeps up on her. Or really…in her. Like, you don't just fucking run away from crying your guts out and wishing it were you." The pounding in my chest and escalation in my voice sends a jolt down my back. I fidget to shake it off.

"Say more about that. Crying, wishing it were you." I know Dr. Ellis sees this as "getting somewhere." He sits up straighter in his chair and writes in his notepad at a furious speed.

"Like, when you're left here with the bullshit and the pain and the…the confusion because you don't know how to…how to even think anymore, you totally fucking wish it were you. Like, with Greg…or, I guess this isn't—" I stop myself and swallow.

"No, go ahead." He nods and motions.

"I mean…I was fucking jealous that he didn't have to deal with, like, Mom anymore! And I know that's so, so fucked up! But…in my mind then, I felt like he'd gotten a free pass or some shit. Take the bullet now so you don't have to later. I know that's really terrible, I…"

"I'm not here to judge you, Valerie. I'm here to help you work through feelings like this."

"I know, I know. I don't feel like you're judging me, I really don't. *I* just judge myself, honestly. Like my twelve-year-old brother fucking *dies* of alcohol poisoning, and I'm somehow fucking jealous? How the *hell* could I be jealous of him?"

"You were severely traumatized and constantly in a state of panic growing up, waiting for the next thing to happen with your mother. It's completely understandable to want a way out of that. I don't know if you truly wanted to take Greg's place or if you just wished you could leave the situation as well." We make eye contact for a little while as I process what he's said before I freak out and blink away, avoiding connection as usual.

"I—I still wish it were me instead of him a lot of the time, though. Greg was so fucking innocent. Like, not even just as a kid or anything. His *personality* was innocent. With everything Mom would do and shit, he was still always happy. I deserved that. *I* should've been the one to…to fuck up badly enough to die choking on my own goddamn vomit in front of that fucking pool!" Currents inside me blast my voice out more clearly than ever, with no insecurity creeping in, no raspy tone or endings of sentences meekly dropped. My words glow and linger in the air, illuminated by the striking sun, and instead of falling to the ground, they ascend and fill the whole room with an opaque sheen. Neither Dr. Ellis nor I can breathe. Then, suddenly, I inhale all of the words and with them the thick, gelatinous substance they emit back into

413

myself. I feel full and whole again, cradling from within what I cannot show to anyone but those who live in me.

"Think of everything you've done and can do because you *weren't* in that position. How does looking into the future, at all your possibilities, make you feel?"

"Like shit, because I don't fucking have possibilities! I could've done so goddamn much at this point, had an *impact*, made a *change*, and instead I'm just a schizophrenic, anorexic mess who can't even look her own father in the eye or say 'I love you' to anyone and mean it." After the statement escapes my lips, I feel lighter than I did when I woke up and weighed my lowest weight and was barely able to balance on two feet. Now, there is not enough of me to prevent myself from being carried away by the wind, swept around the room by the air-conditioning system that always abruptly turns on and off in this room, messing with the normal mechanics of conversation by making everything seem overly dramatic. Or at least that's how I feel. Maybe Dr. Ellis is used to it by now. Maybe it isn't so serious to him, since I'm just another client.

"I think it's important you realize that you've been through a lot that probably kept you from making those huge leaps you think you should've. It's not as if after living in a household like that for so long, you can simply just come out anew. It takes time, and it takes understanding, and that's what I hope to pull out for you here. It's…it's important to integrate, not run away." His dark eyes blink at me slowly. Hands interlaced around his crossed legs. The yellow notepad balancing on his perfectly pressed navy pants. His shoes, the black ones I said I liked a little while ago, sway slightly with the breeze of the buzzing air conditioner. It suddenly turns off and compels me to fill the silent void.

"I just wish I could do all that at once, I guess. Become a healthy, functioning adult without all the work I'm finding out it takes to get there."

"That's so great, though, Valerie. That you *do* want to become a healthy, functioning adult. That you have hope and drive."

"I mean, I definitely don't always. It comes and goes. I get worried…that one day it'll go away forever. And sometimes I even *want* it to, I don't know why… But I guess that's what I'm here for." My brows furrow so tightly as I look at Dr. Ellis's face that I'm convinced they've been stapled.

"And that's what I'm here for. To help you untangle all that."

Chapter 58

I'm firmly five pounds heavier than my lowest weight. Five

pounds fatter than when I was perfect and just didn't realize it. The

scale hasn't budged in almost two weeks, even though I've cut my

calories back even more and am working out twice a day in the

place of my film classes. I see more of my ribs and hips peeking

out when I stand in front of the mirror, naked and unclothed every

morning, but the number isn't going down at all, not even by one-

third of a pound. I should donate a kidney. Maybe my dad will

need a transplant or something. He's getting old.

Dr. Ellis has suggested that my obsession with being thin is

an attempt to identify as something to the most extreme degree. He

says that since my mother never gave me the attention a child

requires to feel they exist, I obsess over labels to compensate. I

don't really know if that's actually what's going on, and I don't

fucking care. All I can think of is moving that number on the right

down one single digit, just *anything* to show me my hard work is

paying off. Because losing weight is the only hard work I've ever

really done for myself; my body is the only art I've ever created;

my suffering is the only passion I've truly dedicated myself to. To give that up would be to wipe away the sand art I've spent centuries carving out. It would be more suicidal than the act itself.

I quietly put my scale back in its place under my bed, making sure to still not wake Patricia. She got back late last night, as is becoming usual, so I assume she'll be asleep for a while longer. The semester has ended anyway, and she should be leaving to go back home soon. If I remember correctly, she lives just a train ride away, so she often decides when to return on short notice. I get dressed quickly and walk over to the gym I've just gotten a monthly membership at, not the one across the street, but one I have to walk farther to. It's more expensive than the one across the street, but it's a fifteen-minute walk away, so it's worth it. Running in the cold hurts my chest too much now, so I figured some weight lifting on the side would be a helpful alternative. Maybe that's why I've gained weight. Maybe I'm putting on muscle. My abs totally *do* appear to be more defined. I'm getting stronger by the minute, hacking the numerical system to defy its very meaning.

Five minutes walking on the treadmill at a pace of 3.5 miles per hour. Then ten minutes jogging at 5 miles per hour. Then ten minutes with a raised incline of 2.0 at 7 miles per hour. Then ten minutes back at five with no incline. As I run, I feel like my ankles are stilts on a tightrope that I'm barely balancing on. Then a seven-minute cooldown, gradually returning to stop. Now on to abs and weights. Twenty minutes on each. I know not having my period for so long is fucking with my bone density. But it feels like that isn't *really* happening to me, and it's all some weird horror film I'm playing out where I see dead people and abusive people from my past while living as a walking skeleton.

With each weight lifted, I'm worried my arms are going to disintegrate at the joint. My abs are so hard yet so thin; a karate kick could chop my body right in two. Exiting the building with my puffy jacket unzipped in front of my black sports bra, the cold winter air strikes my collarbones like a bunch of tiny knives. As I move down the sidewalk closer and closer to my dorm, the knives permeate deeper and deeper into my chest, but I do not zip up my jacket. I want everyone else on these narrow streets, generally uncrowded yet surprisingly active for such an early hour, to notice my artfully decaying corpse. I look each person who passes by me directly in the eye through my oversize, darkened sunglasses. I demand that they acknowledge me and see me as I am, undeniably wounded. I want them to wince at the blood, gasp at my struggle, and question whether or not I am truly alive. Except I don't think a single person even recognizes I'm there, just to the right, on the crooked sidewalk. The morning-shift security guard nods at me, like he does every day, and I pretend that my sunglasses block my peripheral vision.

Back in my dorm, Patricia isn't there, but her suitcase is half filled and her desk is messily covered in toiletries. I'm excited for her to leave just so that I can have two or so weeks in peace, without fear every morning of her noticing that I'm weighing myself. My dad says he wishes I'd come home. I wish I had a home.

As I undress, I jump up at the sight of Greg sitting in my desk chair. His left leg is lifted up onto the seat, and his right is sliding back and forth on the floor. I cover the sports bra over my chest in a panic.

"Jesus, Greg! What the hell?" He giggles and looks down at his right foot. Thankfully, I haven't taken off my leggings yet.

"Relax, Val. Not like there's much there left to cover up, anyway." My face reddens as I look down to small, sad, deflated breasts. I push them up tightly in an attempt to make him reconsider.

"I'm sorry about what I said last time I saw you. I really am, Val. I know you're doing your best."

"I... I'm really not. But thanks. It kind of fucked me up at the time." My right hand falls to my side to animate my speech as my left moves to cover my entire chest. I allow my hair to fall forward to hide my body even more.

"You should come join me, Val. It's easier where I am. You should do it for real. Or else it'll get worse. If you do, it'll be better for you and for everyone. We can be together again, except without Mom this time."

"I want to be with you, Greg. But I'm really fucking scared."

"Are you scared of doing it for real? Because there's nothing to be afraid of. It's not that bad, really," he says nonchalantly. I bite my lip.

"I'm scared of doing it for real and totally not doing it at all. I'm…I'm scared of both living and dying. Neither really seems great. I just want to, like, evaporate and not exist. My doctor even called me about these tests they ran on me. My hormones are ridiculously out of whack, and my heart has a murmur. They want me to come back in. I'm not calling them back. I'm not even going to change on my own. I'm scared either way, but a little less scared for things to end sooner than later." Greg cocks his head to the side and lets his foot stop swaying, and it ends up underneath the chair with the top of his shoe touching the ground.

"If you come with me, you won't be scared anymore, Val. I know it's crazy. But it's your choice. You have to do something. You're going to do something. You just have to."

"I—" My voice cuts off as I hear the door open and Patricia sniffle while holding a laundry basket. I rip my leggings off quickly, grab a towel, and bolt out the door, heading directly to the shower.

It's cold, frighteningly cold, and I can't stop shivering. Greg's right. I'm going to do something. I'm going to make a choice one way or another, to firmly carve my name into the wall of life or to blow it up altogether. It's Wednesday. I have until Friday to decide.

The water begins to turn hot, passing through moderately warm to Lucifer's fury within seconds, but I don't adjust it. The red blotches appearing on my stomach where the water hits look like a red velvet carpet tapering off at the edges into an ivory iceberg. I decide whichever side of me the water hits next will make my decision for me. The left is to remain. The right is to move on.

I close my eyes and inhale and exhale deeply, feeling my organs touch each other in the sharp absence of both air and any food. Every cell in my body debates, having a trial within microscopic walls, the jury going back and forth endlessly for weeks within the span of each breath. I feel the water strike, and I look down to make sure. It's decided. The verdict comes out. Millions of judges in my body hit a single hammer. I reach for shampoo.

Chapter 59

Jett knocks on my door, and my heart races. His combed hair and fresh face peek through. Rolled-up sleeves show the edges of his arm tattoos.

"Hey," I say softly. I bat my eyelashes, hoping the extra highlighter makes him take a longer look at me as I enter.

"Hey, Val. You look pretty."

I smile lightly and shrug. He comes over to give me a hug and kiss me on my forehead as I sit on the edge of my desk chair.

"Are you going out with Di later?" Jett leans against my bed, elbows pressing into the white duvet.

"Oh, uh…no, I just had some stuff earlier. Di's dad, he…he *died*, actually, so…"

"Holy shit. Fuck, I'm so sorry."

"Don't worry, it's not like you had a way to, like, know. It's…it's just what's going on for now. Life shit."

"Yeah. Life shit. Is Patricia already gone for the semester?" He looks at her empty side of the room as he moves up onto the bed, and I come up to join him.

"Yeah." I swallow, "I…I wanted to, like, apologize for basically just…just dismissing you when you were trying to really come through for me the other day. Because I really like you, too, Jett." My eyes feel heavy, and I end up looking down at my hands instead of making eye contact with him like I'd promised myself I would. He puts his arm around my shoulder and rubs my arm with his firm, gentle grip.

"There's literally nothing to apologize for, Val. It's hard to tell someone exactly how you feel, especially with the shit you've been going through."

"I know, but…but yeah. I just… I really like you, Jett. A lot." Our eyes meet, and his chest seems to rise and fall like a puppet pulled by mine. He leans over me, and our mouths meet for an instant before pulling away, then fully committing. Jett's body moves mine down onto the fluffy white sheets, and he rests back on his knees, unbuttoning his white shirt and tossing it to the side. The red-and-black tattoos mesmerize me as he lifts off my thin black sweater and releases his chest onto mine. It's heavy enough to immediately warm my goose-bump-covered abdomen, but his skin has a weightlessness that allows me to breathe more deeply

425

than I could on my own. Our inhales and exhales continue to match, ebbing and flowing along with our mouths, and his hands tangle through my perfectly disheveled curls. They swipe underneath the black tangles onto the white comforter and farther underneath my back, unsnapping my new red lace bra I hope he doesn't fully realize is ridiculously padded. His chest rests on mine, a heavy softness permeating my heart and giving me enough strength to move on top of him. A slight motion of my bony hip against his jeans sends his body the message before his mind can even contribute, and he helps to prop me up. I take off my gray jeans as he unhooks his belt and does the same, his hands meeting my waist. I flinch at first, but he pulls me closer, and I lean on him as he did on me. He breaks his mouth away for an instant and lifts my shoulders up slightly.

"Val, I...I love you." He blinks his long eyelashes slowly.

"I love you, too," I say in a whimpering tone I'd be embarrassed of if I had the time to think about it. Jett pulls my neck toward him, and our breath unites, not needing to breathe solely for ourselves but rather breathing as one unit molded together. He reaches for my lace underwear, which I'm slightly disappointed he didn't get to see match my bra, and the thin fabric slips down my legs with the help of his hands. I do the same for him, hooking my hands underneath his gray boxers until they hit the floor with a soft thud. He pulls my white duvet crookedly on top of me as he slides me below him once again, and in the darkness, our mouths reconnect. He lifts the covers up eventually to get up and reach for my desk, but I put a hand on his shoulder to stop him.

"It's…it's okay," I murmur.

He eyes me, confused. "Are you… Did you get—"

"Yeah, yeah." I cut him off sharply, and he blinks down at my bare chest, then pulls the white covers above us both again. I don't have a drop of energy left to fuel my sex drive, but I can't resist doing any kind of physical activity that might cause a caloric burn, and I appreciate the distraction from even consciously considering those numbers like I do constantly.

Our muscle memory takes over, and with every feeling of his body against and through mine, I forget the sadness I nearly drowned in before he walked into this room, the sadness I felt for a millisecond before greeting him, as all of our memories spun within me so quickly they caught flame. The fire remains, powering the electricity within me manually, the original system having shut down long ago. I'm running on his force, a parasite of a culminating past, ready to allow for his eventual escape from my wrath. Split seconds come rearing back into my mind. The washcloth tearing in the elevator. The raw sweet potato. Skid Row. Matcha lattes. Carrying me after I passed out. I have no conscious bodily control, so I pray that tears do not silently erupt without warning. Thankfully, Jett's body distracts me, and I focus on following the designs of all his tattoos. They are all so beautiful and intricate and complex; I wish I were as delicately constructed as each thin line on his body. The ink, the veins, and each strand of his fine hair consume my attention individually until the morphing body between us slows. I'm above him, but I move, curled, to the side, breathing heavily along with Jett. His eyes are open, softly gazing at the peeling ceiling above us. I notice my window was never closed.

I move closer and lean my head onto his shoulder, and he pulls my leg across his abs so that I'm leaning on him entirely.

"I love you, Val," he whispers in a firm tone that sends more flames to revive my insides.

"I love you, too," I say again, but my mind is taking back control, and the words feel slimy in my mouth. I think of Really Bad, and being in that car with Vic, and wondering how it would sound differently coming from his voice. Not because I wish it were but because my mind is using all of its remaining efforts to pull me away from this moment. I'm thinking about what it will be like when the door shuts behind him soon, when he heads out to the concert he said he could "meet me for a little before" since he has to leave by nine. I'm imposing an even greater limitation on our time soon, so I don't feel as frustrated that he will, too, on a much smaller scale.

He looks at his watch, then smiles and sits up.

"I should go shower and head out soon." Jett shakes his tousled hair and sniffles, still smiling from his dark eyes. I nod and begin to sit up as well, but he quickly jumps down and hands me my underwear for me.

"Thanks," I say, blushing, once again unable to meet his eyes.

"Hey, hey," he says, "I'll text you tonight, or tomorrow if I don't have service, okay? We should...we should do something tomorrow. Just not too early, because I'll definitely be asleep." My jaw lengthens with the weight of knowledge pulling it down. I open my lips to say something, but strings of saliva seem to slam them shut once again.

"Or...we don't..." He looks at me curiously as he pulls up his boxers and jeans.

"No, no! Sorry," I say, pushing back my hair. "Yeah." My mouth forms a smile, but my brows can't seem to unfurrow. "We...we should definitely do something tomorrow." He slides on his white button-down and leans to kiss me one more time. My hands cannot bear to touch his skin, my fingers knowing that experiencing it as the final time would be too much to feel in one grasp.

"Love you. Bye." He closes the door softly. I bite my lip and fall over to the opposite side, with no electricity left inside me to power tears of a true goodbye.

Chapter 60

As the sun has just begun to peek out from behind the clouds, its rays not yet fully reaching the ground, I gingerly pull out my scale and pray that I can see the floor well enough to place it down without waking Patricia up. It doesn't work, and there is a sharp clang. I look up to remember that Patricia's gone. I slam it down once more for good measure and to hopefully wake up whoever's underneath me.

I almost jump as I see the number has dropped a whole pound. *Finally.* Energy rushes to my head, out of my brain, and illuminates my messy dorm room before even sunlight does. Then I also remember that it doesn't fucking matter. The water decided. It was a hard right hit, too, not a little futile sprinkle. A secure omen, confident in its declaration. At least today I don't have to work out now. At least my dad isn't here to fuck it all up again. At least Greg isn't here to convince me to forget everything I've planned.

I wasn't going to have some maintenance man walk in on me, naked and crying, like my dad did on Really Bad. I'm not an amateur anymore.

The pill bottle I picked up the other day ever so slightly reflects the budding sunlight and glows a bright tangerine right at me. I look away, reminded of the plan I created during last night's true last supper. Just as calculated as usual, in case something goes haywire here and I can't pull this off. And just as calculated because I can't be a bloated cadaver.

I turn on my vanity mirror and get out the makeup I'll need. It's the expensive shit I don't typically use day to day. In fact, the last time I'd used most of this was when I went out with Patricia. The fifty-dollar eyeliner pencil is dull. I still can't find my sharpener. Guess it's convenient that it's my last inconvenience.

A thin brush carves out canyons of crimson shadow into the corners and creases of my veiny eyelids. Little lines of purple remind me of how my mother used to always tell me how unfortunate it was that they were so prominent. Now, I highlight them even more, plastering dark powder instead of thick concealer over the area. I hope I make her fucking proud.

The thin tip of black eyeliner feels cold on the corner of my painted lids and jolts my heart rate even higher. My hand, shaking but stiff, makes the winged shape uneven and jagged. Frustrated, I reach for a Q-tip to straighten it out, then take a deep breath and recall Dr. Ellis's breathing exercises. I hope Dr. Ellis doesn't blame this on himself. I hope he knows that, somewhere inside me, he made me kind of rethink shrinks. He was different than all of the female therapists I'd seen before, who seemed to make me feel like a puddle of failure. If I were leaving a note, I'd let him know.

Pale foundation coats my face and glimmers as it remains slightly tacky. My mother's was constantly dry and patchy, so I make sure mine is always oily, a feat for my dry-as-hell skin, and I really hope that it sets enough now to not smear all over my pillow if I happen to move. I want my white sheets painted delicately, exactly how I've planned it. I even washed them yesterday for this. Jett's DNA can't be at such a toxic scene.

Holding the lipstick and looking at all the streaks it has from past applications makes me shudder. It's my favorite color, a dark scarlet called YoungBlood that I've used countless times since I got it years ago. It hits my messily lined lips and yearns to hold on for more, not wanting to let go, but I rip the suction suddenly and toss the lipstick into the trash with the rest of the makeup I've used. I look in the mirror and sigh, wishing my eyeliner were a little straighter and my concealer a little thicker. Next time.

The outfit I picked out hangs prominently at the end of my cramped closet, all of the pieces perfectly organized onto one hanger so that I wouldn't have to make any decisions today. Every decision has already been made. Today I'm just following through.

My hands grip the velvet hanger and slip the black dress off. It's the same one I wore out with Patricia. As I step into its small, slick frame, it inches up my legs and waist, and I'm reunited with the memories of connection. Of color, light, and sound. I was fed enough for a lifetime inside that club, there with Peter, and it's all encapsulated in this synthetic polyester blend. Each time I grip it and slide it up my thighs, a shock of electricity runs through the tired wires inside me. They're barely able to putter out consciousness. They beg for release, to be miserably recycled. As the dress bunches up over my midsection, I clench my jaw. The euphoric sensation passes, and panic replaces it Hopefully, whatever news article I'm in reaches Peter. Hopefully, he thinks he's the reason.

I gently step into the ratty, torn tights I've owned since middle school. They were once whole and untattered. I bought them with my mom at Target, begging her for a pair with feet because I hated the way I felt being the only girl with black ankle leggings instead of full tights. My pleading voice was so high-pitched and creaky, filled with the pain of hoping every day it wasn't cold enough to have to wear tights, and she ended up agreeing, with an eye roll while she muttered about me wasting all of our money. They ripped the first time I wore them, that next day when the temperature dropped down below fifty, and I got a compliment from Hannah Riley. She wasn't the most popular girl in school but was still someone I idealized, and I'd loved the tights ever since. Ripped tights gradually progressed into ripped jeans over the years because of Hannah Riley just saying they were "pretty cool." Today, the thin material barely stretches over my much longer legs, and the small holes are exaggerated into massive craters. I wish my thighs were thin enough not to protrude out of the gapes.

My stomach rumbles as if on cue. My mind laughs, but my body lacks the fuel to tell my vocal cords to release sound. I reach for the thick red belt hanging on the edge of the hanger, faux leather with metal grommets throughout, and latch it around my waist. It fits a tighter hole than the last time I wore it months ago. It still has dried sauce on the right side from when I wore it out to eat with Di on our first time at a restaurant together. Our Thai go-to. I'd ordered some peanut lettuce boats that had more than an acceptable amount of peanut sauce on them. I don't order those anymore.

A heavy silver necklace hangs on the opposite side of the hanger, with a huge lock on the end. I bought it months ago when I'd first moved here, at a tiny thrift shop that shut down not long after. I haven't worn it until now, haven't even tried it on, and it's longer than I hoped. It weighs down my neck. I feel it imprinting on the nape of my spine. At least I'll be lying down.

Finally, I slip on the red satin gloves that perfectly match my lips. I've never worn these, either; I bought them out with Di just recently, but the fact that they're the exact same color as my favorite lipstick justified the insane price that Di had scoffed at. Di.

Oh my God. Poor Di. She's the only reason I was hesitant, the only real reason I debated with myself even after the universe had made its decree with one drop of water. Jett will move on, find someone else, or just go follow a rock band. I don't know if what I feel for him is love or fleeting infatuation; I don't really have a frame of reference for the former. Maybe he'll go tour with some band and end up coming back to school in a few years, graduating eventually and becoming that cool-guy history teacher. Di—Di's who I worry about. Because Di doesn't just move on, she wallows, like me, and I know the depths that wallowing can reach. Trenches so deep that you drown by your own will, suffocating under the oceanic pressures of your own identity built upon exponentially increasing notions of hopelessness. Di's already suffering. She'll understand.

My mind returns to the present as the orange pill bottle glows even brighter, shining like a deity demanding worship. Just shoes, then I can bow down. I slip on red Mary Jane heels that I wore out throughout high school, having bought them online from some sketchy Asian website that took months to deliver them. They're scuffed and smudged with black lines, but the high platform makes them easy to walk in. Not that I'll be going far.

The latches around the tops of my feet snag on my tights, and I have to rip a new hole on the left to get them on. One last mark of evidence that I exist.

In the mirror, I look like I'm ready for a photo shoot. I have that heavily made-up look blaring back at me in the morning sunlight like I've been done up for a TV interview. It's the stage makeup for my final role, the female star of my own comedy show.

The bottle increasingly reflects light and even begins to pulse as if it's begging for me to consume its contents. I sigh and pick it up, reading the freshly placed label. *TAKE ONE PER DAY, WITH FOOD.* I guess I'm breaking both instructions. In my heels, I'm able to rise up onto my bed easily, with the bottle in one hand and YoungBlood in the other. I open the little bottle and look in, my eyes rolling down the orange cavity of memories leading back lifetimes, to bargaining with God for a new mother; to hugging Greg's infant body and wishing, out of mercy, that he hadn't been born; to slamming my own seven-year-old face against my bedroom wall hoping I could get a concussion and leave the hellhole I already knew life to be. The cavern leads me to sit in my childhood bedroom, not among the pink duvet at my dad's place, which was a haven of preemptive anxiety only on weekends and holidays, but the baby-blue Walmart sheets with nail polish stains splattered about. The trail of memories travels at the speed of light until I'm in the hospital after Really Bad, screaming at the nurse and my dad about Vic really existing, a male doctor having to hold me down and sedate me, then my mind surges to Dad, eating with him, or more like just watching him laugh at his phone while I sneer at my dinner plate. Then I finally reach just minutes earlier, painting my face with jagged eyeliner and tacky foundation. The pills jiggle in my shaking hand, and before anything internal can scream *no*, the overpowering momentum behind the movie of my memories propels my hand backward and up toward my mouth, shaking the bottle until every little orange circle has fallen down my dry throat. I look at the empty orange bottle, which no longer encompasses any of my memories, and I place it on the window ledge next to me on my bed.

The shaking in my body has stopped. There is nothing left to power unnecessary movement; the electrical wires within me have long since declared surrender. Their copper has even begun to erode and rust, contaminating my bloodstream and further infecting the gaping wounds covering my whole body. I am a painted clown, not by my makeup but by the various tones and tons of pus now spewing everywhere. I raise a grossly infected arm, hidden behind a crimson glove, and begin to draw on my window with the lipstick. The wax hits the smooth glass and glides like maple syrup dripping down a tree. My hand moves with the vibrancy of an artist, and once again I am Jackson Pollock, painting for an exhibition of my life's best works, but now I have the talented poise to skillfully paint. I drop down, beginning the second word, and look out to see if anyone is watching me. All I see are sleeping bodies in the building next door, each curled up against their window or just sock-covered feet peeking out from unkempt sheets. A small flicker within myself hopes someone will look at me and come crashing in, lassoing me and then launching me far above to my helicopter, so that I could look upon this scene and revel in my finale. But no one notices, no one even moves to prove their existence like I've tried so forcefully all these years to prove my own. I lean back on the edge of the twin mattress and look at my words beaming back at me. *HI MOM.* A heart dotting the *I.*

Suddenly, a pang hits my chest when I realize I've forgotten to grab the razor and safety pin I need. I gingerly drop myself back to the floor, feeling disappointed that what I thought were my final steps must now be replaced by these forgetful waddles to retrieve the instruments I require. I then groan and climb back onto my bed, careful not to place the soles of my heels onto the pristine sheets and dirty them at all. I look back up at my words and muster a slight smile. Finally a true artist.

My stomach squirms violently, and I wince as growing nausea sends acrid fluid up my throat. My eyes begin to focus in and out, unable to remain steady, but I manage to slice my pointer finger with the safety pin as planned and squeeze it with my opposite hand to squirt out little droplets around the frame of my body. Continuously, taking quite some time, I poke my bony finger in different spots until I've spewed out enough blood to create a thin ring circling where I'm lying. With each stab, I feel less pain and less motion in my rising and falling chest. Through hazy eyes, I glide the small razor across my right wrist before being unable to fully separate the skin as planned. My gaze twirls too much to continue. The words to my right spin in concentric circles until they are indecipherable from the rest of my surroundings. A vignette begins to encroach on the remaining light in my peripheral vision until my eyelids renounce any remaining effort and forfeit. However, my ears are still working, taking on the agency of the rest of my senses that have vanished, and I hear a buzzing symphony as if it is in the room with me. The vibration spirals into an echo coming from within. A final note plays. The audience claps. I bow as the curtain falls.

Chapter 61

My eyes flutter open as a thrashing heave erupts from my chest. I stare at the bright lights above me. They remind me of my dorm hallway, and I feel disoriented about what time it is. My mind is too frozen, too calcified, to ponder my location just yet. It must thaw and ooze out of the cracked skull I somehow still seem to possess. An outside voice isn't quite processed by my ears, but its echoes hit the outside of my hollow head, and I turn toward where I hear the sound waves. A tall figure approaches me. I can barely make out red-framed glasses through my hazy eyes.

"Valerie." The voice strikes me right in the heart, and I feel as if I'm being resuscitated. "Valerie," it repeats, louder. The resonance acts as a defibrillator. I inhale sharply as the face comes forward and forms in my vision.

"W-what's…" I trail off into a deep chasm of confusion that no words can fill. A hand rests on my shoulder. The touch is distantly painful, though it isn't firm.

"Your roommate found you. You…overdosed."

"H-how? I…" I can't begin to decide how to finish that thought.

"She forgot her phone, apparently, and...found you. How are you feeling?" Dr. Ellis blinks heavily as he studies my face. I move my lips around and find them to be awfully numb. I'm not sure if I'm bloated or just swollen from dehydration.

"I…I feel dead, so I guess…I got what I was going for?" He doesn't laugh; he just rests his hand more directly on my shoulder until it moves slightly onto the pillow. He draws it back sharply, which scares me, and I notice the blinking line on the monitor in front of me spike up higher. He returns to the seat to the right of my bed and continues to study me as if I'm a petri-dish experiment.

"Your father is coming up later tonight. You probably won't see him until tomorrow, though, if he isn't further delayed by the hurricane. Are you thirsty? Hungry? Cold?" I blink at him, wishing I could laugh. I want to say yes to all of the fucking above. I close my eyes and sigh. Whatever medication I must be on prevents my thoughts from turning into coherent sentences, and instead I seem to be solely able to think in primal terms. Yes. No.

Hmm. Simply speaking requires all of the effort artificially transported into my body through these IVs.

"Hurricane?" I finally ask in a pitch uncomfortably high for my throat.

"Oh yes, there's a major hurricane on its way around there. It should pass in a few days, though, worst case." I don't want to see my father. I hope it lasts more than a few days.

"Hmph." I toss restlessly in the thin hospital sheets.

"Do you need anything?" Dr. Ellis's voice is softer than his usual work tone.

"Why are you here?" It feels as if my words are gauze being pulled off of a wound effortlessly by someone else.

"It didn't take long for word to get to me, so I rushed over. I wanted to be here when you woke up."

I look at him for an extra second. "Thanks." I expect a surge of panic to arrive, but instead, I am busy blinking at each little light flashing on the machines surrounding me. "Are they going to take me off to some crazy asylum now?" I finally ask, mesmerized by my heart beating on the green screen.

"If you do end up going somewhere, it won't be an asylum, I assure you. But I'm not sure about the best action at this point. It's still a discussion."

"I don't want to go away."

"I know. I hope…I hope other options do come to light. I do think you need a break from the pressures of school, and everything that entails, though. Well, I'm getting ahead of myself, I shouldn't… I'm sorry." I notice now he's in Lululemon sweatpants I faintly recognize and a soft-looking gray V-neck that looks like it was overpriced. *Second-Skin Microfiber* was probably the marketing jargon they went with.

I close my eyes and suddenly reimagine myself sitting in Dr. Ellis's love seat our last time together, speaking ominously without him realizing it. Here, in this half-sedated state, I am able to observe my thoughts without my usual judgment. It was as if I was declaring what would happen. An ignorant magician.

Maybe if I imagine it hard enough, or say it with enough conviction, I'll leave this place. I wouldn't return to my dorm, or to my hometown, or anywhere I've been. I'd turn the little cavern inside my skull into my own sanctuary, where Greg and I could live together forever. No one else. No need for money. No need for food.

We'd just play board games and computer games like we did back then. I'd beat him in Scrabble, and he'd kill my favorite Sims character. I'd throw a pillow at him. He'd pretend it hurt his nose, then jump on me while I apologized profusely. I'd complain about my old nose, and he'd matter-of-factly tell me he didn't see any problem, without necessarily trying to make me feel better. Like Greg always did, he acted with the utmost concern without actually being concerned. It was like he understood how to *do life*, straight out of the womb, while life-ing just wasn't really my thing. I don't think it can be.

My mind fades, strung along by intravenous puppeteers, but Greg remains there by my side, making sure I don't stray too far away from him and from our room together inside me. He assures me he'll always be there, even though I probably won't see him as often now. Now, after Really Bad 2.0.

Greg grips my hand tightly, and I feel Dr. Ellis's touch on my shoulder as well. In this vibrant illusion, I eventually arrive in my helicopter and view myself from above. The body I'm looking at, sleeping in her hospital bed, is slowly growing in size. The surrounding sheets tighten around her increasing frame. It can't be me; this is someone else, someone larger. I don't have those pus-filled wounds and jagged scars or the soft fat. Nothing of the sort. In the helicopter, I reach to feel the back of my ribs and the corners of my hips. Instead, I feel alien mounds of flesh. I gasp and look down at myself, seated in the cockpit, and see a protruding stomach and bloated arms. I scream, writhing, as Greg and Dr. Ellis are down below silently viewing my swollen frame.

"No! No! No! No!" I'm becoming so violent that the aircraft is shaking. I slam my fists against the glass windshield, but my hands are now too padded for it to break. *"Let me go! Let me go! I want to get out!"* My obese body is flailing everywhere as I struggle to exit the aircraft. Finally, under the heavy weight of myself, the exit opens, and I look down at the thousands of feet between me and the girl in the hospital bed below. Wind pulls me out, and my eyes shut against the air pressure. The closer I get to the resting, overweight patient, the more disgusted I am by her appearance. Nausea, from the sight of her and from this traumatic fall, pulls me to curl into a ball as I descend even farther.

My eyes dart open. I yank my arm back immediately to check for my ribs and hips, but the IVs in place stop me with a sharp pain. Gritting my teeth, I do so with the opposite, less restrained arm, little droplets of blood dribbling out anyway from the tension on my veins. Out of the corner of my eye, I see Dr. Ellis lift his head up sharply from leaning on his shoulder, and he darts over to help me. When he arrives at my side, I've already lifted up my entire hospital gown to verify the presence of my bones, and he stops in fear. My fingers slide over the sharp bolts on either side of my body and run up to feel strong stripes along my back. In relief, I drop my arm down and allow the little streams of blood to watercolor my gown. Dr. Ellis runs out in his Lululemon pants.

"Nurse? Nurse!"

Chapter 62

"We have to make sure your vitals are restored before we can move you. Then it's up to your team to decide how and when to release you. I don't have authority on that." The nurse hangs her clipboard up on the white hook on the wall, having to balance on her tiptoes to reach. She's small, with a spherical body that stretches her pastel scrubs. I bet her vitals are worse than mine.

Apparently, my heart rate isn't too concerning. I'm convinced they're completely inept, but at least it keeps them off my ass about eating. Dr. Ellis has been bringing me some food in, and I've been eating mostly salad-bar lettuce and cold oatmeal, since I don't have much of an appetite right now anyway. I roll over to the opposite side in the hospital bed and sigh into the limp pillow as I change the channel on the TV. I've watched so many episodes of outdated TLC reality shows that I feel like a paralyzed sloth.

Every day, a twitch inside me grows and grows from not being able to weigh myself. All anyone seems to care about here is *flushing out my system*. I wish my arms were small enough for them to notice me. I wish my collarbones were prominent enough for them to reconsider how much treatment I probably need. No one even fucking weighed me; they just cared about my blood pressure and whatever other shit the numbers on the green monitor mean. My ribs still feel as rough as they did before I came; I know there's no way I've gained any considerable weight with how little I've been eating. I want to rip off this hospital gown and curl up so that when the nurse comes in, my spine looks like it might tear the skin along my back in two. Maybe she'll do something then.

I hear a soft knock and pray it isn't my father. I assume his flight has been delayed, as I haven't seen him yet, and I hope it's just Dr. Ellis. Red glasses peek past the door, and my chest warms.

"Is my dad still back home?" I ask before he gets the chance to say anything.

"Yeah, it looks like it'll be another two or three days before airports open back up. I'm sorry about that."

"It's...it's okay. I don't really want to see him like this anyway."

"I understand. Do you want anything to eat? I have a banana with me." I look into his tired, dark eyes and feel warm.

Maybe they've just upped whatever I'm on, if anything. I have no fucking idea what's going on anymore.

"Okay," I finally muster.

"Okay?" His surprise makes me blink away nervously. It's the first time I've agreed to have anything besides the meals of watery oats and soggy romaine.

"Um, yeah, sure."

He hands me the banana. It is spotty and soft, just how I like them, and I can't help but smile. Our eyes meet fleetingly as we make the trade-off.

"Thank you," I say, peeling the skin. Dr. Ellis smiles through his small lips and sits down in his usual chair.

"Do you have, like, clients you're missing to be here?" My speech is somewhat muffled by half-chewed banana.

"Don't worry, I've taken a few days off. Nothing major that can't be rescheduled. You look…you look like you're doing better. Brighter." My face flushes as he watches me eat. It's not so much that I'm eating a banana, in particular, but eating in front of others is terribly humiliating. However, narcotic-induced numbness prevents a full shutdown from happening, and I finish the banana.

He gets up and takes the peel from me, putting it in a plastic bag he pulls out from his briefcase. I furrow my brows in confusion.

"Compost. June and I…"

"Oh, oh. Cool. Is June, like, okay with you being here?"

"She…she thinks someone else is having a medical emergency."

"Who?"

"No one, just a friend of mine."

"Oh, okay."

"I'm sorry if you wish I'd told her it's you."

"I'm probably getting enough attention as is. But I appreciate the thought. Really."

He rolls his eyes at me playfully, and I gasp as much as my fatigued respiratory system allows.

"Did you just *roll your eyes* at me?"

"What, it can't be my turn now?"

I purse my lips and prop myself up on the disappointingly thin pillow. "I don't roll my eyes at you. I don't think I've *once* rolled my eyes in all the times we've met."

"Maybe you just don't notice." He seals the ziplock bag. I roll my eyes in fabulous grandiosity and flop back on the mattress. The plastic hospital bed creaks. I wish I wasn't big enough for it to make that sound. The half smile on my face sinks.

"Are…are they going to move me to, like, a psych ward? I…I want to leave, Dr. Ellis." My head turns to the right so I can look at him. From how I'm lying, his whole body looks sideways in the black chair.

"They'll keep you for a few days, most likely, until making a decision on whether to release you or refer you to a program. If…if you do take your medication regularly, though, I do not see an inpatient program as being necessary, as opposed to something day to day."

I stare at him, blinking, from my fetal position. He looks into me, as he often does during our sessions when I choose silence. He tries to read me as if it my stillness is dialogue. I always wonder what he's getting from it.

"I'm sorry I lied."

The words whisper out and taper off at the end. I see them floating through the air, like a piece of paper, before finally landing onto Dr. Ellis's brain and settling. His eyes soften. He glances down at his hands and cups one over the other.

"Lied... How?"

"I—I told you I would do my part, and all. 'Put forth effort' was how you phrased it, I think." I'm staring at my pulse on the green monitor. It's increased slightly. I hope he doesn't notice. Dr. Ellis continues to look at my eyes as I refuse to meet his, pretending that the jolting line is truly captivating.

"You did put forth effort, Valerie. No one... There isn't a perfect journey to dealing with mental illness. You did your best." I clench my jaw and look up to stop the burning in my eyes. It's sudden and overwhelming. I pray Dr. Ellis doesn't notice the tears welling up in my right eye, closest to the pillow. I turn onto my back to stop any from falling.

"I..." I sniffle aggressively. "I'm sorry, though. I *didn't* do my best, I know that, I just...I just can't; I—" My throat cuts me off sharply to prevent my voice from crashing into hysteria. Dr. Ellis walks over and grabs my hand. Upon feeling his touch, the tears cascade from the sides of my face. My eyes and jaw slam shut so hard, I'm worried the force will yank the IVs straight out of my arms. He says nothing, just stands there and holds my hand, as tiny dribbles paint the sides of my face and warm the tips of my ears. My hand is limp, all of the energy in my body focused on my face, but Dr. Ellis's grip remains warm and firm.

Chapter 63

Two days later, my father makes it into town. Dr. Ellis warned me last night and also let me know that *they* have agreed to let me go on the condition I go to an outpatient program during the week. I still don't have a clear picture of who *they* is, but apparently *they've* been talking to my dad, too.

"It was a compromise. I really had to talk it out with your father. It wasn't an easy decision to come to," Dr. Ellis told me.

"Oh. Um, thank you."

"Yeah. Sleep well."

"Do you have another banana?" I asked him right before he walked out of the room.

"No, but—"

"Oh, it's fine—"

"No, no, wait right there."

"I can't really leave."

He rushed out, came back in a minute with a disappointingly green banana, and handed it to me with a smile.

Dr. Ellis then stood there. I looked at him uncomfortably without even peeling the banana.

"Sorry, I'll... I just don't want to leave and turn the light off on you, you know..." He sat down. I finished my banana, then handed him the peel, and he left as he put it into another plastic bag.

My stomach rumbles, and I wish I had another banana. They seem somewhat friendly to me since I've been here. I'm not sure why. It feels liberating yet incredibly scary to have a *whole* banana instead of the allotted half I would usually eat with my portioned oatmeal for breakfast. Two voices inside me scream with every bite, warring it out until my stomach rumbles fiercely. The voices are quiet in my hungry state. I relax in the familiar peace.

"Miss Updike, you have a visitor," the nurse quickly says before my dad's eyes peer down from behind her. They are small, bright lasers that startle me. I shudder and look down at the thin bedding on top of me. I hope it covers my body enough for him not to notice me much.

The nurse jumps as she turns around and sees him there, and he unapologetically swerves around her stout frame to enter the room. His footsteps slow as he approaches me. I see and hear a heavy swallow. I have to remind my forgetful chest to breathe. As he approaches, I keep my mind focused on evenly inhaling and exhaling, following a precise rhythm, but as he fills more and more of my vision, my thoughts start to wander. They increase to a scream until he's standing directly in front of me, peering down, with a complicated gaze I find too angry to meet for more than half a second. I want to apologize, but I know if I say anything at all, his reaction will probably send my whole body into a state of catatonic shock. My dad rests his hand on the edge of the hospital bed, which creaks slightly under the weight he dumps onto it. I hope the creaking I make when I get onto the bed isn't as loud.

"How are you feeling?" I can feel his gaze on the top of my scalp. Suddenly, it itches, but I feel paralyzed and tormented under the growing discomfort.

"A little tired. A little…yeah, tired." I stop myself before I say *hungry*.

"Are you…are you… I…" He sighs and removes his hand. I blink twice. I don't want him to finish whatever his question was.

"I don't have to go off and live anywhere, right?" I finally ask through my tense, almost-shut vocal chamber. Suddenly, I hear a huge inhale and a strong sniffle that echoes off the walls sharply.

"No, no…" I have never heard his voice so wobbly, so unstable. *Inhale. Exhale. Inhale. Exhale.* Another sniffle so loud it might as well be from Zeus's nostril. I lay there, blinking and alternating between watching my chest rise and fall and watching my heart rate on the monitor peak and plummet as I hear my dad quietly sniffling. I don't want to look up and see what's actually happening, but I imagine that he is just holding back mucus. Allergies. He's always had bad allergies.

My loosely meandering train of thought sharply turns back to the present when the nurse comes in and motions to my father, who speaks to her at the door. They half whisper, but I don't want to hear or listen anyway. I just want a goddamn banana.

Finally, my dad returns, his eyes glowing red. I regrettably meet them with my own and feel inflammation in my own body.

"You're going to get to leave tomorrow. I…I got us a hotel room. A suite kind of thing. So we could be together for a little while." *So I can keep an eye on you in case you try to kill yourself again.*

I nod my head. I hope Dr. Ellis comes back again before I have to leave.

My dad sits down in one of the chairs and stares out the window. The direct sunlight on his rugged face highlights wrinkles I've never noticed before. He looks older than I've ever seen and more tired than I remember. Probably tired from thinking about me. I wish he hated me so I wouldn't feel so bad about my ambivalence.

I wish I had my phone so I could text Di or Jett. Someone just to talk to. My stomach lurches forward as I realize I'll have to explain what has happened to both of them. Maybe I won't, though. Maybe they'll already know. Maybe that's worse.

"Have...have you told anyone?" I ask, keeping my head directly upright but turning my eyes toward him ever so slightly.

"No. I wanted to respect your privacy." My heart sinks, pulled down by thankfulness and regret. If I were him, I'd probably have packed up and left even before Really Bad happened. I don't understand how he can be compelled to still be here for me throughout all this shit, "family" or not.

"Thanks." I look away, but his tired eyes remain fixated on me. He blinks a few times.

"Valerie, I think maybe we should have you back home for a little while." My jaw clenches, stopping me from either asking what he means by *we* or defensively pushing for the outpatient day-only program. As if I'm alone and no one has spoken, I remain staring straight ahead through unfocused eyes.

"I think some time to get back on your feet and relax would be best for you. You can always return to school when you're ready." At first, I feel sympathetic with needing a break, but feelings of overwhelming repugnance flood me all at once when I consider boarding a plane back there. There is too much there trying to suffocate me, and in my weakened state, it may just do that. My heart pulls me forward and forces me to sit up. The wires are still plugged into me, like I'm some kind of fucking electrical outlet funneling energy into an electronic device long overdue to be replaced, are not strong enough to keep me down. IVs pinch my arm, but not quite hard enough to pull me back.

"I'm not going home."

"I knew you wouldn't be cooperative at first."

"Dad, Dr. Ellis said you'd decided on an outpatient program. I'll do that, I'm okay with that."

"Do you want to get better, Valerie?" My father's voice is solemn. As it permeates the hospital room, I hear it harmonizing with the buzzing machines. It's an orchestra I was dragged to unwillingly.

"I…" I start to say *yes*, then stop myself. "For some reason, I don't know. I don't know if getting better…would actually be better."

"I think coming home, recuperating, and resting would help you get better, and we can discuss your school and finances, and, well, we'll get to that. But I can't force you. You… You're an adult."

"I don't feel like one. I'm still such a child."

"I don't think you got the childhood to ever really know what being a child is like." I meet his eyes, then feel my gaze drop as if gravity itself is forcing it to bow down to the deluge of sorrow overcoming me. A memory of me, not even eight years old, pops into mind. I was sitting on the floor of my bedroom at my mother's house. The dark-green carpet of the room I had no say in decorating looked back at me solemnly, and I began to wonder if I could do something worthy enough to trade my mother in for someone else. All of the scenarios of what I thought was "good enough" flood my brittle, nearly demolished cavern of a skull. I remember promising to do so well in school, they'd send me straight to college before I hit double digits. I remember saying I'd become the most beautiful-looking, most perfectly tiny girl in the world so that I would be swept away by fame. I remember pleading to God to take me away from the hellhole I was in in exchange for never thinking one sinful thing again. Little trails of snot fell from that face, a chubby face with sun-kissed freckles. A face with a nose I had eradicated, with light hair rimming it I couldn't bear to keep visible once all I could see was my mother in both of those things.

Now, I gaze down at my calves and ankles. They probably aren't too much larger than the size they were at when I was crying on that green carpet. I wonder if, after a few days here, my millimeters of remaining muscle have withered away. I know for certain there has been no healing; every cell in my body has been more focused on the areas recently traumatized.

"I'm so sorry, Dad," I say, and little dribbles of snot fall from this artificial nose of mine as if they never stopped trailing down over a decade ago. My sinuses blast open so readily that it shakes me. The bed creaks, reminding me of the space I'm taking up. I wish I didn't take up any space here. I wish I didn't take up any space at all.

My dad gets up to grab a tissue and hand it to me. His attempt to lovingly pass on the Kleenex is so painfully foreign to both of us that I openly wince and turn away from him, emitting a small giggle. It is inappropriate. My face flushes.

"Don't apologize to me, Valerie. *I'm* sorry… I'm sorry I didn't know about what you were going through…"

"I'm tired of you saying that," I blurt out with strained vocal cords. "How the hell did you not know? How the *hell*?" I'm not yelling, but my throat is crying out.

"I know, I know. I'm sorry—"

"You… Just… You're apologizing for feeling guilty about being a *bystander* to your *child*. Your own daughter was…fucking suicidal before she was six, and you're *sorry*? I don't..." I shake my head calmly, having thought this out in my head too many times before to become overwhelmed by the emotions keeping me alert in the absence of food. His jaw drops, probably at the statements I'm making and at the detachment present within them.

"What was I supposed to do, Valerie?" he finally spits out.

"Save me! Save me from the hell that was Mom, and her drinking, and her hurting me! All she did was hurt me, Dad! The years of drinking and yelling and hitting me and *hating* me! Do you know what it's like to have someone put all of their energy into killing the light inside of you for your whole entire life and then be expected to be *okay* in the head after that? I shut down for eighteen fucking years, and you're *sorry* that you didn't do anything during that whole time. You knew. Maybe not everything, but you knew something was wrong, and that's on you now that you didn't have the courage to save your own daughter from two decades of hell." I gasp for breath and swallow. "I never got the life I needed to stay alive. I could never feel love at home, so I tried to make a home for myself with stories inside me instead. But once even those films weren't enough, my mind was too desperate to let me know it would take over and make those stories for me. And maybe they aren't real to you. But they're real to *me*. And maybe they'll kill me eventually. But at least I'll be succeeding at killing myself after all these years of you letting it come to that."

Suddenly, he slams his skull tightly onto his palms and exhales so loudly that his nostrils must be filled with dried mortar. He places his wrinkled hands on his khaki-covered knees, stands, and slowly walks out of the room. The door closes, and the reassuring beeping from the monitor brings me back into my own breath.

My eyes close, and I'm reintroduced to that little girl bargaining with God. The same language comes back into mind. *What could I do, God I don't even believe in, to blow all of this away?* Except I don't even know what I want instead. This crisis is all I can imagine myself surviving in. I would be a shark forced to live in the desert. An environment of peace would surely kill the body I've grown to inhabit.

Maybe if I were small enough, adequate enough, then things would untangle. An opposing voice in my mind realizes how unending these ideas about disappearing are, then floats away.

I am not starving to reach a physical ideal. I don't think I ever was.

I think I was bargaining with God, indirectly, and testing out new

creations of myself to win some game that I thought could grant

me a grand prize. But I will never win.

Chapter 64

Somehow, a set of fresh clothes has appeared in the now-empty chair when I wake up. They are my own clothes, nothing characteristically *me*, but still familiar enough to be startled by. A purple sweater I last remember wearing in Dr. Ellis's office. Not-too-ripped gray jeans I last remember wearing with Jett. I had them on them that first time Di and I got Thai, too; there's still a small stain from the peanut sauce on the left thigh. The way they're folded, the stain is staring right at me with intoxicating eyes, drawing me in to feel the guilt of trying to leave a classroom without being noticed. Except, I disrupted the whole goddamn lecture, and now the course isn't repeatable in the slightest.

A nurse comes in to briefly tell me that I can check out today once I'm ready, but it has to be before noon. It's nine now, according to the news channel on the TV. I tell her that won't be a problem, and I can be out soon. She disconnects me from the various IVs and wires, and as I step onto the ground to get dressed, the lightness in my arm makes it feel like a phantom limb.

I yawn and catch a glimpse of myself in the mirror in the bathroom across the room as I begin to step into the jeans. I am no longer imagining the wounds on my body; I see them bandaged up along my arm. Pulling on my sweater, I roll up the sleeves instead of covering up the messiness of my forearm. Now everyone who sees me can see what I always see.

I ring for the nurse, and she walks me through the narrow, winding hallways without a word. We reach the waiting room, where my father sits in the corner picking at his nails. His eyes dart up immediately once I walk into the room. They fixate on my arm, then meet mine, then fly to the nurse's a few inches below me. As I watch every movement he makes to gauge what he's going to do next, my ears seem to turn off and allow for precision in my vision. The nurse goes up to speak with him, pointing at some things on a clipboard and getting his signature, but all the noise coming through to me sounds as if I'm underwater. Finally, the nurse walks away, and my dad approaches me slowly.

"You ready?"

My instinct is to respond with something challenging and underhandedly snarky, but I simply nod, looking down at my black

Vans I thought I wouldn't ever see again. I keep anticipating a huge wave of panic to come over me, one of shame and embarrassment, but I feel withdrawn and numb. The nurse rushes back holding a white paper envelope stapled closed at the top.

"I almost forgot!" she shrieks as my father takes the shiny envelope from her hands. A wave does come over me, but this time, it is a wave of knowing that what is in that bag is what is keeping me soulless.

We make our way, side by side, to a taxi at the front of the queue waiting in front of the hospital. As we move outside, I imagine what I looked like being rushed through these large doors a few days ago. If I was hanging limply on a stretcher, my head tossing as the frame shook, with doctors yelling orders around me. Now, my father holds open the taxi door for me to get into, just like he did last time he came to visit me.

"D-do you have your luggage this time?" I whimper flatly. He laughs meekly and nods.

"We're going to the hotel now. Dr. Ellis suggested you two meet tomorrow, so we set up something at eleven. Is that okay with you?"

"Mm-hmm." I bite my lip as the car jolts over a bumpy road. I hear the pills in the envelope shaking, and the noise startles my numb, dreamlike state. I don't quite understand how we're here now, not talking like everything's totally okay or anything, but not really acting as if yesterday happened, either. Maybe my dad's in denial. But I don't have the energy or even really the desire to change that right now.

After Really Bad, my dad broke down and tried to become everything he thought he should be for me. Surprising me with donuts in bed every weekend morning. Offering to proofread my English papers, even though he couldn't understand them in the slightest. Submitting my shitty films to every contest he could. Buying me knickknacks every fucking day just to surprise me with something he thought would make me smile. I remember one of those days he got me a Wonder Woman USB drive that I never ended up using. It's still on my desk in my old room underneath piles of school papers I never seemed to be able to get rid of.

Now, he sits in tense silence, probably feeling such a concoction of emotions that he doesn't know which one to act upon, so he lets them fester and eat him alive while I'm eaten from the outside in. The memory of yesterday increasingly permeates the air of the car. My arm seems to call out menacingly to those eyes of his, which are painfully trying to remain fixated on the taxi driver's neck ahead of him. They dart to the side and down like a fish being horrifyingly yanked by a fisherman's hook. I feel more at ease with him, like this, than if he were trying to make me feel better, thinking that if he did enough, I'd suddenly do the one-eighty he's dreamed about. Except it isn't even about him, it wasn't ever, and so he can't even begin to reroute the pendulum swinging inside me with so much momentum it might just throw my body to the ground.

My mind comes to an aggressive halt as the taxi stops in front of a modestly lit hotel. It is small and narrow but seems to scale hundreds of floors as I gaze up from my seat in the taxi. Suddenly, a doorman opens the door I'm leaning on and says, "Good afternoon," while pretending not to notice my arm. My mind wanders as my dad checks us in, drifting off to thoughts about my clothes, toiletries, and even makeup I wish I could have right now. *Will they let me back in my dorm to get any of my shit?* Probably not. I'm probably seen as a threat to the premises at this point. *How am I thinking of this so cleanly, in such a straightforward way?* Probably because of whatever inhuman amount of medication is pumping through my veins right now. I'm probably going to feel like this, a smooth yet boring cruise down a man-made amusement park river, until I've forgotten what it's like to be free.

The room we're in has a bedroom with two double beds and a separate living room. I haven't stayed in something like this since probably middle school, when trips with my father were still simple, and I when I was young enough not to need a separate room. I wonder if he still snores ever so slightly like he did those years ago. I'd always wake him up and complain, then he'd apologize, fall asleep, and do it all again. I'd eventually fall asleep myself and whine about it to him the next morning over the room-service breakfast he somehow always had waiting for me. Every hotel memory I can possibly conjure up includes that breakfast on a tray, usually pancakes or waffles, because those were my favorite, with berries and maple syrup. I look down at my body now, which cannot fathom living in such a way. I want to reach out and pull on the costume of my old self for just one day, to remind myself why I no longer do those things. Something must've gone horribly wrong for me to be here now. Something I'm forgetting. My memory of having those blueberry pancakes without much thought must be missing the painful catalyst to propel me forward to what brought me to how I am now. Maybe I'm trying to create the story I always wanted. The story I didn't get with my mom, that I tried to make through film but never could manage, and which I've now turned into a story so real it's taking over what is apparently truly real. That tarot reader's voice echoes in my mind, telling me that I'm "running into the same wall." I think I'm ramming into it over and over, not hoping to get somewhere but hoping that every hit will be my last. I wonder if there really is a way to create stories that can keep me alive instead of lead to my demise.

There's so much to unpack before I can imagine what it is I want. I just know what I *don't* want, which is building more and more shaky infrastructure to cover up a swampy, unstable foundation. There is no "inner me" to return back into after all this made-up shit: there is only a lot of made-up shit to get rid of before making up what the inner me has to be. And I don't know if anything can remain if I do that. I don't know if I have it in me to do that.

"You…you can wear some of my things to sleep in tonight. I've asked the hotel to send up a toothbrush and everything for you until…until we can go to your room tomorrow and get what you need," my dad says tightly.

"Okay. Thank you." I give him a long stare until he looks up to meet my gaze and lifts the corners of his mouth to smile. I do the same, then notice a banana on the far side of the suite in a clear bowl on the living room coffee table. I walk over, pick it up, then look at it as the two voices in my head throw verbal daggers at each other. Through the underwater murkiness, I cannot even make out what they are saying to each other, and instead I just continue to look at the banana, just wishing it were riper.

Chapter 65

My dad doesn't accompany me to Dr. Ellis's office. He just hands the cab driver a twenty and walks back inside the hotel, still in his pajamas at ten thirty. I've never seen him not being completely put together by eight.

I start tapping my foot on the floor of the car, the frame thin enough to make the whole vehicle shake with my movement. The driver, a not-too-old Indian man, glares back at my legs. I stop and pull my knees up into my chest immediately.

The meter rises steadily, and I start to twitch again, making no sound this time, with my knees just rising and falling in my cross-legged position to barely touch the seat cushion. The meter is at nineteen fifty, and I don't have any money on me.

"You can just stop right up there. I don't have any more than a twenty."

"I stop at the next light."

"Okay." I know where we are. This is the route I used to take, walking here from my dorm. The busy avenue curves to the right, and all I need to do is follow the curve, take a left, and cross the street. His office building is as secluded as a building can possibly get from the inherent loitering of such a busy neighborhood, and the huge windows all over allow for voyeurism in this privileged isolation. When I push against the familiar revolving doors, my arm fires up in acute pain. The sleeve of my purple sweater, the same one I wore yesterday, isn't rolled up this time, so the security guard inside simply stares at me curiously. The door has needed some kind of repair for months; it's incredibly difficult to push open, especially for me. I manage to power through with my other arm and walk through the seating area to get to the opposite side where the elevators are. Though filled with students and building employees at this hour, I feel even more underwater. I cannot seem to look at anyone through a clear lens; everything is filtered and softened and unfocused. I keep blinking to snap back into myself, into liveness, into presence, but a haze is cast over my entire consciousness.

The elevator ticks, and I exit, walking directly into Dr. Ellis's waiting room. It looks the same as always, with outdated family-friendly magazines piled on the several side tables around the dimly lit area, but I feel as if this is the first time I'm seeing all of it. As I sit down, I anticipate feeling panic from this unfamiliarity where there should be déjà vu, but I cannot even pick up the pace of my mind from a slow meander to a decent trot. I gaze at my gray jeans glumly.

"Valerie?" I jolt up, frightened, at Dr. Ellis's voice. With his hair freshly combed and still slightly wet, he peers through the door he leans against. I swallow and stand up.

"Hi." I follow him back into the space I feel I can most depend on. Everywhere else, whether it be of my own construction or real life, seems to unfailingly crumble to pieces, but this light-filled room high up near the clouds remains unchanging. The same books, in the same alphabetical and topical order, rim the wall opposite me. Now that I think about it, it's an awfully large office for just one therapist.

"You're at your hotel with your father now, right?" He clicks the end of his pen against the yellow notepad and blinks at me through his red-rimmed frames. The pages of the notepad are loose and wrinkled but still managing to stay together.

"Yeah," I finally say, my brain feeling like it's lagging behind its usual pace. "We're in a suite, I think so he can see everything I do. No, I *know* so he can see everything I do. Which I get at this point." We both emit a soft laugh and sink farther into our seats.

"Have you spoken much with him? About what happened or anything at all?" Dr. Ellis jumping right into discussing my suicide attempt doesn't send the expected shock of electricity through my body. Instead, I continue to blink at him flatly as if I'm watching a professor lecture.

"Just like we usually would, except it felt heavier, I guess. He can't ask me what I want for dinner or anything without, like, looking at me with so much sadness. I feel so…like, not only bad, but so fucking uncomfortable."

"I wouldn't expect anything less at this point. Fortunately, this is only temporary."

"Yeah, I…I just want to know what's going to happen to me. My dad wants me to go back home, even though you both discussed an outpatient program, I thought, and I don't really know where I'm supposed to, like, live if I go to that program? I don't…I don't know. I'm just tired and done." We gaze at each other for an extra beat or two, just sitting in everything I'm bringing with me to this conversation. The offerings of chocolate on our first few meetings. The asking him about his family months ago. The passive-aggressive tests I employed, manifesting through backhanded comments or winding thought forms he'd have to track sufficiently for me to open up. He clears his throat, and we snap back into the now.

"Ultimately, it is up to you, Valerie. You are an adult in this instance, even if…even if there are lots of moving parts outside of you."

"I don't think my dad wants me to know that."

"I'm sure you know this, but he also is…going through a lot with this."

"I know, and that's why I can't even let myself *feel*, because then I'll probably just crumble. If I could feel guilty. I don't think these fucking meds let me."

"You should, though, have a better idea of what you really do want, with a clearer mind. Wouldn't you say?"

"I try and kill myself, I'm basically mentally hijacked, and now I'm meant to just, like, fucking go on? I don't…I don't think a *clearer mind* is at all what's happening here. A *silenced mind* is more like it." Small raindrops begin to patter against the windows to my right. I normally always have an umbrella in my backpack when I come here. *Came* here. Now, I don't want to ask whoever needs to be fucking asked if I can go get my backpack and all my other shit.

"When do I get my phone back? How do I get my phone?" I blurt out quickly as Dr. Ellis begins to inhale and reply to my statement. He sits back midbreath and blinks down at me.

"Your father was supposed to have retrieved some of your basic personal belongings yesterday. Maybe he's going today. We spoke to some dorm administration." I roll my eyes and sigh. If I were him, I wouldn't want to do shit for me, either.

"I just want to fucking talk to Di and Jett, to see how they're doing, to tell them why I've been basically dead—" Our eyes meet, and then we shudder together. "I mean, like, why I haven't been able to answer. You know." He nods and scribbles a few lines in his notepad.

"Maybe…just bring this up to your father. So it's all sorted out."

"Can I not go back and get my things myself?"

Dr. Ellis sighs and massages his temples. "I'm afraid not."

"I…I get it," I say flatly. My eyes continue to watch the rain falling without thought.

"I'm sorry, too," I add. "I mean…it must feel kind of like a fucking *failure* to you. All these *strategies* and *therapy methods* and everything that seemed so promising…" The rain patters, filling the deep void between my voice trailing off and his silence. I look at his tailored khakis, his perfectly shined black shoes that he mentioned June doesn't like, and I see a sad attempt at control within it all. Like how my eating issues probably are for me. Like how treating me like shit probably was for my mom.

"I don't feel like a failure. And you shouldn't, either. Mental health is…like physical health. It ebbs and flows."

"Physical health tends to always deteriorate over time."

"So maybe I wasn't using the best analogy."

"Really, though. I mean, why bother if I'm doomed? Because I'm paying you?"

"Valerie…"

"Really. Like, what *must* it be like for a therapist once your client tries to commit suicide? Do you just continue on like it's just another bump in the road? Like a bad day?"

He looks at me straight through the thick lenses encapsulated in those red rims without blinking or wavering. The force of my words, though not felt by me in any emotional sense, lure my eyes to meet his in this visual push-pull. Finally, he raises his shoulders with a sharp inhale and swallows. His Adam's apple wiggles inappropriately for such an interaction.

"I see it as an incident, though extreme and intense, that requires thought and working through to understand, like any unfortunate mental-health flare-up. The difference is the gravity of it. And...I keep seeing you because I care about my clients, Valerie. I hope you can see I obviously don't do this just for payment."

"So you'd do this shit for free?"

"I didn't say that."

"I know. I'm sorry. I'm...I'm really fucking mad, I think," I say, an undesired laugh accompanying my words. Dr. Ellis, shaken up and jittery, sits up taller. Before he can say anything, I continue.

"I'm fucking mad because I didn't have a say in any of this! I'm fucking mad because I'm, like, being thrown around by my own goddamn mind and people who don't even goddamn exist except in my head, and I *feel* shit about them! They get to me; they're so fucking real; I fucking hate it; I fucking *hate it*!" I'm leaning over my knees now, my face in my hands and scrunched together between tense knuckles. I stand up and walk over to the windows.

Slowly, I place my hands on the glass and watch as the rain begins to strike harder. There is a slight vibration, and it begins to raise the electricity within me, not dead but dormant. Looking toward Dr. Ellis now, he sees that internal charge and simply looks at me without speaking. Words have never solved me; words will never solve me.

A crisp page of notepad paper flips in the background.

Chapter 66

As I walk out of the building, I see my father waiting in a cab, a large green van with a billboard sign on top for a gentlemen's club.

"We should get my things from my dorm," I say firmly as I slide into the back seat, leaving more than enough room between us.

"The door isn't closed!" the driver booms across the plexiglass divider. I slam it several times until it clicks. My father has, by now, returned to his phone.

"Dad, please, Dr. Ellis... I know I'm not supposed to go back there, but you can. I just want to get my phone, and...and my clothes. Please. I don't know why you're putting this off." He looks back up at me and sighs. It is silent for far too long, in my opinion, until I open my mouth to add more and he interrupts me mid-inhale.

"I don't think you are ready to have everything back yet, Valerie."

"*Ready?* What? I'm an adult, it's my say in this matter. I don't even really want to go back there, but I—I need my things—"

"So I have to go back and get them for you?"

"Who the hell else is going to? I'm really sorry, Dad, but what else am I going to do here?"

"Valerie, why?" His face reddens with tension. I can finally see his anger toward me, denied for years, decades, maybe even lifetimes, beginning to seep out of his aging pores. I almost begin to salivate, in euphoric relief, at seeing my mind's conclusions and beliefs finally manifesting in real life.

"Why? Because I'm your daughter, and—and I'm not allowed into my place of residence, which contains all of my belongings because I tried to *kill* myself there, so I need my *dad* to—"

"What's the point if you're just going to do it all over again, anyway, Valerie? I can give you everything back, give you the damn world with my own hands…Christ himself could come down and bring you back up into the clouds with him, and you'd *still* be like this. Why should I keep going around and around in this never-ending circle that will always end up the same for you?" After everything has seeped out of his face, all of the gallons of liquid hatred, he is left empty and porcelain. The redness in his face has paled into a lifeless gray. Flickering electrical wires inside me shut down, no longer able to withstand any conductivity whatsoever. I look to the ratty black leather seat cushion beneath me and begin to focus on its creases, wondering if they came from the dead animal's own body or from years of wear. I wonder if this is even real leather at all. I hope not.

I follow a thick crease beginning right at the middle of my thigh. It twists and bends where the seat-belt clicker, which has probably never really been used, forms an indent down the middle of the cushion. It then reroutes and jumps upward. My eyes, tracing it, see it meet my dad's cream pants. They are ugly. They have been ugly for as long as I can remember. He has photos in them with me, when I was much younger, not even as tall as the pants themselves. I wonder if he brought them on the trip we took to Arizona when I was little. The one where I was eating that strawberry. I wonder if these pants have been around my mom, then, too. I wonder if they understand.

My ears suddenly absorb everything that has been said. The words coalesce in a plume from my father's mouth, then hit the roof of the van, then eventually enter my airspace. There is no sharp feeling, no shock or hurt. There is only agreement, which lifts my eyes up heavily to meet his.

"You're right. But you're going to still act as if I could, I know it." We hit a bump, and his head nails right into the ceiling with a sharp thud. The formaldehyde vial preserving that moment has suddenly burst, liquid settling in a puddle on the street far behind us now.

"Change of address," he bellows angrily at the divider. I wonder what cabs were like before these panels alienated us from the drivers. Before it felt like we were animals at risk of lashing out against our handlers. My father continues on to repeat the address of my dorm several times, which I'm surprised to find he seems to know by heart.

Minutes later, without speaking, my dad exits the car even before it's come to a full stop. His brittle hips wobble as he tries to regain stability after half jumping onto the sidewalk. The door is still open, and the taxi driver stops in the middle of the road, running back to close it. He curses and backs into the curb.

"You getting out?" he booms with a raise of his hand.

"N-no. He's coming back down. We're going somewhere after this." He grunts, and the meter keeps running. I watch it as if it might suddenly double and betray me.

About fifteen minutes later, my father comes back down, carrying two trash bags and my phone. The security guard runs out and opens the van door for him. I hide my head in my face.

"Thanks," I blurt as I take my phone from my dad's hand. He throws the trash bags in the trunk. I can see the clothes are folded, and I know he wouldn't do that. I wonder who packed my things. I wonder who cleaned my room. I wonder what they were thinking of me.

My phone's battery is almost dead, but I am able to open it and see dozens of notifications, most of them mindless and trivial. There are texts from Di rolling in from days ago. I stop at the last few on the list.

u ok?

hello?

jesus val i'm getting worried. respond !!! pls

did i do something? while i've been gone? god dammit val

Furiously typing, I begin to send a message back.

oh my god di. oh my god. i'm calling you tonight, i'm ok,
i'm not mad

i tried to o.d. on my meds. im calling you later

I refresh my messages to see if some from Jett will come
in, but nothing happens. The service here must be spotty. As we
continue driving, I keep refreshing, over and over again, until my
finger feels permanently pressed into the screen. Finally, I open up
my conversation thread with Jett to see if maybe there are texts
there. Except, there are only my texts from days and even weeks
ago. They're all coupled with little red exclamation points on the
side, as if they weren't delivered. My feet begin tapping. I'm
hunched over the screen scrolling in a panic to the very top of our
conversation, but I see nothing but green messages on my side that
look unsent.

"What the hell?" I cry out. My dad's eyes look at my
shaking body with worry. I call Jett's number and put the phone to
my ear, but instead of a dial tone, I only hear my heart echoing

inside my brain, the hollow wood creating a chamber for the sound to increase.

"We're sorry, the number you dialed is no longer in service. Please try again."

The phone falls from my hands and clangs against the metal on the door. My father's eyes are wide and intrusive, seeing every part of me. I reach down to pick it up and expect to see something different on the screen. The call is still on, with the time passed blinking at me.

As if inhabited by a demon, I am pulled out of the van by a force not within me, directly as the driver slows to a stop at a red light. I leap out of the cab and ever so slightly hear my father's voice yelling from the distance, but I am still underwater. Only now, I am on fire, too, though unlike ever before. I am raging blue and purple flames from within crystallized liquid, existing outside of the parameters of nature. My legs, like they know all too well, begin to run without thought. Each step that hits the ground ignites me further.

Chapter 67

I burst through the revolving doors that I just exited from not thirty minutes earlier. The neckline of my purple sweater is falling down on one side, my right breast almost fully exposed, but I do not stop to pull it up until I'm panting in the elevator. A few moments earlier, the security guard had yelled, "*Wet floor!*" at me, but it registers just now. *Oh.*

All those mentions of Jett that Dr. Ellis dismissed and uncomfortably rerouted, all those rigid questions he asked as if he had something to contain, all that lack of eye contact to prevent him from seeing what my eyes were implying. I do not have the space in my mind to mourn Jett. The only thing remaining is the fury in my brittle bones, which cannot pinpoint who or what exactly to blame, or latch on to Dr. Ellis as a metonymy for it all. For being a parasite feeding off of my imagination.

The elevator finally reaches its destination. I feel the currents of blood in my veins coursing at the speed of light, overtaken by a foreign generator. This outside power is straining me, as my body isn't used to such a strong current, and fear rises within me at the thought of short-circuiting and giving out, here in this waiting room, as I shuffle through the chairs. The fear is like acid rain being poured down on me, unapologetic and total, without regard for its landing.

The door I'm about to open at the end of the waiting room slams open as a tall black woman walks through, whispering on her phone. She almost falls back in surprise upon seeing me, then blinks and scurries by. I continue on, an animal unwaveringly set on its prey. My feline pupils have dilated to encompass the whole planet; I can see every possible enemy who could stand in my way. I do not feel the slick door handle as I ram it open with my Hulkean arm. Suddenly, as the whoosh of air exits and I hear the familiar rattle of the air conditioner, the water from my brain drains in an instant. I am no longer underwater; I am heaving above the waves and gulping down air with the might of a thousand men. My brain is starving for oxygen, for ignition, for its own life. I must grip, with every neuron, the fulfillment I came for.

I'm heaving and out of breath as I burst into his office, but I don't even stop to inhale before blasting out of myself.

"You knew! You could tell, and you never said anything! Anything! For months, hundreds of— Not even— Nothing! I was just a goddamn *specimen* for you to fucking psychoanalyze and watch self-destruct! *How...could...you?*"

He doesn't even look *at* me, he looks *through* me, beyond me. As I stand there, with the residual smoke of betrayal fumigating the space between us, he says nothing. He simply sits on a pedestal made of a PhD and inauthentic professionalism, not responding. I might as well be as inanimate as the parquet-framed photos scattered along his office walls. An overwhelming urge to rip these images off comes over me. I run behind his green leather armchair and slice at all of the little glass boxes like a rock climber with talons. If he won't look at me as an actual person, if not something more meaningful, then I will not act as such. Three, four, five, of these perfect little cells fall to the ground and do not shatter but still crack the air with the noise of glass hitting laminate. A wife and son gaze up at me from the posed Easter photograph that always used to catch my eye as I looked at the clock obsessively each time we met. Jarringly reentering reality, I turn back to make eye contact. Now, his eyes brim slightly with the gleam of tears, and he opens his mouth to speak but chokes on his breath, swallowing reflexively. His sadistic control has crumbled into animalistic surrender.

Without my permission, his display of grief catalyzes my own, and I cannot contain the silent streams of tears that instantly race down my sunken cheeks. What feels like a lifetime's worth of experiences flashes between us as our gazes fuse in a momentary slice of immortality. I fracture even more, becoming torn, trapped, melted, consumed. All I am is a prisoner of memory, locked in the cell of my own mind.

The air conditioner turns off, and I run to it, wanting to hit it and punish it for making this even more dramatic, but I stop myself below the wall-mounted device and fall to the floor. My tears are internal, thick and mucousy, running down my throat. Dr. Ellis begins to walk over to me, slowly, like an animal unsure about a human. Streams fall slowly from his dark eyes. I choke on the globs in my throat and audibly swallow the snot back down. We're both sniffling and sitting on the carpet. I'm curled into a ball with my knees pulled up to my chest, and he's in front of me with his legs off to one side, trying to breathe heavily and plug the sorrow from flowing out of him even more.

He begins to scoot closer to me. My eyes hazily move upward, and I can only bear to meet his with an unfocused gaze that distorts everything but the red rims of his glasses. He reaches his hands out to take my left hand, the one flowering out from etches of incompletion of what I had hoped to finish off once and for all.

"I-I'm sorry," Dr. Ellis whispers. "*I'm* s-sorry this time." I can now see small smile lines peeking out from the red frames, as stark as the day I first saw them. We sit in silence. Like I'm experiencing a sugar crash, I feel hijacked and artificially drained. There is no energy remaining for my senses to be activated. My hand is numb. I wish I could feel it being held, though I am pretty certain if that were the case I would not be allowing him to do so.

This all feels strangely like déjà vu, as if it were me and Vic again, talking about how depressed we were and feeling sorry for ourselves together. Or me and Jett, meandering on and on about how scared we were about growing older. The sadness numbed out by the unity. The togetherness canceled out by the discomfort.

But I remember that I am here, and not with Vic, and not with Jett, and my eyes well up again. My arm suddenly burns, as if I'm Harry Potter with the forehead scar and Dr. Ellis is Voldemort. I snap my hand back, as he might as well be. Slowly, I begin to stand up and wipe snot from my face. The rain is still pouring. The air conditioner is on. But nothing is coming out of me. I do not know how I am walking to the door; I do not know if within me exists an autopilot setting unbeknownst to me or if there is another being taking over my body. Maybe it's Greg.

Before opening the door, I look at Dr. Ellis, who is still on the floor. He is blinking down at his lap before finally jerking his gaze up to meet my eyes. I hope to never see his face again. I hope to only see red-rimmed glasses on someone else, someone who doesn't wear shiny black loafers, loafers that his wife doesn't like. Someone who doesn't sit in a goddamn green armchair balancing a yellow notepad on his perfectly tailored pants while gripping a fucking Mont Blanc pen in the opposite hand. In one instant, as I'm peering down at him, months of memories within this room lock me in even closer. Every single question, response, and silence replays in the space of one exhale. After the cinematic rush,

Dr. Ellis gazes up at me like a dog at its owner. Except I run away, softly shutting the office door behind me. I feel as if I have just broken up with my psyche, in love with my own codependent abuser. The keys have been handed back over. Rightfully.

Chapter 68

Each step I take after leaving Dr. Ellis's feels as if I am dragging the entire building behind me, with thick chains coiled around each ankle. I can barely walk the block to the busy avenue before having to sit down on the curb with my head between my knees. A taxi honks at me as it tries to pull over. I don't even flinch.

I feel something digging into my butt and remember my phone is there. I pull it out, and immediately upon opening it, Jett's contact appears. I bite my lip and try calling it again. Once again, the female operator's voice greets me unwelcomingly. As I watch dozens of brightly colored cars drive by, I feel as if I am in a bad dream where everything is realistic but just can't be real. It's like a nightmarish fun house. Every person I see driving seems to have a grimace on their face, smiling in a garish, disturbing way that I have to look away from. A huge truck suddenly whips past, its force blowing my hair back and knocking me off-balance as well. My phone falls down and clicks on again. This time, I pick it up and scroll up to Di's contact, dialing it as I sniffle to hold back more tears.

"Val? Val?" she answers. "*Val!*"

"Di! Di, I'm here, I-I'm…" A car horn blares, and I wait for it to pass. A deluge of tears conveniently demands my silence at the same time.

"Val, what the hell is going on?" Her scratchy voice is tired and sounds muffled, like she's in bed.

"I tried to OD, b-but it didn't work; it was so bad, D-Di, a-and…" I choke on my tears. Out of the corner of my eye, I see an Asian family holding tourist maps and gazing at me as they pass by.

"What! Jesus! Val, oh my God! A-are you, like, physically okay?"

"I mean, I'm fine, my arm is just really fucked up because I—I…" Her long exhale on the other side of the line completes my statement for me. "I'm sorry I didn't text you a lot, Di, I just th-thought I wasn't going to ever…ever see you ag—" I'm choking so much on my tears now that I'm worried my phone is going to incur water damage. It is painstakingly silent on Di's end until I begin to hear her sniffle in the background.

"Oh my God. I… I'm so glad I still have you, Val. You little shit." Di coughs, the sound of phlegm still sharp through the call. A light smile appears on the edges of my mouth, which is quickly weighed down again by surges from deep within that I didn't even know I could conduct in my nearly dead wiring.

"D-Di…it's so fucked, th-though…"

"How?"

"I…I don't even… Jett…"

"Jett? Shit, did he do something? *Jesus* Chr—"

"*No! No!*" My head falls between my knees again. My gray jeans are soaked in slobber, my speech contorted by the wires of mucus trailing across the inside of my throat.

"Val. I'm here. I'm listening." It's her version of *calm down* when she knows there's no way in hell for me to listen to her say that.

"J-J-Jett isn't real!" Every blaring car horn goes quiet as my words echo across the galaxy, reverberating against each other until I am sure my brain is on the verge of combustion.

"*Aaaaagggghhhh!*" I scream into the phone. It's quiet for several seconds before I hear Di inhale to speak and then retreat again.

"Val. *I'm* real. And I'm here for you." A wave of choking hysteria fills my body where tears have run out. I have nothing left in me to produce them.

"I just…I can't do this anymore, Di! I can't be me, but I can't not be me; I can't be what they want me to be. I just want to fucking curl into a ball inside of my own shitty goddamn mind and die, and starve to death until there's nothing left of me!"

"Breathe, Val!" Di screams. "Just breathe," she adds softly as she rethinks her tactic. I begin to calculate my responses, sensing her rising agenda.

"Please, I'm here. Just breathe, you don't need to talk," she continues. I start coordinating my breath with each passing car in the traffic in front of me, but the pace is too slow, and I start heaving again to catch up. Di's soft, wispy inhales and exhales are the only thing keeping me grounded. Otherwise, I truly would have gone up in flames and burned to death, by my own doing, right here. For real this time, no schizo shit. No schizo shit ever again.

"I… I'm sorry, for piling this on top of everything else you have right now. I never even really was there f-for you with your—
"

"Val, this isn't about me right now. Don't try and think about me. We can deal with that another time, another time soon, because I miss talking to you, dude, but right now you don't need to be thinking about any of that. Fuck, where are you?"

"I… I'm near my therapist's office. I'm just on, like, the fucking curb."

"Were you just seeing your therapist?"

"Um…y-yeah, I, like…" I exhale loudly and close my eyes. "I saw him, then found out about Jett, and…I ran back in…" My breathing is slowing, and a wave of exhaustion passes over me.

"You ran back in?"

"I…I was so mad, Di, I w-wanted…I wanted to *kill* someone…"

"Did you hurt him?"

"No, no! I just…I just cried, mostly. He cried, too. Then I ran out."

"Oh my… Where are you staying now, Val?" She's saying my name more than usual. I'm getting annoyed by her scripted motives. Not that they're rude, but they're just scripted, so I must be, too, or, at least, as scripted as I can be in this state.

"My dad got us a hotel room so he can, like, watch over me. I don't really know what's happening after. I thought I was going to an outpatient program, but he wants me to come home, so… Yeah, I'm staying at a hotel with my dad. But I really don't want to fucking go back there now after jumping out of a cab with him, like, however long ago."

"I…I wish I could tell you another place to go, but I think you need to go back to see him, Val. It's not like there's much else you can do, or someplace better, right now."

"I could just run away. I could figure out how to come to you, o-or—" My voice escalates until it cracks. A couple whispers as they point and pass by me, and I tilt my head away.

"After all this, I think you need to give… Maybe you should let go. Maybe you should go to your dad, cry it out, or whatever you need, and let him take the reins from here." *The reins.* I fucking hate her metaphor.

"I'm s-so scared, Di; I feel like I'm always going to die, I'm so fucking scared…"

"Stay on the phone with me." She clears her throat, and I hear bedsheets rustling. "Do you know how to get back to where you're staying?" I pull the phone from my ear and look up how far the hotel is from here.

"Y-yeah, it's, like, a thirty-minute walk. I'll…I'll head over there, I guess." I begin to stand and brush off my butt. As I begin to head down the block and reach more people, I feel like I blend in more, and I begin to breathe steadily again. My swollen face is shadowed by the dozens of taller people walking swiftly around me.

"Okay, that's good, it'll give you some time to think," Di says. I continue to walk, mesmerized by avoiding every crack in the sidewalk. "I'm here," she restates.

"Mm-hmm, I know, sorry, I'm just…I don't know. I feel wiped," I grunt out through glop-covered vocal cords. Di continues to reassure me, asking meaningless questions about where I am along the way. She tries to lighten the mood and make comments about places I say I'm near, which takes my mind off of everything in the moment but also make me feel tricked. I don't know if I'd want it any other way at this point, though.

I've begun to work up a sweat when I see the black hotel down the long block.

"Oh my God, Di, it's there, I... Okay. I'll go in, I'll just...just answer whatever my dad asks. Get something to eat. Go to bed." I repeat that in my head a few times. *Get something to eat. Go to bed.*

"You can keep me on the phone during everything, if you want. If it'll make you feel better, Val." My heart booms and shakes my whole body as I move through into the hotel, greeted by smiling doormen despite blotchy redness all over my cheeks.

"I...I need to just do this myself and go in there, Di. I hope I see you again," I mutter quietly as not to be heard in the silent lobby. I painfully push the elevator button.

"At least you're still overdramatic." I purse my lips in a pathetically contained smile, then furrow my brows at the opening doors to my right. I don't know if she's right about that.

"Bye, Di. Thank you. I love you."

"I love you, too, Va—" The phone call cuts off as the

elevator shoots up. My ears pop, and my heart sinks.

Chapter 69

As I enter, my father is sitting in one of the two cream armchairs on the opposite side of the living room, staring at the floor. He doesn't so much as breathe at my presence.

"H-hey." I shut the door behind me, but it's slightly uneven with the frame, and I have to slam it in. The walls shake some, and I subsequently shudder with the force. My arm stings.

"I...I don't really k-know what's best for me. A-and if you think I need to go home, m-maybe..."

His eyes lift up slowly. "I don't think you should come home, Valerie. I wanted you to be close to me so I could watch over you. But I can't watch over you anymore." He swallows and clenches his jaw without looking me directly in the eyes, still. His childish text ringtone dings twice.

"Earlier...I jumped out because...something like V-Vic happened again." Now, my dad's eyelids drop down and he winces as if he is in physical agony. "I realized it... I tried to call when we were..." My overworked mind can only form short, stout phrases with little explanation. His cold apathy provides little to bounce off of. I wish I could still be angry. I wish I could even still be sad and crying. Instead, there is truly nothing left besides a barely functioning physical frame: Di isn't here, and no one else in my head has a life outside of my own. I do not have enough in me to keep myself alive, let alone them.

"What do you think you need to do, Valerie?" His voice is soft. His eyes are closed. His phone rings again, which causes him to swallow once more. It's his work ringtone, a country guitar melody he's had since I was a little kid. I don't even know how he's managed to keep that ringtone. I rub my temples and realize how hungry I am, my stomach rumbling now that I've stopped moving.

"I want to get away from all this, I don't know…start new again."

"Wasn't that what you did coming here? Move away, start again?" Finally, he looks to me, and this time, I look down in defeat. "You can't move on from this. You have to fix whatever you need to fix." Blunt words like *fix* are never used by therapists and medical professionals, at least not to me, so his borderline-inconsiderate terminology freezes me up a little. I sigh and nod.

"I know. You're right. I just don't know how to."

"I can tell you over and over to take your medication."

"I know. It's just… It's like becoming a different person."

"Isn't that what needs to happen, Valerie?" Never have I felt unaccepted by him until now. My hands tense up. I want to both shout at him and cower in defeat. Instead, I stand there looking at my gross gray jeans. My stomach rumbles, the sound waves echoing between our two bodies.

"Maybe I need to start new away from you, Dad." A thin thread connects my mouth to his heart, and the string vibrates back toward my throat. I shake in tune with another stomach rumble.

"So that I can figure that out. Because I can't, with you. Not because of you… I…" I look to the side and see the two trash bags filled with my clothes, paid for with his money, carried through his hands.

"After *everything*? Everything I… *Valer*—"

"Dad, it's not because of anything you did! *Don't you get it?* I just can't do any of this anymore, the bullshit, any of it! I have to do this myself." I notice a heel poking out from one of the black bags. It's scuffed and dark. It takes me a moment to recognize it, but it's one of the heels I wore out with Patricia weeks ago. A residual amphetamine charge seeps out from the tiny stilt and connects with my energy center within, supercharging me and sealing up each and every wound on my body, including the visible cuts on my arm. It forces me to take a deep inhale, tipping me almost over the edge before I root down and exhale with a loud, uncharacteristic howl-sigh combination. I lean down, rip the shoe from the bag by its heel, and hold it in my hands like a newborn child. The second half of the pair then falls out of the hole and lands in front of my feet. I pick it up and eye it cautiously. From the gaping opening, I see other clothes of mine, mostly workout sets, which pain me to remember wearing. I dart my eyes away to land on my father's eyes again. In front of me, my helicopter lands for me to enter, but I slam the door and refuse. In fact, the electricity emitting from within me shoots toward the aircraft and combusts it in an instant. A flash of blue flame leaves behind floating ashes, which, in their reflected sunlight, display fractals of memories trapped within that helicopter, looking down upon me from miles above.

I reflexively swallow. Both of the heels are hooked around my right pointer finger on their ankle strap. The imprint of my father's reddened, sunken face is branded into the back of my cavernous mind and smokes from the hot branding tools. The fumes cloud my vision, and I turn away to breathe. My free hand opens the hotel door to escape. A final gush of tears, powered by every living soul living inside of me, dribbles down the purple sweater covering my flaming, immortal body.

Acknowledgements

I would like to thank all of my writing teachers and mentors who pushed me to believe in myself from the very beginning. I also thank my familly – blood-related or not – who have stuck with me along this journey and lovingly agreed to workshop some of this novel's material with me. I appreciate your honesty and your encouragement.

I also deeply appreciate everyone who assisted me on this project at The Artful Editor: especially Naomi Eagleson, Katie McCoach, and Michelle Hope. This manuscript could not have come to live without your input.

About the Author

Maren Altman is an author, astrologer, and yoga instructor based in Manhattan, New York. At the time of this writing, she is completing her undergraduate education at New York University, where she is studying Philosophy, Creative Writing, and Psychology. Along with being a professional consulting astrologer and vinyasa yoga instructor, she is currently finalizing her second novel, *Badflower,* with no plans to stop writing in the future. Outside of these pursuits, Maren is a vegan activist, planning on opening her own vegan restaurant and yoga center in Manhattan.

www.marenaltman.com

Printed in Great Britain
by Amazon

50563373R00292